STOP!

This is the back of the book. You wouldn't want to spoil a great ending!

This book is printed "manga-style," in the authentic Japanese right-to-left format. Since none of the artwork has been flipped or altered, readers get to experience the story just as the creator intended. You've been asking for it, so TOKYOPOP® delivered: authentic, hot-off-the-press, and far more fun!

DIRECTIONS

If this is your first time reading manga-style, here's a quick guide to help you understand how it works.

It's easy... just start in the top right panel and follow the numbers. Have fun, and look for more 100% authentic manga from TOKYOPOP®!

1
2
3
4
5
6
7
8
9
10

THE MANGA REVOLUTION · LEADING · 漫画革命

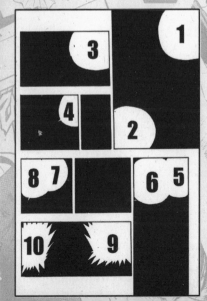

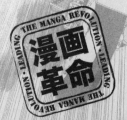

From the creator of *Peace Maker*

vassalord™
ヴァッサロード

+

Nanae Chrono

The Vatican has employed a new assassin who's a vampire, *and* a cyborg. If you think he sounds nasty, wait 'till you see his master! When these two hot guys collide, the good times and carnage will roll like a head off a guillotine!

© NANAE CHRONO/MAG Garden

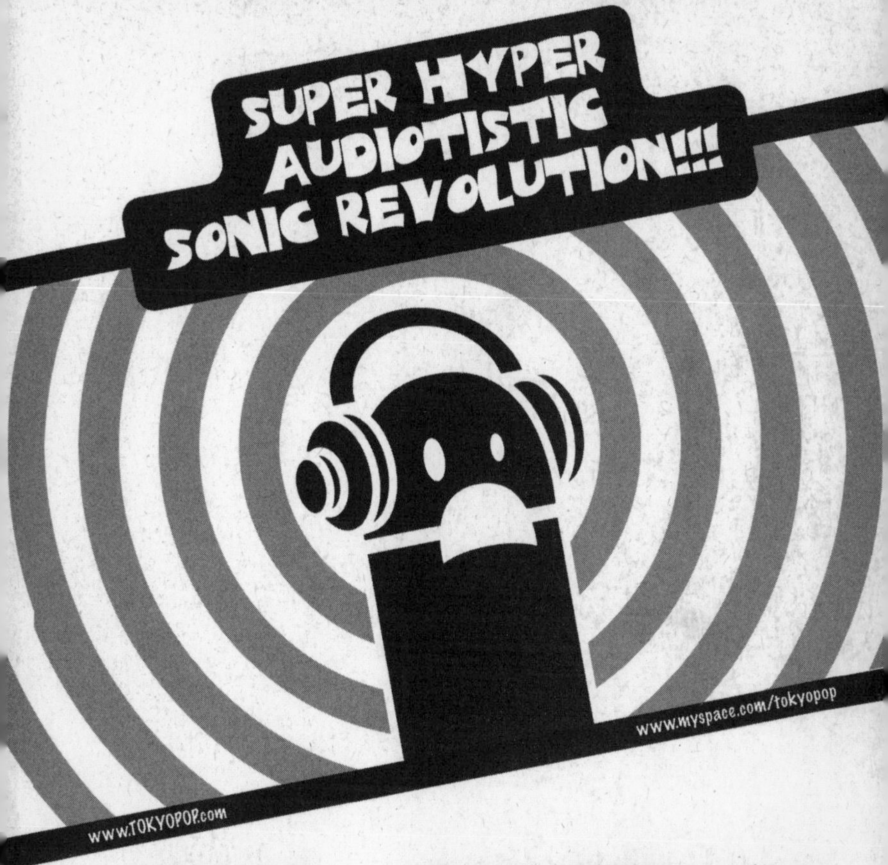
SUPER HYPER
AUDIOTISTIC
SONIC REVOLUTION!!!
www.myspace.com/tokyopop
www.TOKYOPOP.com

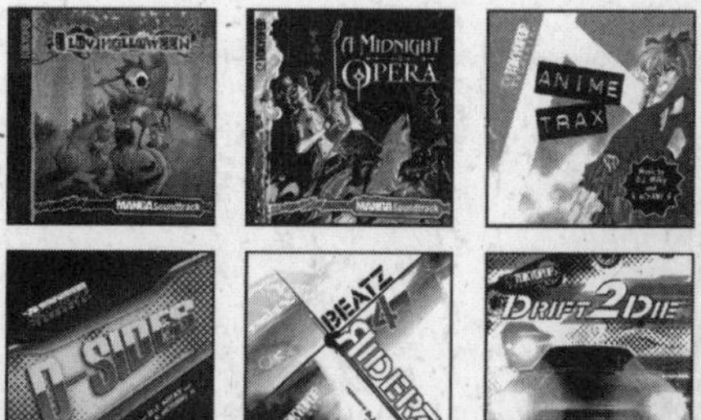
A MIDNIGHT OPERA
ANIME TRAX
BEATZ 4 RIDERZ
DRIFT 2 DIE

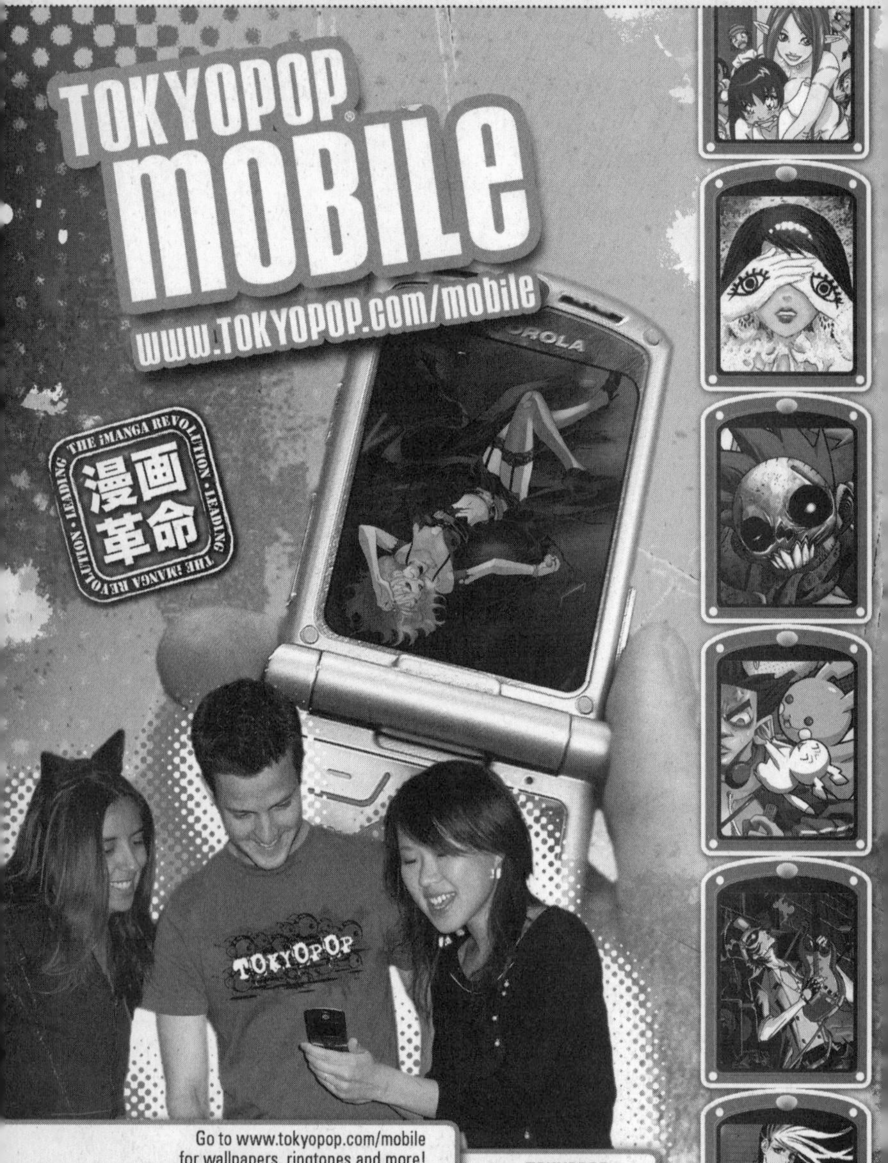

TOKYOPOP
MOBILE
www.TOKYOPOP.com/mobile
THE iMANGA REVOLUTION · LEADING THE iMANGA REVOLUTION · LEADING
漫画革命
TOKYOPOP
Go to www.tokyopop.com/mobile
for wallpapers, ringtones and more!
www.TOKYOPOP.com

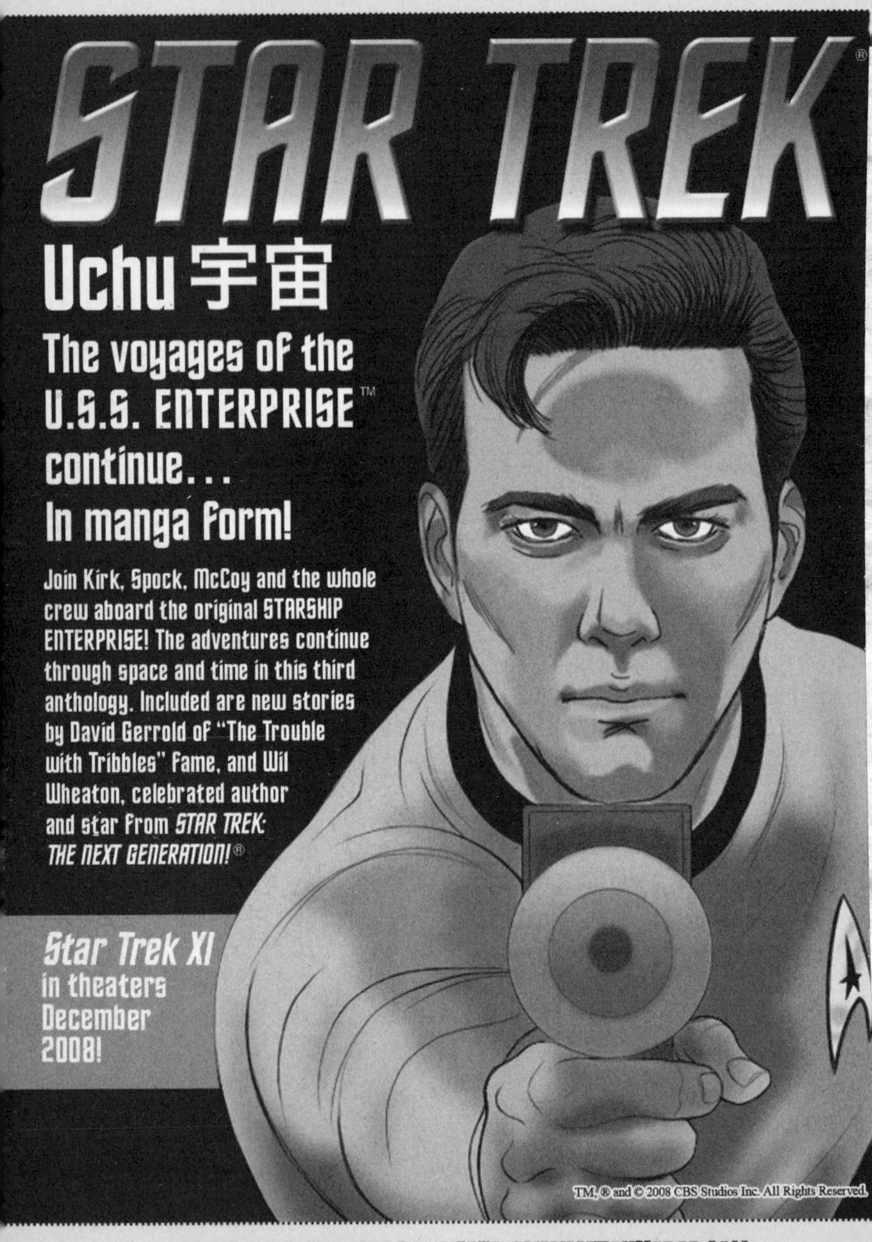
STAR TREK®
Uchu 宇宙
The voyages of the U.S.S. ENTERPRISE™ continue...
In manga form!
Join Kirk, Spock, McCoy and the whole crew aboard the original STARSHIP ENTERPRISE! The adventures continue through space and time in this third anthology. Included are new stories by David Gerrold of "The Trouble with Tribbles" fame, and Wil Wheaton, celebrated author and star from *STAR TREK: THE NEXT GENERATION!*®
Star Trek XI in theaters December 2008!
TM, ® and © 2008 CBS Studios Inc. All Rights Reserved.

YURIYA'S SECRET WHICH SHE WANTS TO HIDE ♥

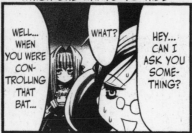

HEY... CAN I ASK YOU SOMETHING?
WHAT?
WELL... WHEN YOU WERE CON-TROLLING THAT BAT...
I HEARD THAT WHEN A VAMPIRE IS CONTROLLING A BAT, HE OR SHE CAN SEE WHAT IT SEES.
WHISPER WHISPER
SO... UM...THE OTHER DAY...
OH, DON'T WORRY. I WAS THE ONLY ONE CONTROLLING IT THAT TIME.
SO RELAX. NOBODY ELSE SAW YOUR BODY
PHEW.
FLATTY... TEE HEE!
!!!

--FLAT AS A BOARD--

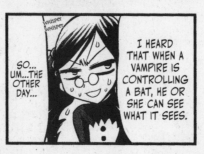

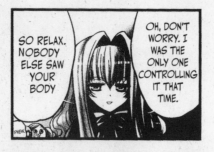

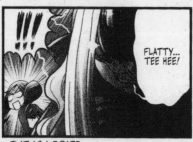

IN OUR NEXT VOLUME...

chibi Vampire
TOKYOPOP
Created By:
Yuna Kagesaki
10

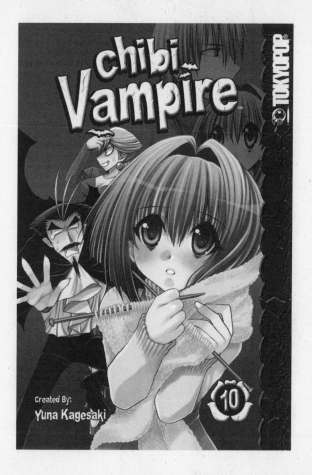

FOR ONCE, KARIN'S LIFE ACTUALLY SEEMS TO BE GOING LIKE SHE WANTS IT TO. SHE AND KENTA HAVE DECLARED THEIR LOVE FOR ONE ANOTHER, AND KARIN'S EVEN MET ANOTHER VAMPIRE WHO HAS A SIMILAR BLOOD PROBLEM. BUT WILL KARIN'S TRAIN OF GOOD LUCK BECOME DERAILED WITH THE RETURN OF HER GRANDMOTHER, ELDA MARKER? WHAT WILL ELDA DO WHEN SHE FINDS OUT KARIN'S NOT A NORMAL VAMPIRE? AND WHEN IT'S FINALLY REVEALED WHY LOVE BETWEEN VAMPIRES AND HUMANS IS TABOO, WHAT WILL BECOME OF KARIN AND KENTA?

S-O-SAN~HER HIDDEN DESIRES~

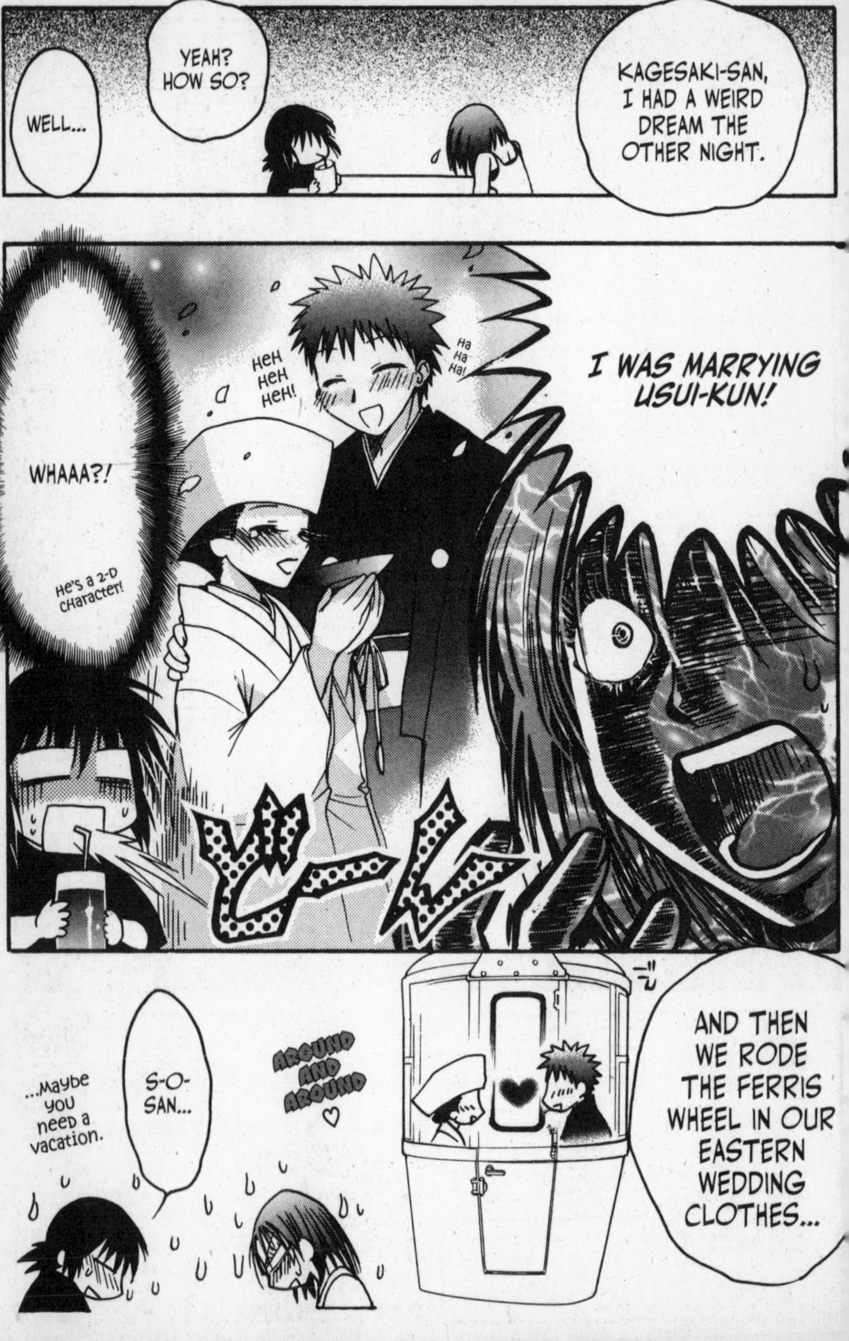
KAGESAKI-SAN, I HAD A WEIRD DREAM THE OTHER NIGHT.
YEAH? HOW SO?
WELL...
I WAS MARRYING USUI-KUN!
HA HA HA!
HEH HEH HEH!
WHAAA?!
He's a 2-D character!
AND THEN WE RODE THE FERRIS WHEEL IN OUR EASTERN WEDDING CLOTHES...
AROUND AND AROUND
S-O-SAN...
...Maybe you need a vacation.

AND THEN 1

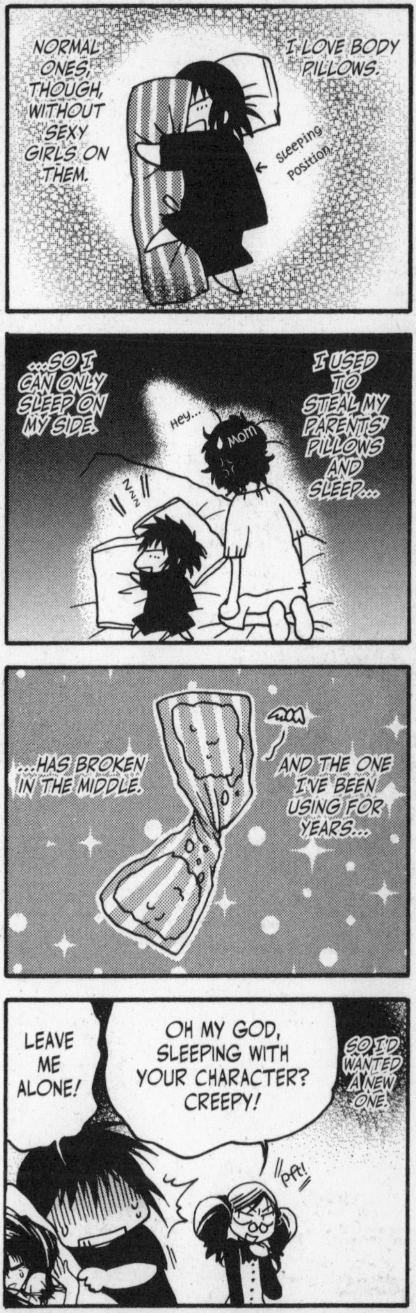
I LOVE BODY PILLOWS.
NORMAL ONES, THOUGH, WITHOUT SEXY GIRLS ON THEM.
Sleeping Position
I USED TO STEAL MY PARENTS' PILLOWS AND SLEEP...
HEY...
MOM
...SO I CAN ONLY SLEEP ON MY SIDE.
AND THE ONE I'VE BEEN USING FOR YEARS...
...HAS BROKEN IN THE MIDDLE.
SO I'D WANTED A NEW ONE.
OH MY GOD, SLEEPING WITH YOUR CHARACTER? CREEPY!
LEAVE ME ALONE!
pft!

AND THEN 2

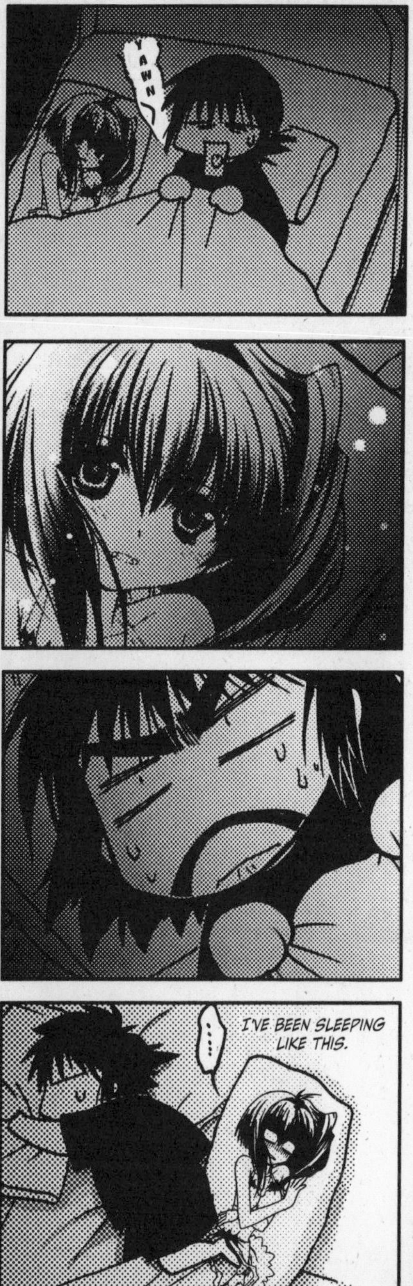
YAWN
....
I'VE BEEN SLEEPING LIKE THIS.

THEY SAW 1

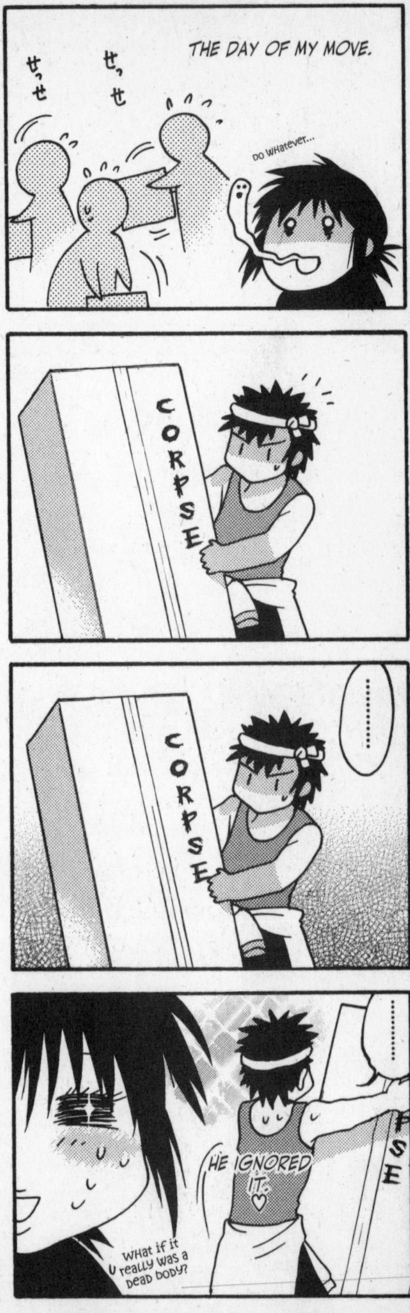
THE DAY OF MY MOVE.
せっせ
せっせ
DO WHatever...
CORPSE
....
CORPSE
....
HE IGNORED IT. ♡
WHat if it really was a DEAD BODY?

THEY SAW 2

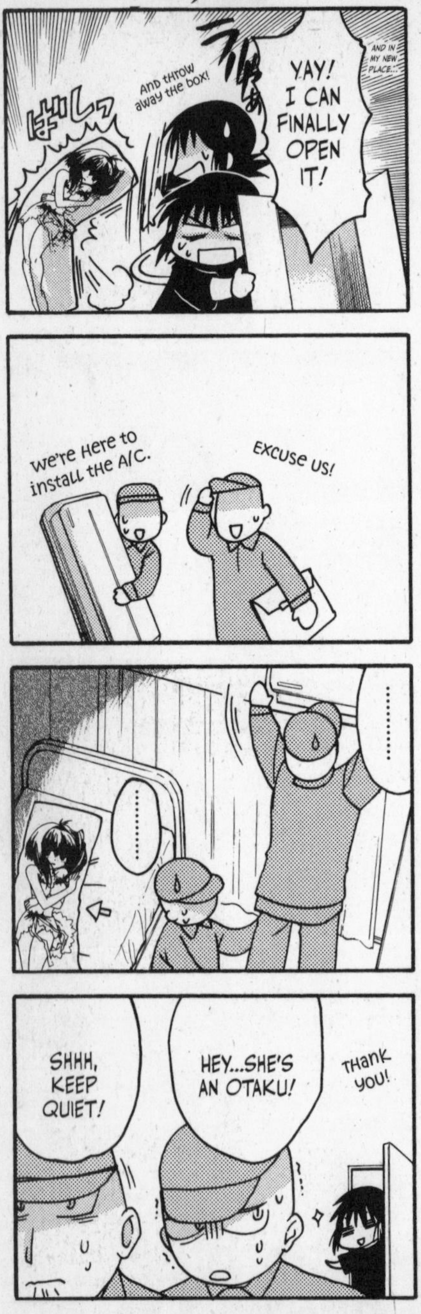
AND IN MY NEW PLACE...
YAY! I CAN FINALLY OPEN IT!
AND THROW away THE box!
ばしっ
EXCUSE US!
We're Here to install the A/C.
....
....
THank you!
HEY...SHE'S AN OTAKU!
SHHH, KEEP QUIET!

Crazy Move

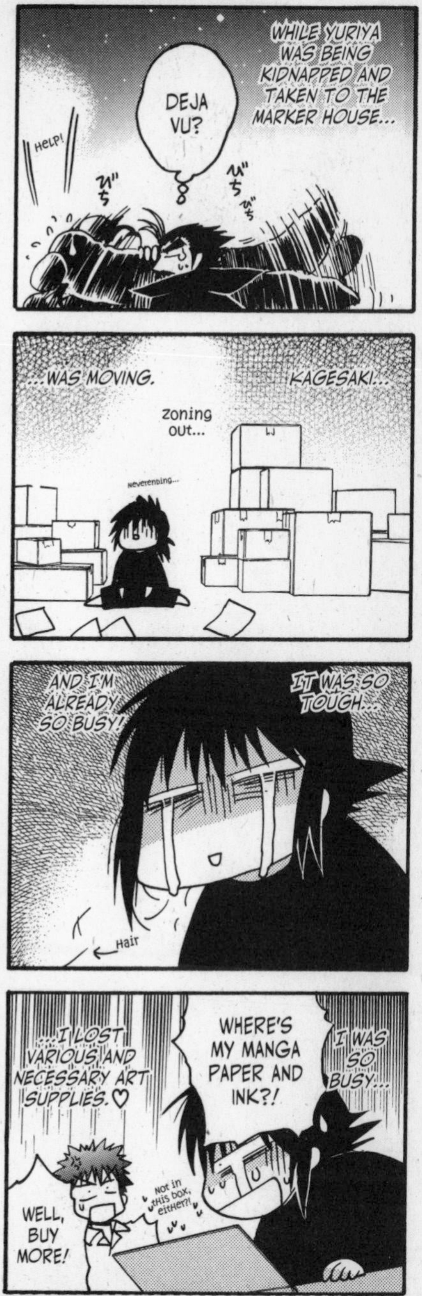

WHILE YURIYA WAS BEING KIDNAPPED AND TAKEN TO THE MARKER HOUSE...
DEJA VU?
HELP!
KAGESAKI...
...WAS MOVING.
zoning out...
neverending...
IT WAS SO TOUGH...
AND I'M ALREADY SO BUSY!
Hair
I WAS SO BUSY...
WHERE'S MY MANGA PAPER AND INK?!
...I LOST VARIOUS AND NECESSARY ART SUPPLIES.♡
Not in this box, either?!
WELL, BUY MORE!

I DIDN'T WANT TO HAVE TO PAY TO REPLACE THEM...

Large Enough for a Person

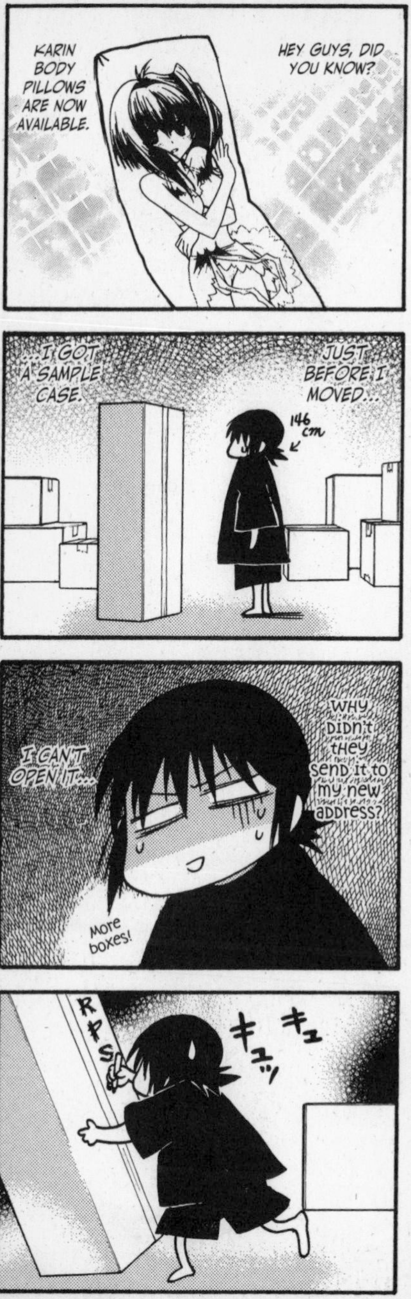

HEY GUYS, DID YOU KNOW?
KARIN BODY PILLOWS ARE NOW AVAILABLE.
JUST BEFORE I MOVED...
...I GOT A SAMPLE CASE.
146 cm
WHY DIDN'T THEY SEND IT TO MY NEW ADDRESS?
I CAN'T OPEN IT...
More boxes!
RPS
キュ
キュッ

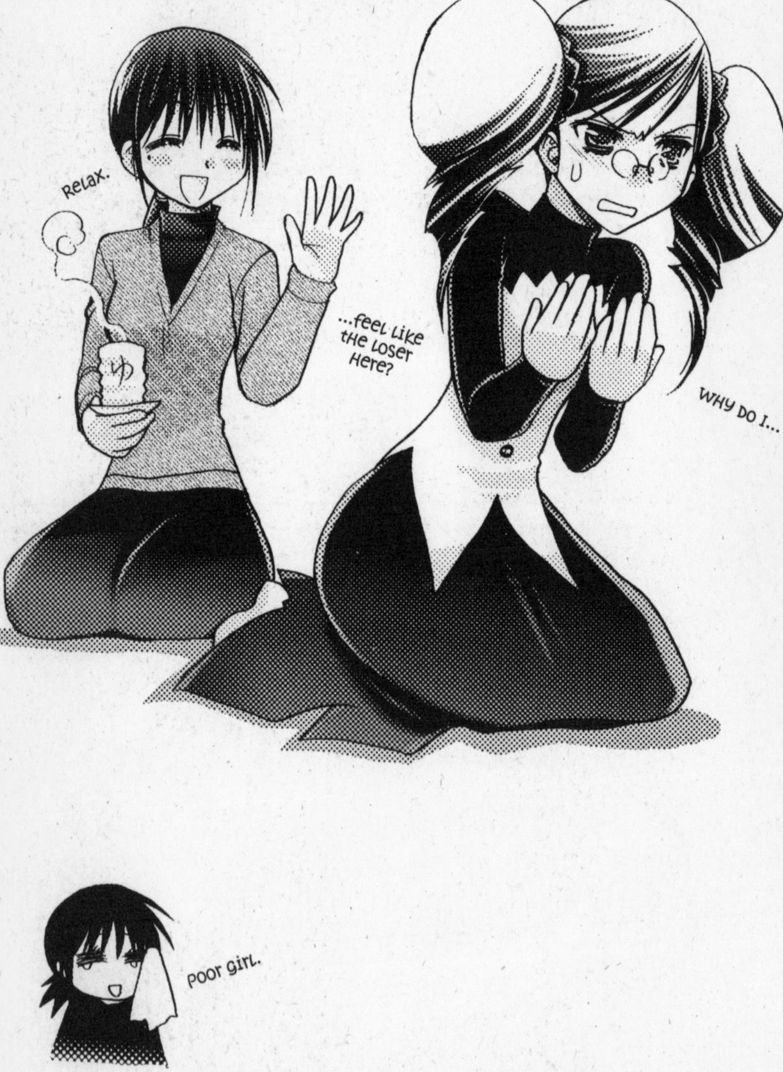
WHY DO I...
...feel like the loser here?
Relax.
ゆ
Poor girl.

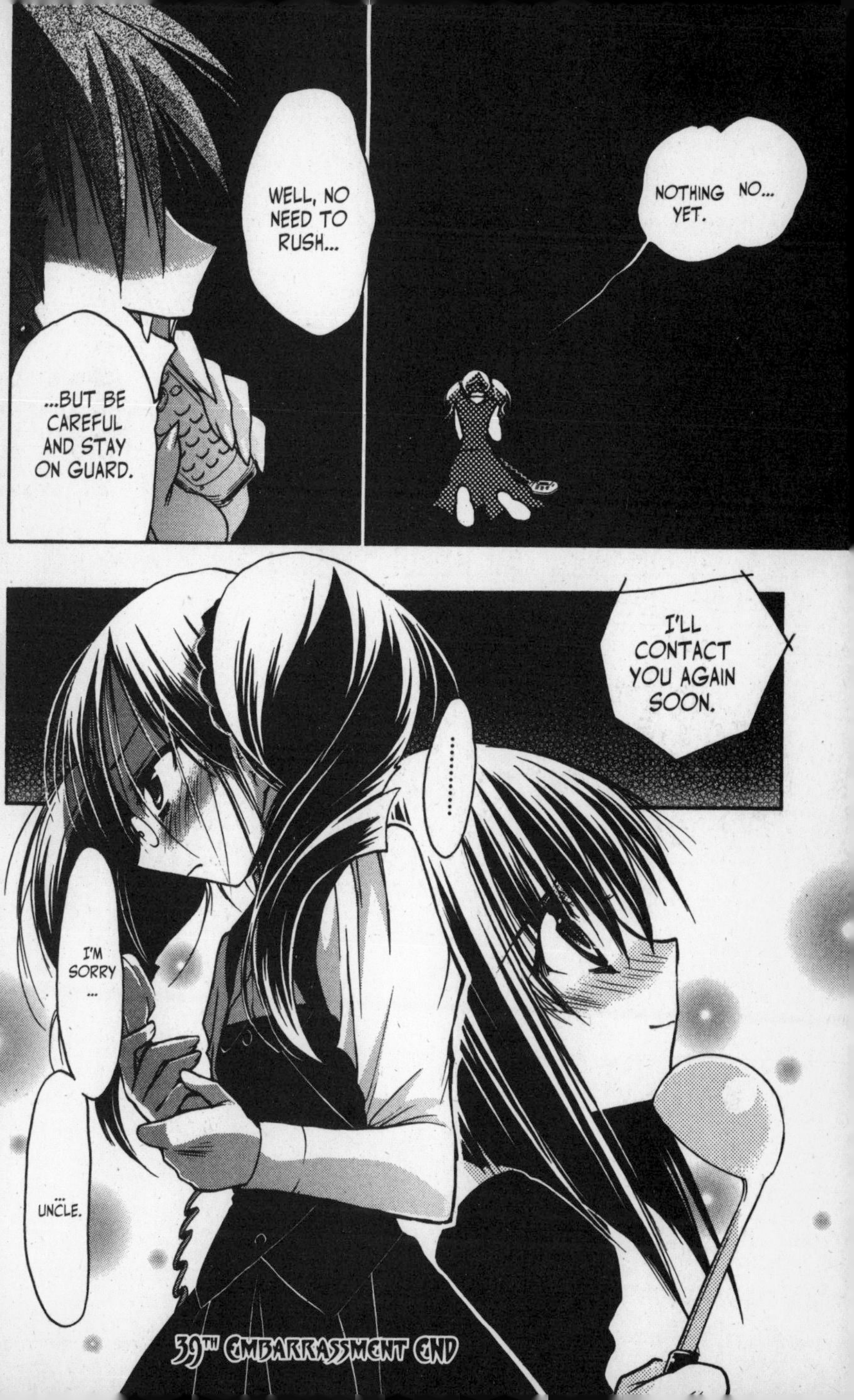
NO...
NOTHING YET.
WELL, NO NEED TO RUSH...
...BUT BE CAREFUL AND STAY ON GUARD.
I'LL CONTACT YOU AGAIN SOON.
....
I'M SORRY ...
... UNCLE.
39TH EMBARRASSMENT END

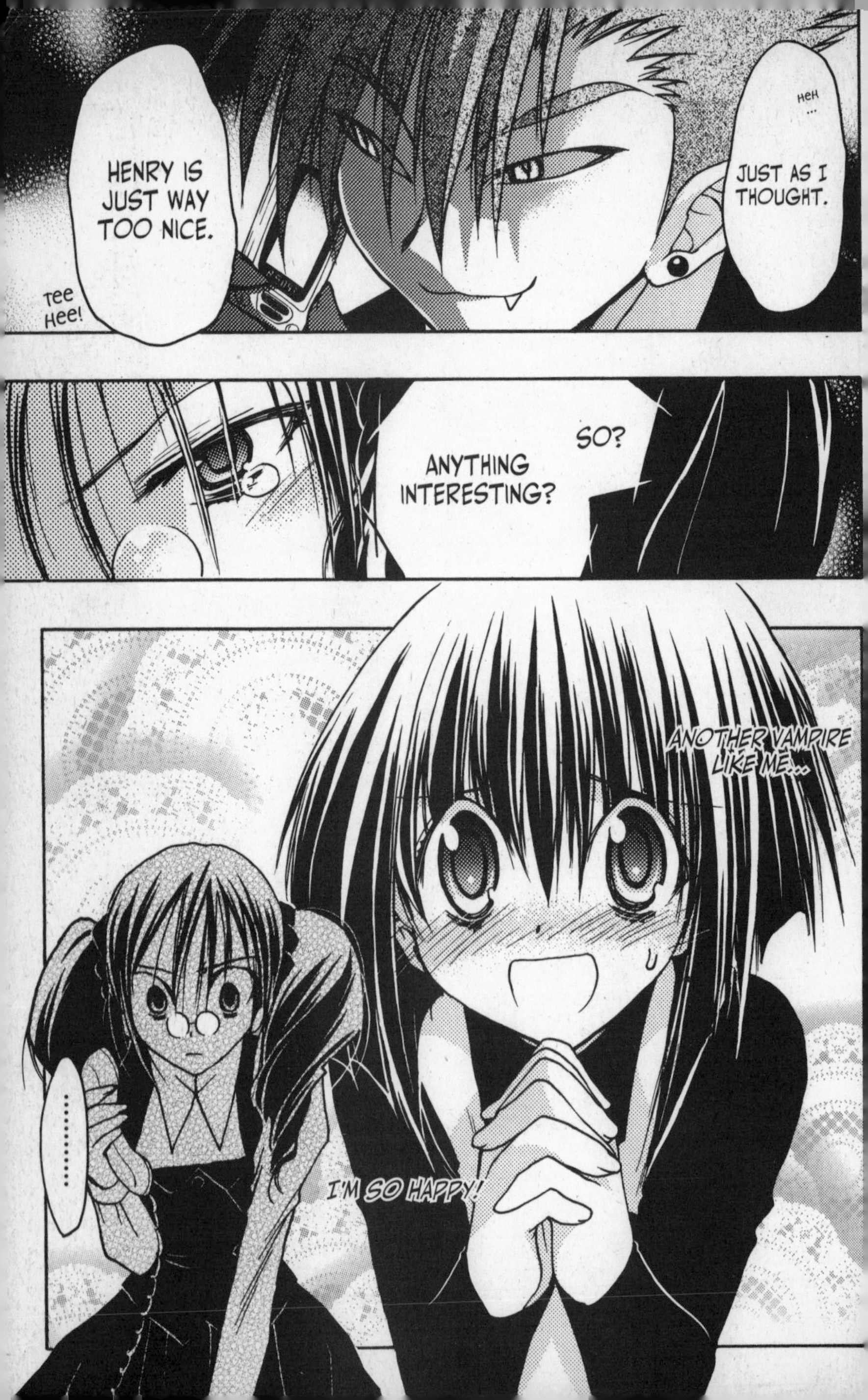
HEH... JUST AS I THOUGHT.
HENRY IS JUST WAY TOO NICE.
TEE HEE!
SO? ANYTHING INTERESTING?
ANOTHER VAMPIRE LIKE ME...
I'M SO HAPPY!
....

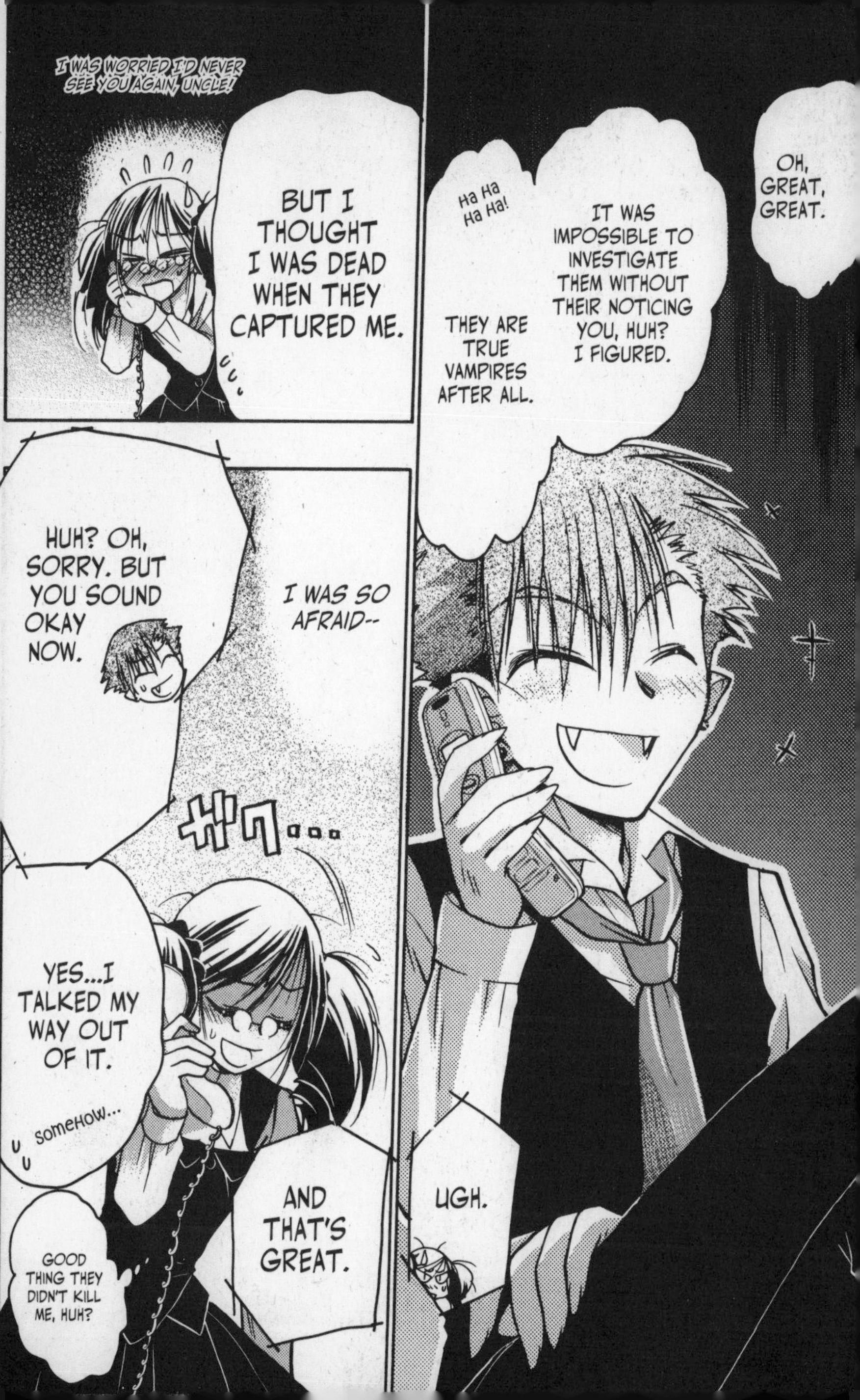
OH, GREAT, GREAT.
IT WAS IMPOSSIBLE TO INVESTIGATE THEM WITHOUT THEIR NOTICING YOU, HUH? I FIGURED.
Ha Ha Ha Ha!
THEY ARE TRUE VAMPIRES AFTER ALL.
UGH.
I WAS WORRIED I'D NEVER SEE YOU AGAIN, UNCLE!
BUT I THOUGHT I WAS DEAD WHEN THEY CAPTURED ME.
I WAS SO AFRAID--
HUH? OH, SORRY. BUT YOU SOUND OKAY NOW.
ガク...
YES...I TALKED MY WAY OUT OF IT.
somehow...
GOOD THING THEY DIDN'T KILL ME, HUH?
AND THAT'S GREAT.

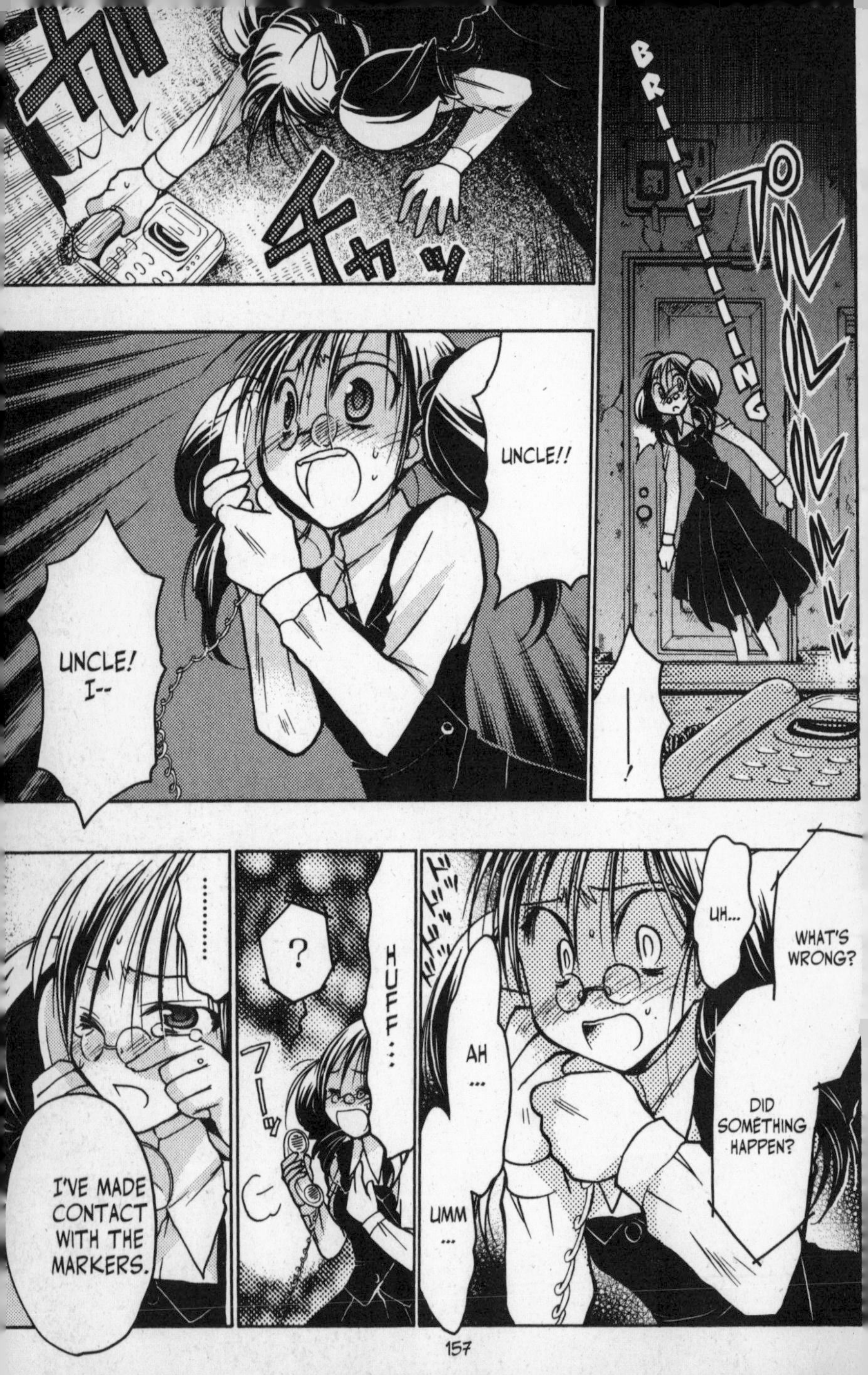
BRIIIING
!
UNCLE!!
UNCLE! I--
UH...
WHAT'S WRONG?
DID SOMETHING HAPPEN?
AH...
UMM...
?
HUFF...
......
I'VE MADE CONTACT WITH THE MARKERS.

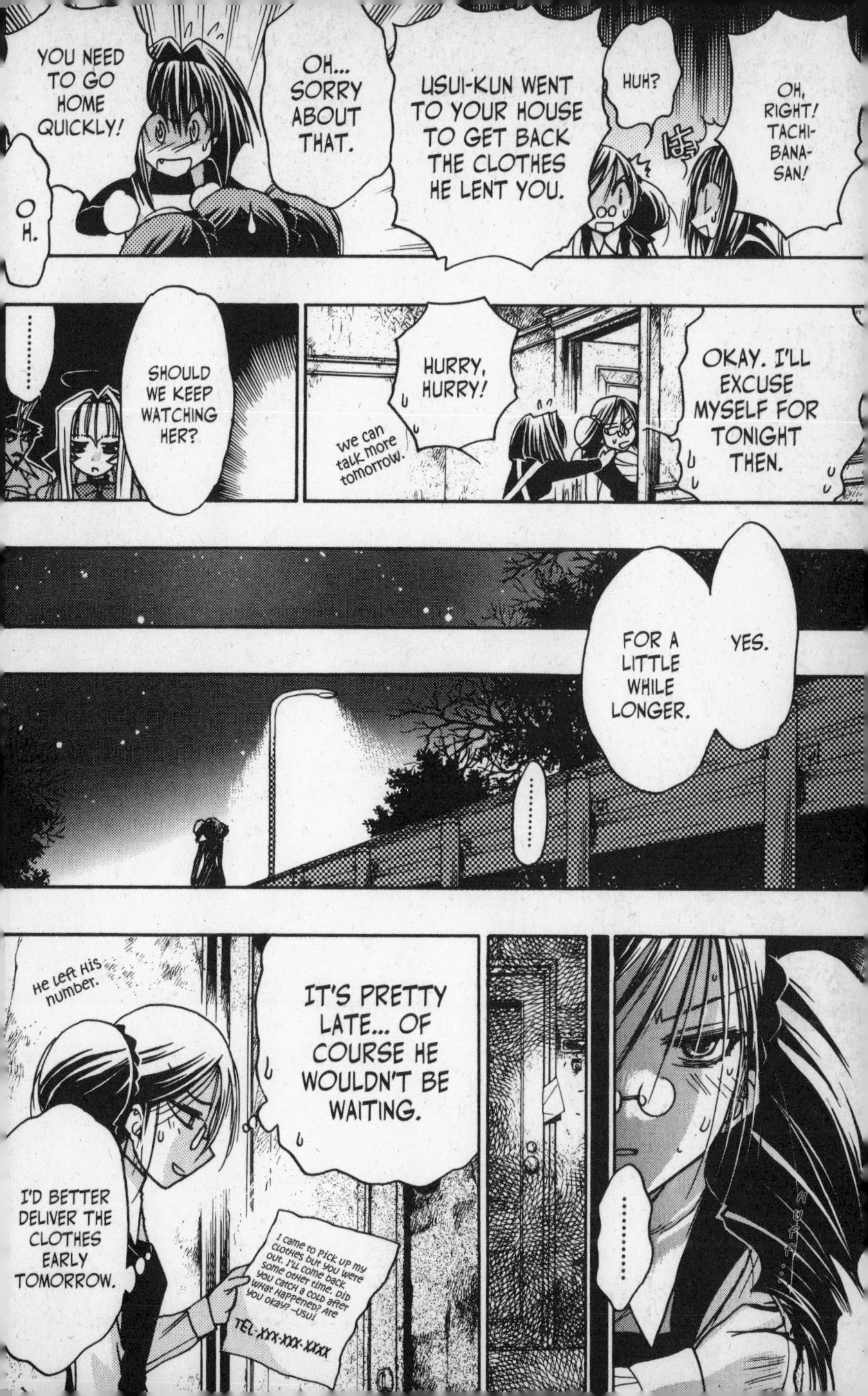
OH, RIGHT! TACHIBANA-SAN!
HUH?
は
USUI-KUN WENT TO YOUR HOUSE TO GET BACK THE CLOTHES HE LENT YOU.
OH... SORRY ABOUT THAT.
YOU NEED TO GO HOME QUICKLY!
OH.
OKAY. I'LL EXCUSE MYSELF FOR TONIGHT THEN.
HURRY, HURRY!
We can talk more tomorrow.
SHOULD WE KEEP WATCHING HER?
......
YES.
FOR A LITTLE WHILE LONGER.
......
......
Huff...
IT'S PRETTY LATE... OF COURSE HE WOULDN'T BE WAITING.
He left His number.
I'D BETTER DELIVER THE CLOTHES EARLY TOMORROW.
I came to pick up my clothes but you were out. I'll come back some other time. Did you catch a cold after what Happened? Are you okay? —Usui
TEL-XXX-XXX-XXXX

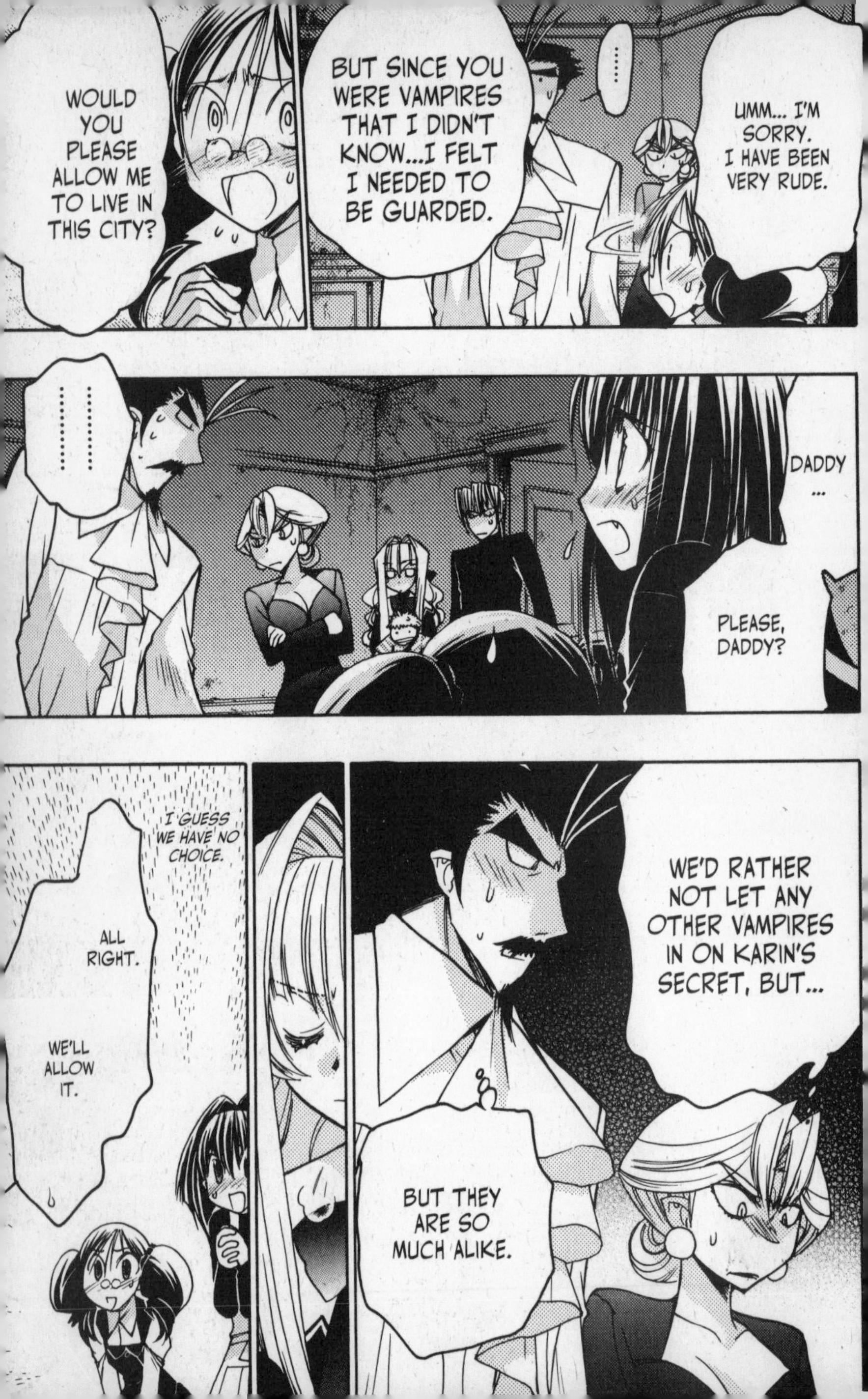
UMM... I'M SORRY. I HAVE BEEN VERY RUDE.
......
BUT SINCE YOU WERE VAMPIRES THAT I DIDN'T KNOW...I FELT I NEEDED TO BE GUARDED.
WOULD YOU PLEASE ALLOW ME TO LIVE IN THIS CITY?
DADDY ...
PLEASE, DADDY?
......
WE'D RATHER NOT LET ANY OTHER VAMPIRES IN ON KARIN'S SECRET, BUT...
BUT THEY ARE SO MUCH ALIKE.
I GUESS WE HAVE NO CHOICE.
ALL RIGHT. WE'LL ALLOW IT.

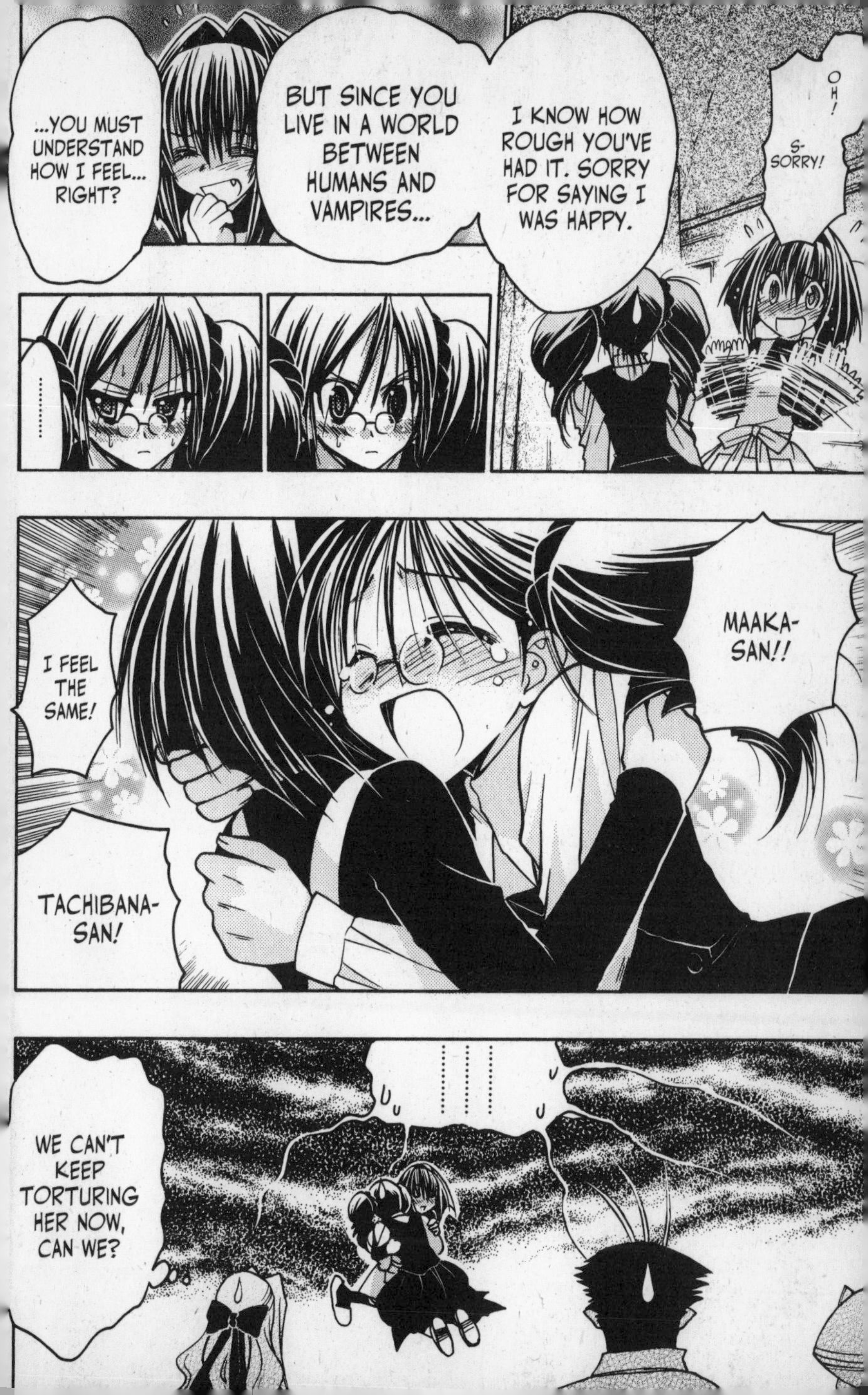
OH! S-SORRY!
I KNOW HOW ROUGH YOU'VE HAD IT. SORRY FOR SAYING I WAS HAPPY.
BUT SINCE YOU LIVE IN A WORLD BETWEEN HUMANS AND VAMPIRES...
...YOU MUST UNDERSTAND HOW I FEEL... RIGHT?
......
MAAKA-SAN!!
I FEEL THE SAME!
TACHIBANA-SAN!
......
WE CAN'T KEEP TORTURING HER NOW, CAN WE?

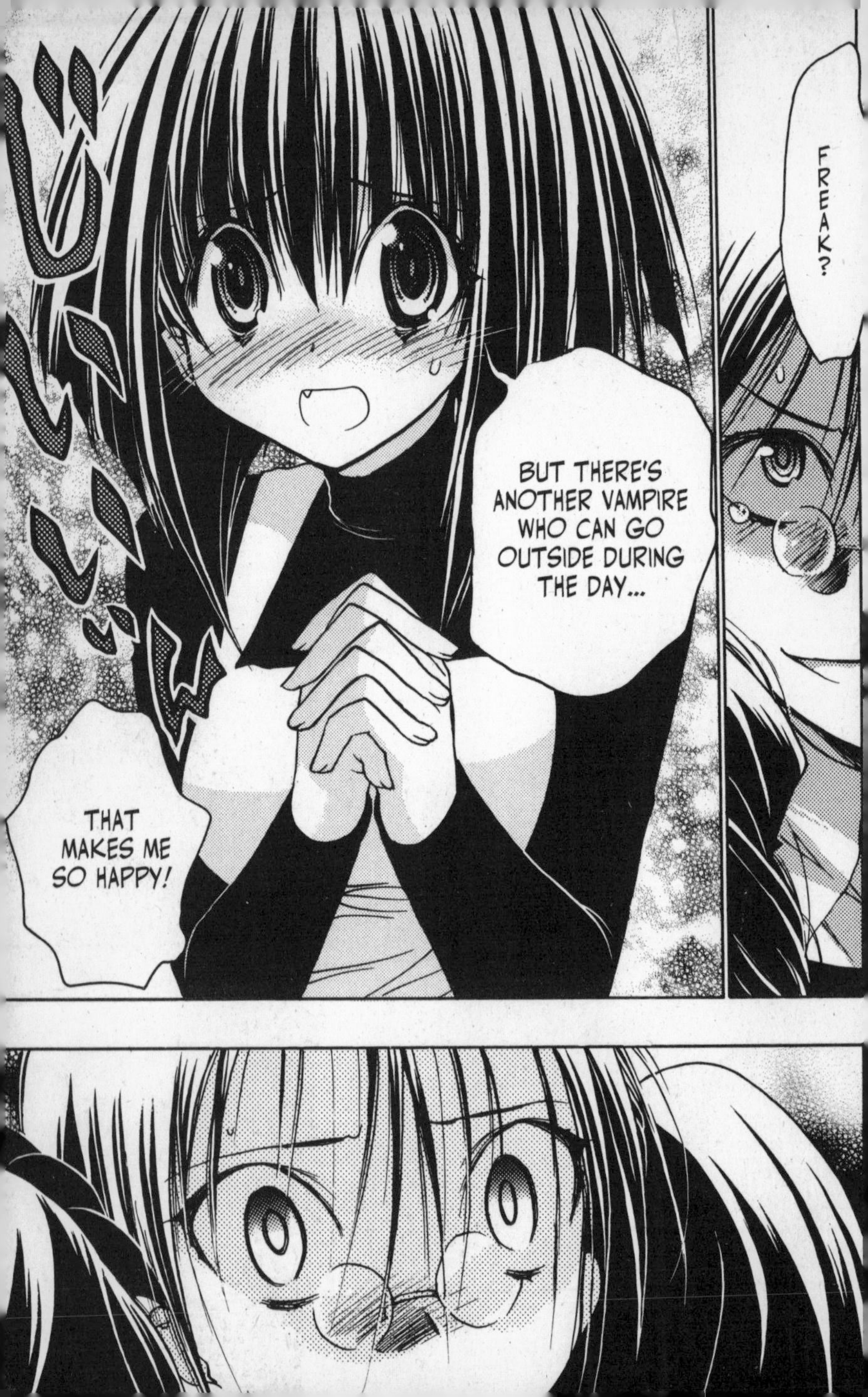
FREAK?
BUT THERE'S ANOTHER VAMPIRE WHO CAN GO OUTSIDE DURING THE DAY...
THAT MAKES ME SO HAPPY!

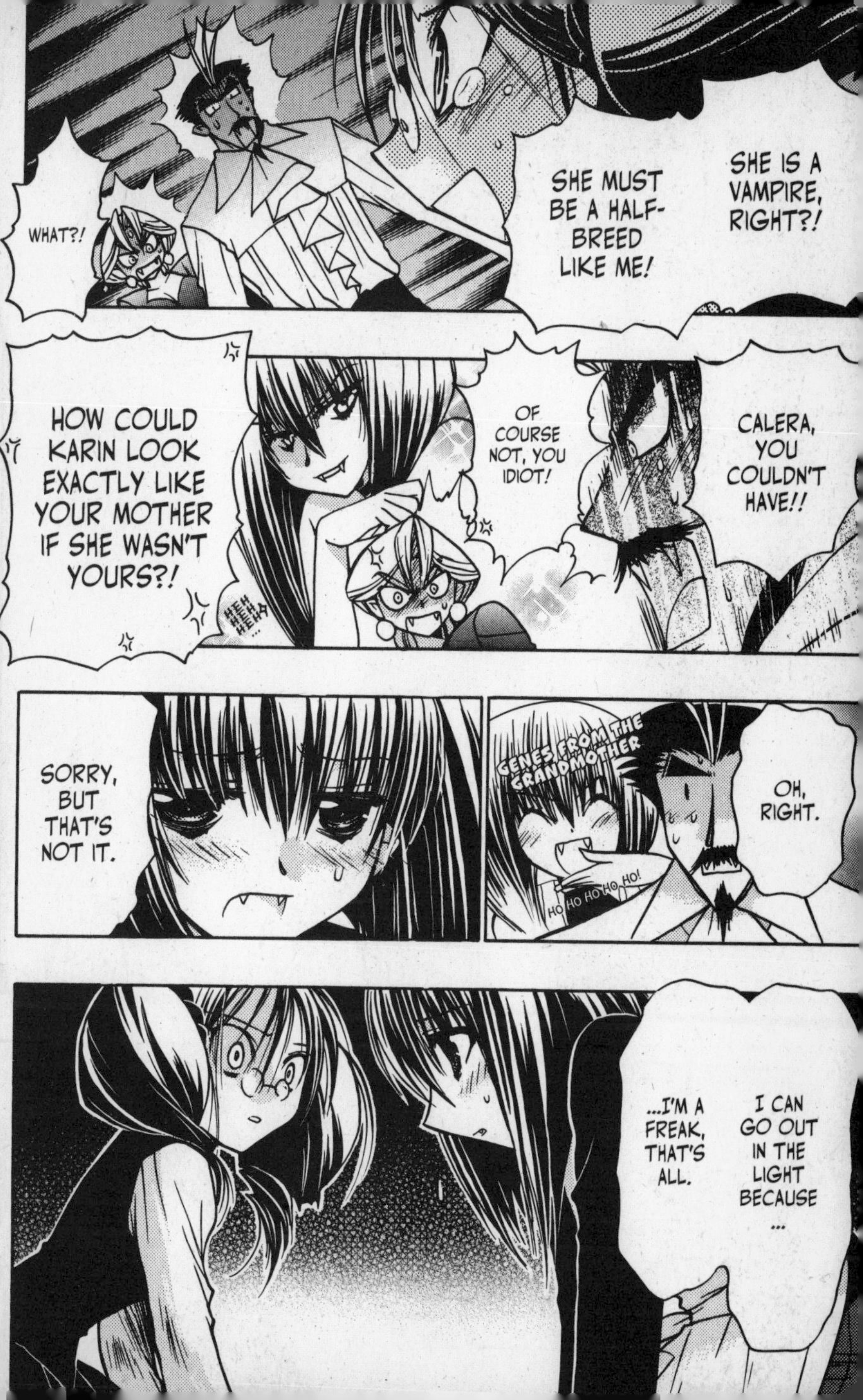
SHE IS A VAMPIRE, RIGHT?!
SHE MUST BE A HALF-BREED LIKE ME!
WHAT?!
CALERA, YOU COULDN'T HAVE!!
OF COURSE NOT, YOU IDIOT!
HOW COULD KARIN LOOK EXACTLY LIKE YOUR MOTHER IF SHE WASN'T YOURS?!
HEH HEH HEH...
OH, RIGHT.
GENES FROM THE GRANDMOTHER
HO HO HO HO HO!
SORRY, BUT THAT'S NOT IT.
I CAN GO OUT IN THE LIGHT BECAUSE ...
...I'M A FREAK, THAT'S ALL.

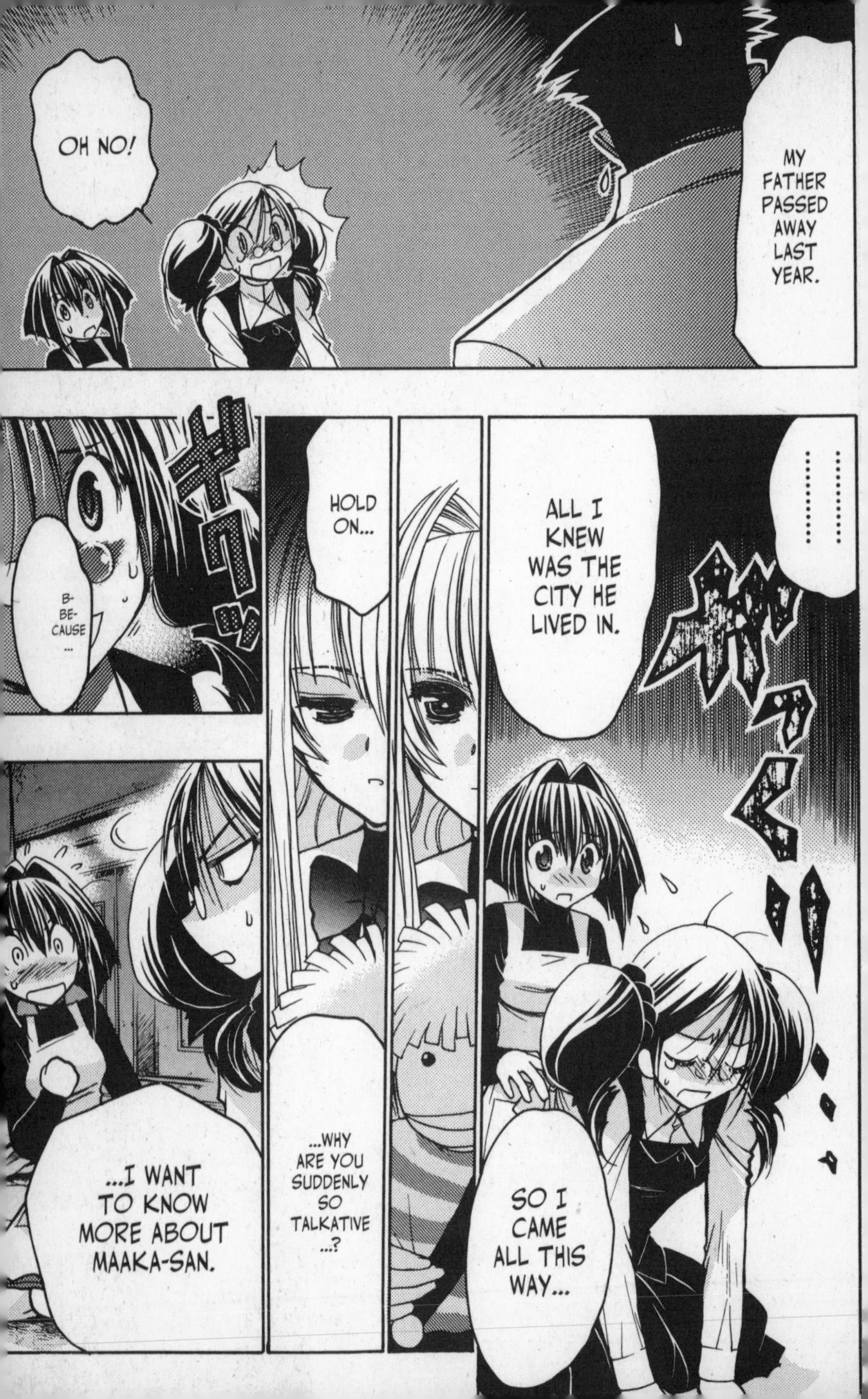
MY FATHER PASSED AWAY LAST YEAR.
OH NO!
......
ALL I KNEW WAS THE CITY HE LIVED IN.
SO I CAME ALL THIS WAY...
HOLD ON...
...WHY ARE YOU SUDDENLY SO TALKATIVE...?
ギクッ
B-BE-CAUSE...
...I WANT TO KNOW MORE ABOUT MAAKA-SAN.

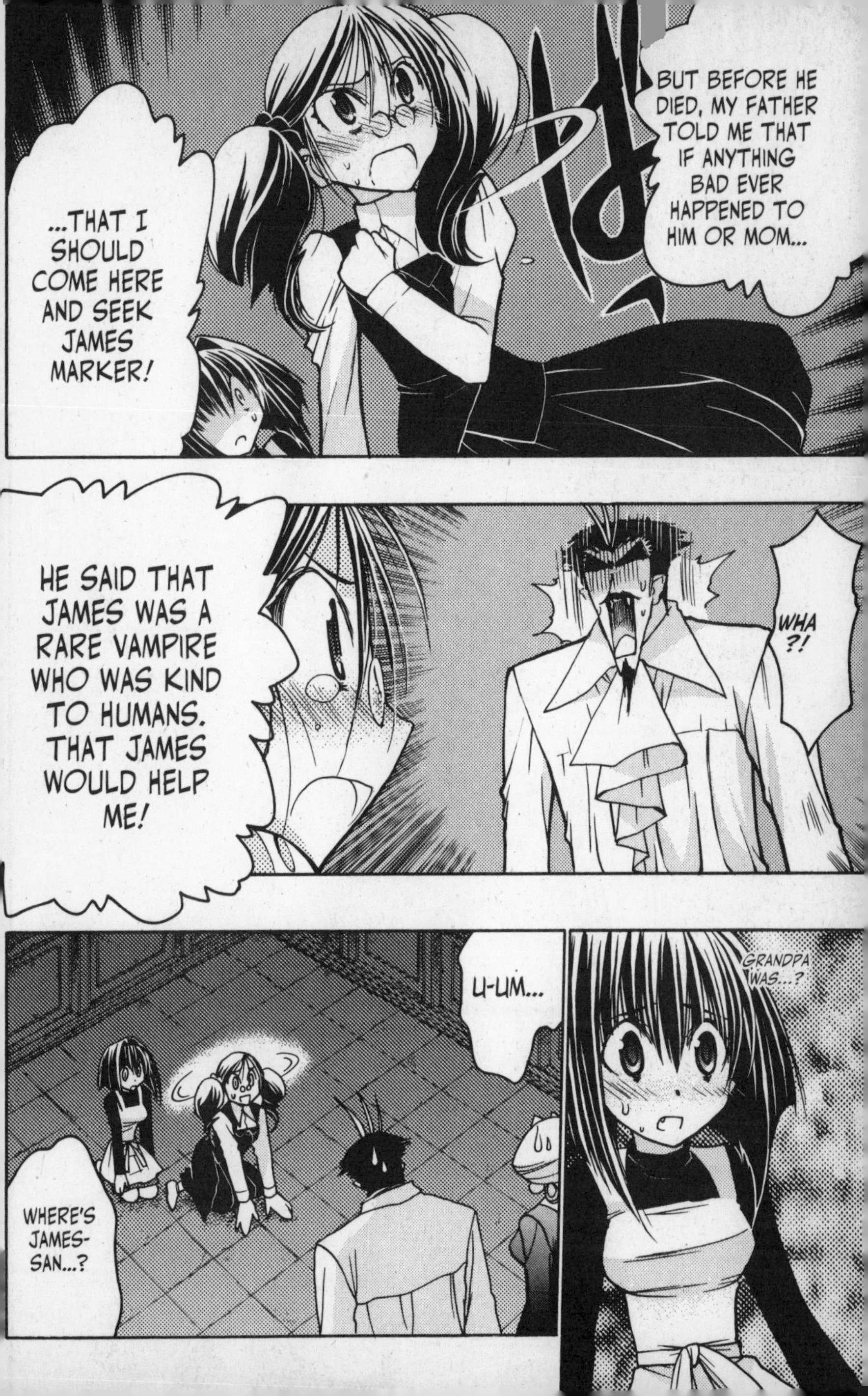
BUT BEFORE HE DIED, MY FATHER TOLD ME THAT IF ANYTHING BAD EVER HAPPENED TO HIM OR MOM...
...THAT I SHOULD COME HERE AND SEEK JAMES MARKER!
HE SAID THAT JAMES WAS A RARE VAMPIRE WHO WAS KIND TO HUMANS. THAT JAMES WOULD HELP ME!
WHA ?!
GRANDPA WAS...?
U-UM...
WHERE'S JAMES-SAN...?

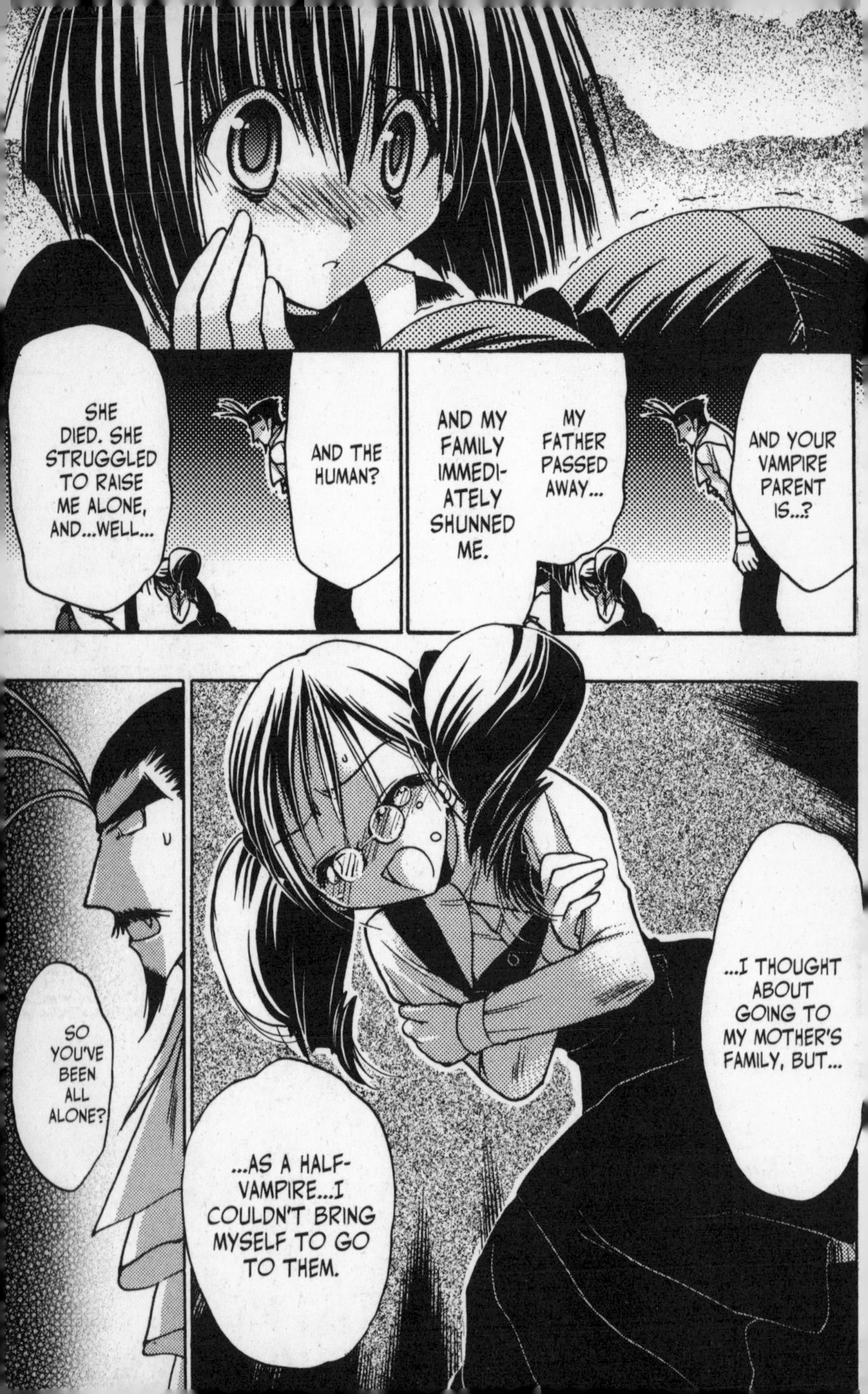
AND YOUR VAMPIRE PARENT IS...?
MY FATHER PASSED AWAY...
AND MY FAMILY IMMEDI-ATELY SHUNNED ME.
AND THE HUMAN?
SHE DIED. SHE STRUGGLED TO RAISE ME ALONE, AND...WELL...
...I THOUGHT ABOUT GOING TO MY MOTHER'S FAMILY, BUT...
...AS A HALF-VAMPIRE...I COULDN'T BRING MYSELF TO GO TO THEM.
SO YOU'VE BEEN ALL ALONE?

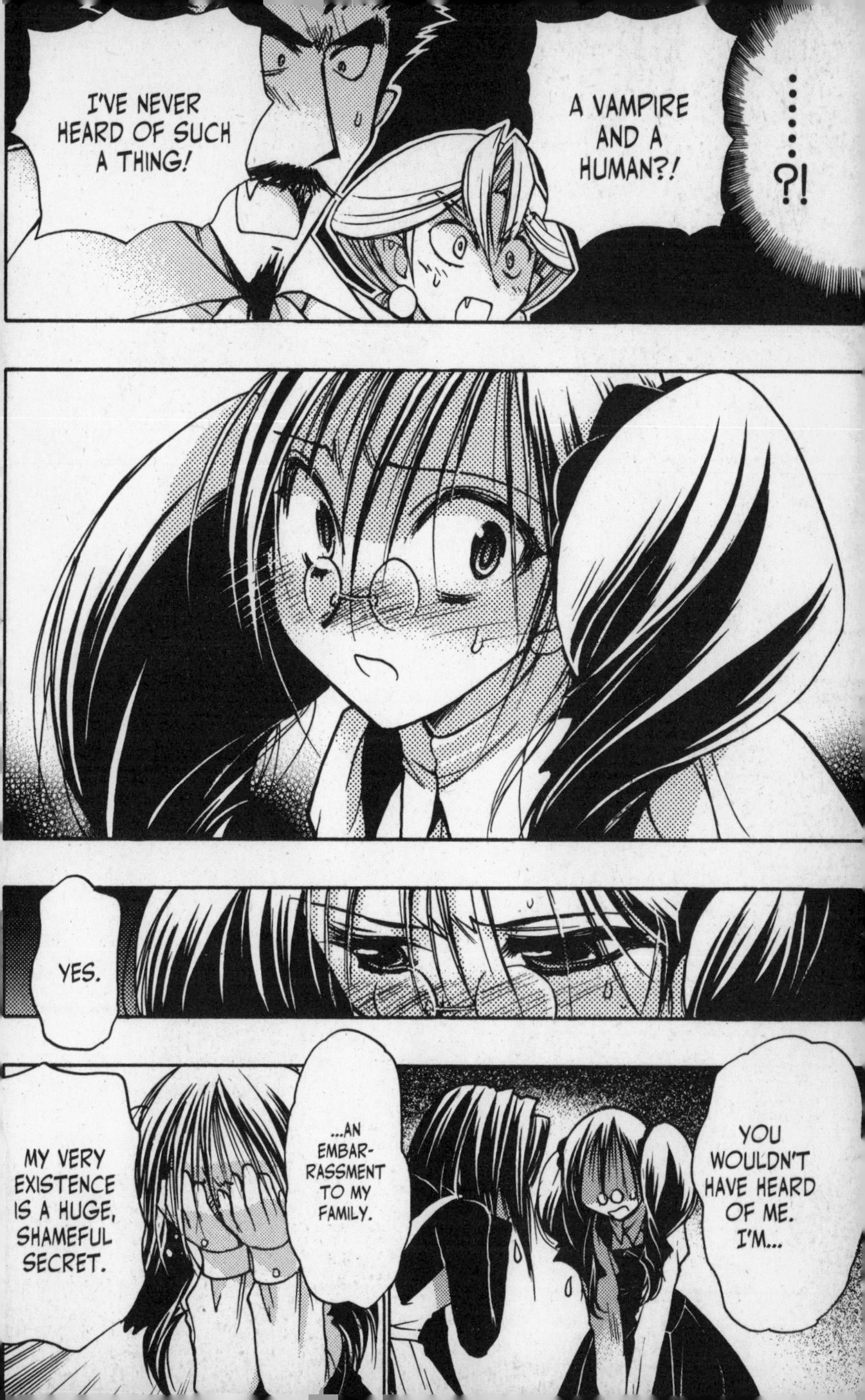
......?!
A VAMPIRE AND A HUMAN?!
I'VE NEVER HEARD OF SUCH A THING!
YES.
YOU WOULDN'T HAVE HEARD OF ME. I'M...
...AN EMBAR-RASSMENT TO MY FAMILY.
MY VERY EXISTENCE IS A HUGE, SHAMEFUL SECRET.

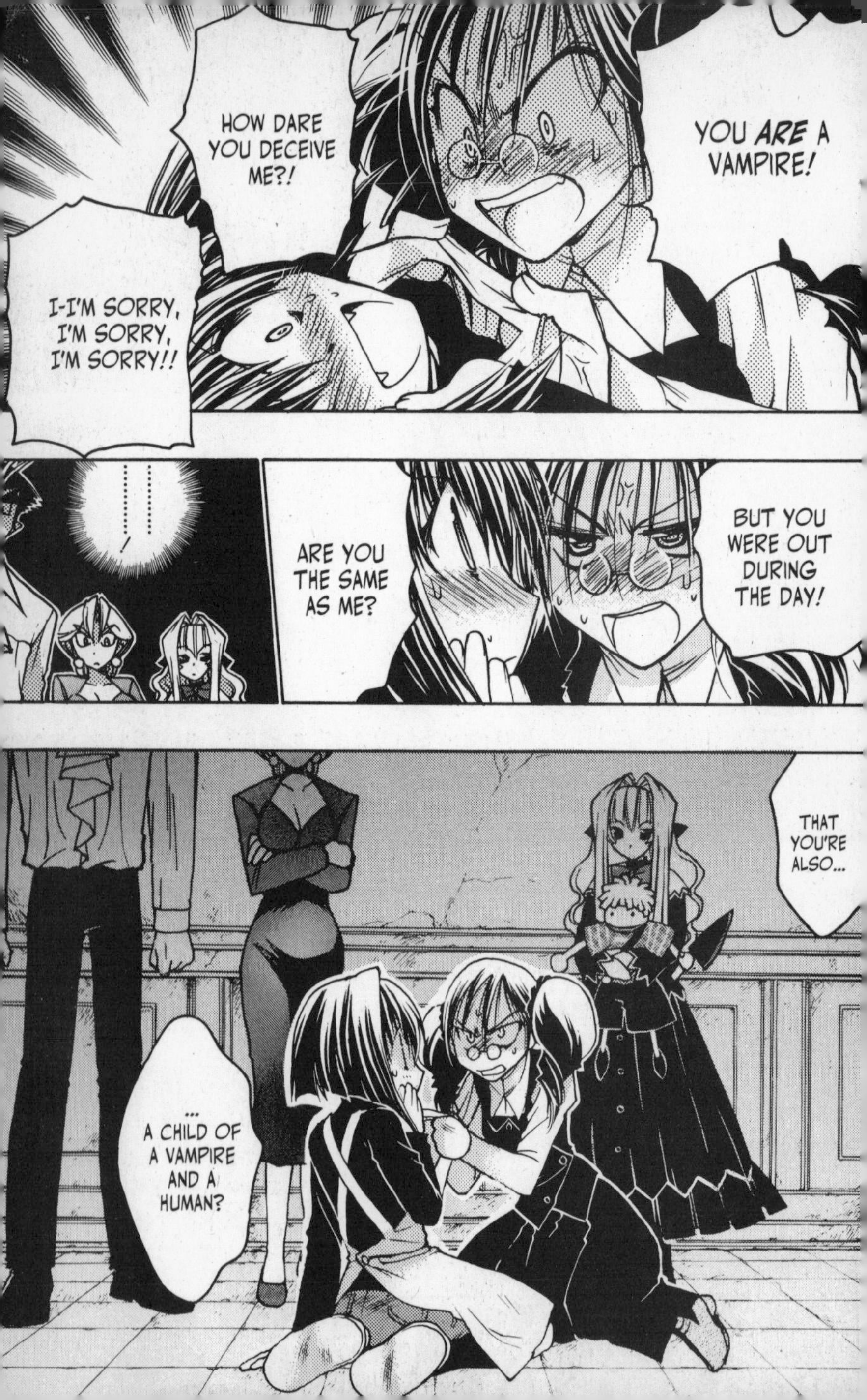
YOU *ARE* A VAMPIRE!
HOW DARE YOU DECEIVE ME?!
I-I'M SORRY, I'M SORRY, I'M SORRY!!
BUT YOU WERE OUT DURING THE DAY!
ARE YOU THE SAME AS ME?
......
......!
THAT YOU'RE ALSO...
... A CHILD OF A VAMPIRE AND A HUMAN?

YUNA KAGESAKI

chibi Vampire

9

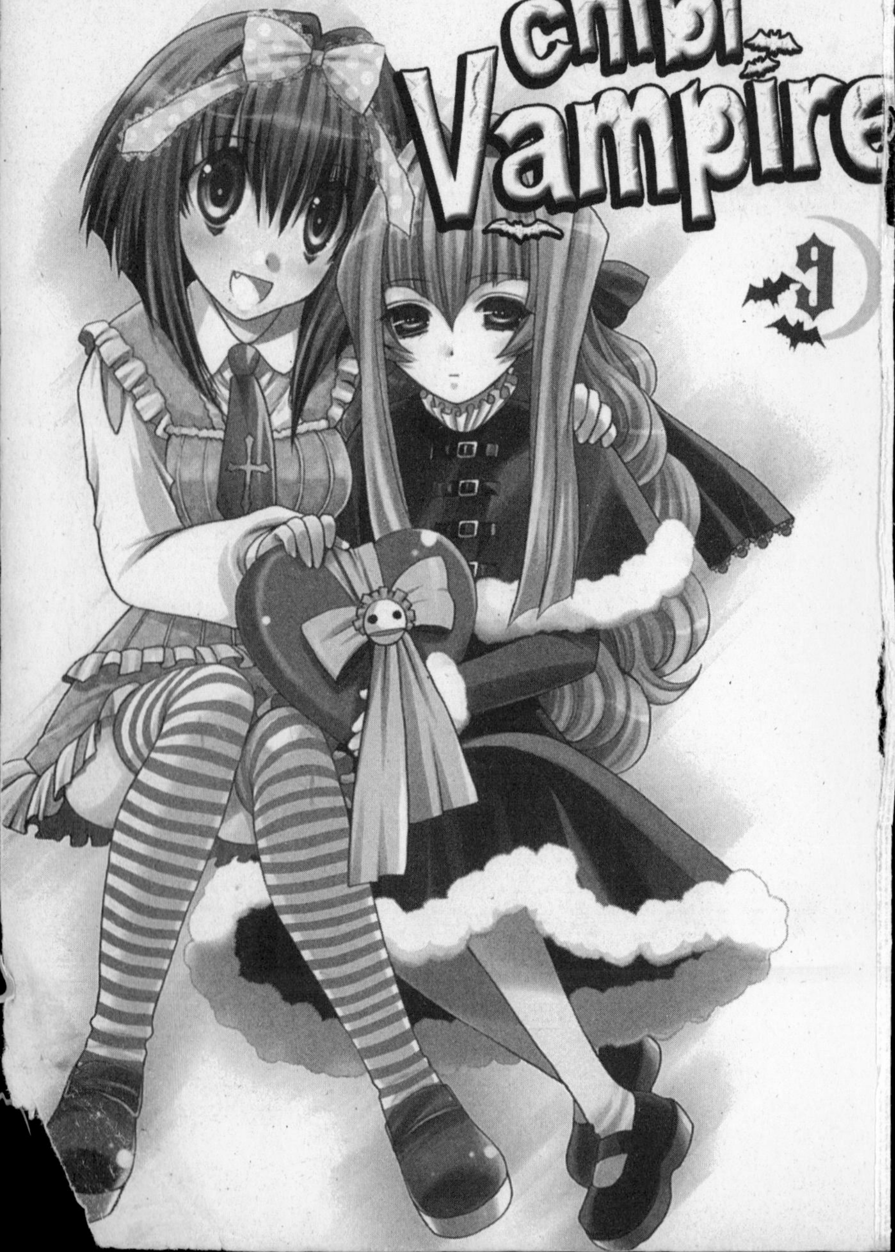

Chibi Vampire Volume 9
Created by Yuna Kagesaki

Translation - Alexis Kirsch
English Adaptation - Christine Boylan
Copy Editor - Jessica Chavez
Retouch and Lettering - Star Print Brokers
Production Artist - Keila N. Ramos
Graphic Designer - Colin Graham

Editor - Nikhil Burman
Digital Imaging Manager - Chris Buford
Pre-Production Supervisor - Lucas Rivera
Production Manager - Elisabeth Brizzi
Managing Editor - Vy Nguyen
Creative Director - Anne Marie Horne
Editor-in-Chief - Rob Tokar
Publisher - Mike Kiley
President and C.O.O. - John Parker
C.E.O. and Chief Creative Officer - Stu Levy

A  Manga

TOKYOPOP Inc.
5900 Wilshire Blvd. Suite 2000
Los Angeles, CA 90036

E-mail: info@TOKYOPOP.com
Come visit us online at www.TOKYOPOP.com

KARIN Volume 9 © 2006 YUNA KAGESAKI
First published in Japan in 2006 by FUJIMISHOBO CO., LTD.,
Tokyo. English translation rights arranged with KADOKAWA
SHOTEN PUBLISHING CO., LTD., Tokyo through TUTTLE-MORI
AGENCY, INC., Tokyo.
English text copyright © 2008 TOKYOPOP Inc.

ISBN: 978-1-4278-0197-5

First TOKYOPOP printing: July 2008
10 9 8 7 6 5 4 3
Printed in the USA

Chibi Vampire

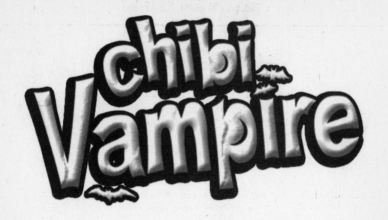

Volume 9

Created by
Yuna Kagesaki

TOKYOPOP®

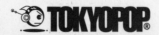

HAMBURG // LONDON // LOS ANGELES // TOKYO

OUR STORY SO FAR...

KARIN MAAKA ISN'T LIKE OTHER GIRLS. ONCE A MONTH, SHE EXPERIENCES PAIN, FATIGUE, HUNGER, IRRITABILITY—AND THEN SHE BLEEDS. FROM HER NOSE. KARIN IS A VAMPIRE, FROM A FAMILY OF VAMPIRES, BUT INSTEAD OF NEEDING TO DRINK BLOOD, SHE HAS AN EXCESS OF BLOOD THAT SHE MUST GIVE TO HER VICTIMS. IF DONE RIGHT, GIVING THIS BLOOD TO HER VICTIM CAN BE AN EXTREMELY POSITIVE THING. THE PROBLEM WITH THIS IS THAT KARIN NEVER SEEMS TO DO THINGS RIGHT...

KARIN IS HAVING A BIT OF BOY TROUBLE. KENTA USUI—THE HANDSOME NEW STUDENT AT HER SCHOOL AND WORK—IS A NICE ENOUGH GUY, BUT HE EXACERBATES KARIN'S PROBLEM. KARIN'S BLOOD PROBLEM, YOU SEE, BECOMES WORSE WHEN SHE'S AROUND PEOPLE WHO HAVE SUFFERED MISFORTUNE, AND KENTA HAS SUFFERED PLENTY OF IT. MAKING THINGS EVEN MORE COMPLICATED, IT'S BECOME CLEAR TO KARIN THAT SHE'S IN LOVE WITH KENTA... SOMETHING THAT CAN ONLY BRING TROUBLE. LOVE BETWEEN HUMANS AND VAMPIRES IS FROWNED UPON IN VAMPIRE SOCIETY, AND KARIN'S FAMILY DECIDES THAT A RELATIONSHIP BETWEEN THEIR DAUGHTER AND A HUMAN BOY IS TOO DANGEROUS. THEY FORBID KENTA FROM EVER SEEING KARIN AGAIN. UPSET AND ANGRY, KARIN SEEKS OUT KENTA TO APOLOGIZE AND BEG HIM TO IGNORE HER FAMILY'S DEMAND, BUT IN THE PROCESS, SHE REVEALS WHY HER BLEEDING IS WORSE WHEN HE'S AROUND. AFTER SOME MUTUAL HEARTACHE, KENTA FINALLY LETS KARIN BITE HIM AND RELEASE HER BLOOD INTO HIM. AT LEAST FOR NOW, KENTA CAN BE NEAR KARIN WITHOUT HER BLOOD LEVEL INCREASING, AND THESE TWO CRAZY KIDS ARE CLOSER THAN EVER. WHEN WE LAST LEFT OFF, THE BUMBLING LOVERS WERE AT THE ZOO ON THEIR FIRST OFFICIAL DATE. AND ANJU HAS SURREPTITIOUSLY SHOWN UP TO KEEP AN EYE ON HER DISASTER-PRONE SISTER.

THE MAAKA FAMILY

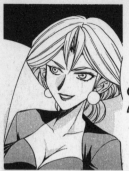

CALERA MARKER

Karin's overbearing mother. While Calera resents that Karin wasn't born a normal vampire, she does love her daughter in her own obnoxious way. Calera has chosen to keep her European last name.

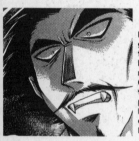

HENRY MARKER

Karin's father. In general, Henry treats Karin a lot better than her mother does, but Calera wears the pants in this particular family. Henry has also chosen to keep his European last name.

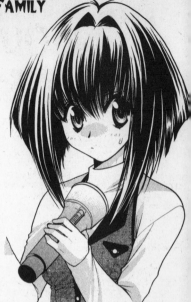

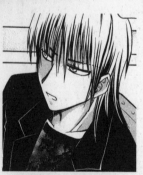

REN MAAKA

Karin's older brother. Ren milks the "sexy creature of the night" thing for all it's worth and spends his nights in the arms (and beds) of attractive young women.

KARIN MAAKA

Our little heroine. Karin is a vampire living in Japan, but instead of sucking blood from her victims, she actually GIVES them some of her blood. She's a vampire in reverse!

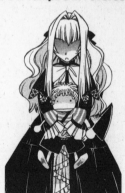

ANJU MAAKA

Karin's little sister. Anju has not yet awoken as a full vampire, but she can control bats and is usually the one who cleans up after Karin's messes. Rarely seen without her "talking" doll, Boogie.

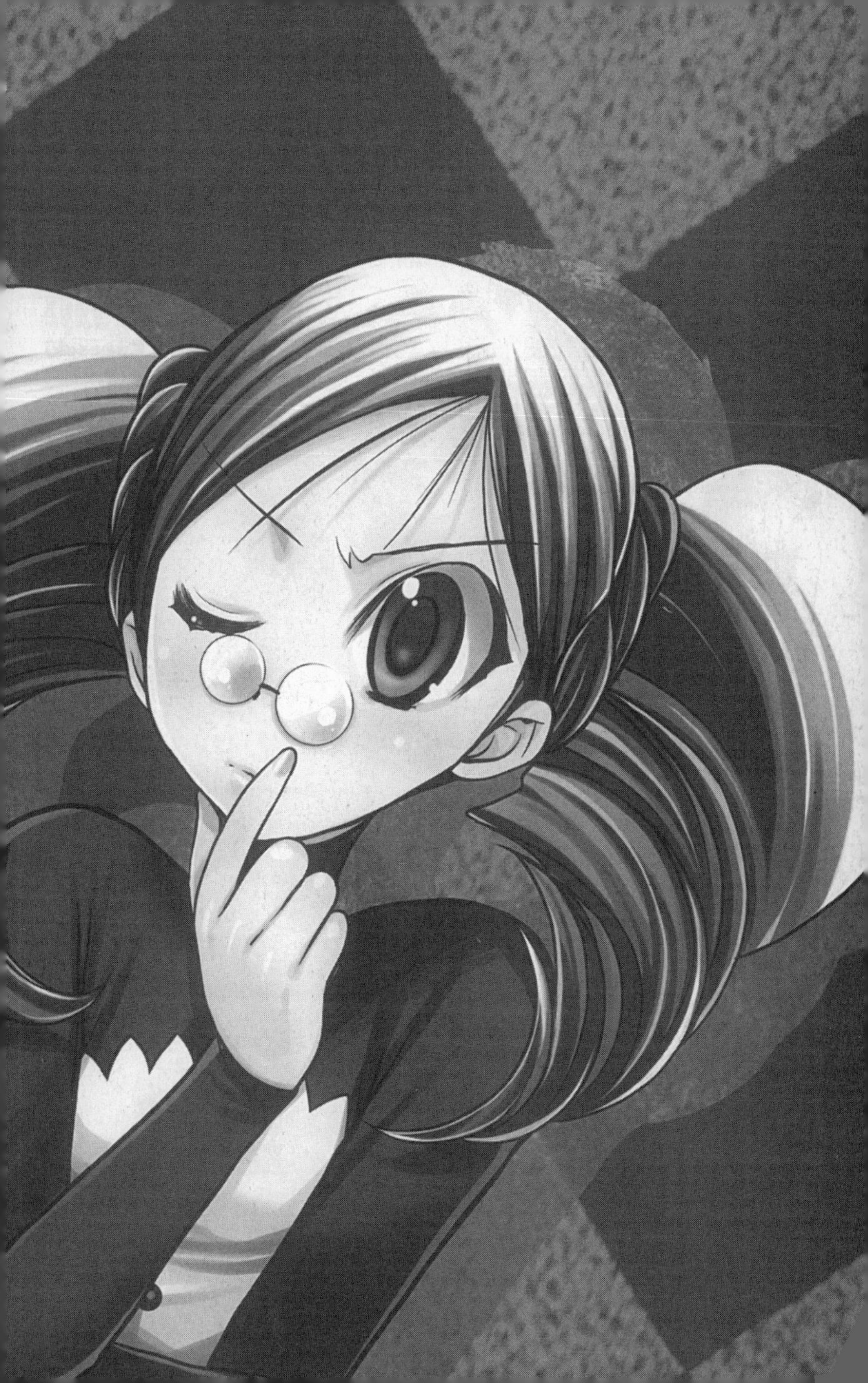

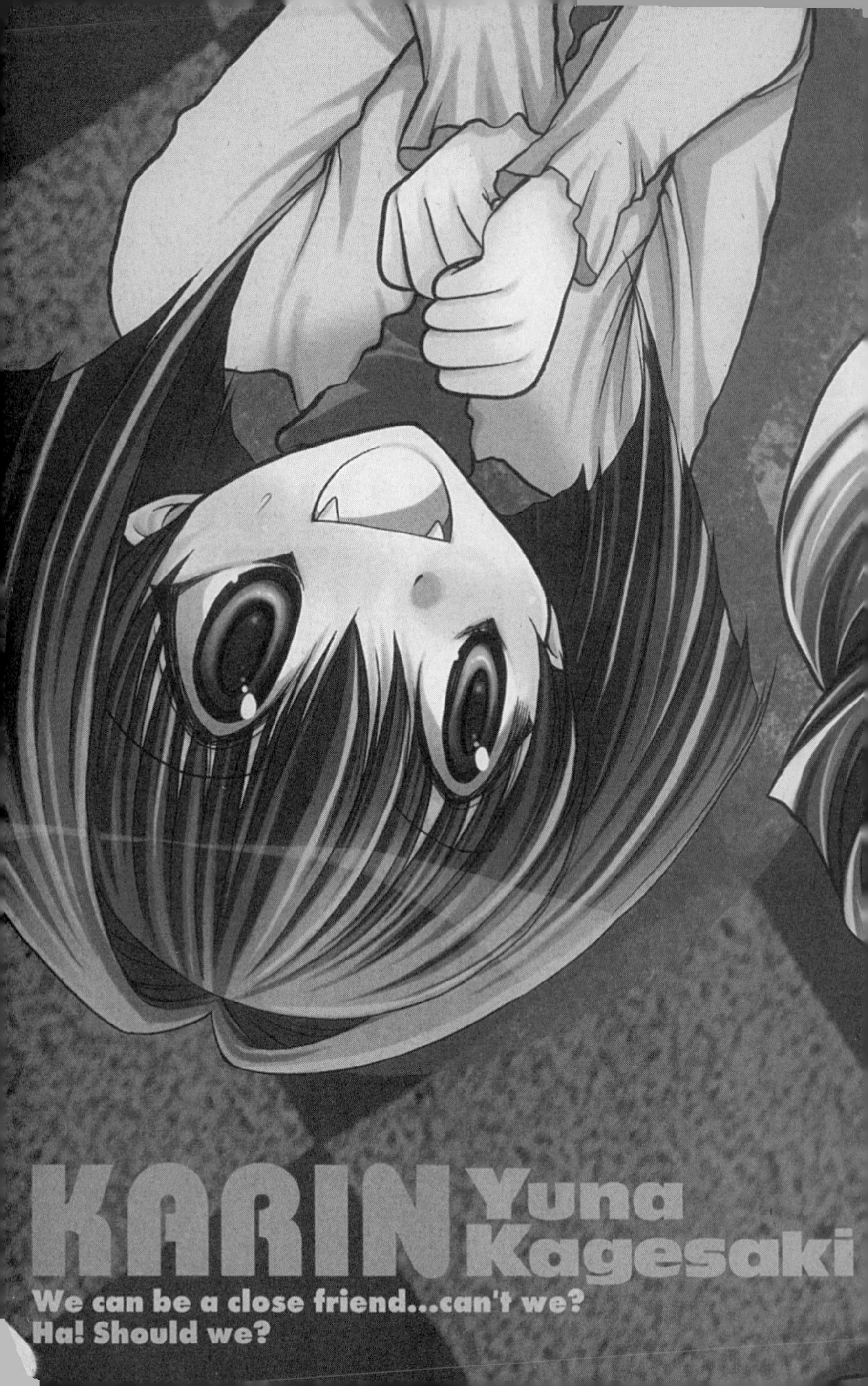
KARIN
Yuna Kagesaki
We can be a close friend...can't we?
Ha! Should we?

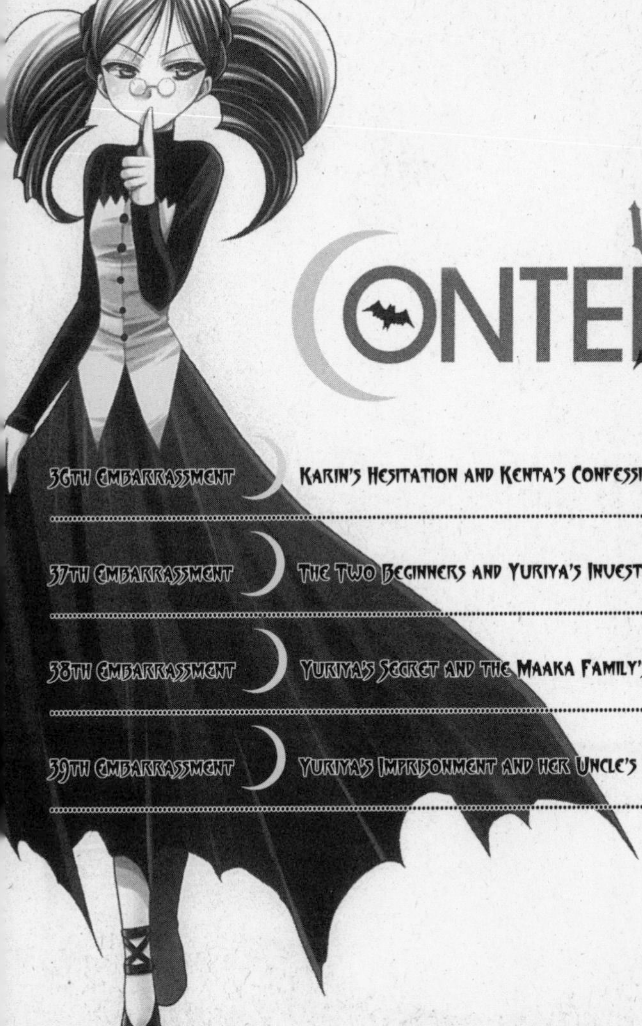

VOL. 9 CONTENTS

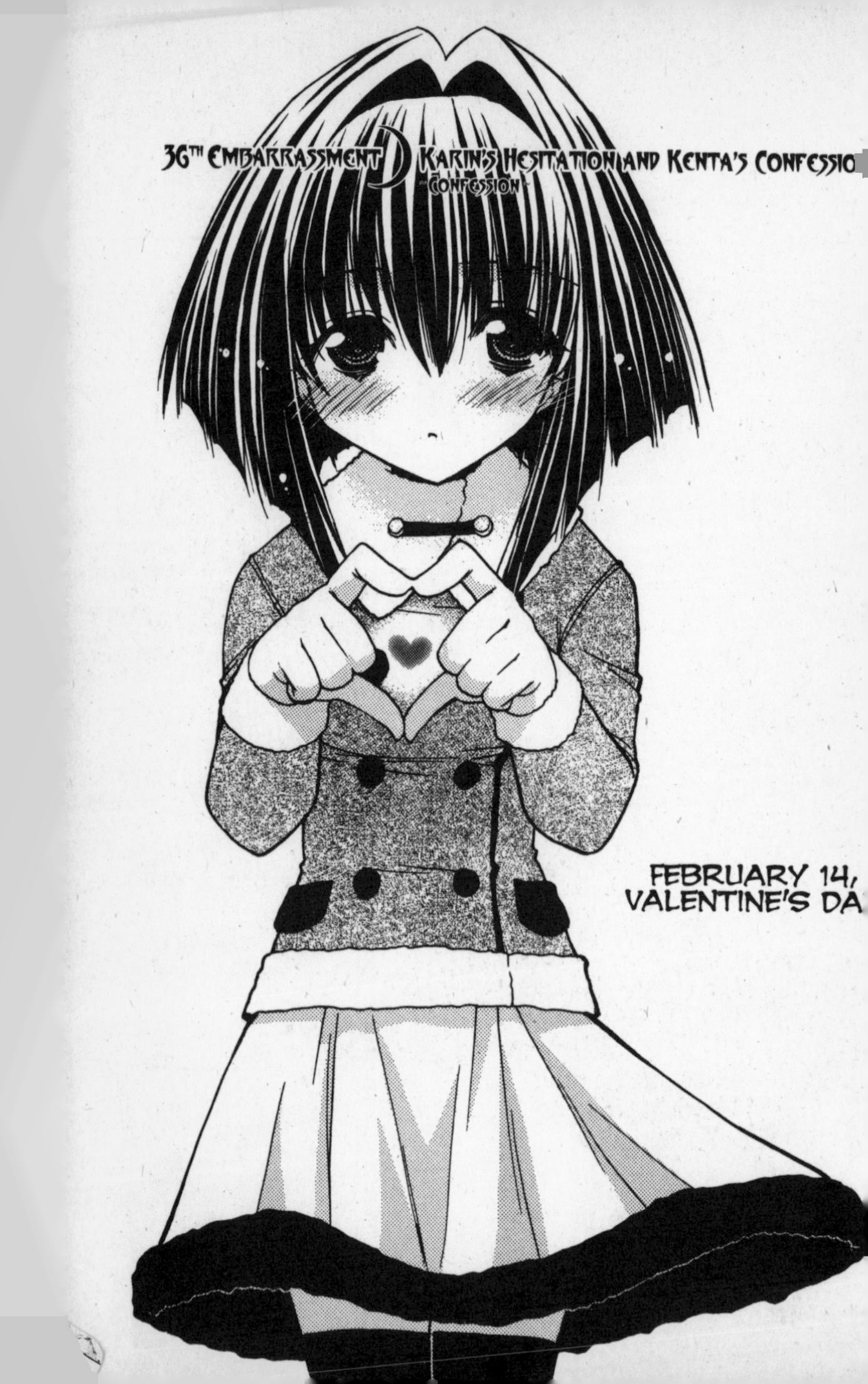
36TH EMBARRASSMENT KARIN'S HESITATION AND KENTA'S CONFESSIO
~CONFESSION~
FEBRUARY 14,
VALENTINE'S DA

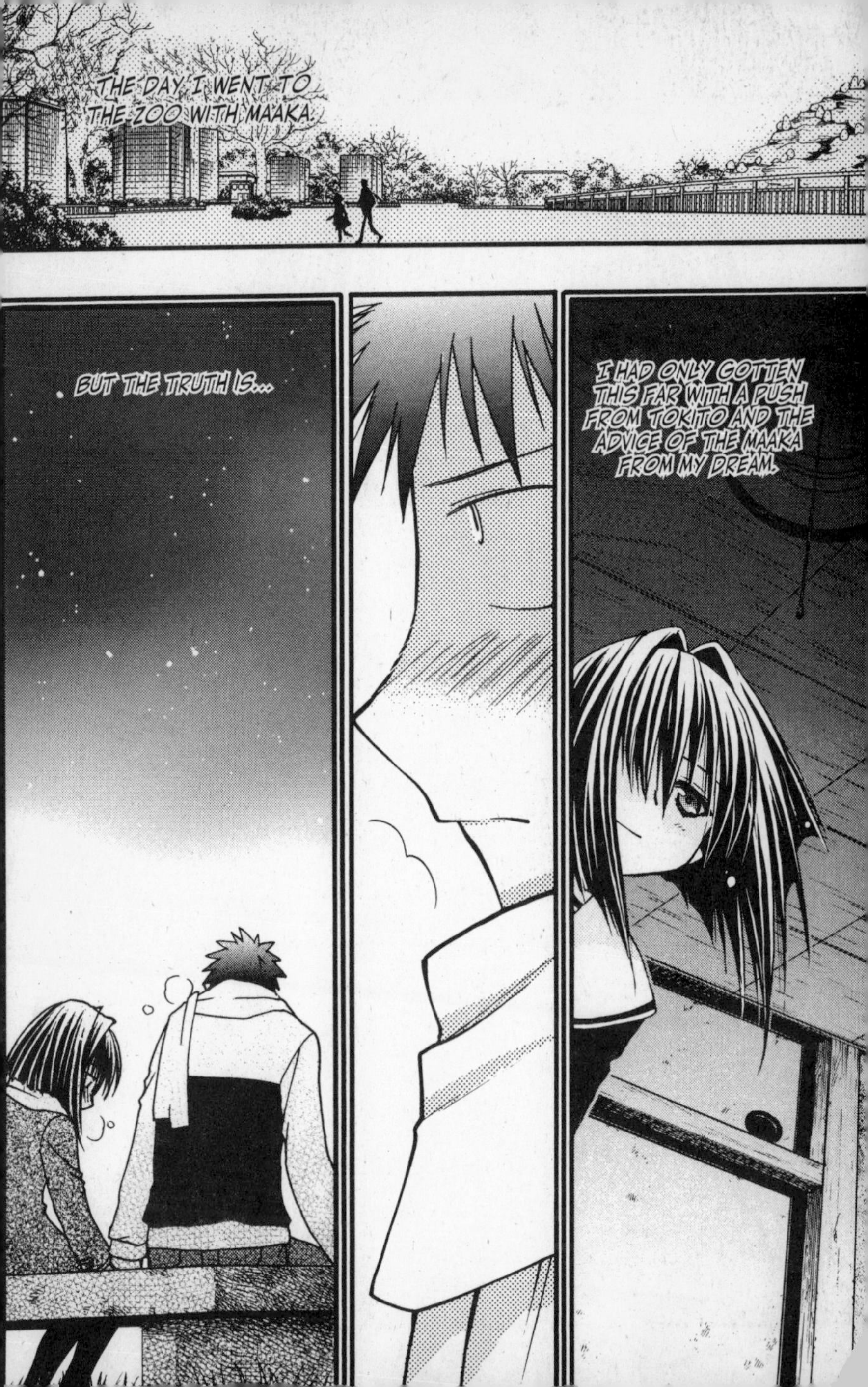
THE DAY I WENT TO THE ZOO WITH MAAKA.
I HAD ONLY GOTTEN THIS FAR WITH A PUSH FROM TOKITO AND THE ADVICE OF THE MAAKA FROM MY DREAM.
BUT THE TRUTH IS...

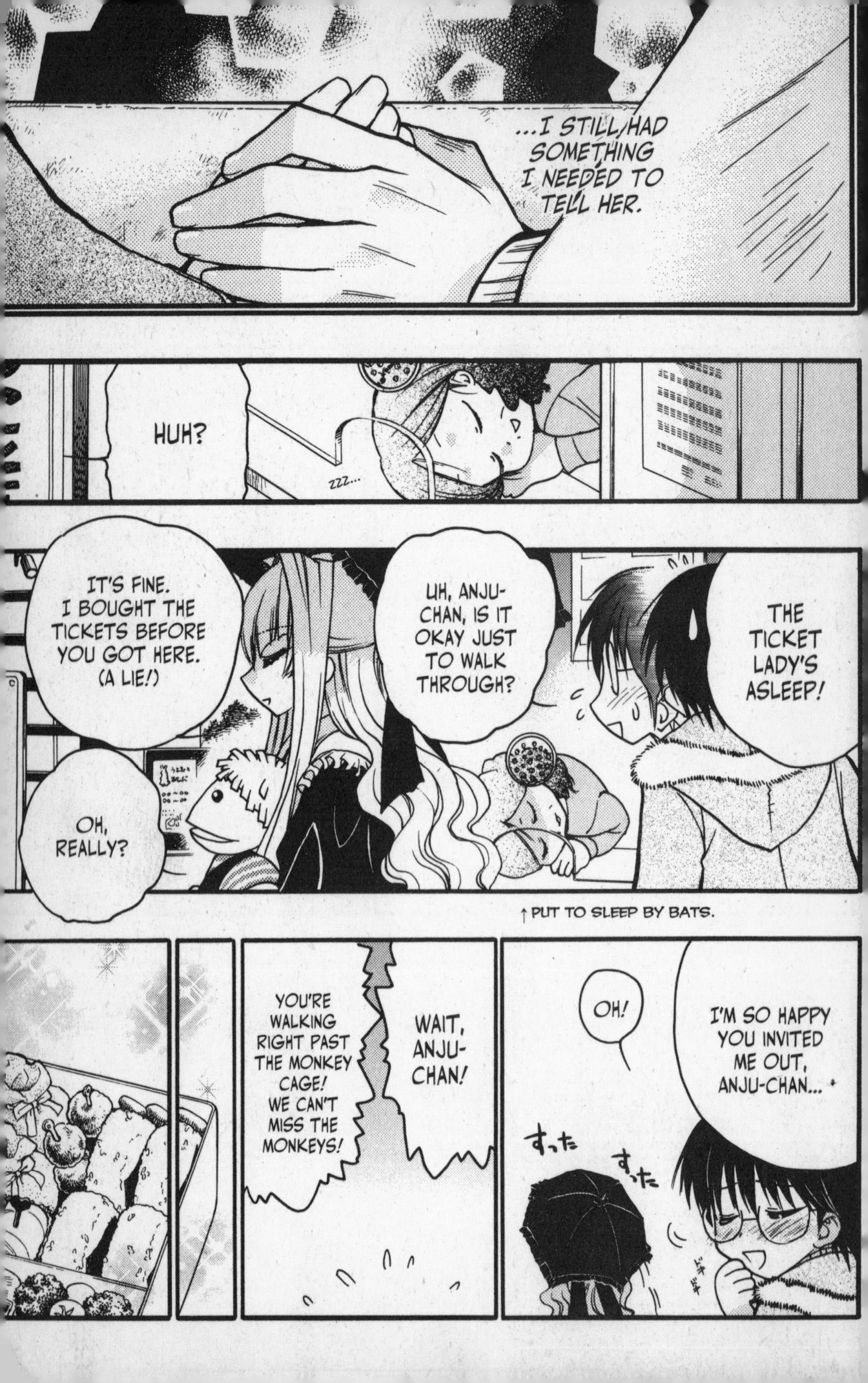
...I STILL HAD SOMETHING I NEEDED TO TELL HER.
HUH?
ZZZ...
THE TICKET LADY'S ASLEEP!
UH, ANJU-CHAN, IS IT OKAY JUST TO WALK THROUGH?
IT'S FINE. I BOUGHT THE TICKETS BEFORE YOU GOT HERE. (A LIE!)
OH, REALLY?
↑ PUT TO SLEEP BY BATS.
I'M SO HAPPY YOU INVITED ME OUT, ANJU-CHAN...
OH!
すった
すった
WAIT, ANJU-CHAN!
YOU'RE WALKING RIGHT PAST THE MONKEY CAGE! WE CAN'T MISS THE MONKEYS!

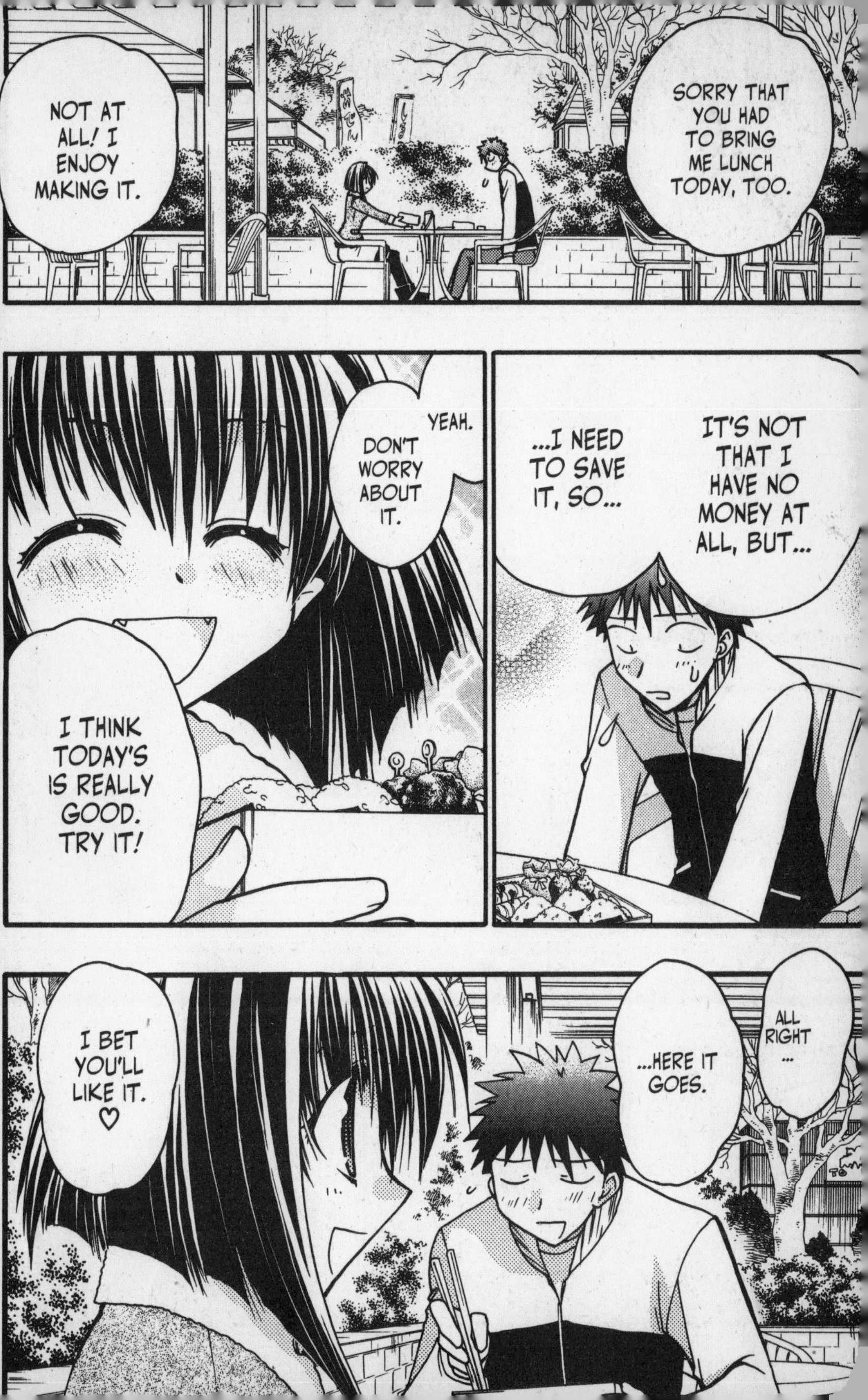
SORRY THAT YOU HAD TO BRING ME LUNCH TODAY, TOO.
NOT AT ALL! I ENJOY MAKING IT.
IT'S NOT THAT I HAVE NO MONEY AT ALL, BUT...
...I NEED TO SAVE IT, SO...
YEAH. DON'T WORRY ABOUT IT.
I THINK TODAY'S IS REALLY GOOD. TRY IT!
ALL RIGHT...
...HERE IT GOES.
I BET YOU'LL LIKE IT. ♡

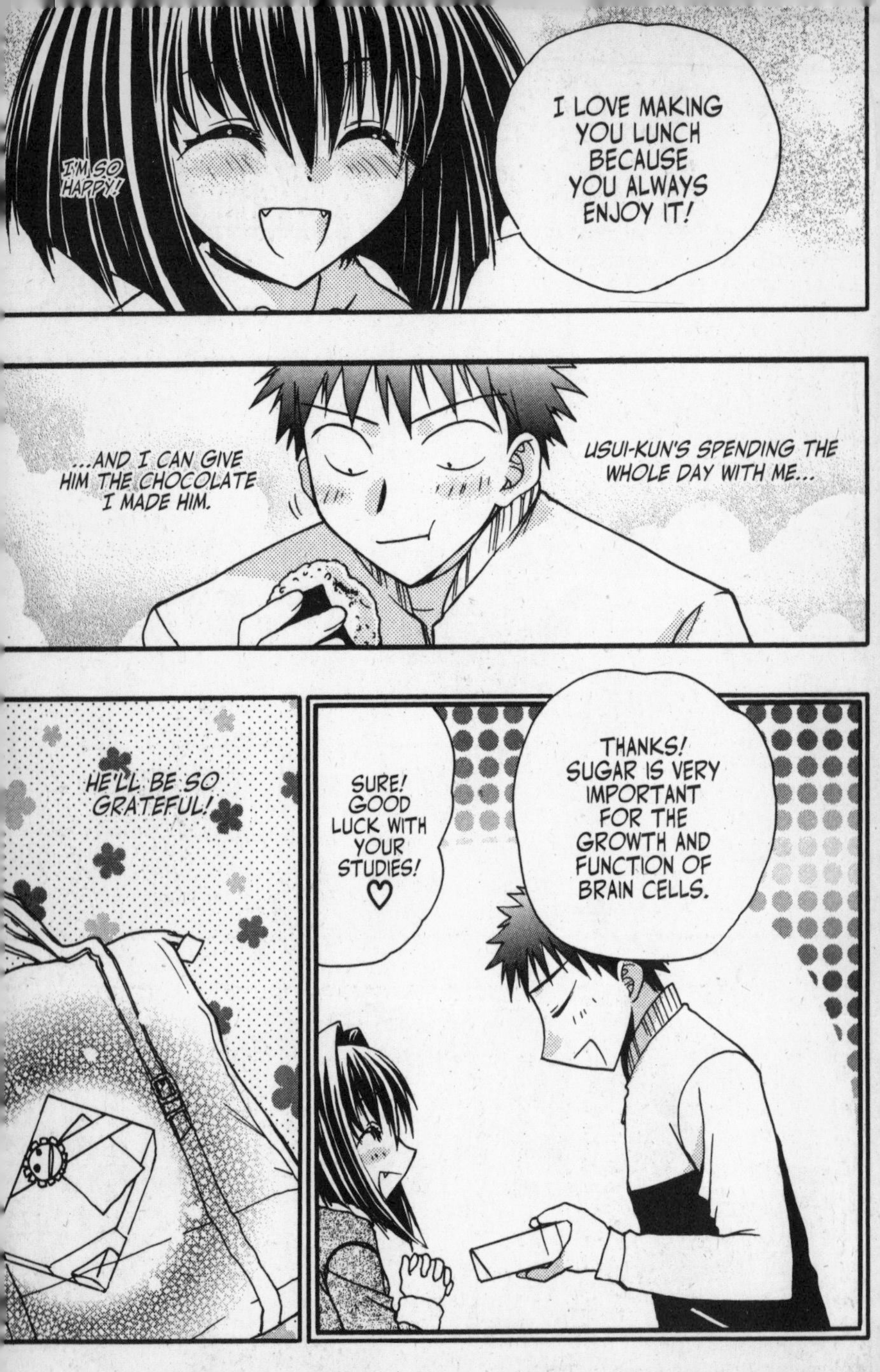
I LOVE MAKING YOU LUNCH BECAUSE YOU ALWAYS ENJOY IT!
I'M SO HAPPY!
USUI-KUN'S SPENDING THE WHOLE DAY WITH ME...
...AND I CAN GIVE HIM THE CHOCOLATE I MADE HIM.
THANKS! SUGAR IS VERY IMPORTANT FOR THE GROWTH AND FUNCTION OF BRAIN CELLS.
SURE! GOOD LUCK WITH YOUR STUDIES! ♡
HE'LL BE SO GRATEFUL!

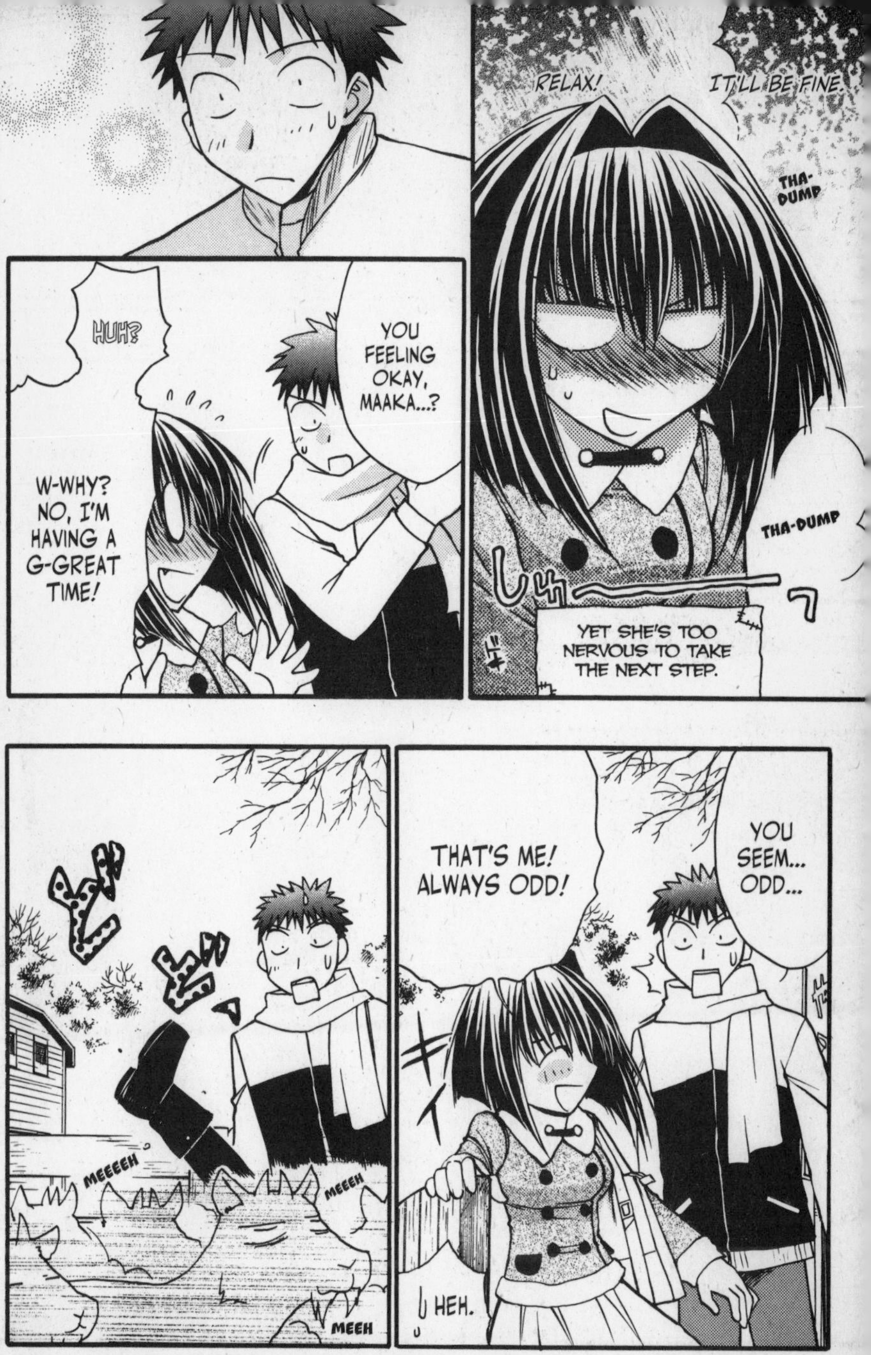

RELAX!
IT'LL BE FINE.
THA-DUMP
THA-DUMP
YET SHE'S TOO NERVOUS TO TAKE THE NEXT STEP.
YOU FEELING OKAY, MAAKA...?
HUH?
W-WHY? NO, I'M HAVING A G-GREAT TIME!
YOU SEEM... ODD...
THAT'S ME! ALWAYS ODD!
HEH.
MEEEEH
MEEEH
MEEH

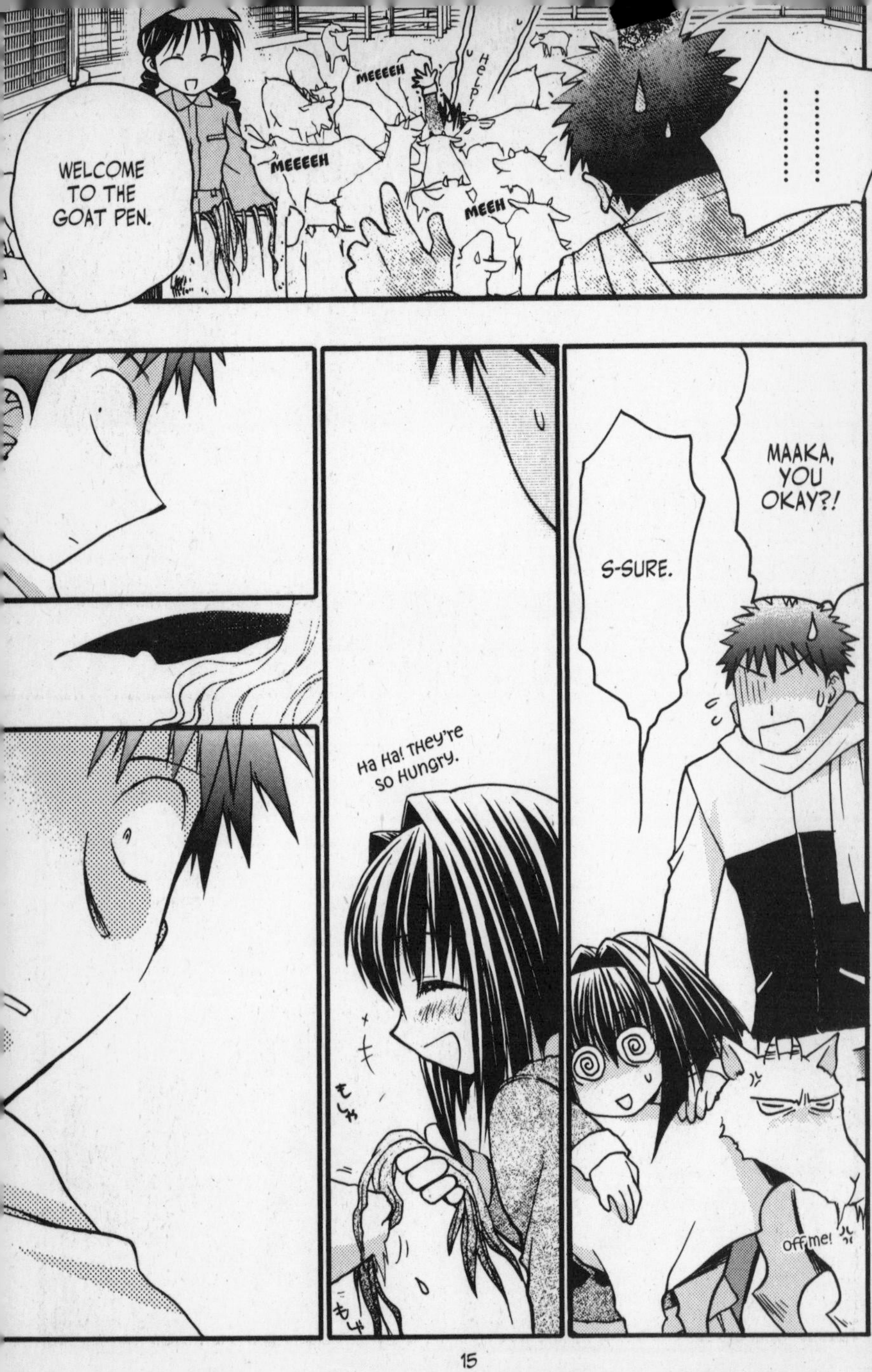
......
HeLP!
MEEEEH
MEEEEH
MEEH
WELCOME TO THE GOAT PEN.
MAAKA, YOU OKAY?!
S-SURE.
off me!
Ha Ha! They're so Hungry.

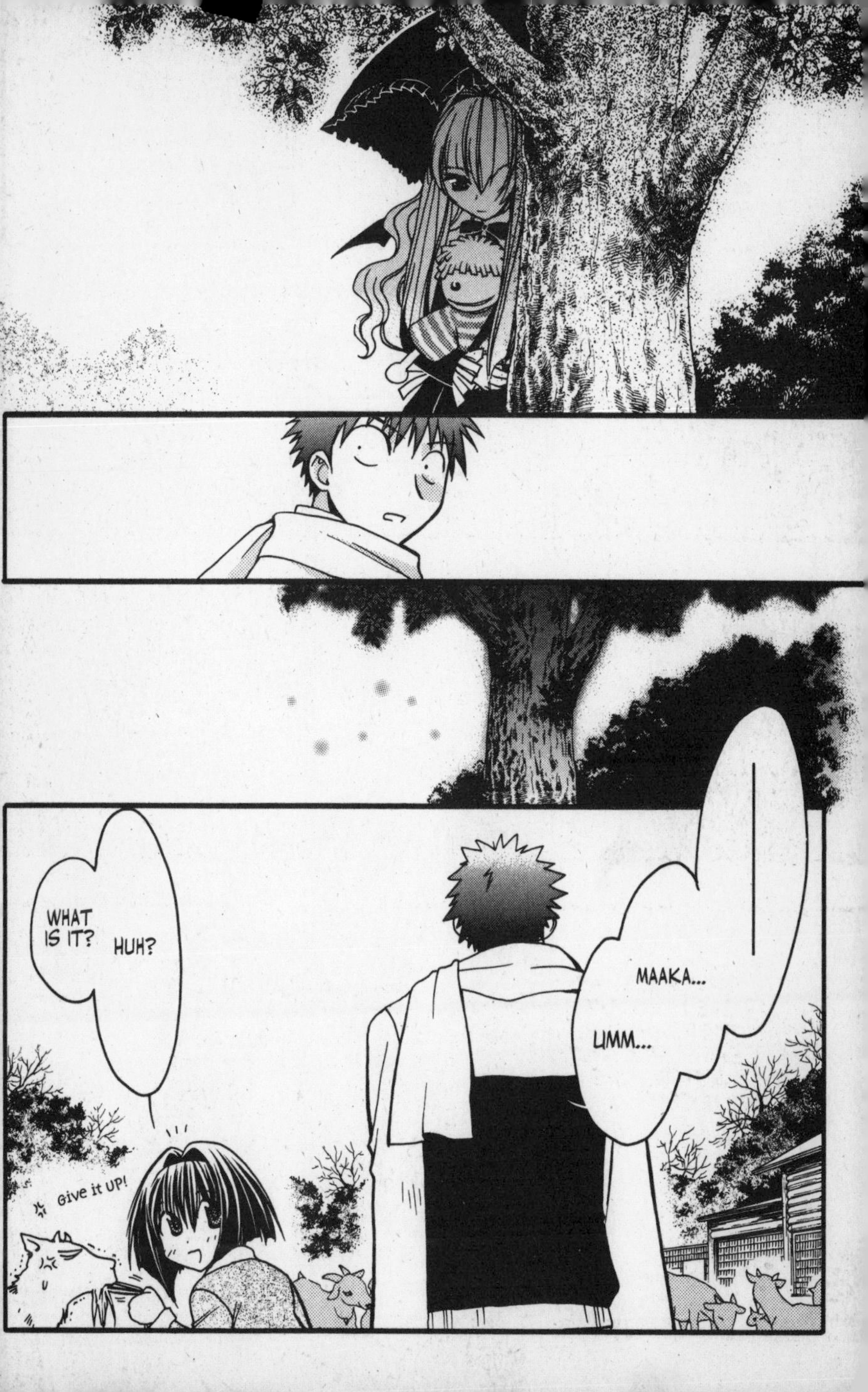

MAAKA... UMM...
HUH? WHAT IS IT?
Give it UP!

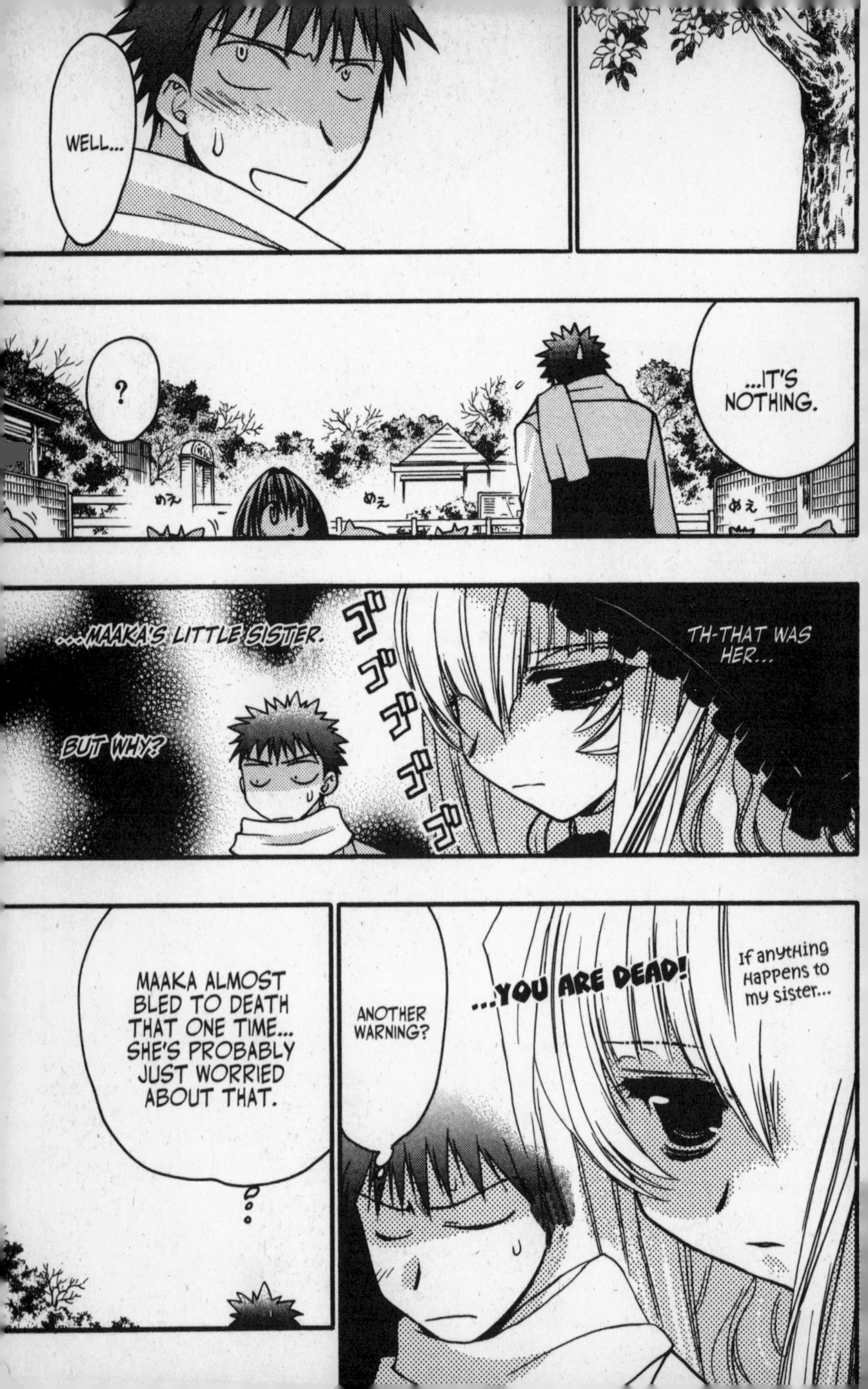
WELL...
...IT'S NOTHING.
?
めえ
めえ
めえ
TH-THAT WAS HER...
ゴゴゴゴゴ
...MAAKA'S LITTLE SISTER.
BUT WHY?
If anything happens to my sister...
...YOU ARE DEAD!
ANOTHER WARNING?
MAAKA ALMOST BLED TO DEATH THAT ONE TIME... SHE'S PROBABLY JUST WORRIED ABOUT THAT.

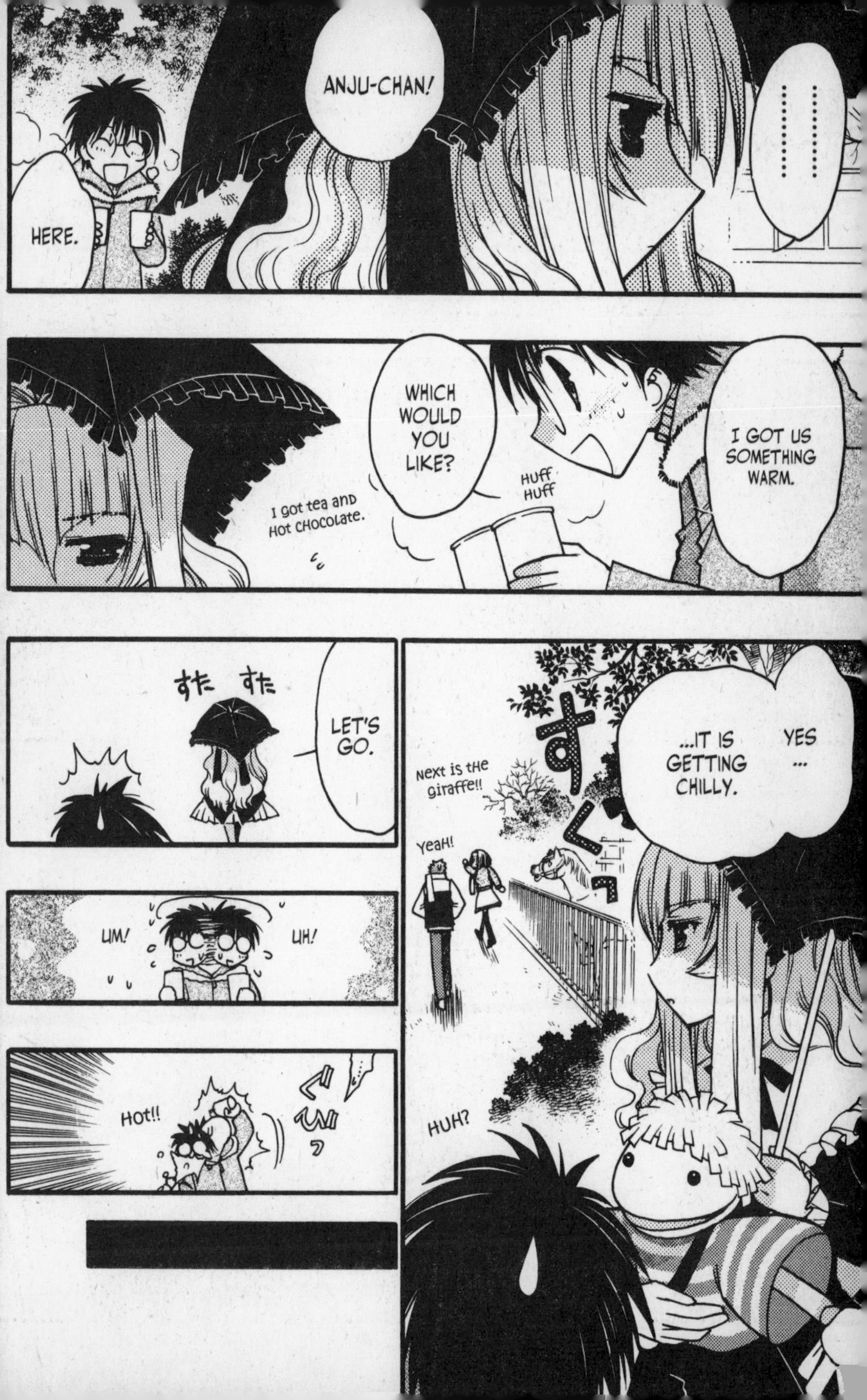
......
ANJU-CHAN!
HERE.
I GOT US SOMETHING WARM.
HUFF HUFF
WHICH WOULD YOU LIKE?
I got tea and hot chocolate.
YES ...
...IT IS GETTING CHILLY.
すくっ
Next is the giraffe!!
Yeah!
HUH?
LET'S GO.
すた すた
UM!
UH!
ぐいっ
Hot!!

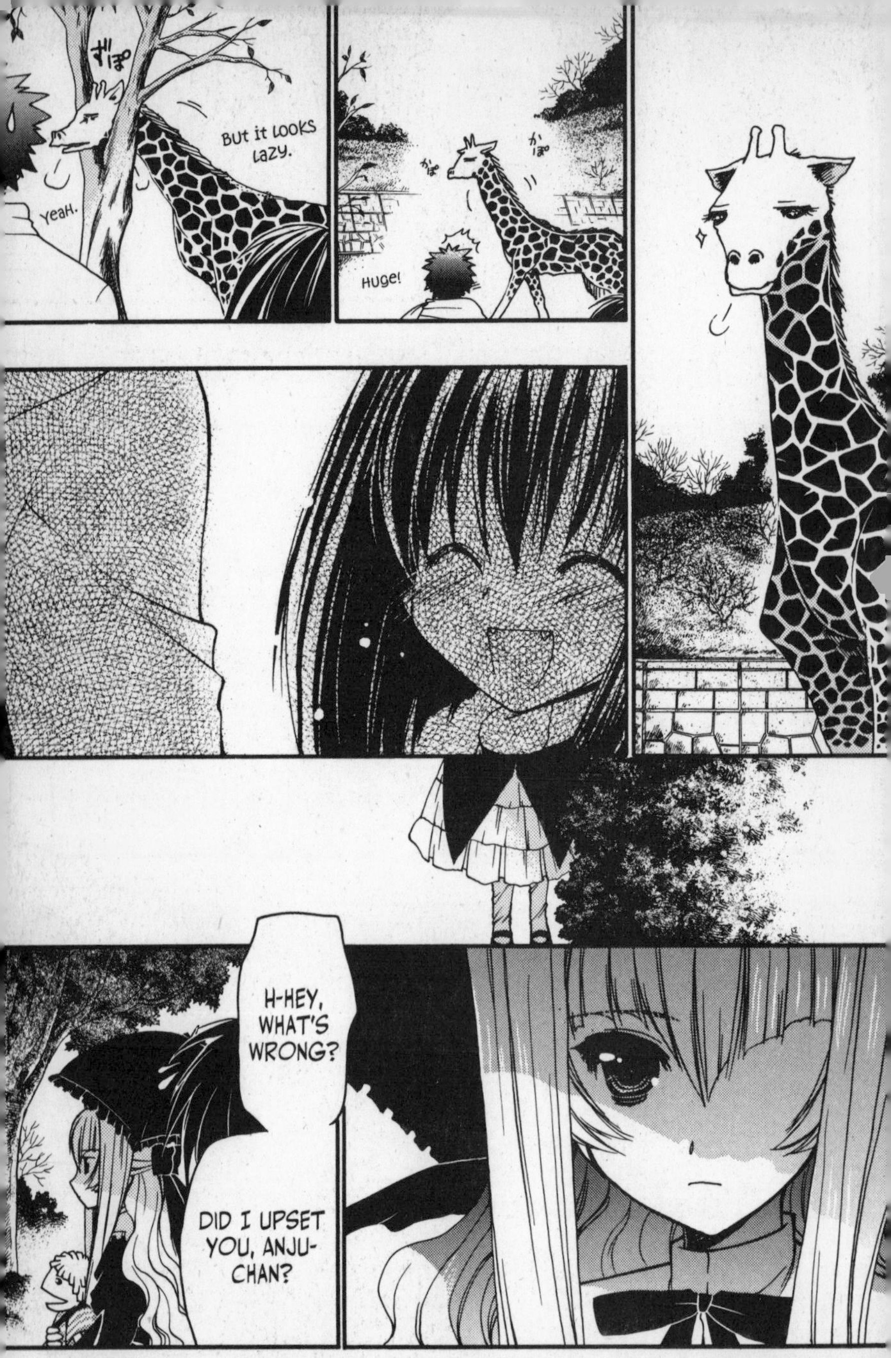

かぽ
かぽ
Huge!
ずぽ
But it LOOKS lazy.
Yeah.
H-HEY, WHAT'S WRONG?
DID I UPSET YOU, ANJU-CHAN?

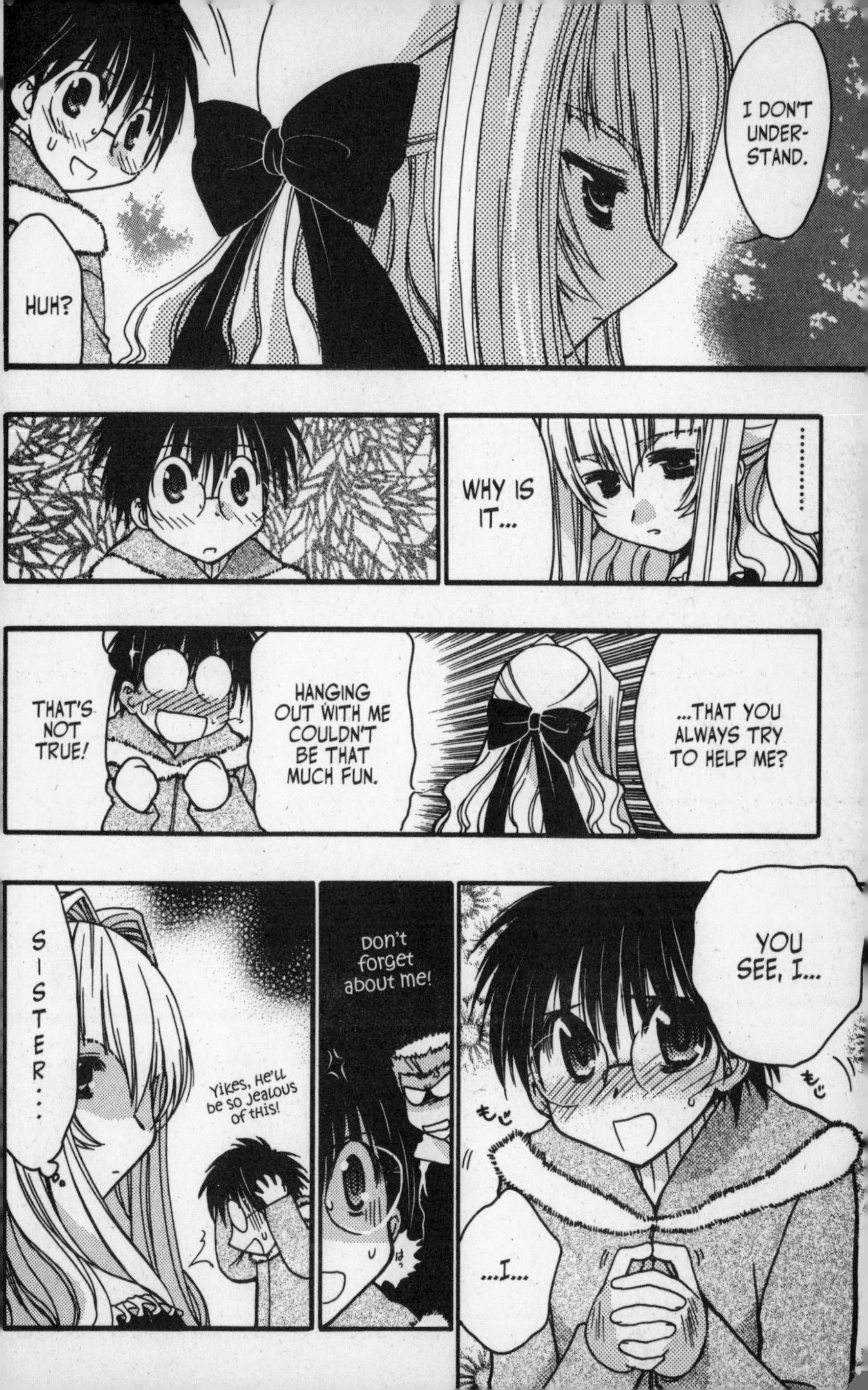
I DON'T UNDER-STAND.
HUH?
......
WHY IS IT...
...THAT YOU ALWAYS TRY TO HELP ME?
HANGING OUT WITH ME COULDN'T BE THAT MUCH FUN.
THAT'S NOT TRUE!
YOU SEE, I...
もじ
もじ
...I...
Don't forget about me!
はっ
SISTER...
Yikes, He'll be so jealous of this!

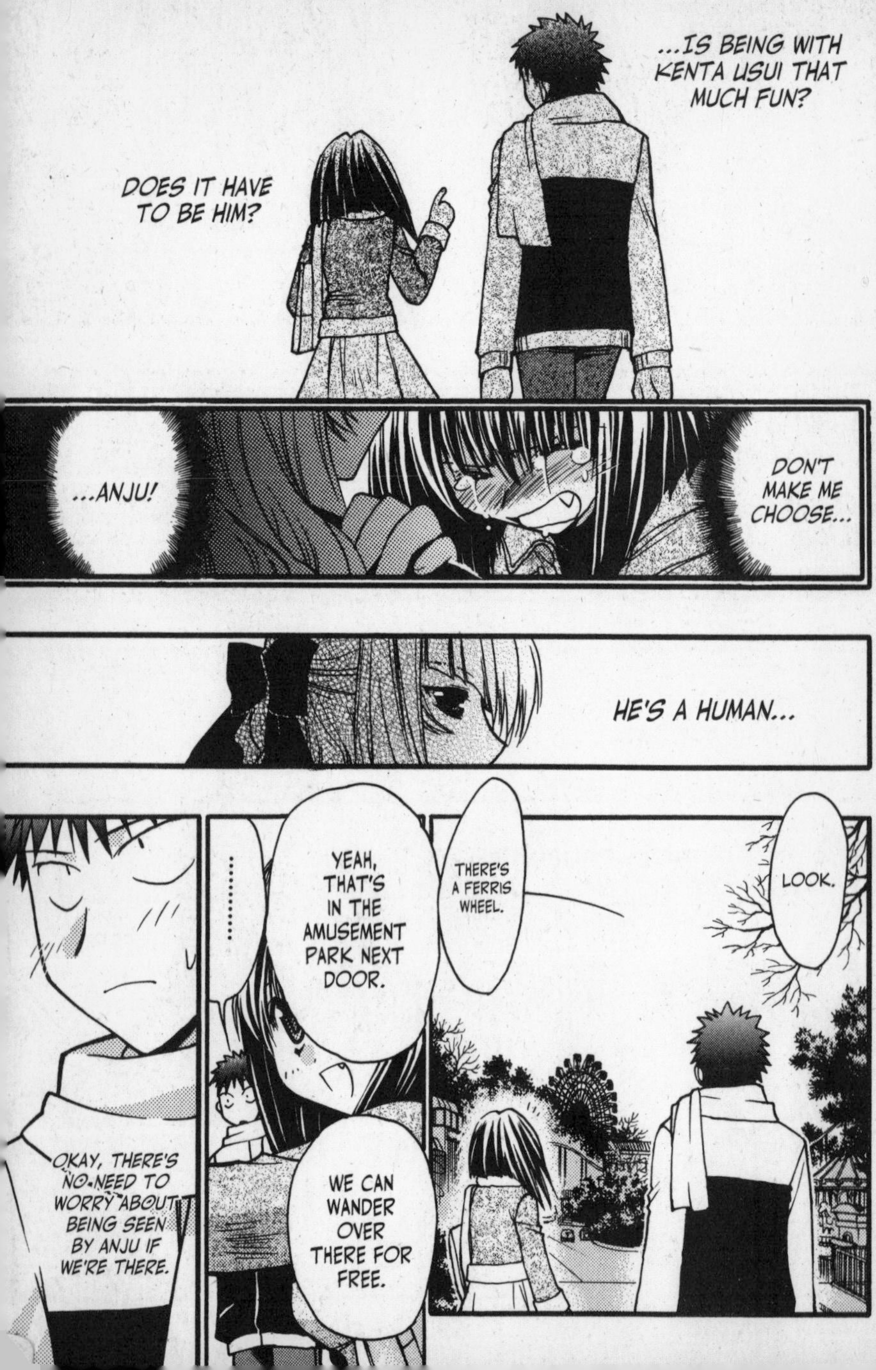
...IS BEING WITH KENTA USUI THAT MUCH FUN?
DOES IT HAVE TO BE HIM?
DON'T MAKE ME CHOOSE...
...ANJU!
HE'S A HUMAN...
LOOK.
THERE'S A FERRIS WHEEL.
YEAH, THAT'S IN THE AMUSEMENT PARK NEXT DOOR.
....
WE CAN WANDER OVER THERE FOR FREE.
OKAY, THERE'S NO NEED TO WORRY ABOUT BEING SEEN BY ANJU IF WE'RE THERE.

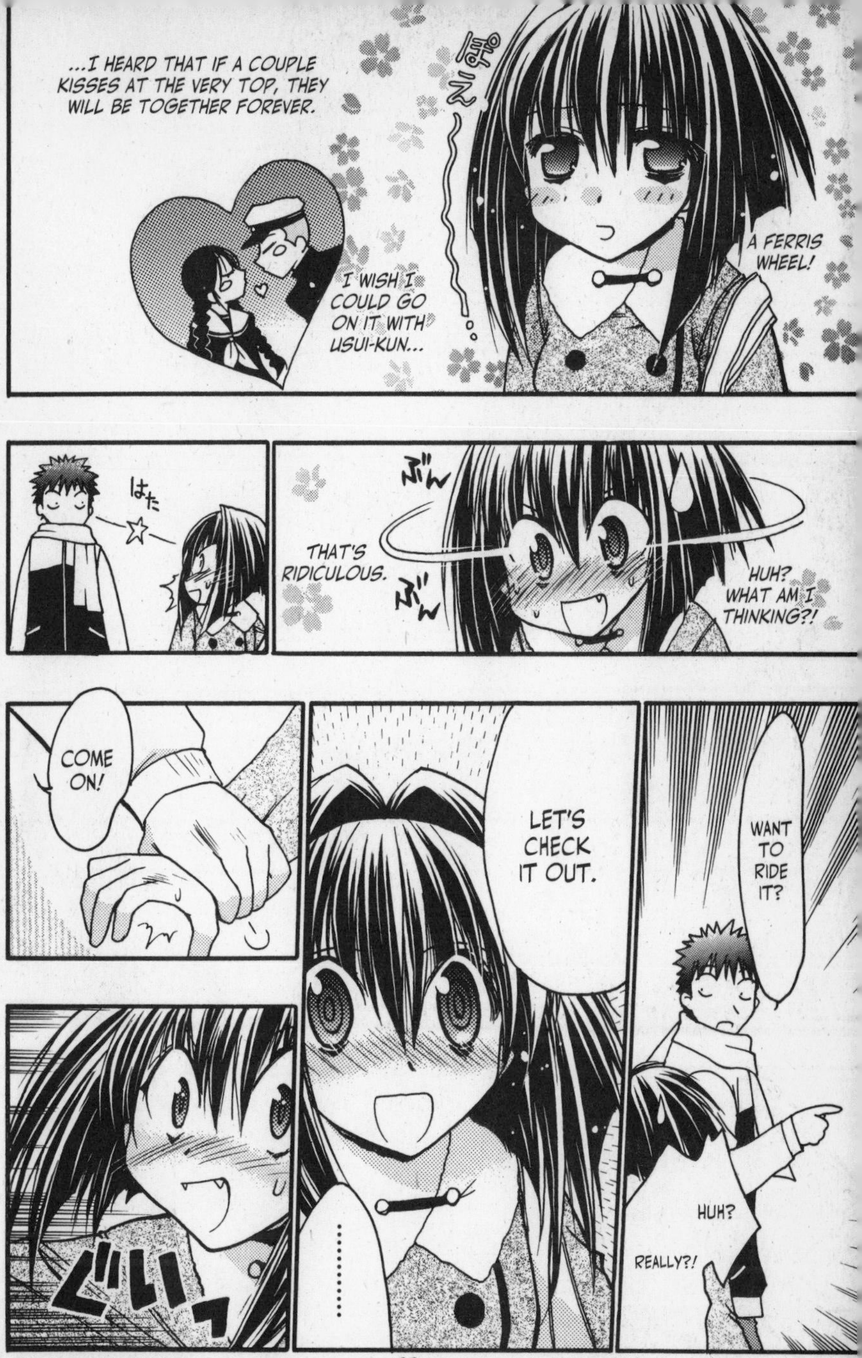
A FERRIS WHEEL!
ぽえ〜
I WISH I COULD GO ON IT WITH USUI-KUN...
...I HEARD THAT IF A COUPLE KISSES AT THE VERY TOP, THEY WILL BE TOGETHER FOREVER.
HUH? WHAT AM I THINKING?!
ぶん
ぶん
THAT'S RIDICULOUS.
はた
WANT TO RIDE IT?
HUH?
REALLY?!
LET'S CHECK IT OUT.
......
COME ON!
じぃっ

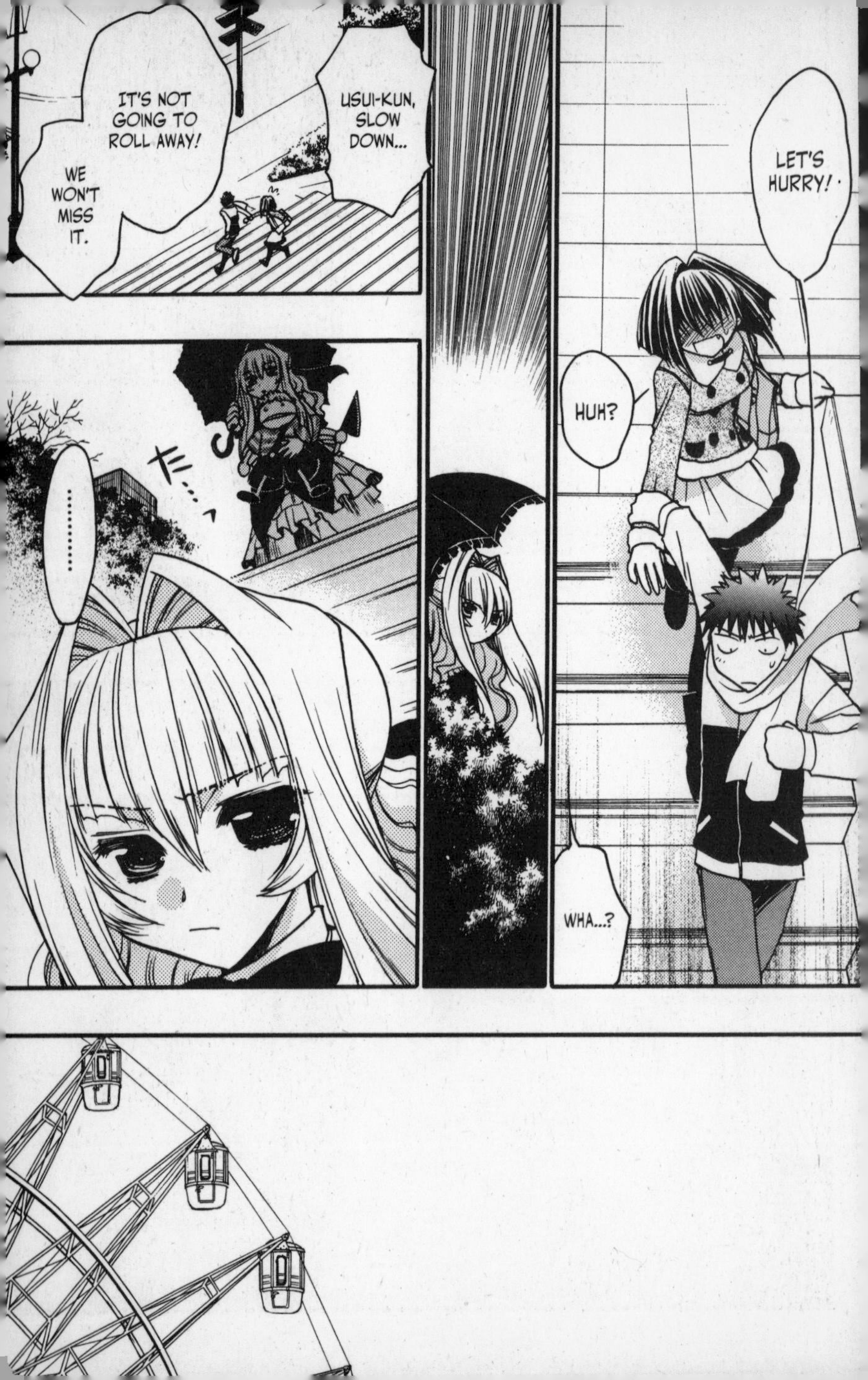
LET'S HURRY!
HUH?
WHA...?
USUI-KUN, SLOW DOWN...
IT'S NOT GOING TO ROLL AWAY!
WE WON'T MISS IT.
......

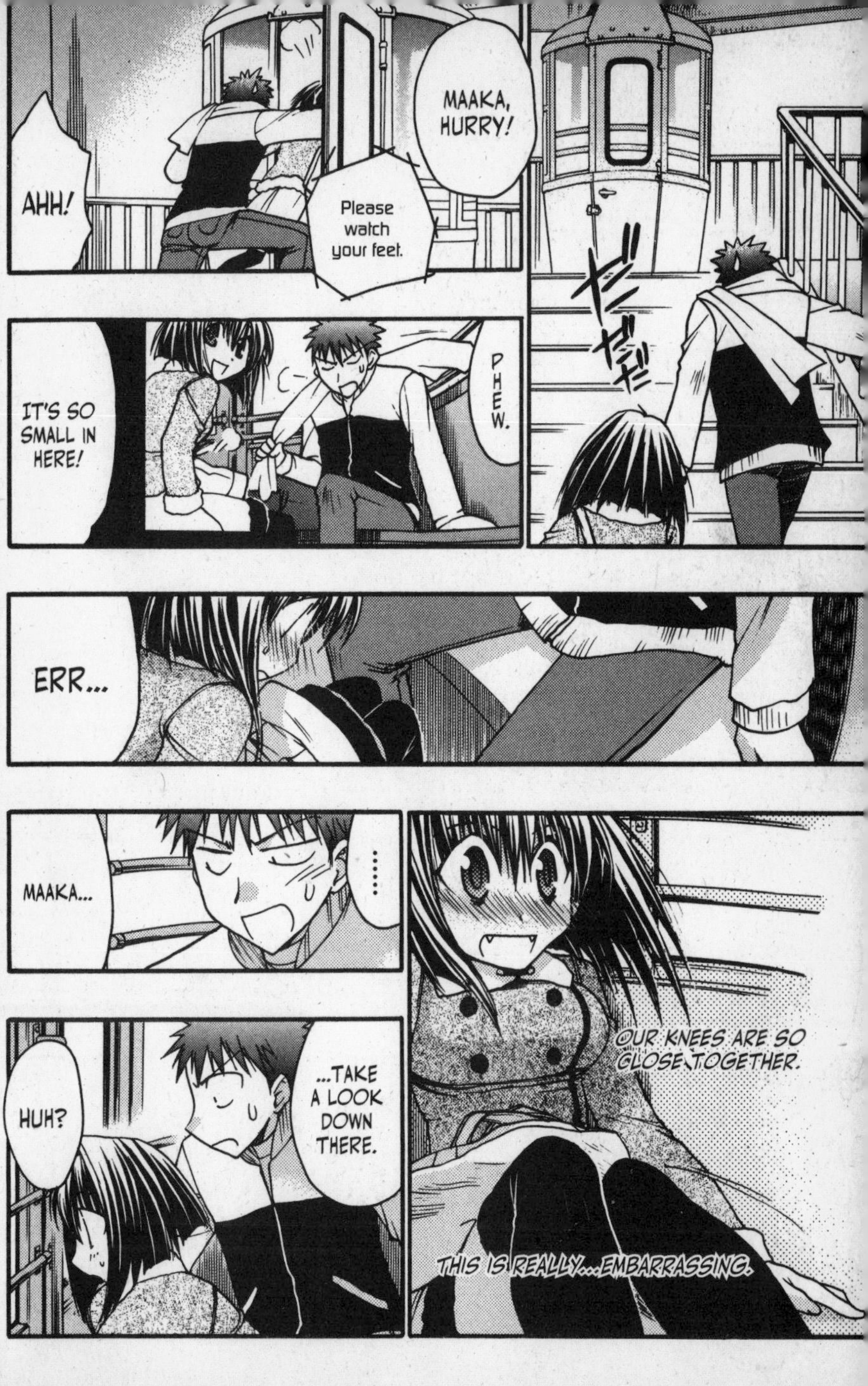
MAAKA, HURRY!
Please watch your feet.
AHH!
PHEW.
IT'S SO SMALL IN HERE!
ERR...
OUR KNEES ARE SO CLOSE TOGETHER.
THIS IS REALLY...EMBARRASSING.
......
MAAKA...
...TAKE A LOOK DOWN THERE.
HUH?

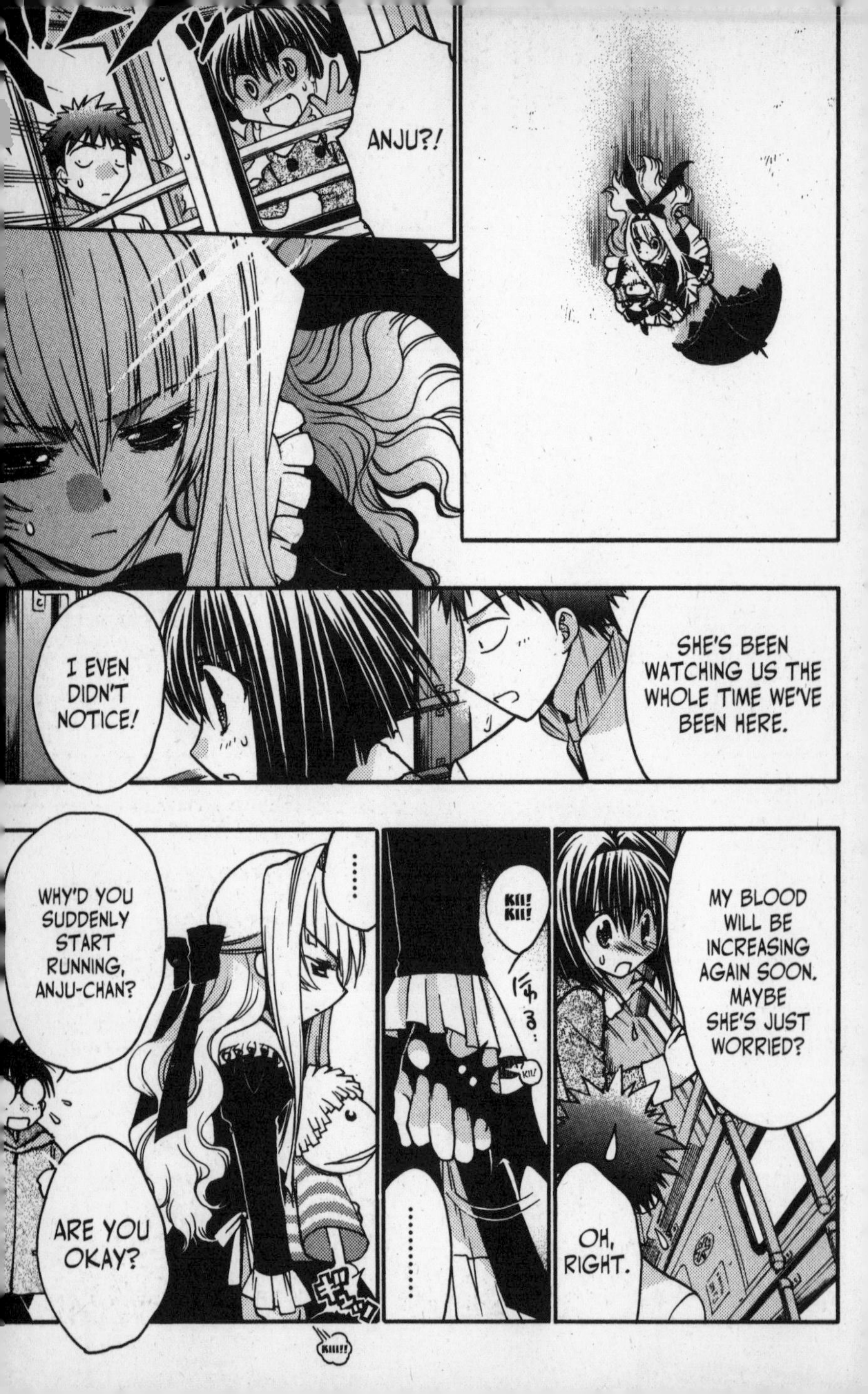
ANJU?!
SHE'S BEEN WATCHING US THE WHOLE TIME WE'VE BEEN HERE.
I EVEN DIDN'T NOTICE!
MY BLOOD WILL BE INCREASING AGAIN SOON. MAYBE SHE'S JUST WORRIED?
OH, RIGHT.
KII! KII!
KII!
......
......
WHY'D YOU SUDDENLY START RUNNING, ANJU-CHAN?
ARE YOU OKAY?
KIII!!

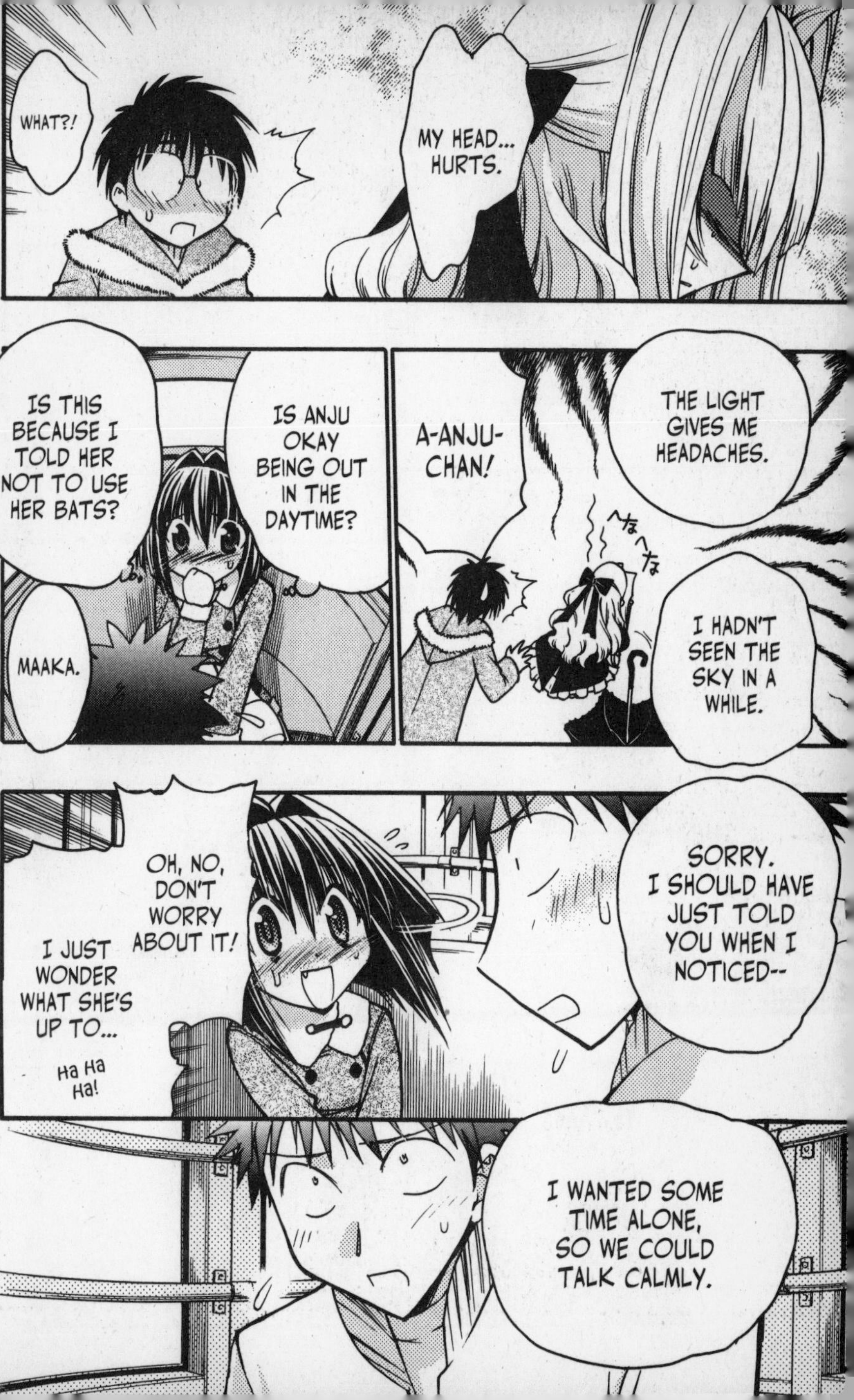
MY HEAD... HURTS.
WHAT?!
THE LIGHT GIVES ME HEADACHES.
I HADN'T SEEN THE SKY IN A WHILE.
A-ANJU-CHAN!
へなへな
IS ANJU OKAY BEING OUT IN THE DAYTIME?
IS THIS BECAUSE I TOLD HER NOT TO USE HER BATS?
MAAKA.
SORRY. I SHOULD HAVE JUST TOLD YOU WHEN I NOTICED--
OH, NO, DON'T WORRY ABOUT IT!
I JUST WONDER WHAT SHE'S UP TO...
Ha Ha Ha!
I WANTED SOME TIME ALONE, SO WE COULD TALK CALMLY.

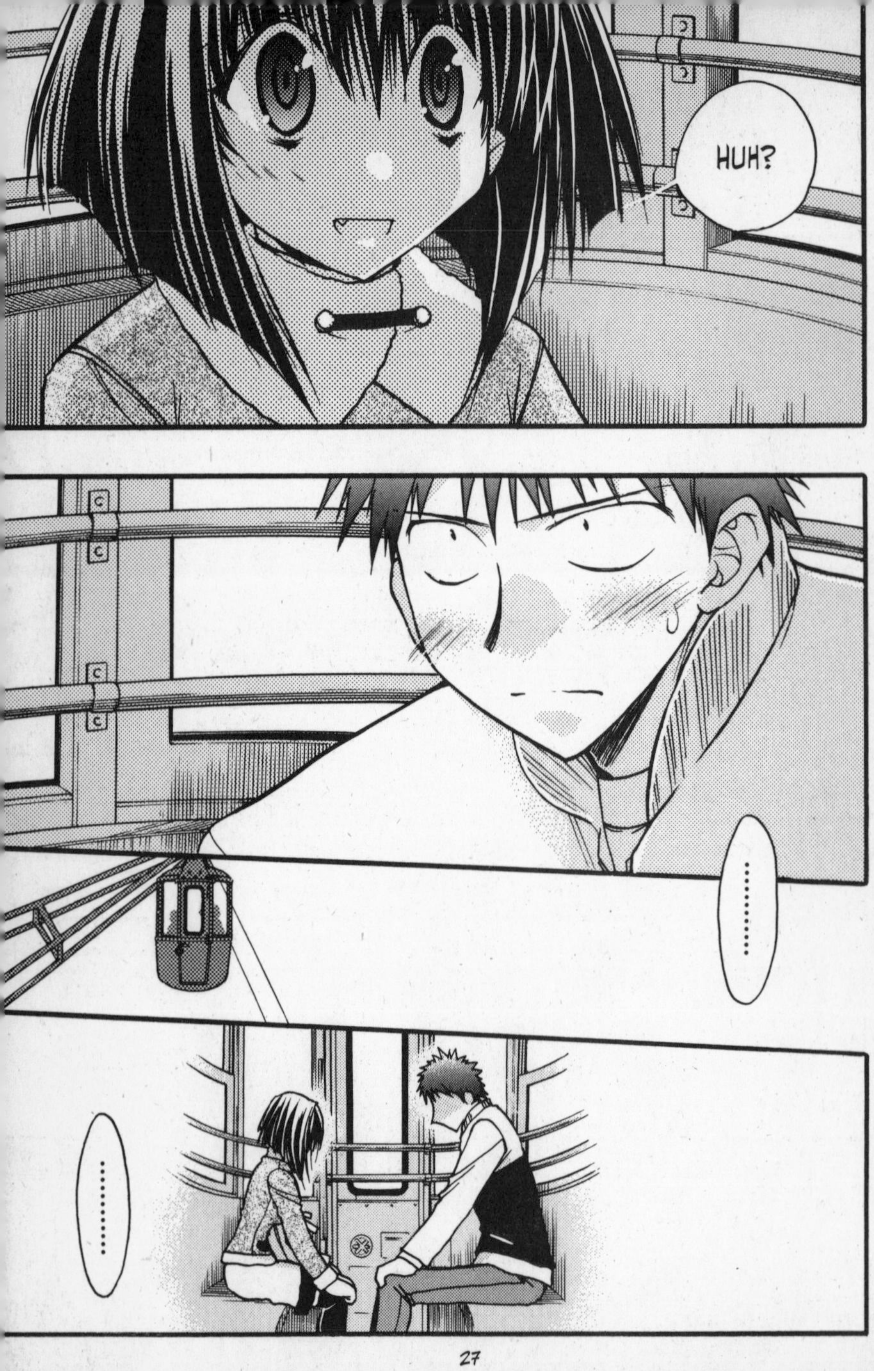
HUH?
......
......

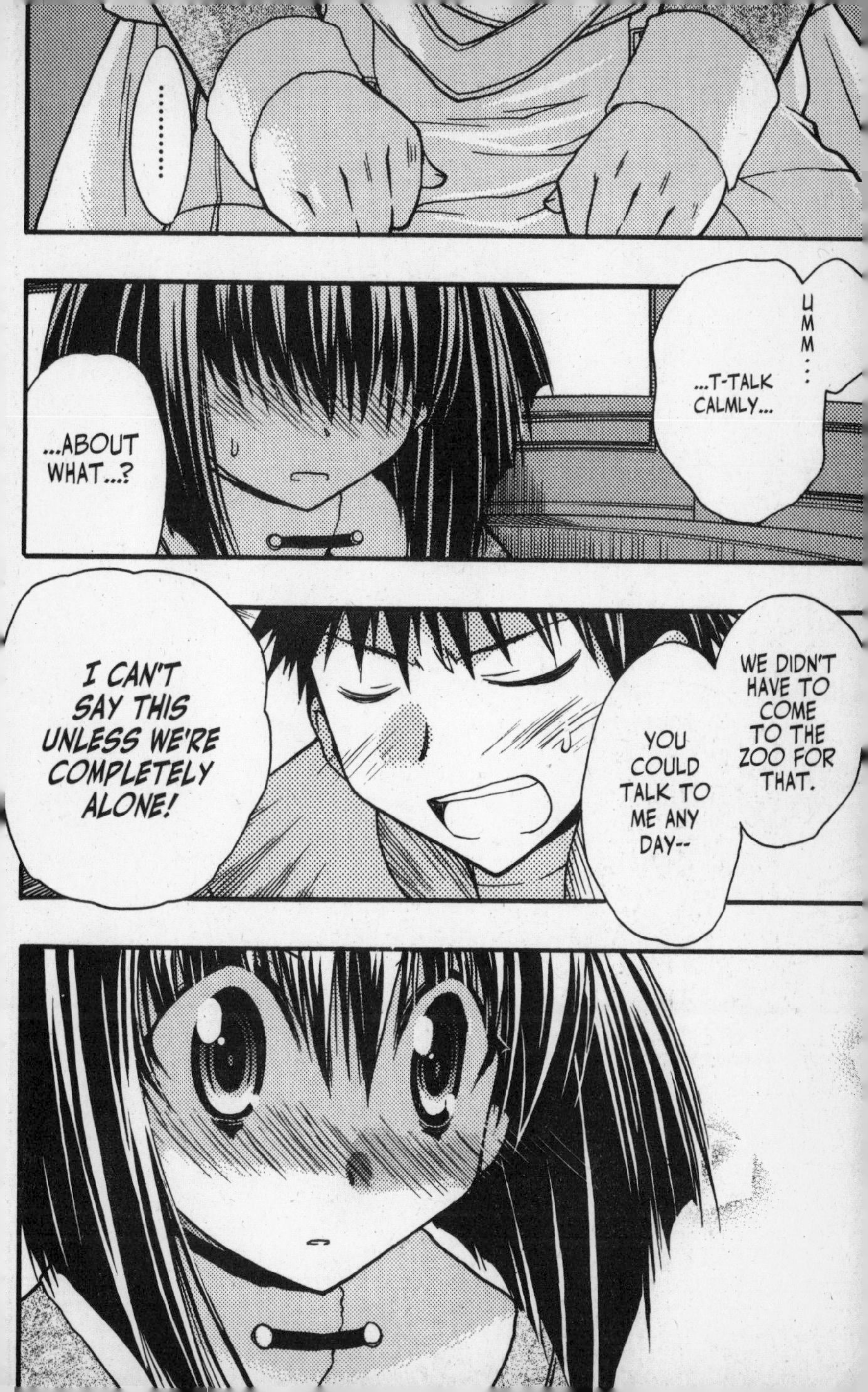
....
UMM...
...T-TALK CALMLY...
...ABOUT WHAT...?
WE DIDN'T HAVE TO COME TO THE ZOO FOR THAT.
YOU COULD TALK TO ME ANY DAY--
I CAN'T SAY THIS UNLESS WE'RE COMPLETELY ALONE!

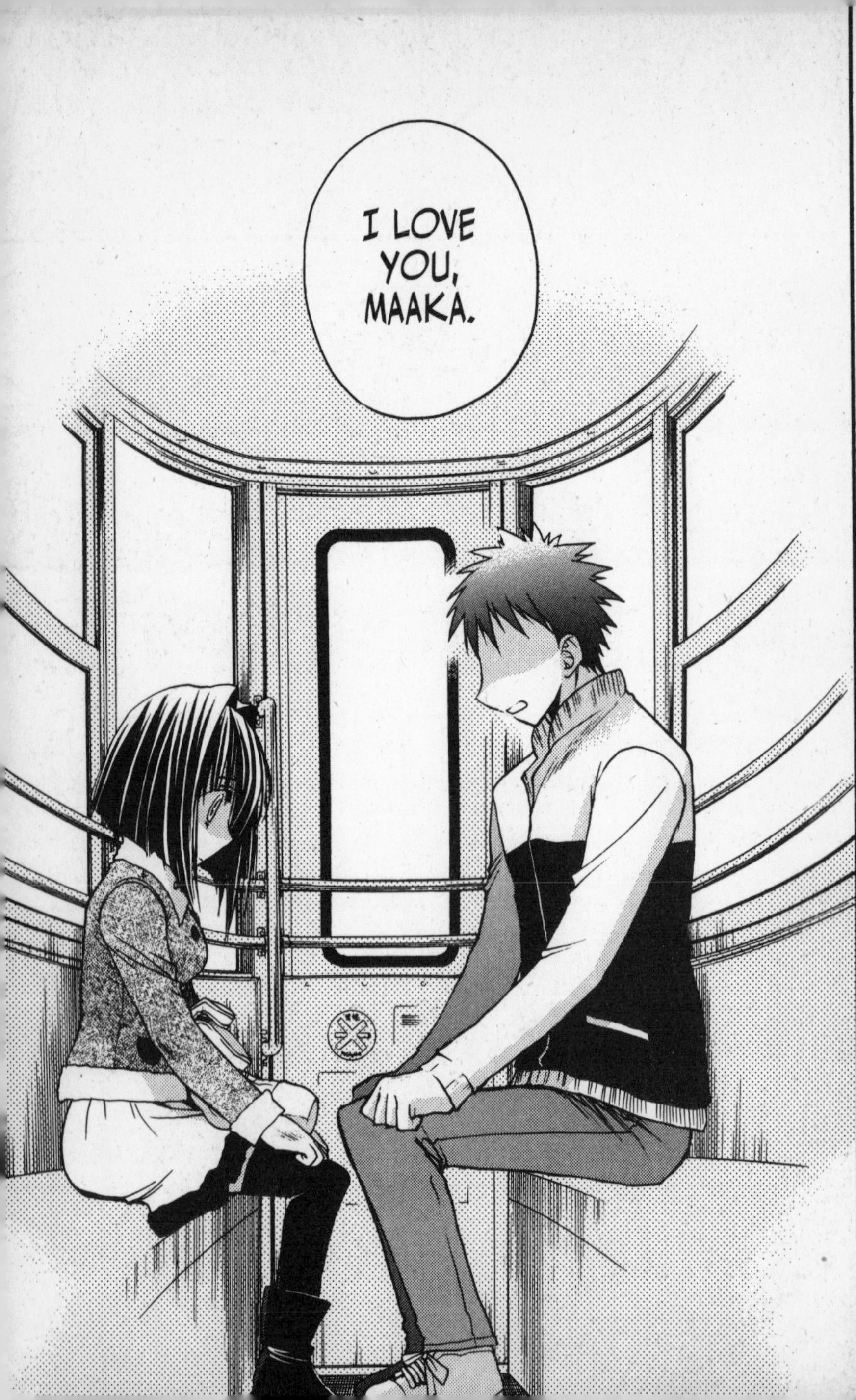
I LOVE YOU, MAAKA.

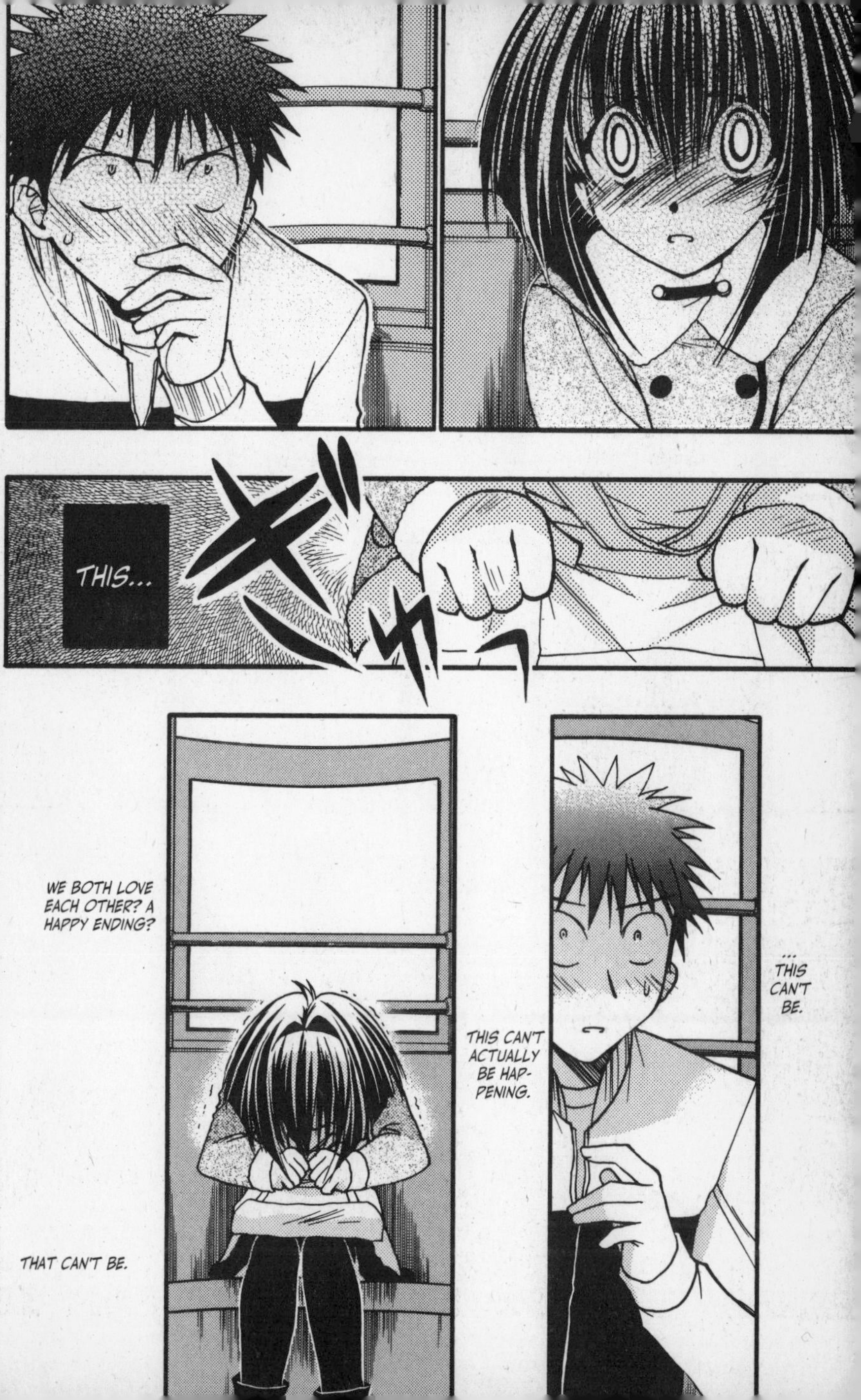
THIS...
... THIS CAN'T BE.
THIS CAN'T ACTUALLY BE HAP- PENING.
WE BOTH LOVE EACH OTHER? A HAPPY ENDING?
THAT CAN'T BE.

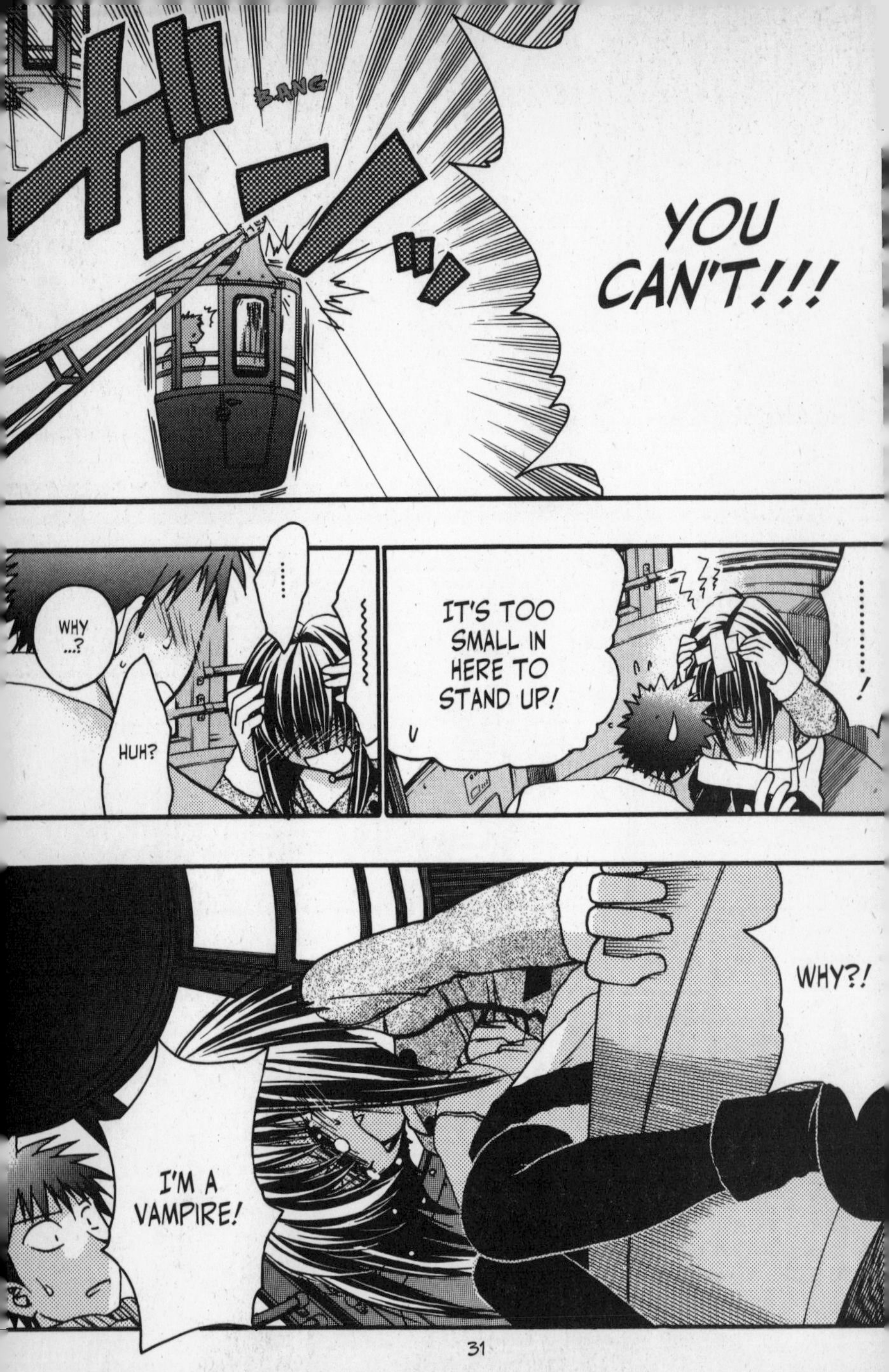
BANG
YOU CAN'T!!!
......!
IT'S TOO SMALL IN HERE TO STAND UP!
......
WHY ...?
HUH?
WHY?!
I'M A VAMPIRE!

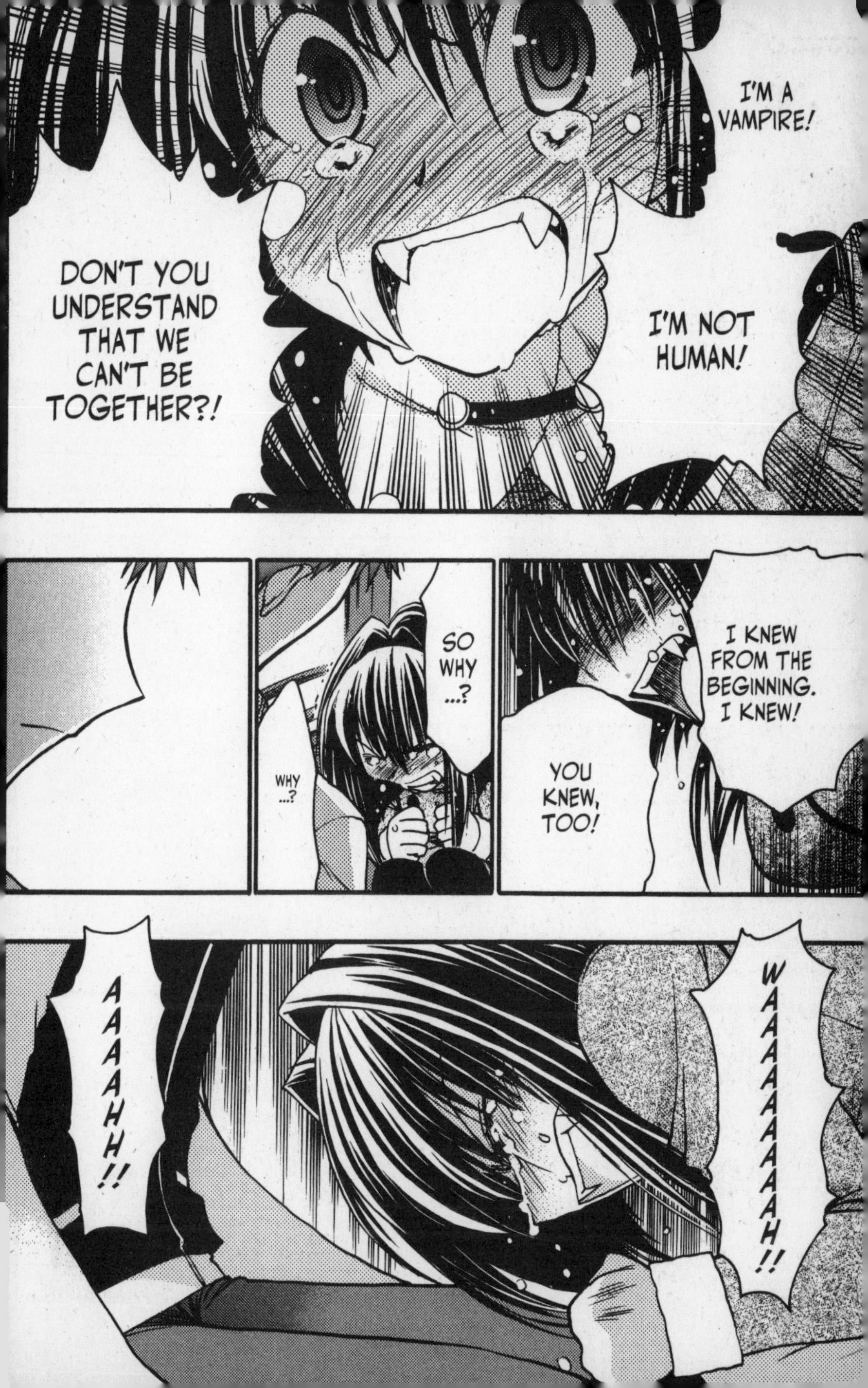
I'M A VAMPIRE!
I'M NOT HUMAN!
DON'T YOU UNDERSTAND THAT WE CAN'T BE TOGETHER?!
I KNEW FROM THE BEGINNING. I KNEW!
YOU KNEW, TOO!
SO WHY ...?
WHY ...?
WAAAAAAAAAH!!
AAAAHH!!

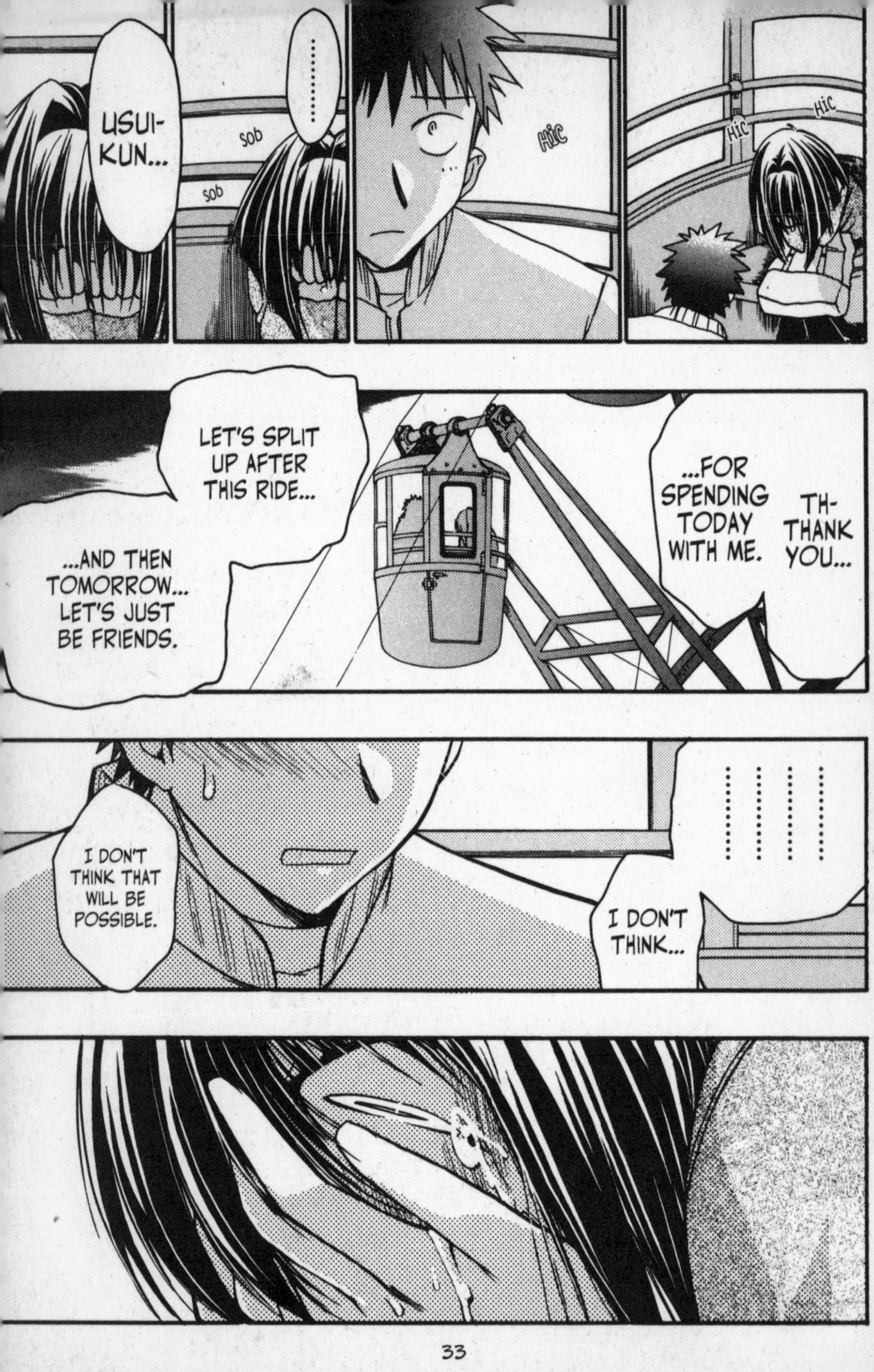
HIC
HIC
HIC
......
SOB
SOB
USUI-KUN...
TH-THANK YOU...
...FOR SPENDING TODAY WITH ME.
LET'S SPLIT UP AFTER THIS RIDE...
...AND THEN TOMORROW... LET'S JUST BE FRIENDS.
....
I DON'T THINK...
I DON'T THINK THAT WILL BE POSSIBLE.

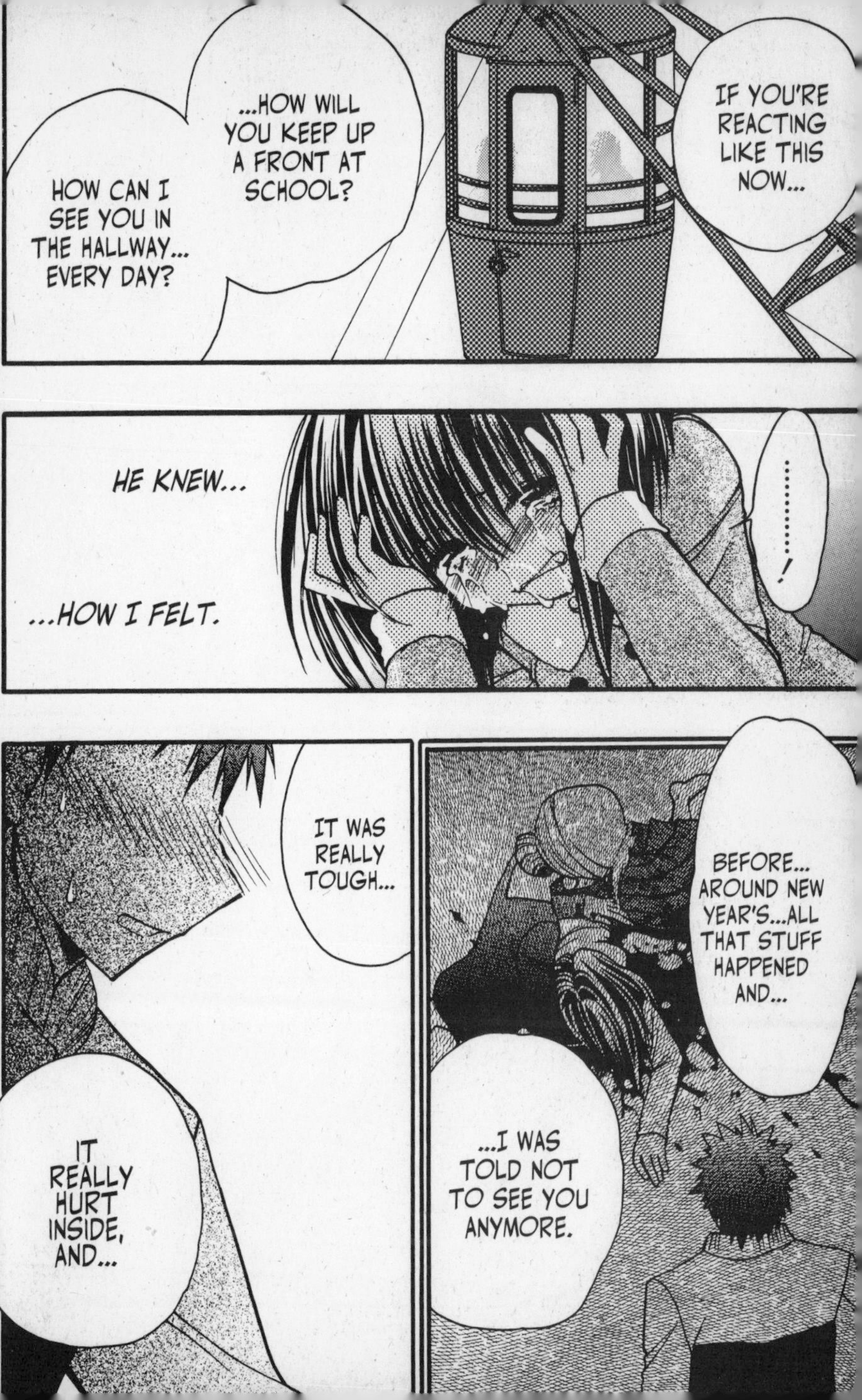
IF YOU'RE REACTING LIKE THIS NOW...
...HOW WILL YOU KEEP UP A FRONT AT SCHOOL?
HOW CAN I SEE YOU IN THE HALLWAY... EVERY DAY?
......!
HE KNEW...
...HOW I FELT.
BEFORE... AROUND NEW YEAR'S...ALL THAT STUFF HAPPENED AND...
...I WAS TOLD NOT TO SEE YOU ANYMORE.
IT WAS REALLY TOUGH...
IT REALLY HURT INSIDE, AND...

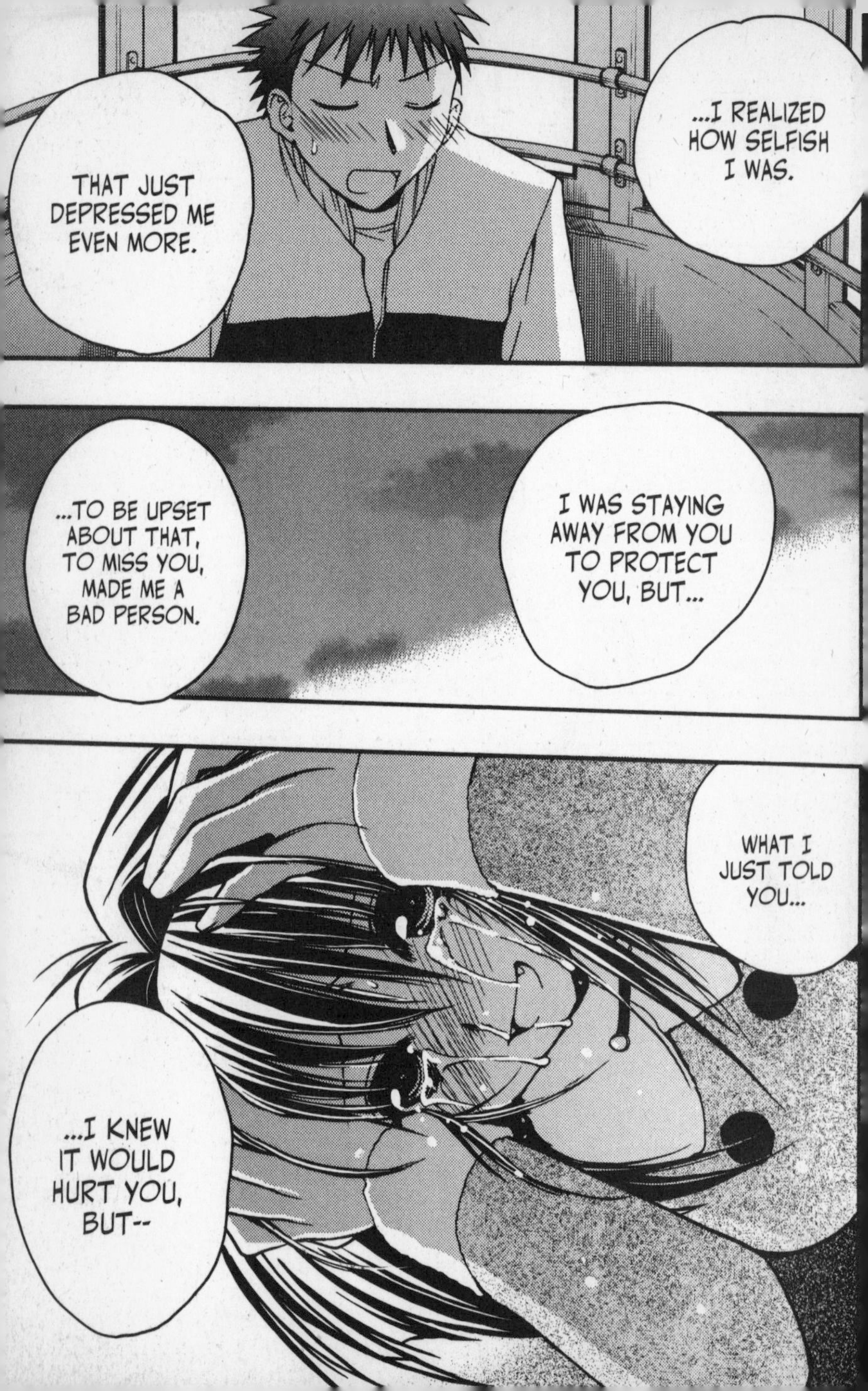
...I REALIZED HOW SELFISH I WAS.
THAT JUST DEPRESSED ME EVEN MORE.
I WAS STAYING AWAY FROM YOU TO PROTECT YOU, BUT...
...TO BE UPSET ABOUT THAT, TO MISS YOU, MADE ME A BAD PERSON.
WHAT I JUST TOLD YOU...
...I KNEW IT WOULD HURT YOU, BUT--

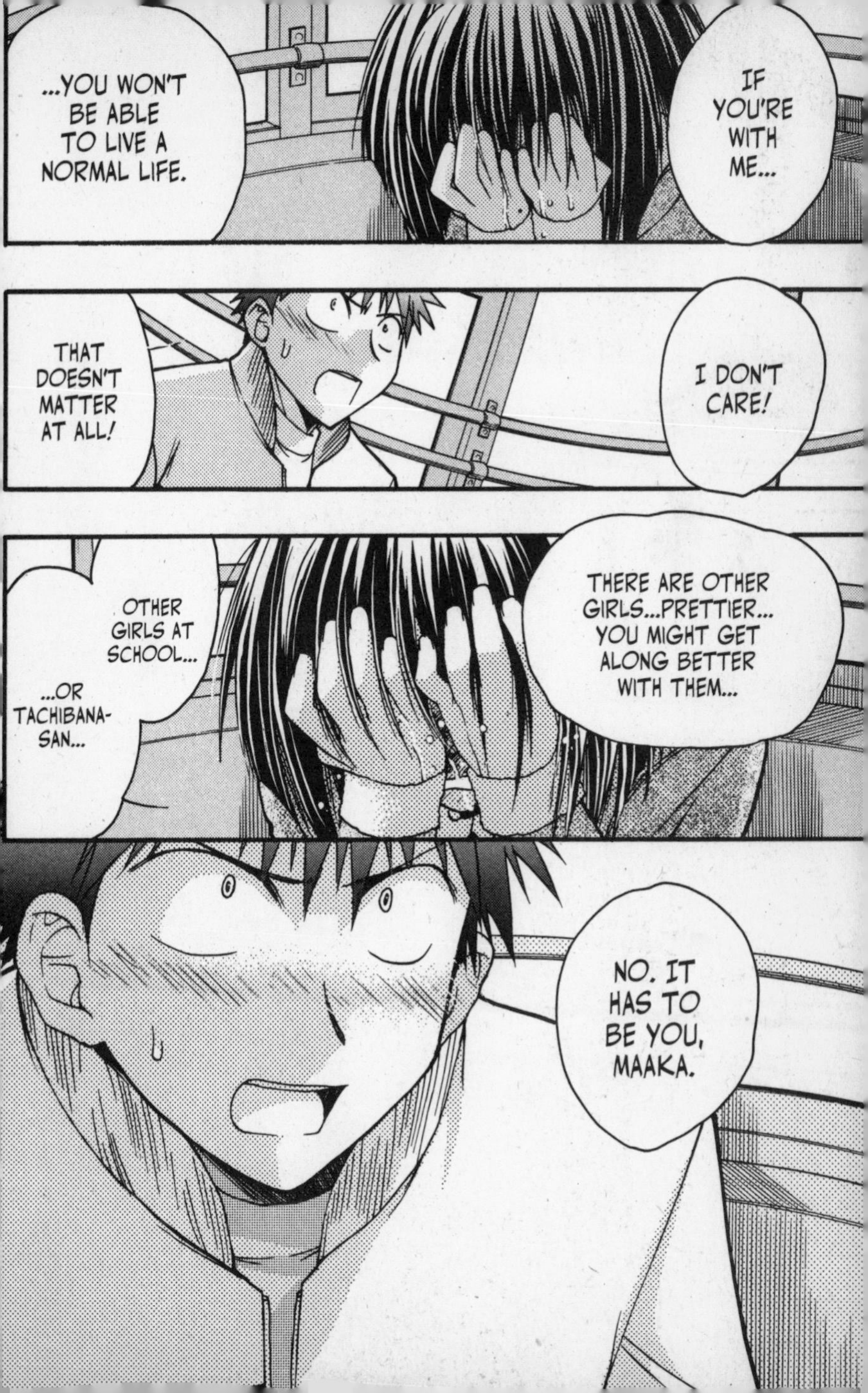
IF YOU'RE WITH ME...
...YOU WON'T BE ABLE TO LIVE A NORMAL LIFE.
I DON'T CARE!
THAT DOESN'T MATTER AT ALL!
THERE ARE OTHER GIRLS...PRETTIER... YOU MIGHT GET ALONG BETTER WITH THEM...
OTHER GIRLS AT SCHOOL...
...OR TACHIBANA-SAN...
NO. IT HAS TO BE YOU, MAAKA.

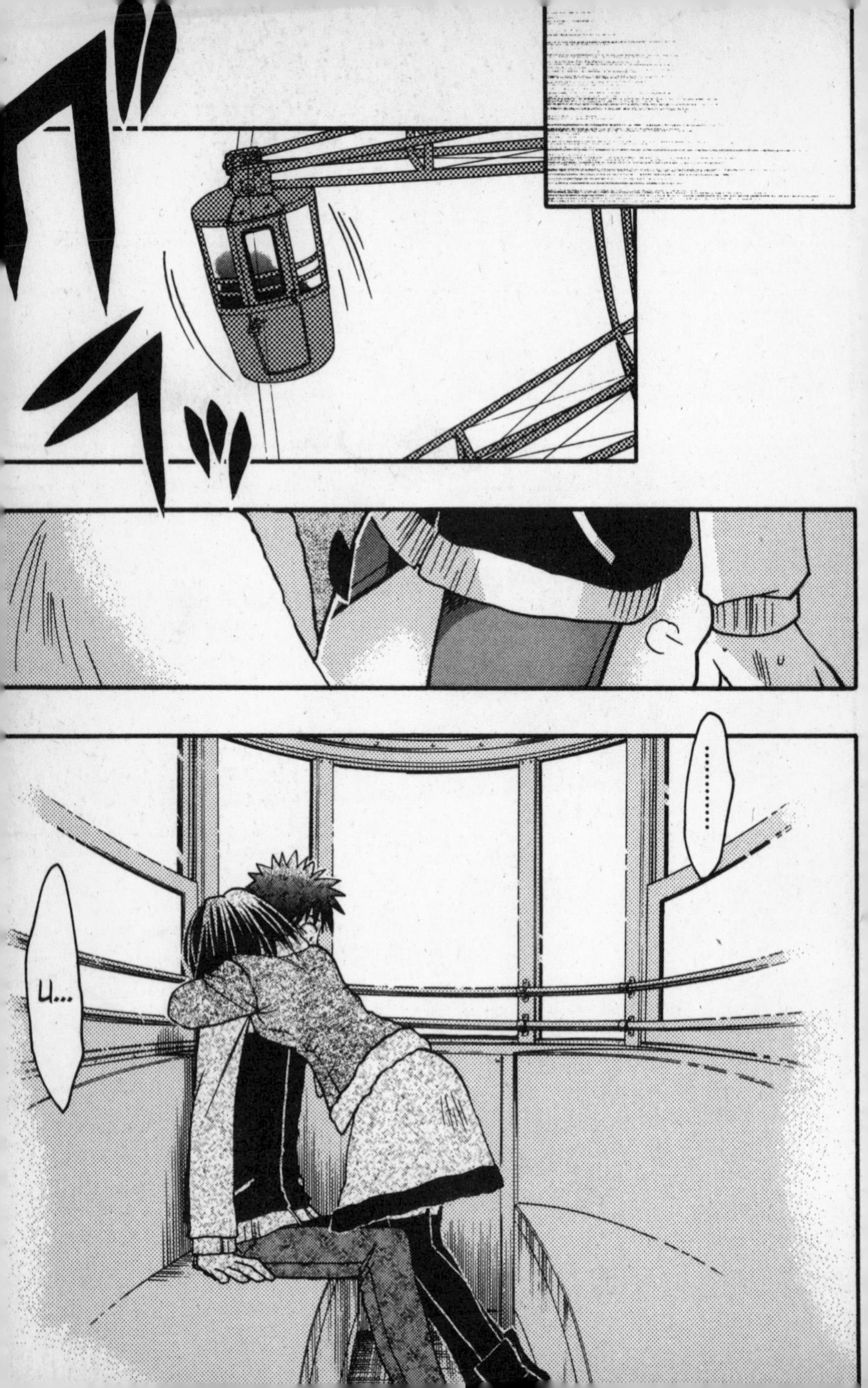
グラッ
......
u...

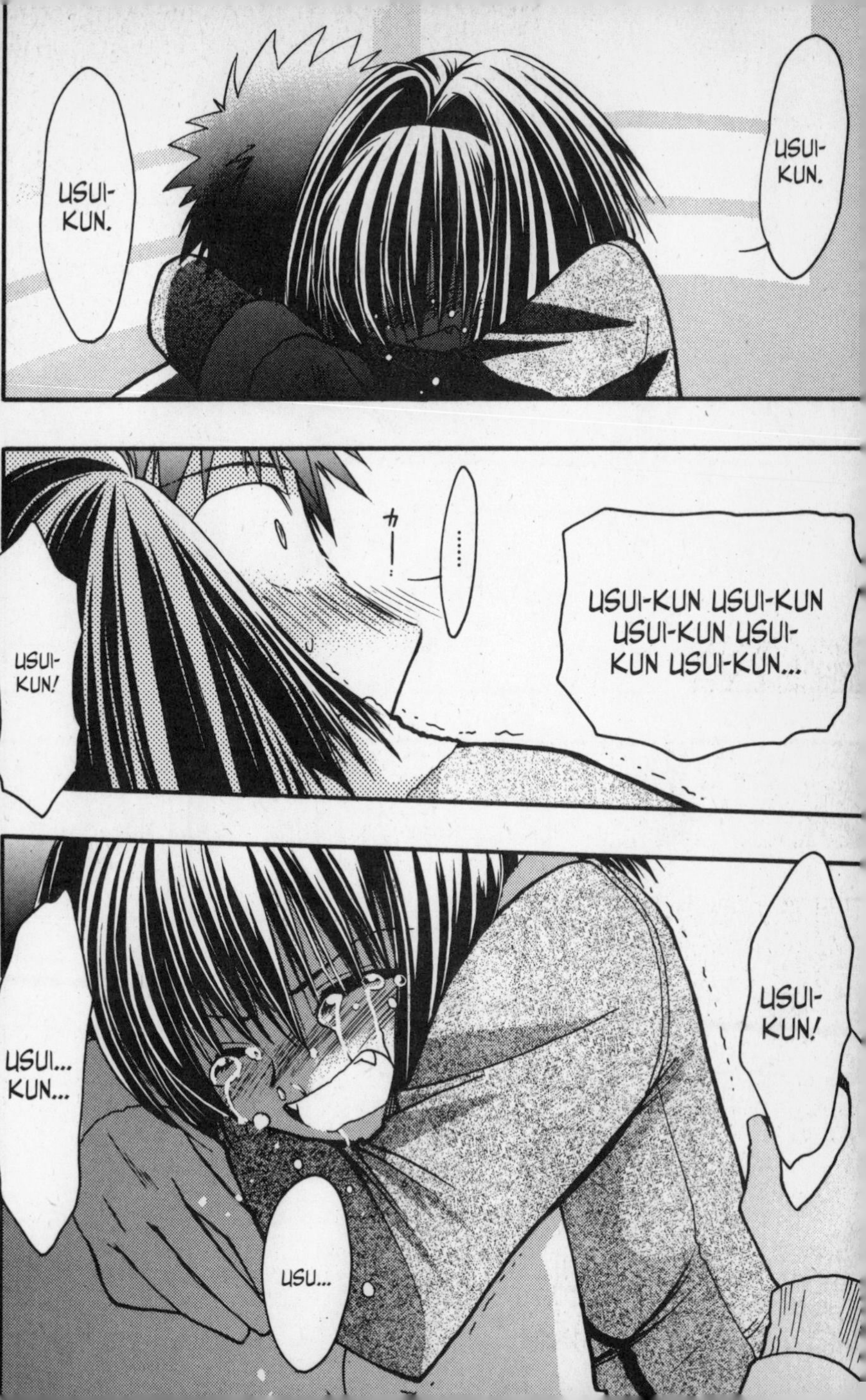
USUI-KUN.
USUI-KUN.
USUI-KUN USUI-KUN USUI-KUN USUI-KUN USUI-KUN...
......
USUI-KUN!
USUI-KUN!
USU...
USUI... KUN...

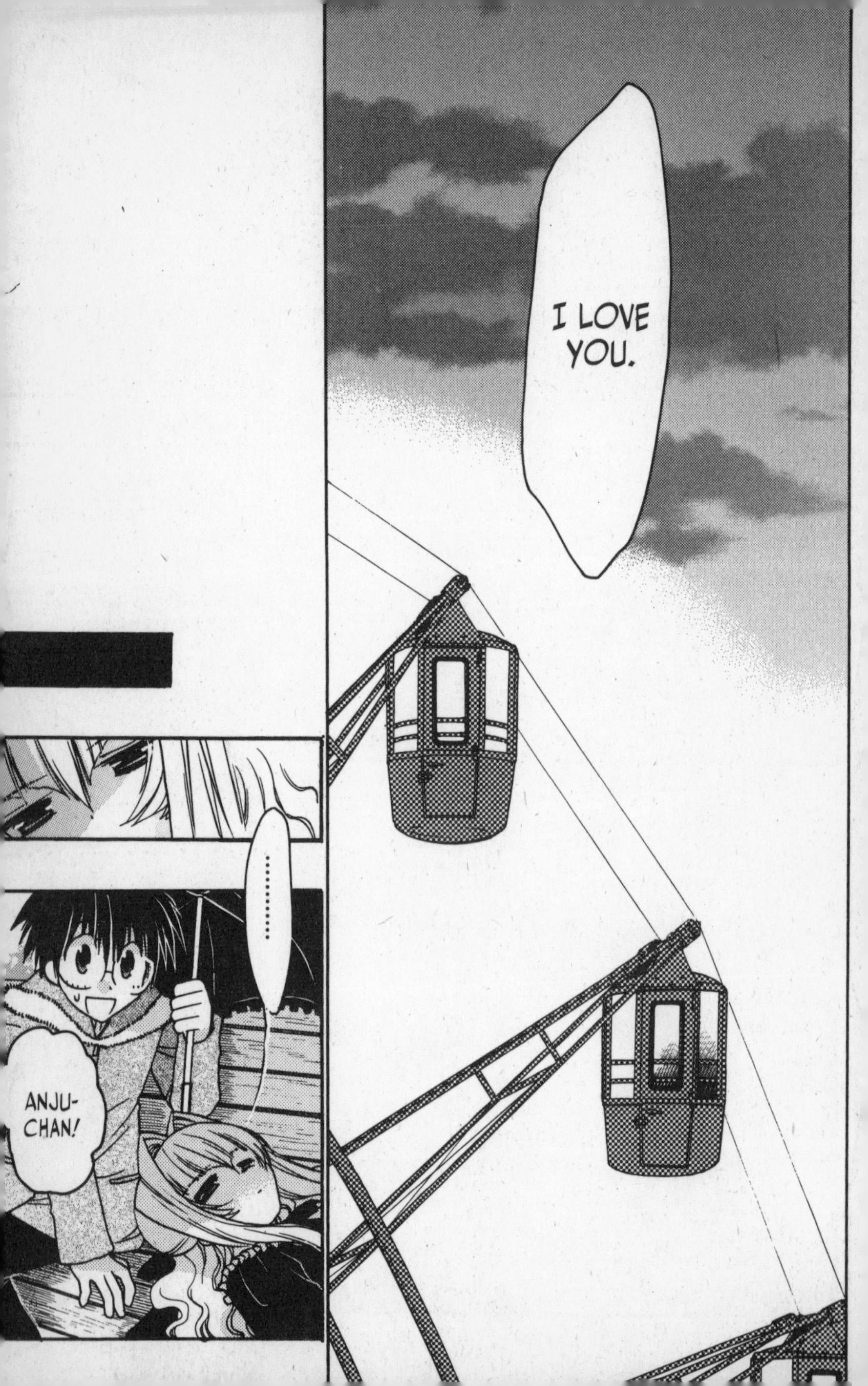
I LOVE YOU.
......
ANJU-CHAN!

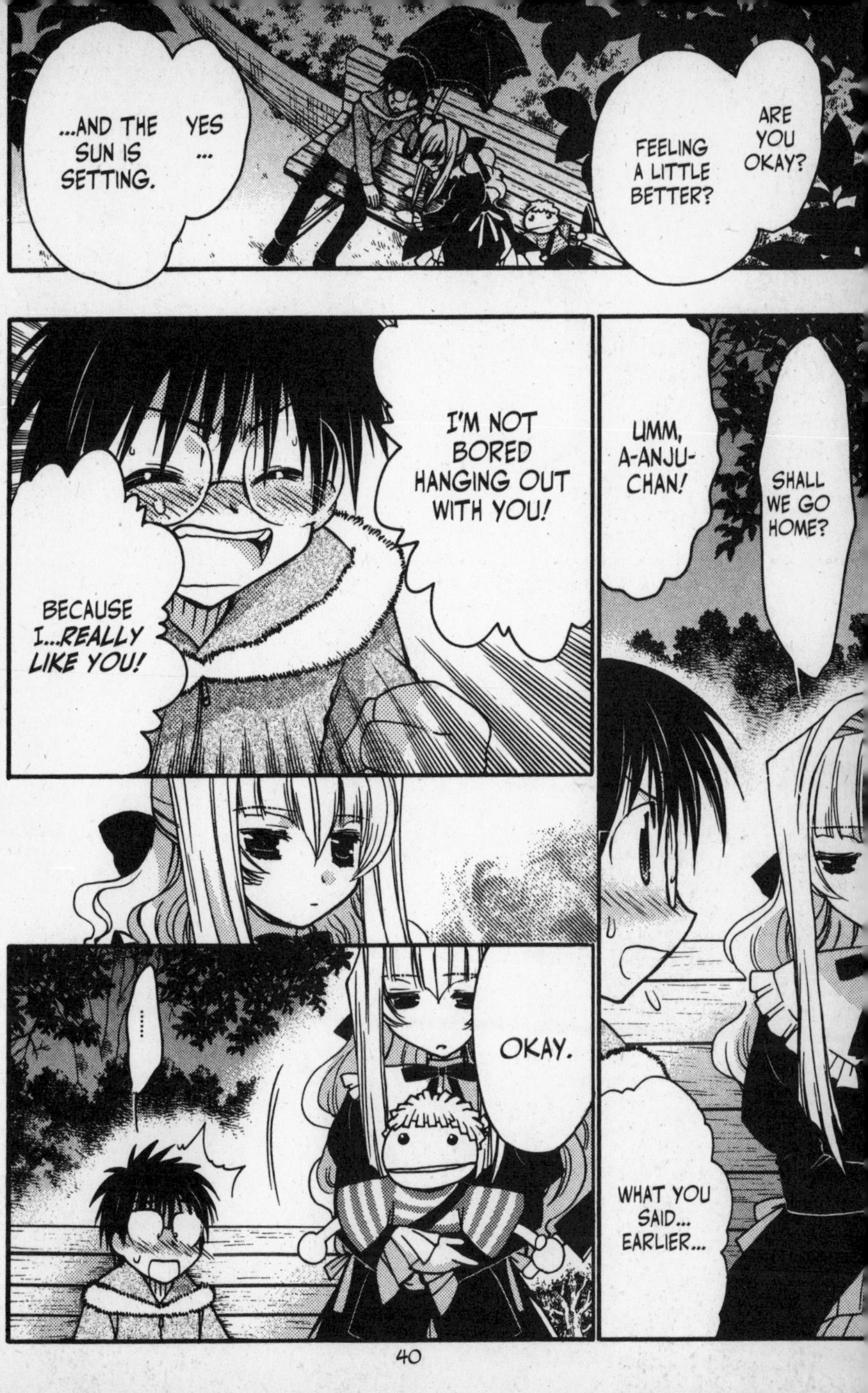
ARE YOU OKAY?
FEELING A LITTLE BETTER?
YES ...
...AND THE SUN IS SETTING.
SHALL WE GO HOME?
UMM, A-ANJU-CHAN!
WHAT YOU SAID... EARLIER...
I'M NOT BORED HANGING OUT WITH YOU!
BECAUSE I...*REALLY LIKE YOU!*
OKAY.
.....

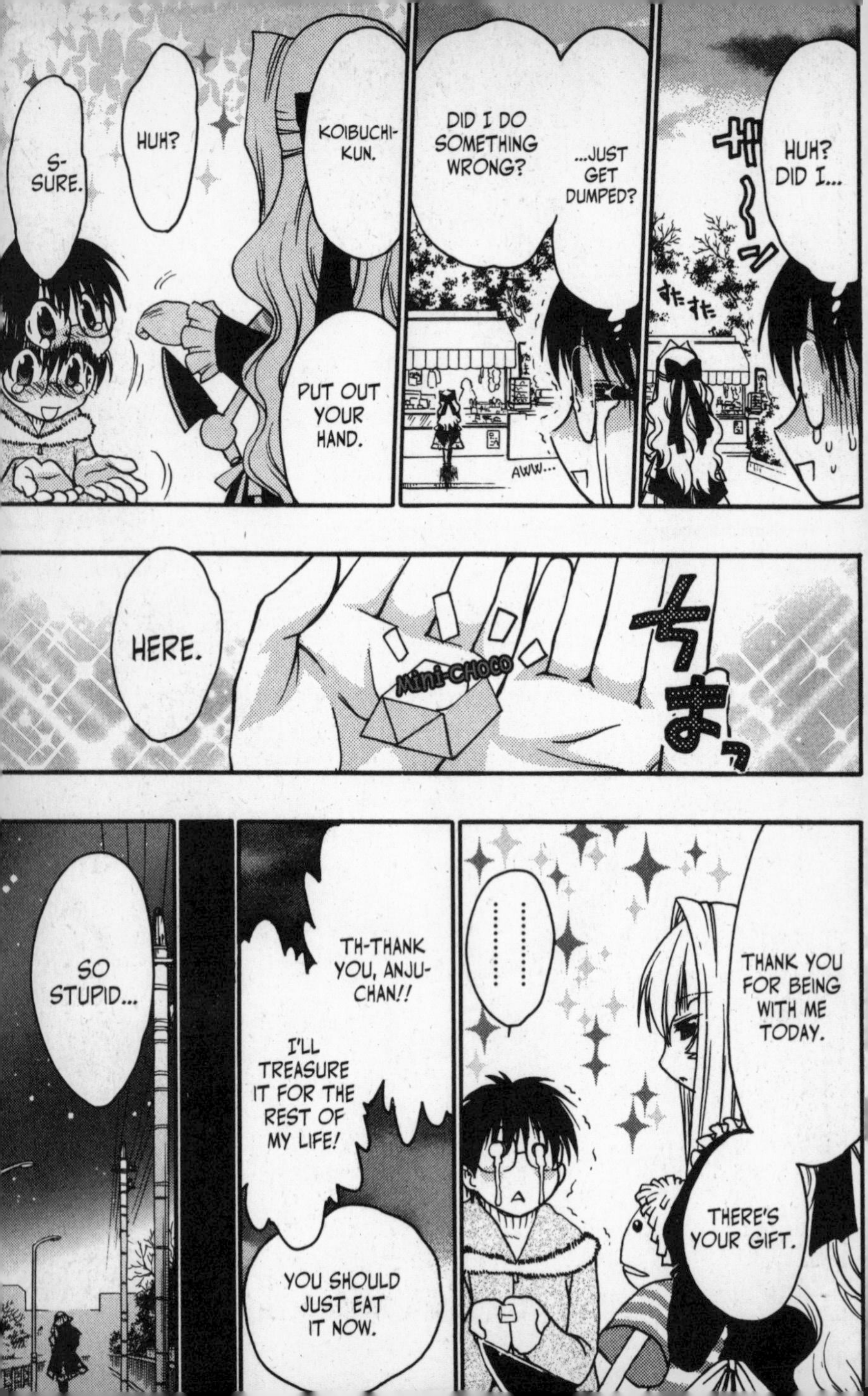
HUH? DID I...
ガ～ン
すたすた
...JUST GET DUMPED?
DID I DO SOMETHING WRONG?
AWW...
KOIBUCHI-KUN.
PUT OUT YOUR HAND.
HUH?
S-SURE.
ちまっ
Mini-CHOCO
HERE.
THANK YOU FOR BEING WITH ME TODAY.
THERE'S YOUR GIFT.
......
TH-THANK YOU, ANJU-CHAN!!
I'LL TREASURE IT FOR THE REST OF MY LIFE!
YOU SHOULD JUST EAT IT NOW.
SO STUPID...

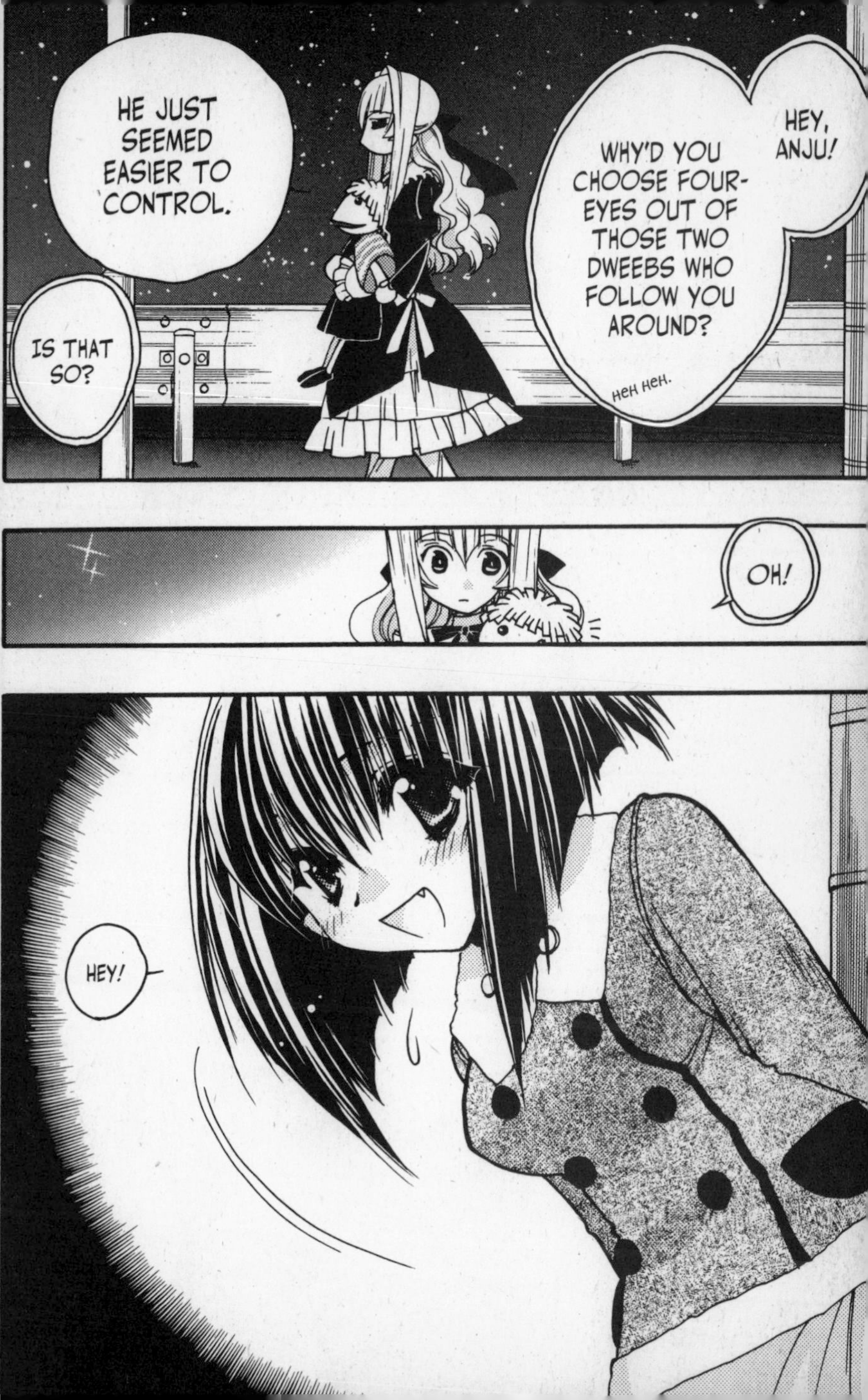
HEY, ANJU!
WHY'D YOU CHOOSE FOUR-EYES OUT OF THOSE TWO DWEEBS WHO FOLLOW YOU AROUND?
HEH HEH.
HE JUST SEEMED EASIER TO CONTROL.
IS THAT SO?
OH!
HEY!

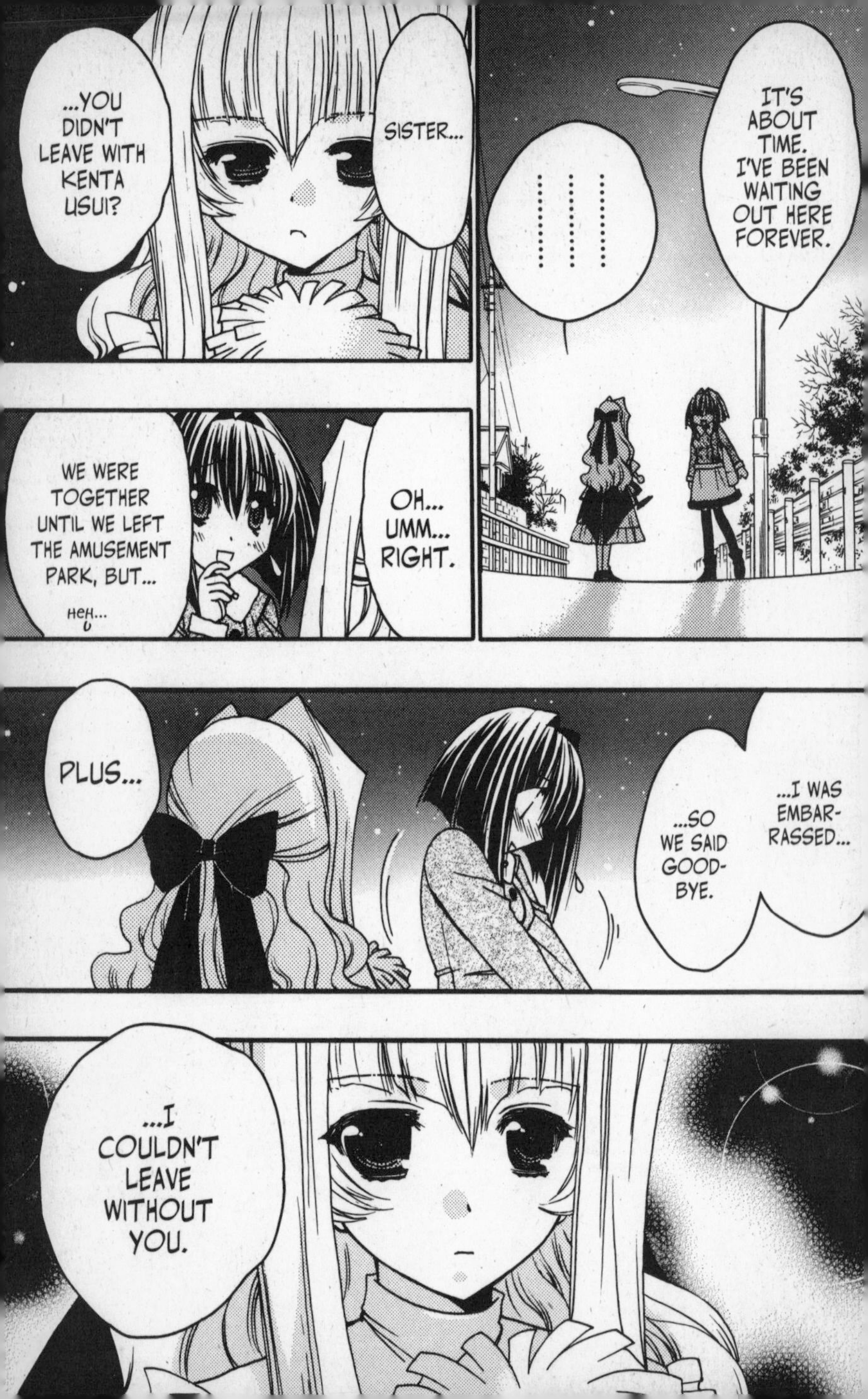
IT'S ABOUT TIME. I'VE BEEN WAITING OUT HERE FOREVER.
......
SISTER...
...YOU DIDN'T LEAVE WITH KENTA USUI?
OH... UMM... RIGHT.
WE WERE TOGETHER UNTIL WE LEFT THE AMUSEMENT PARK, BUT...
HEH...
...I WAS EMBAR-RASSED...
...SO WE SAID GOOD-BYE.
PLUS...
...I COULDN'T LEAVE WITHOUT YOU.

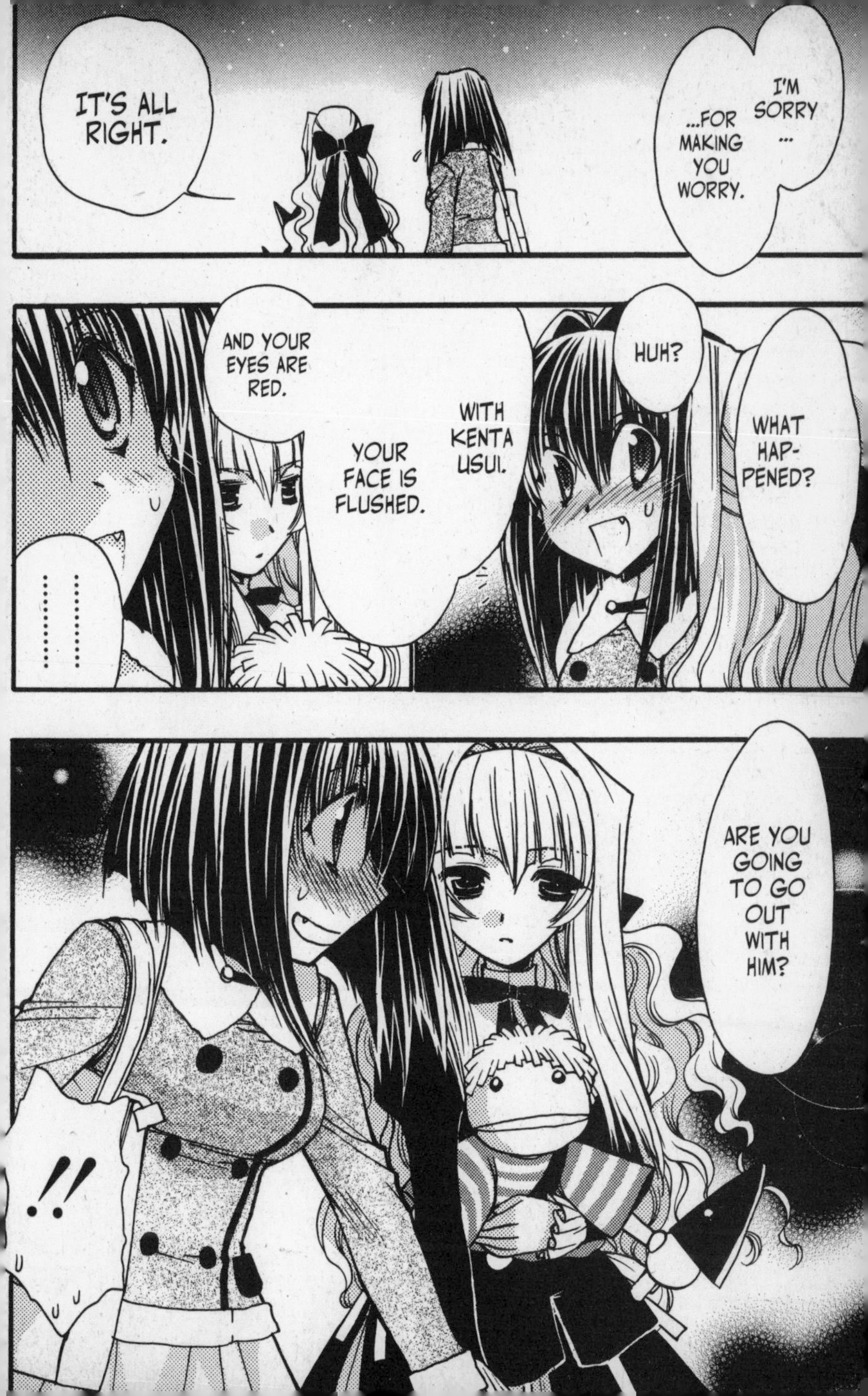
I'M SORRY ...
...FOR MAKING YOU WORRY.
IT'S ALL RIGHT.
WHAT HAP-PENED?
HUH?
WITH KENTA USUI.
YOUR FACE IS FLUSHED.
AND YOUR EYES ARE RED.
......
ARE YOU GOING TO GO OUT WITH HIM?
!!

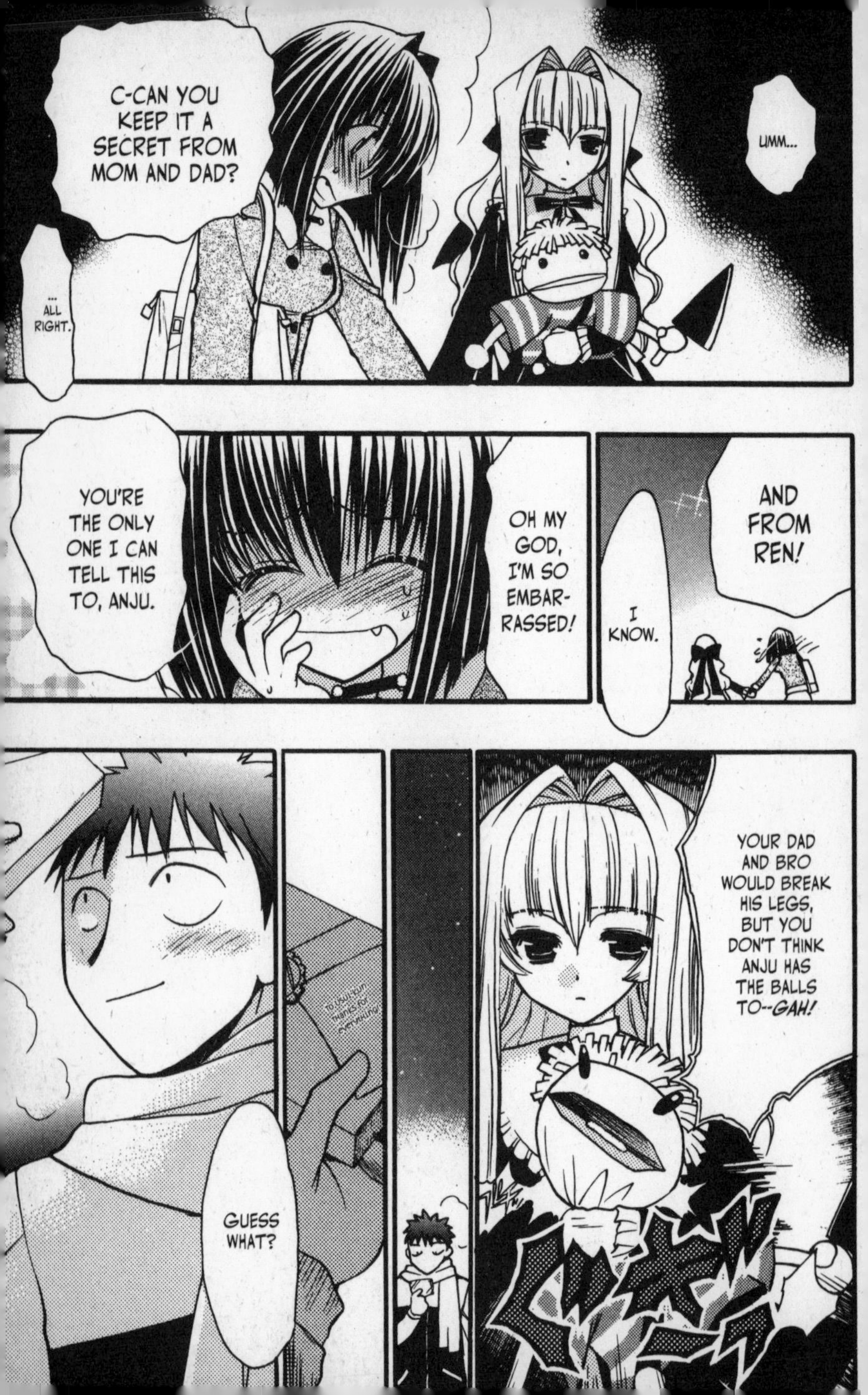
UMM...
C-CAN YOU KEEP IT A SECRET FROM MOM AND DAD?
...ALL RIGHT.
AND FROM REN!
I KNOW.
OH MY GOD, I'M SO EMBARRASSED!
YOU'RE THE ONLY ONE I CAN TELL THIS TO, ANJU.
YOUR DAD AND BRO WOULD BREAK HIS LEGS, BUT YOU DON'T THINK ANJU HAS THE BALLS TO--GAH!
To Usui-kun Thanks for everything!
GUESS WHAT?

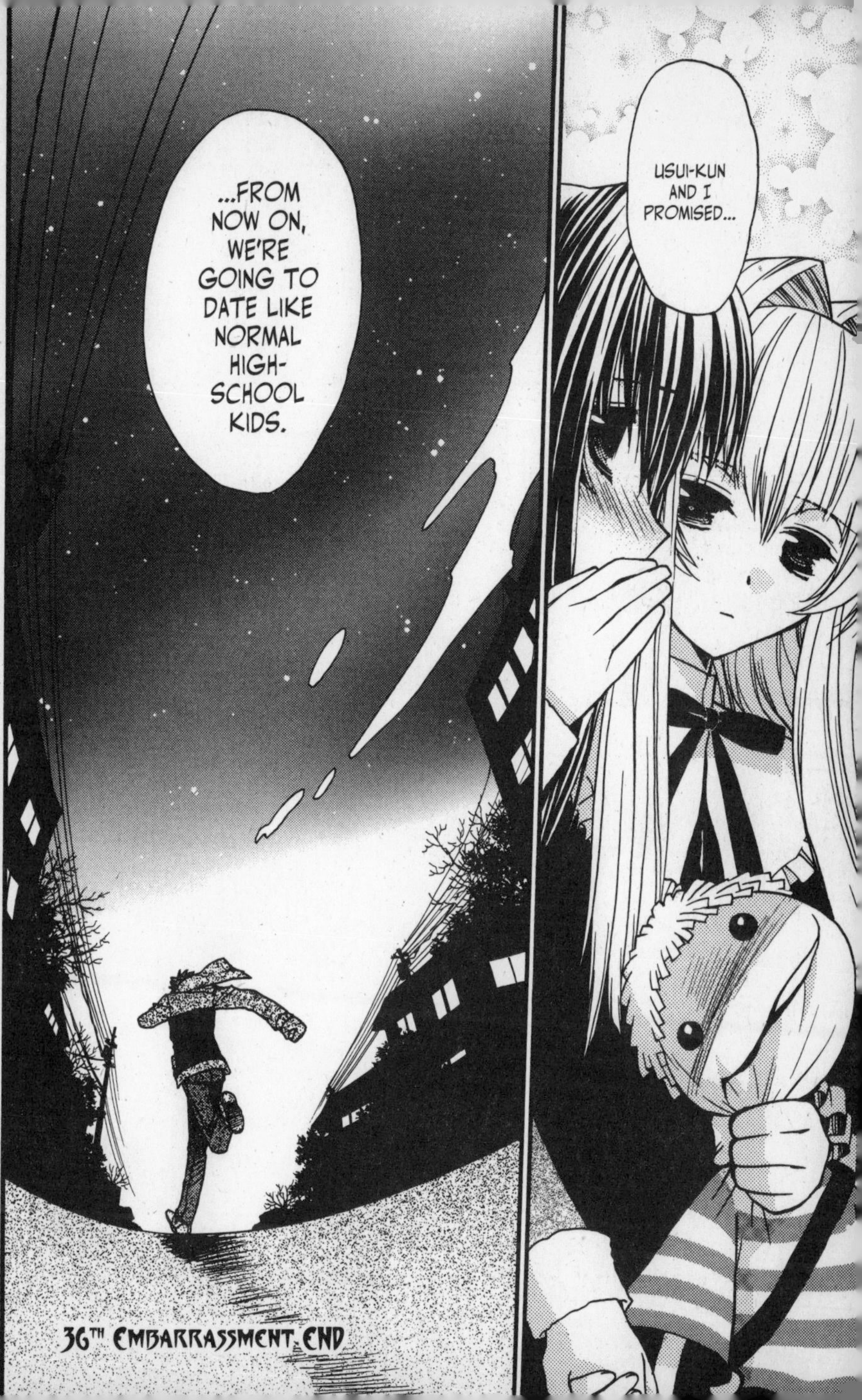
USUI-KUN AND I PROMISED...
...FROM NOW ON, WE'RE GOING TO DATE LIKE NORMAL HIGH-SCHOOL KIDS.
36TH EMBARRASSMENT END

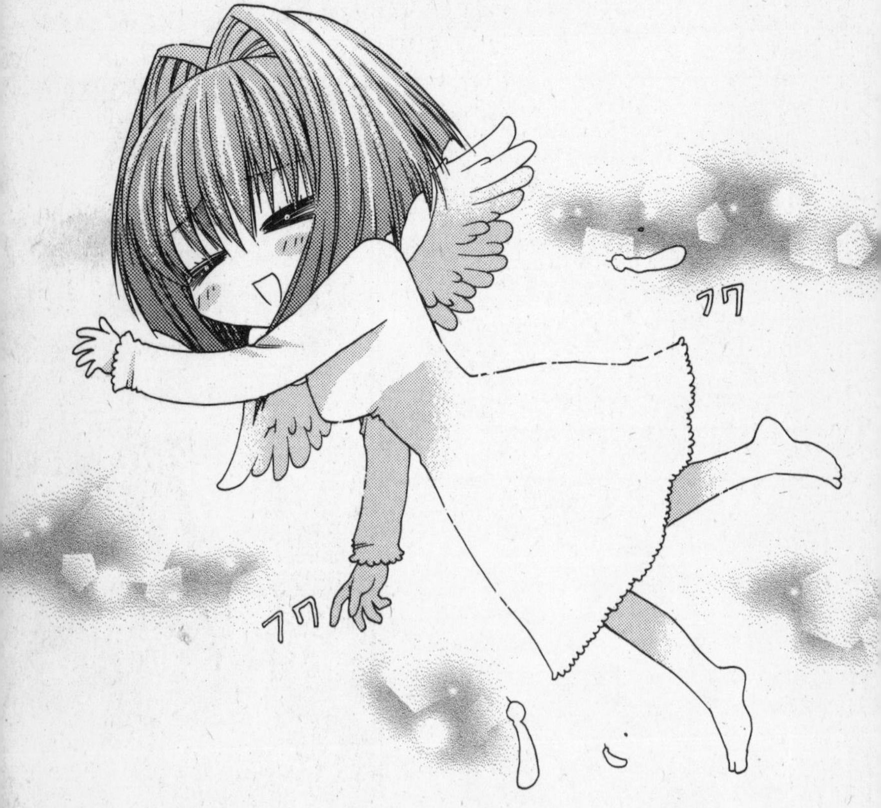

37TH EMBARRASSMENT) THE TWO BEGINNERS AND YURIYA'S INVESTIGATION

~BEGINNERS~

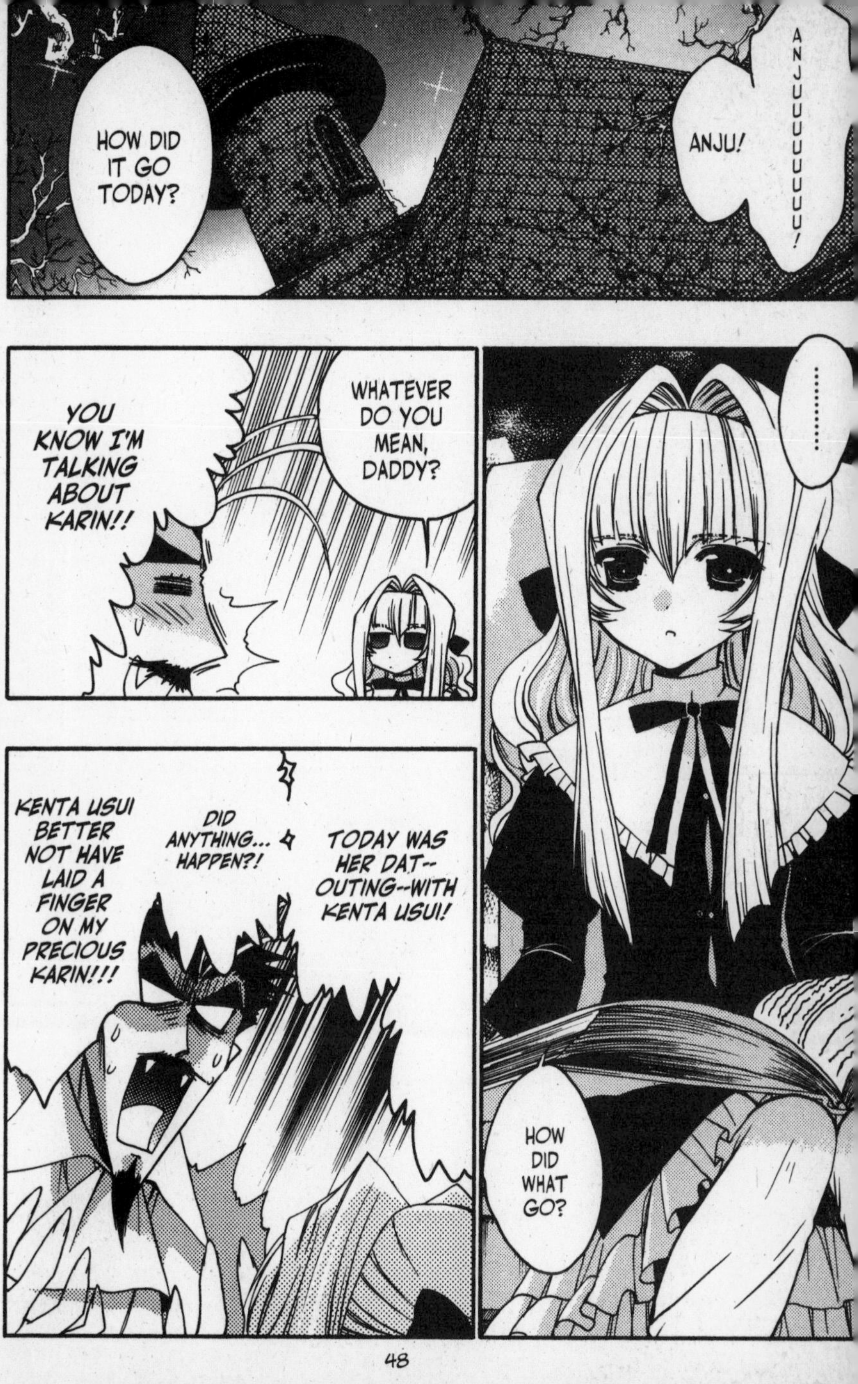
ANJUUUUUUUU!
ANJU!
HOW DID IT GO TODAY?
......
HOW DID WHAT GO?
WHATEVER DO YOU MEAN, DADDY?
YOU KNOW I'M TALKING ABOUT KARIN!!
TODAY WAS HER DAT--OUTING--WITH KENTA USUI!
DID ANYTHING... HAPPEN?!
KENTA USUI BETTER NOT HAVE LAID A FINGER ON MY PRECIOUS KARIN!!!

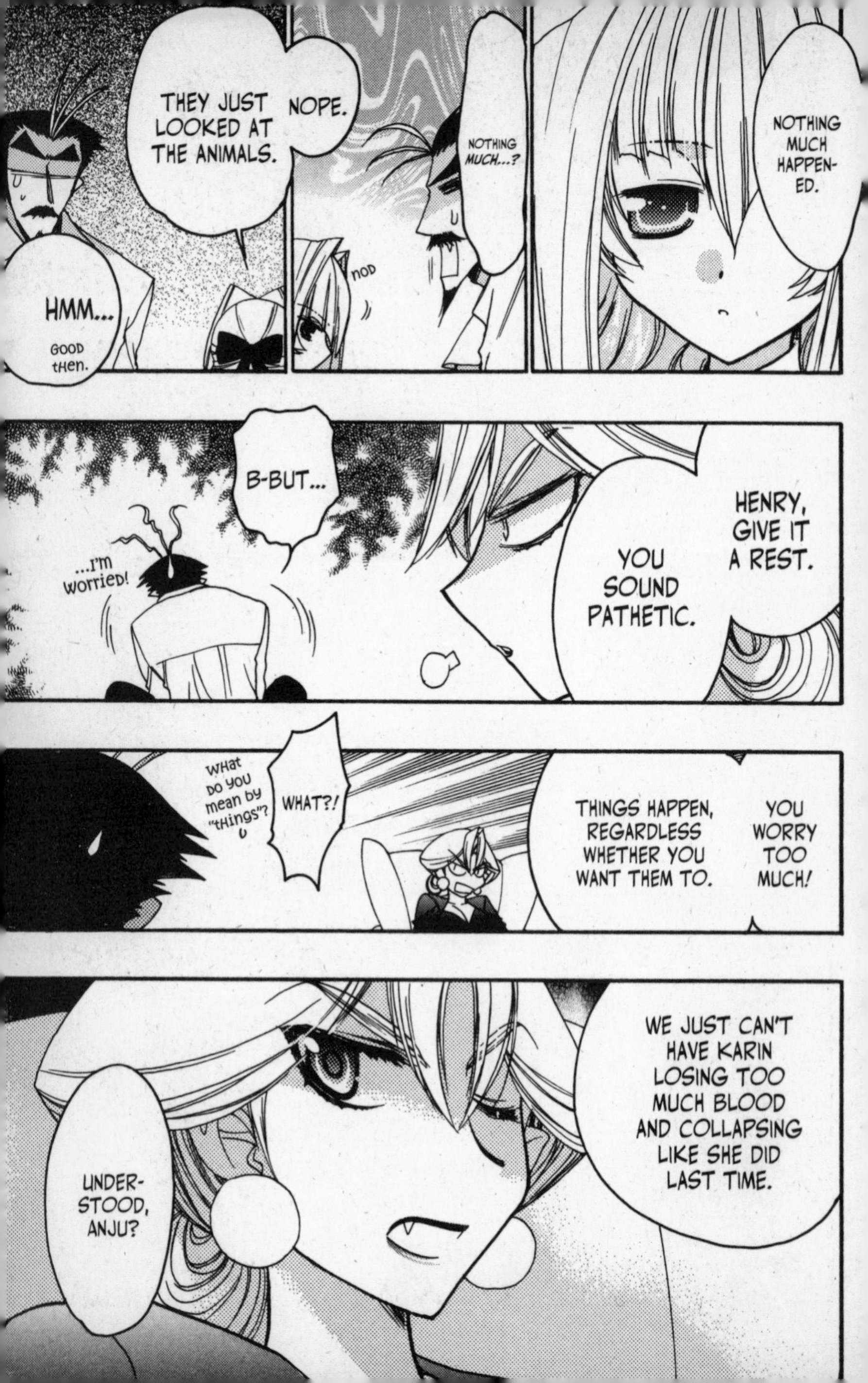
NOTHING MUCH HAPPENED.
NOTHING MUCH...?
nod
NOPE.
THEY JUST LOOKED AT THE ANIMALS.
HMM...
GOOD then.
HENRY, GIVE IT A REST.
YOU SOUND PATHETIC.
B-BUT...
...I'm worried!
YOU WORRY TOO MUCH!
THINGS HAPPEN, REGARDLESS WHETHER YOU WANT THEM TO.
WHAT?!
What do you mean by "things"?
WE JUST CAN'T HAVE KARIN LOSING TOO MUCH BLOOD AND COLLAPSING LIKE SHE DID LAST TIME.
UNDERSTOOD, ANJU?

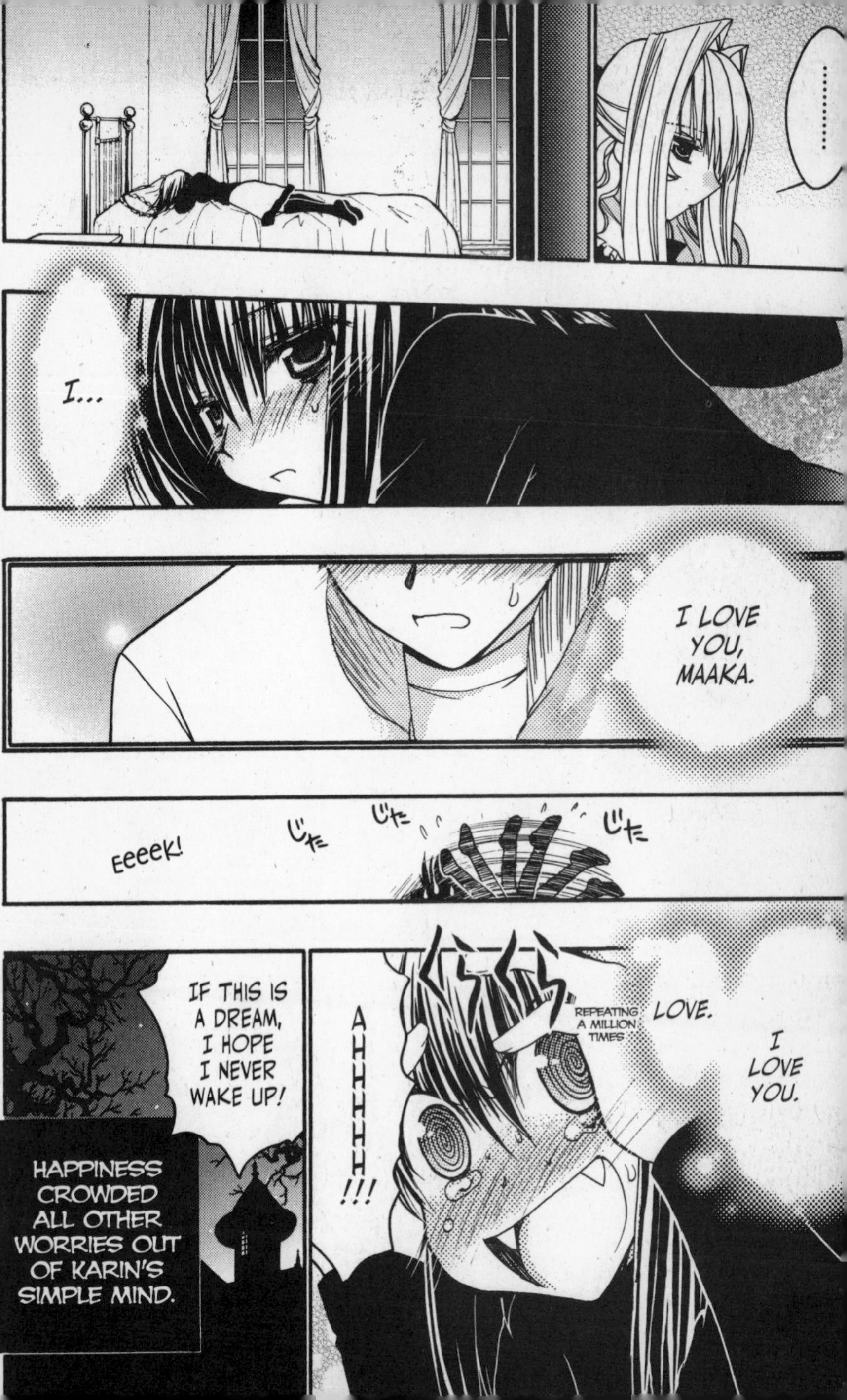
......
I...
I LOVE YOU, MAAKA.
じた
じた
じた
Eeeek!
I LOVE YOU.
LOVE.
REPEATING A MILLION TIMES
AHHHHHHH!!!
IF THIS IS A DREAM, I HOPE I NEVER WAKE UP!
HAPPINESS CROWDED ALL OTHER WORRIES OUT OF KARIN'S SIMPLE MIND.

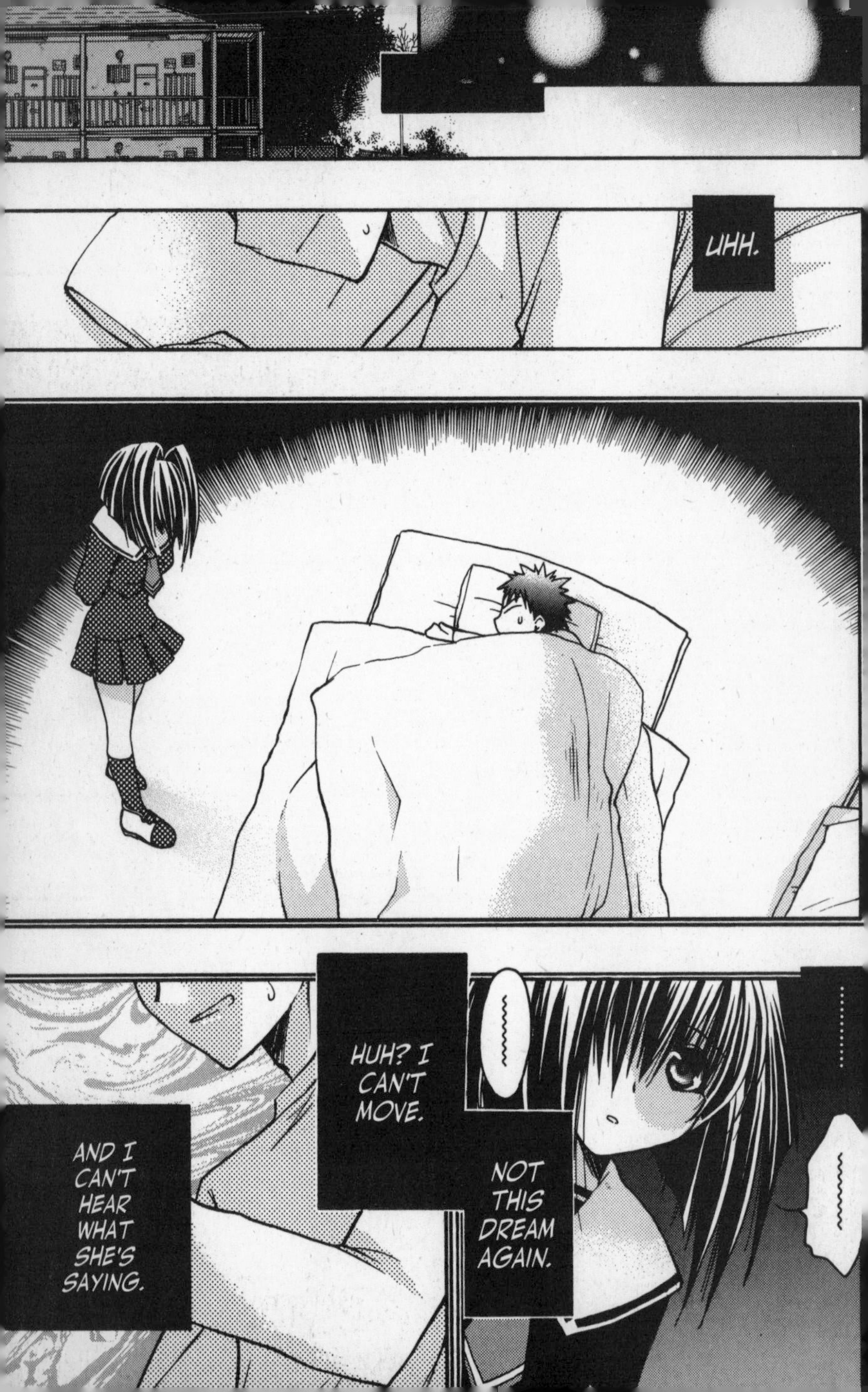
UHH.
......
HUH? I CAN'T MOVE.
NOT THIS DREAM AGAIN.
AND I CAN'T HEAR WHAT SHE'S SAYING.

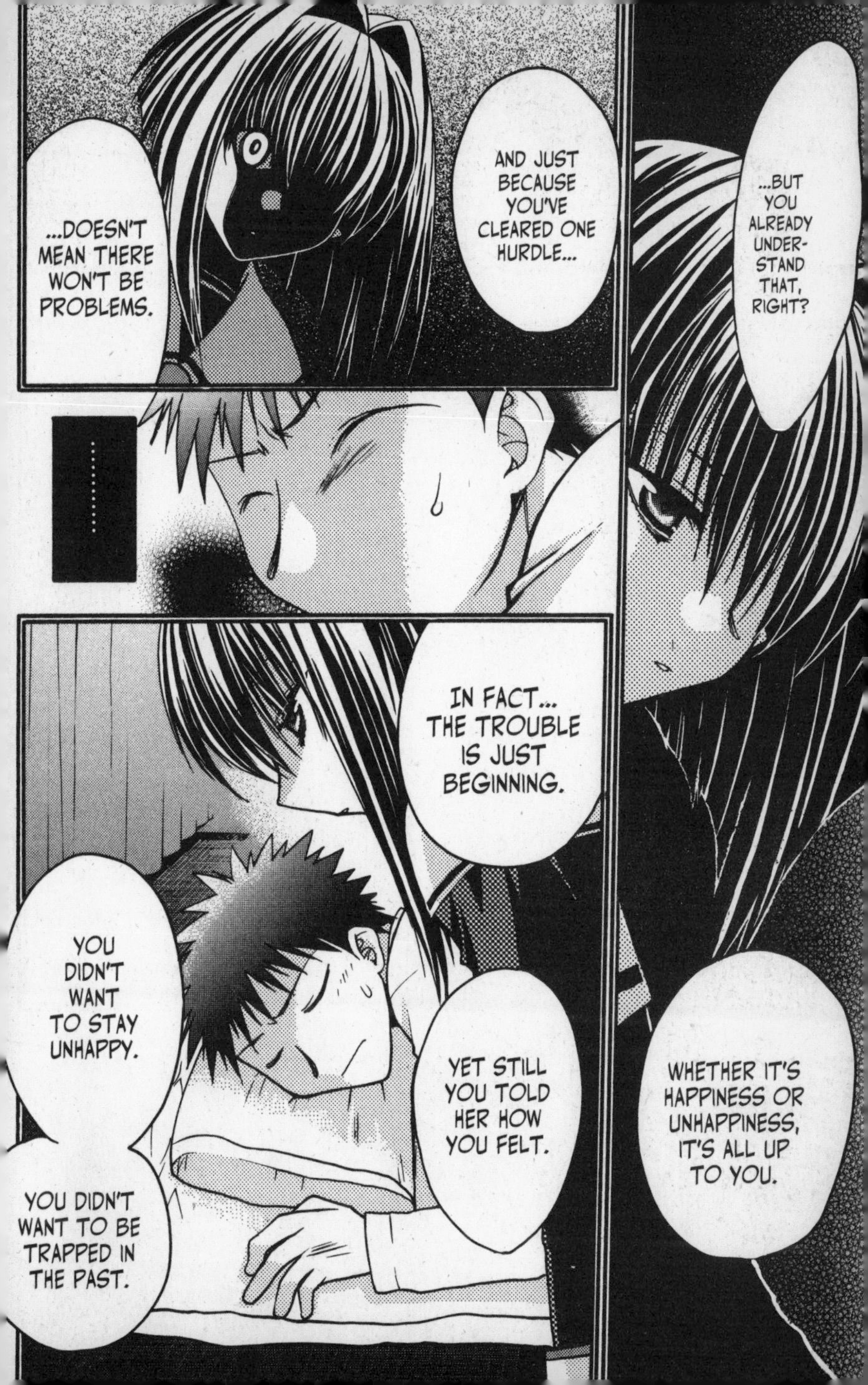
AND JUST BECAUSE YOU'VE CLEARED ONE HURDLE...
...DOESN'T MEAN THERE WON'T BE PROBLEMS.
......
IN FACT... THE TROUBLE IS JUST BEGINNING.
YOU DIDN'T WANT TO STAY UNHAPPY.
YOU DIDN'T WANT TO BE TRAPPED IN THE PAST.
YET STILL YOU TOLD HER HOW YOU FELT.
...BUT YOU ALREADY UNDER-STAND THAT, RIGHT?
WHETHER IT'S HAPPINESS OR UNHAPPINESS, IT'S ALL UP TO YOU.

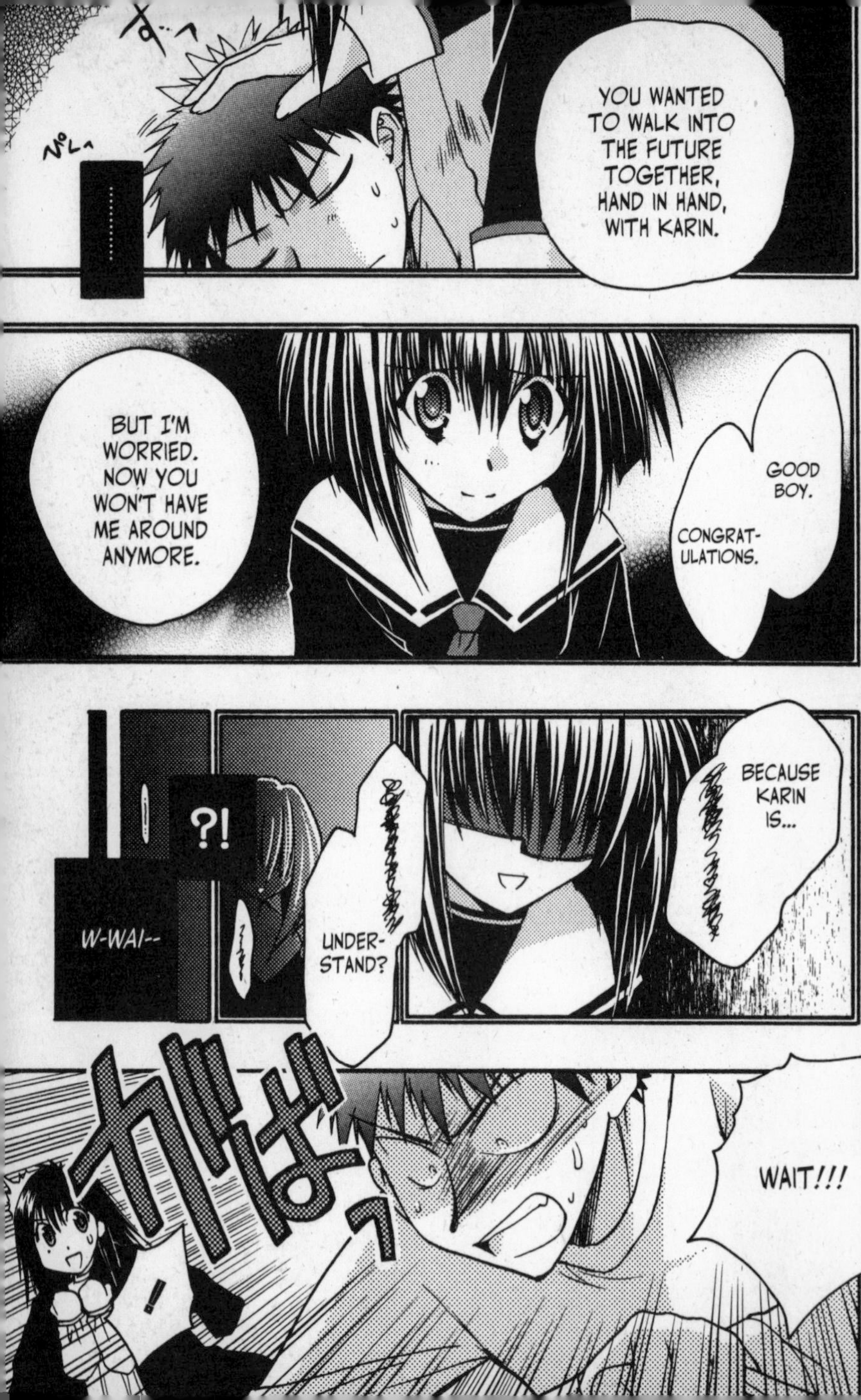
YOU WANTED TO WALK INTO THE FUTURE TOGETHER, HAND IN HAND, WITH KARIN.
......
GOOD BOY.
CONGRAT- ULATIONS.
BUT I'M WORRIED. NOW YOU WON'T HAVE ME AROUND ANYMORE.
BECAUSE KARIN IS...
UNDER- STAND?
?!
...!
W-WAI--
WAIT!!!
!

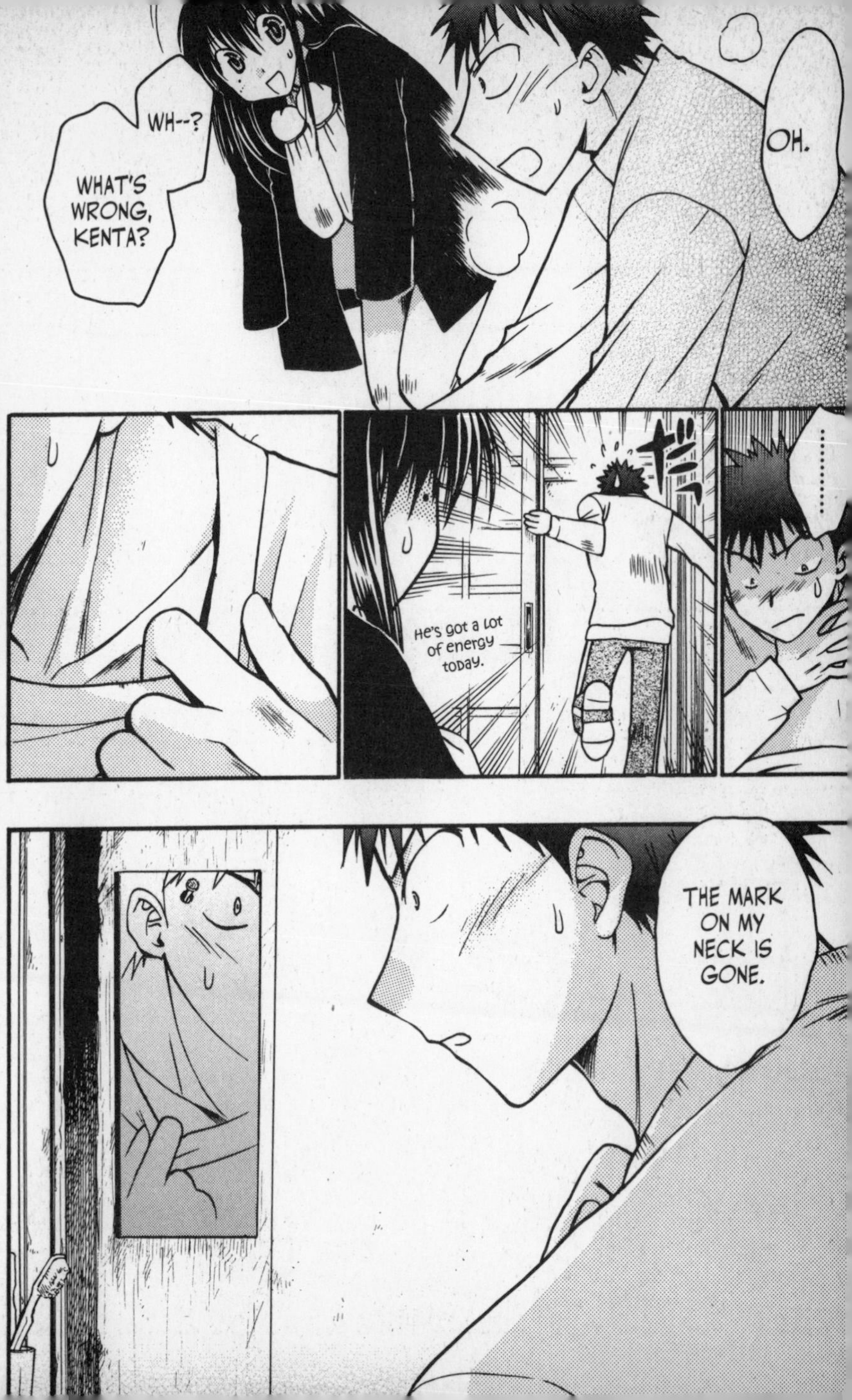
OH.
WH--?
WHAT'S WRONG, KENTA?
......
He's got a lot of energy today.
THE MARK ON MY NECK IS GONE.

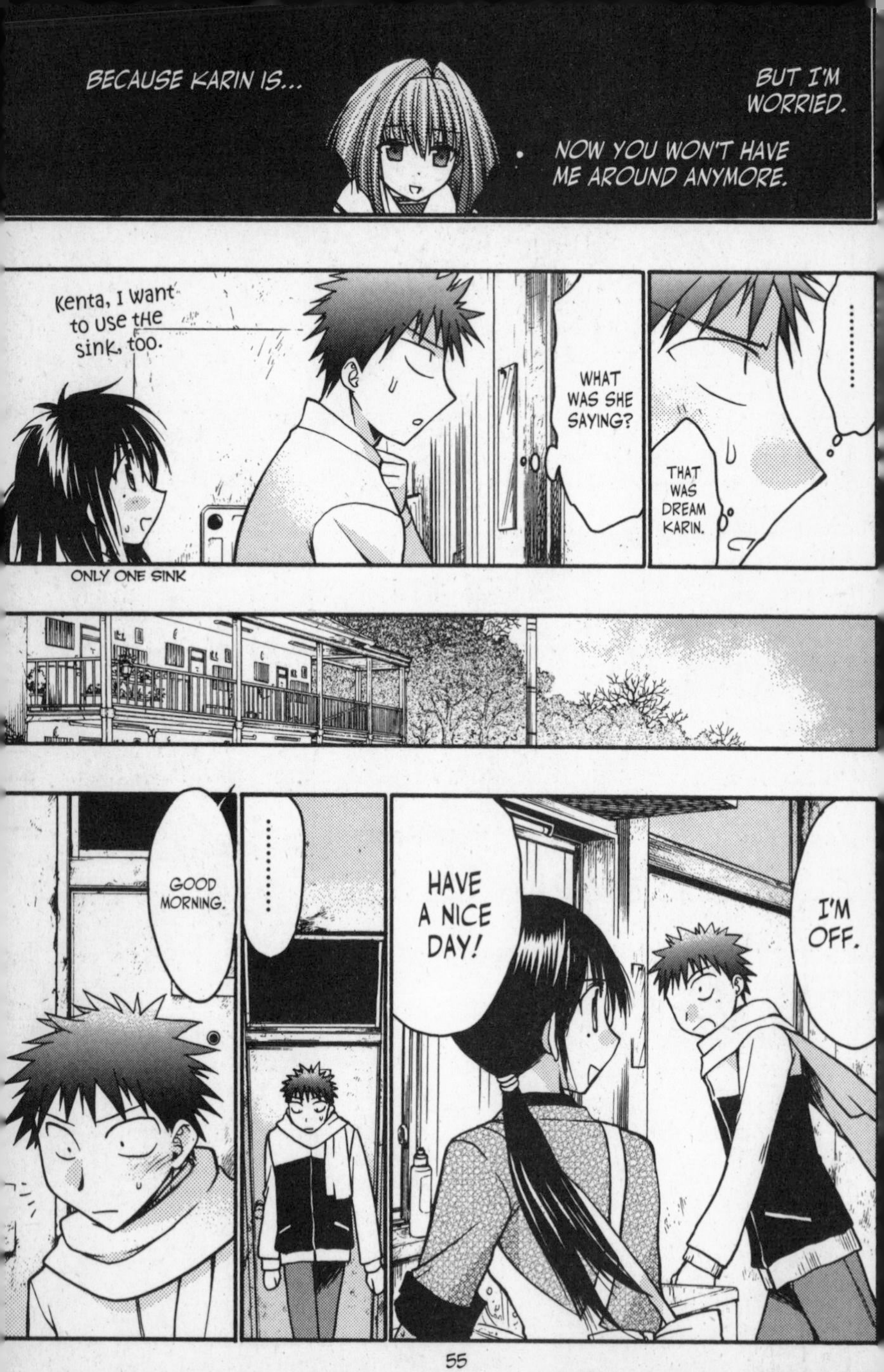
BUT I'M WORRIED.
NOW YOU WON'T HAVE ME AROUND ANYMORE.
BECAUSE KARIN IS...
......
THAT WAS DREAM KARIN.
WHAT WAS SHE SAYING?
Kenta, I want to use the sink, too.
ONLY ONE SINK
I'M OFF.
HAVE A NICE DAY!
......
GOOD MORNING.

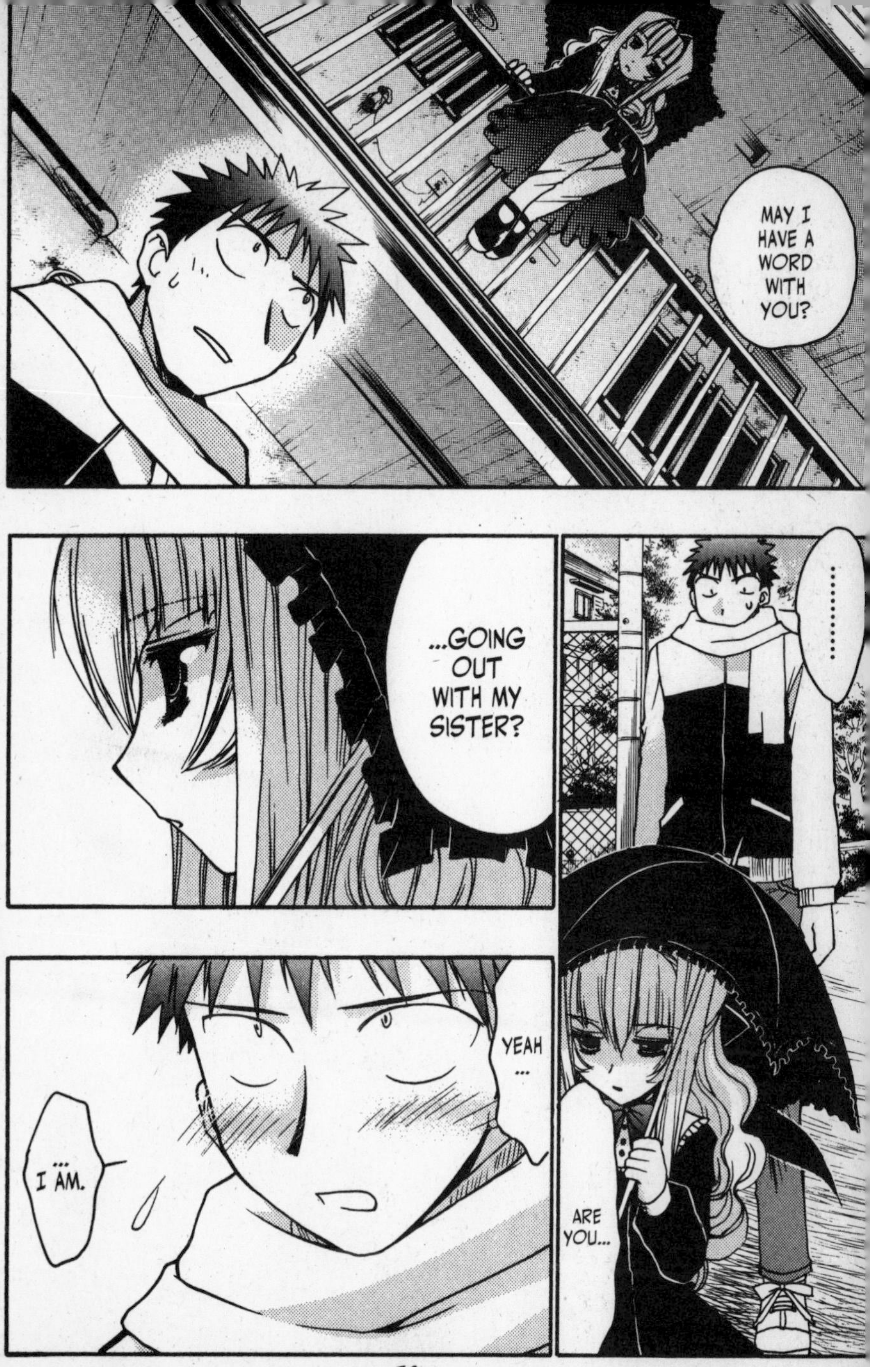
MAY I HAVE A WORD WITH YOU?
......
ARE YOU...
...GOING OUT WITH MY SISTER?
YEAH ...
... I AM.

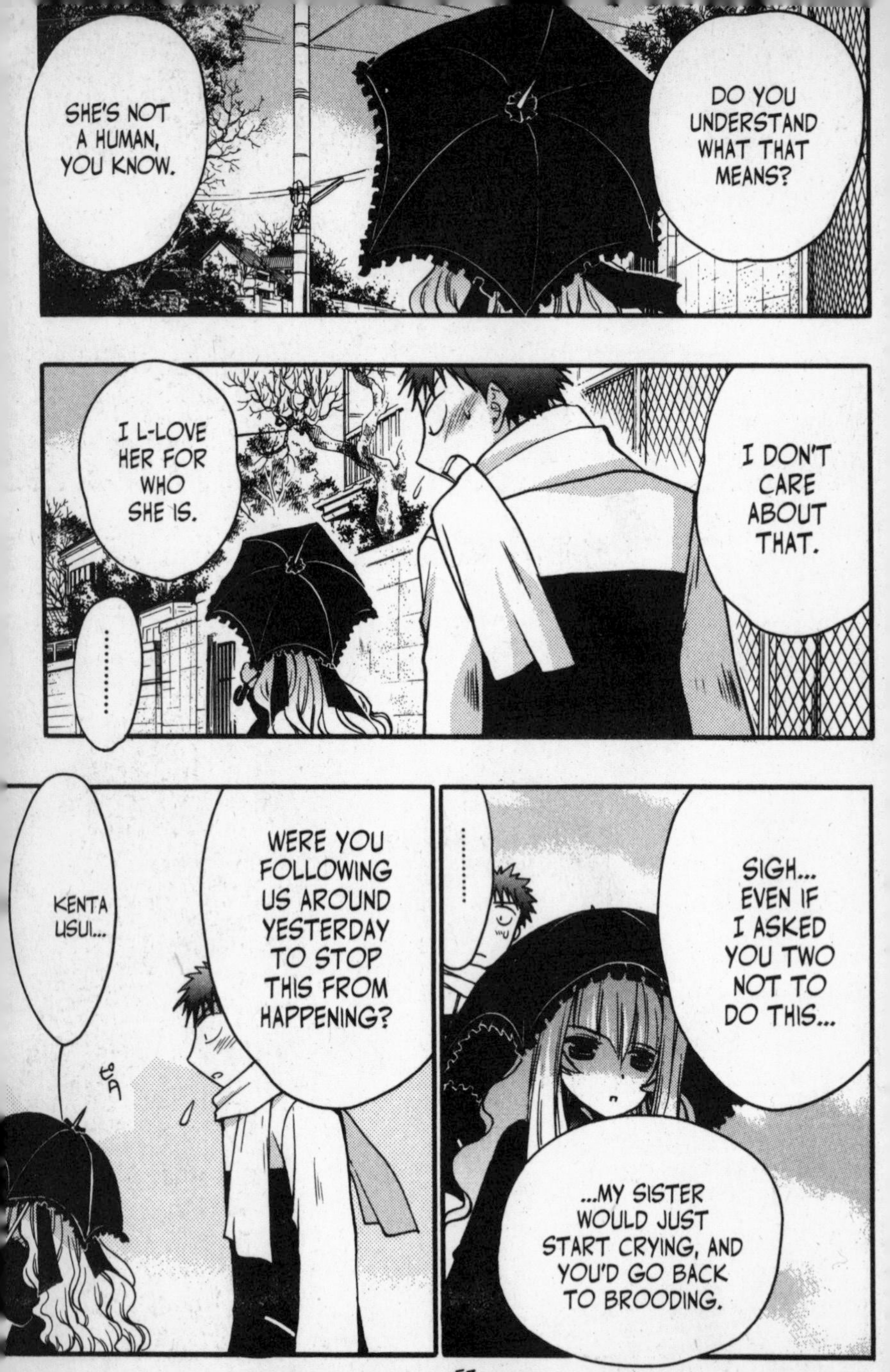
DO YOU UNDERSTAND WHAT THAT MEANS?
SHE'S NOT A HUMAN, YOU KNOW.
I DON'T CARE ABOUT THAT.
I L-LOVE HER FOR WHO SHE IS.
......
SIGH... EVEN IF I ASKED YOU TWO NOT TO DO THIS...
......
...MY SISTER WOULD JUST START CRYING, AND YOU'D GO BACK TO BROODING.
WERE YOU FOLLOWING US AROUND YESTERDAY TO STOP THIS FROM HAPPENING?
KENTA USUI...

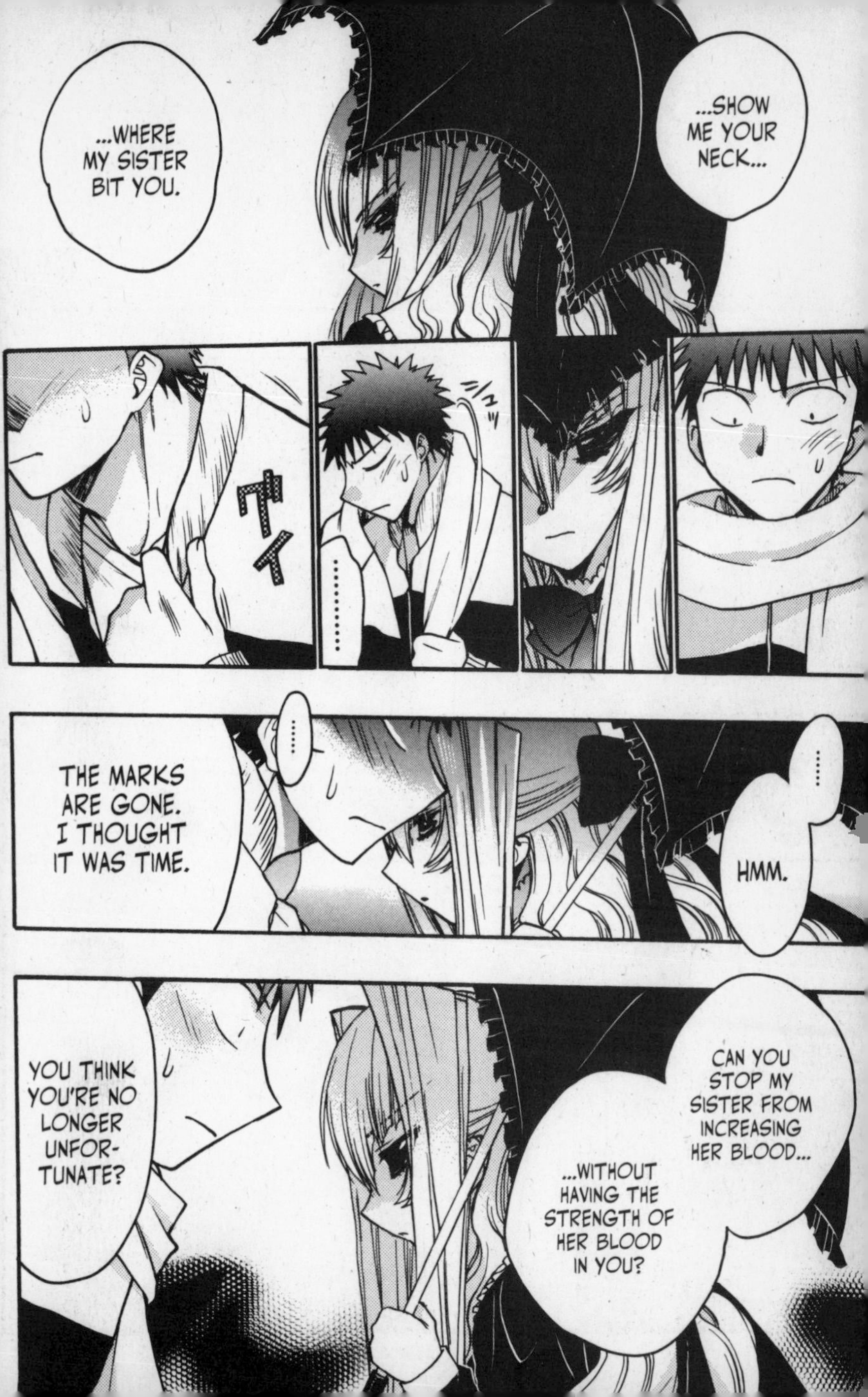
...SHOW ME YOUR NECK...
...WHERE MY SISTER BIT YOU.
......
......
HMM.
......
THE MARKS ARE GONE. I THOUGHT IT WAS TIME.
CAN YOU STOP MY SISTER FROM INCREASING HER BLOOD...
...WITHOUT HAVING THE STRENGTH OF HER BLOOD IN YOU?
YOU THINK YOU'RE NO LONGER UNFOR-TUNATE?

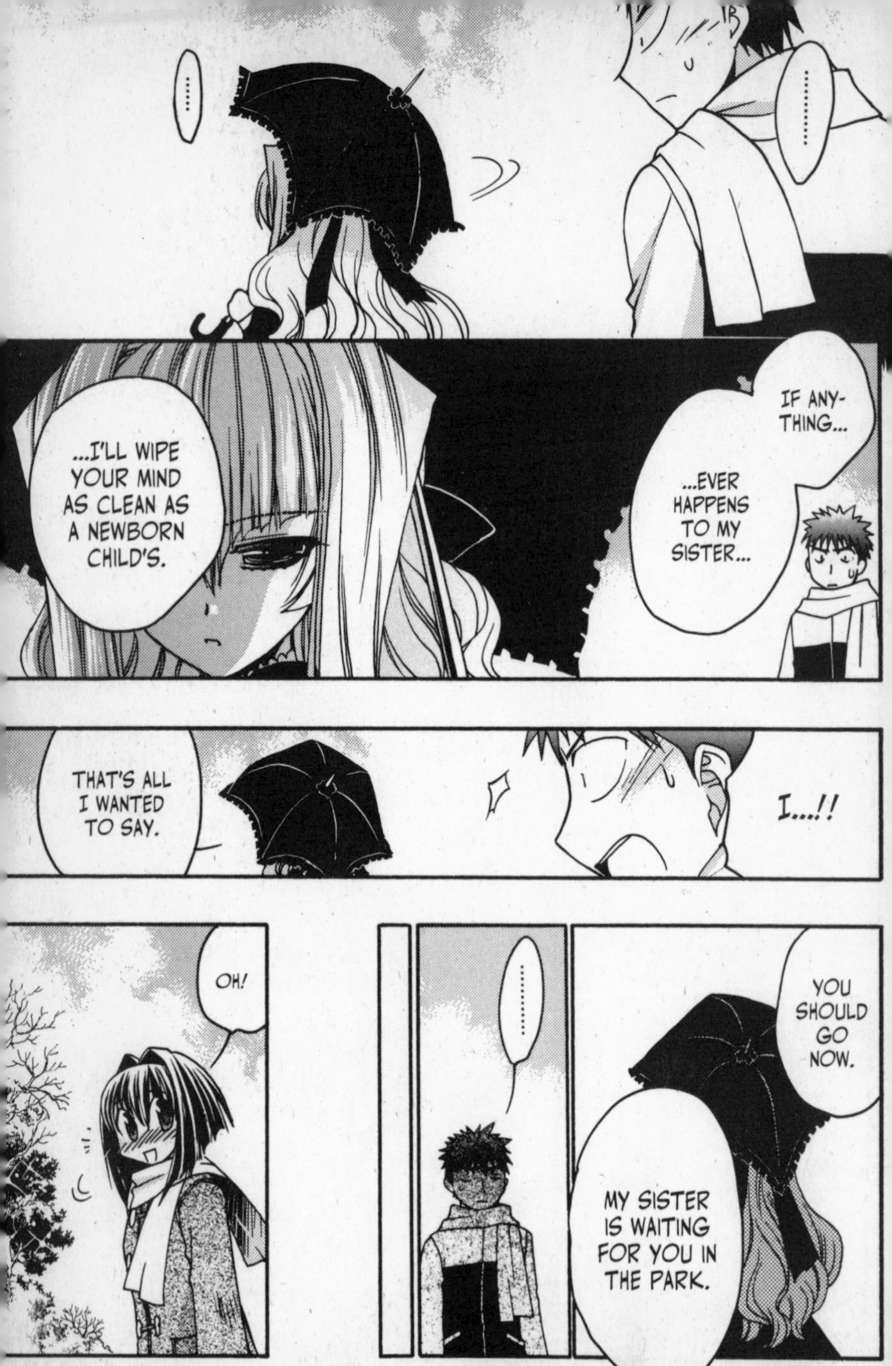

....
......
IF ANY-THING...
...EVER HAPPENS TO MY SISTER...
...I'LL WIPE YOUR MIND AS CLEAN AS A NEWBORN CHILD'S.
I...!!
THAT'S ALL I WANTED TO SAY.
YOU SHOULD GO NOW.
MY SISTER IS WAITING FOR YOU IN THE PARK.
....
OH!

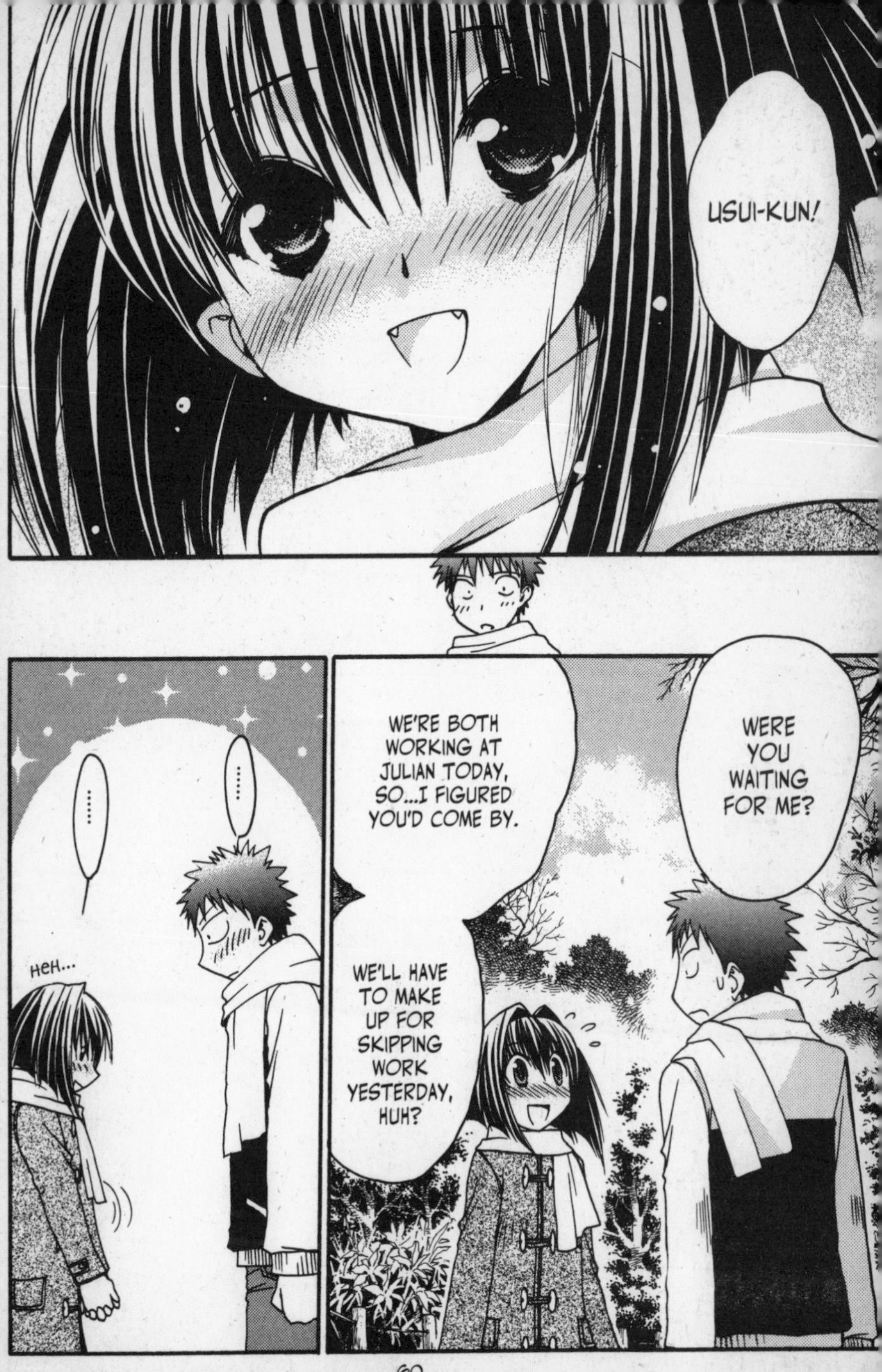
USUI-KUN!
WERE YOU WAITING FOR ME?
WE'RE BOTH WORKING AT JULIAN TODAY, SO...I FIGURED YOU'D COME BY.
WE'LL HAVE TO MAKE UP FOR SKIPPING WORK YESTERDAY, HUH?
......
......
HEH...

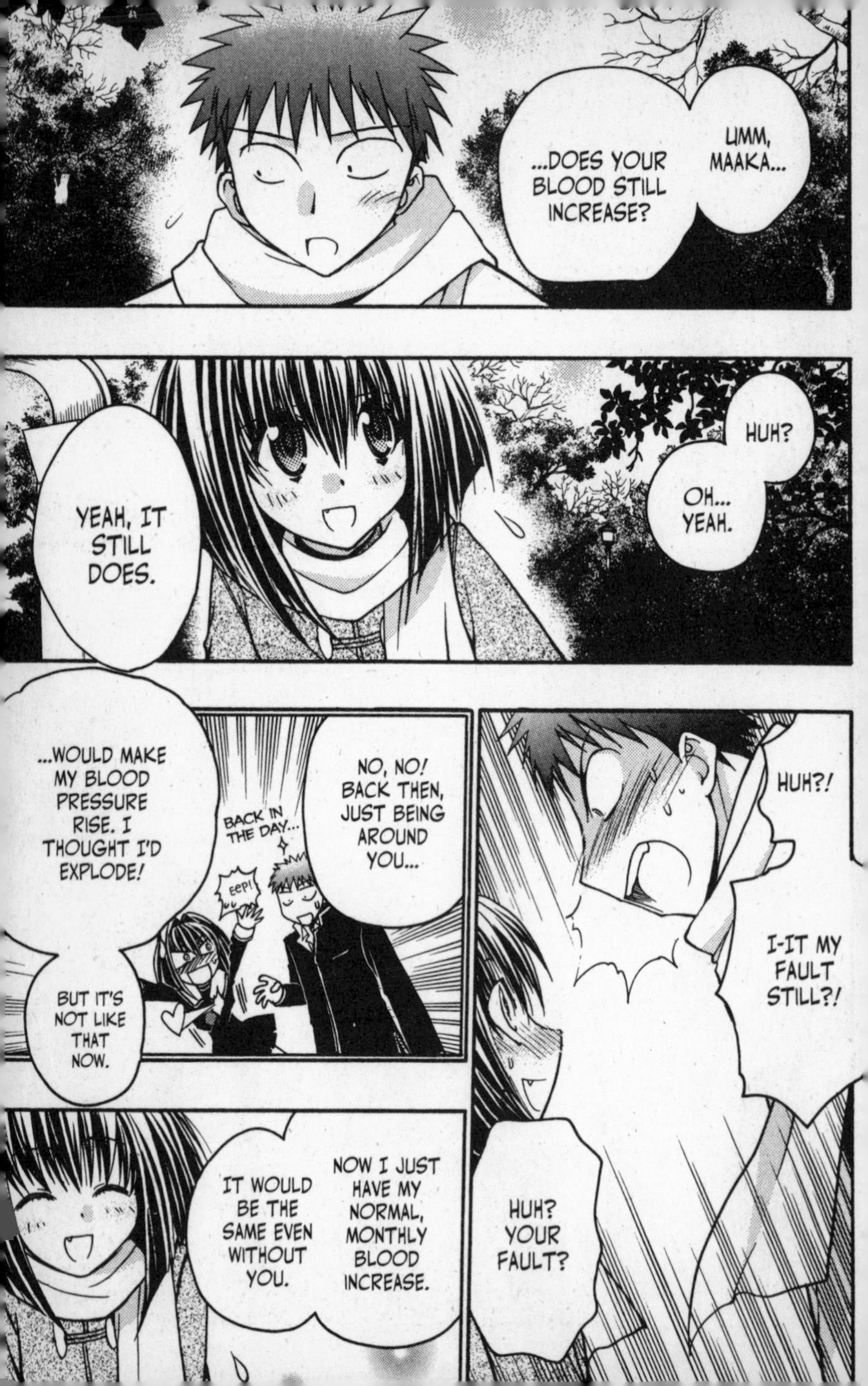
UMM, MAAKA...
...DOES YOUR BLOOD STILL INCREASE?
HUH?
OH... YEAH.
YEAH, IT STILL DOES.
HUH?!
I-IT MY FAULT STILL?!
HUH? YOUR FAULT?
NO, NO! BACK THEN, JUST BEING AROUND YOU...
BACK IN THE DAY...
EEP!
...WOULD MAKE MY BLOOD PRESSURE RISE. I THOUGHT I'D EXPLODE!
BUT IT'S NOT LIKE THAT NOW.
NOW I JUST HAVE MY NORMAL, MONTHLY BLOOD INCREASE.
IT WOULD BE THE SAME EVEN WITHOUT YOU.

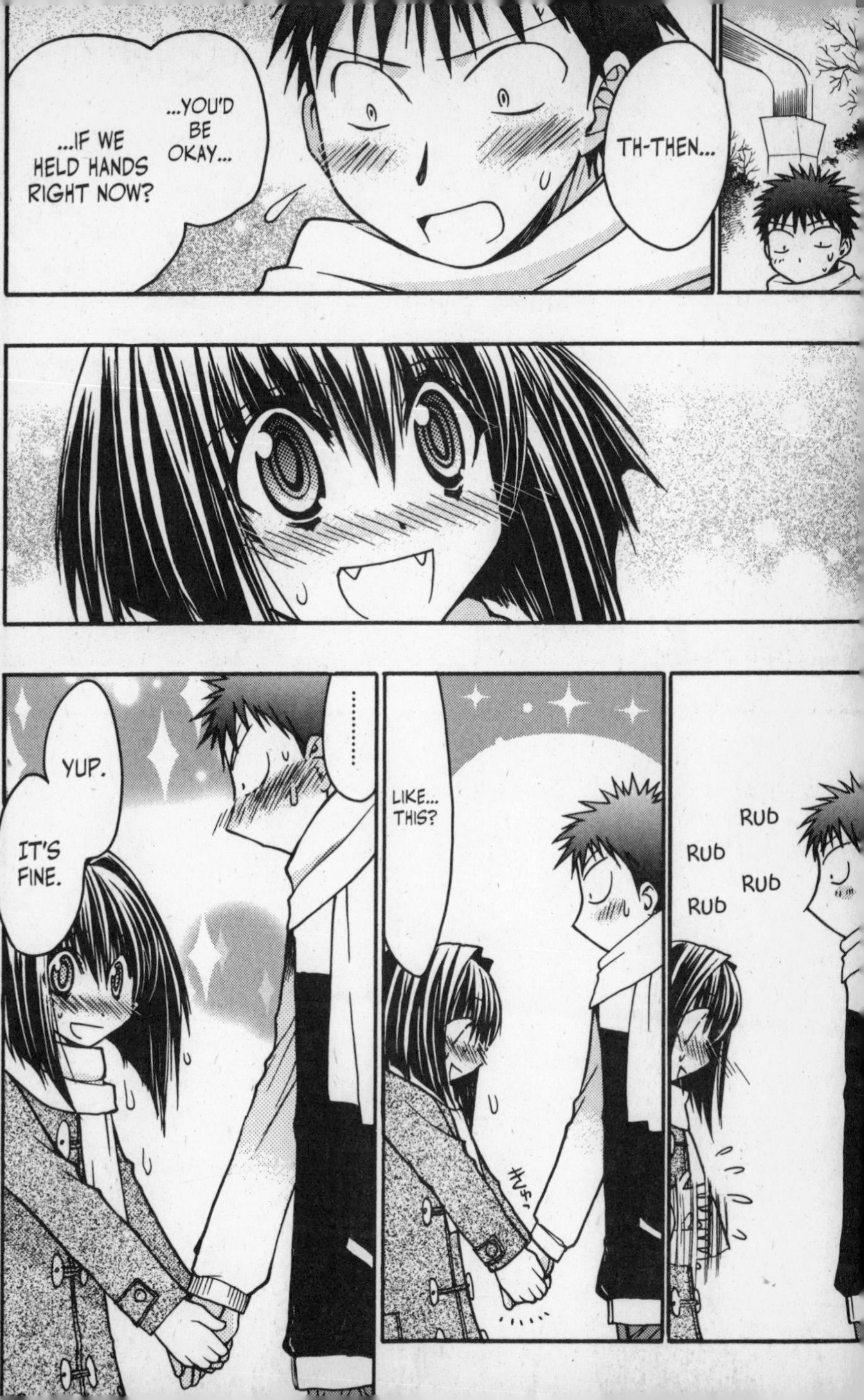
TH-THEN...
...YOU'D BE OKAY...
...IF WE HELD HANDS RIGHT NOW?
Rub
Rub
Rub
Rub
LIKE... THIS?
....
YUP.
IT'S FINE.

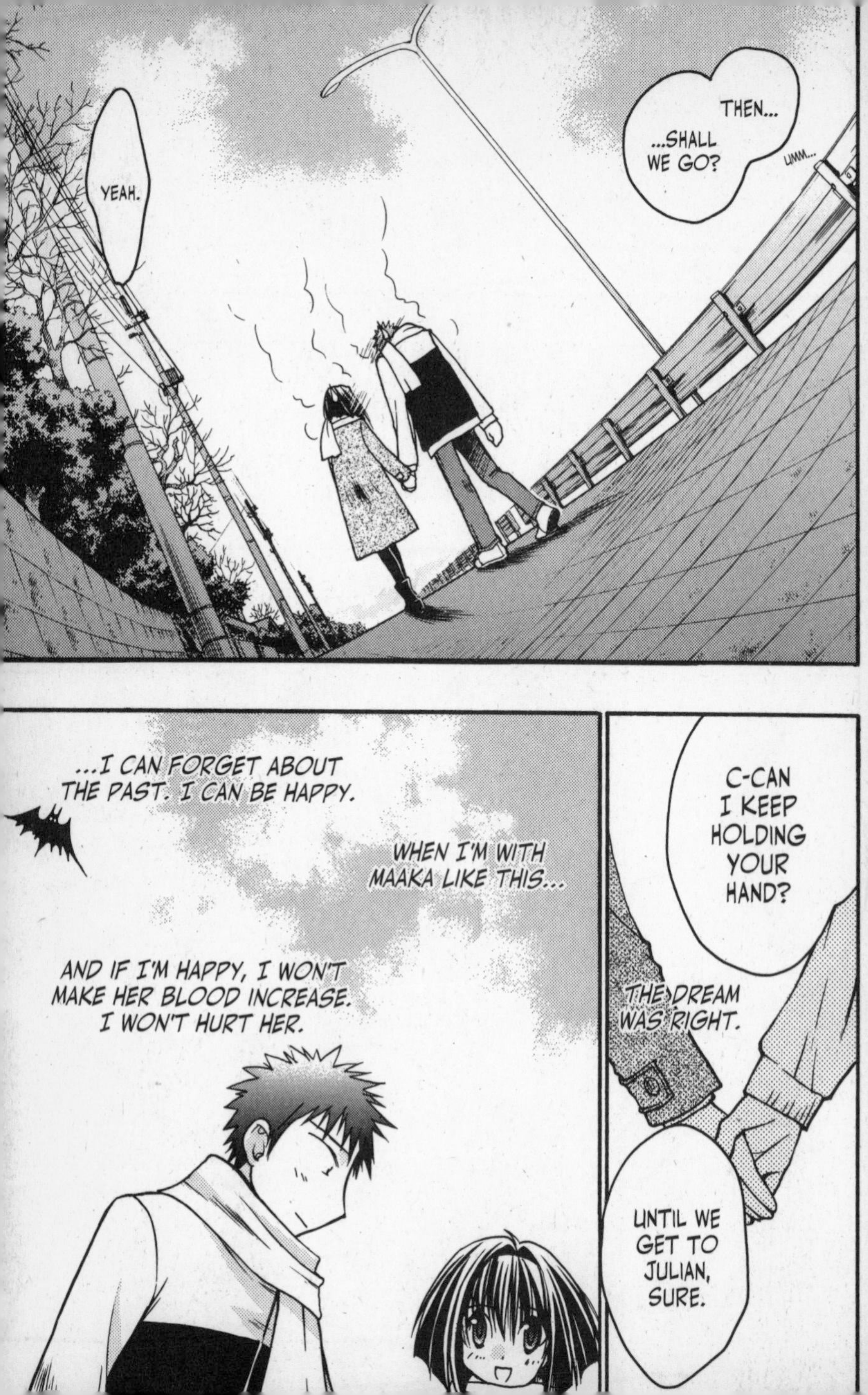
THEN...
...SHALL WE GO?
UMM...
YEAH.
C-CAN I KEEP HOLDING YOUR HAND?
THE DREAM WAS RIGHT.
UNTIL WE GET TO JULIAN, SURE.
WHEN I'M WITH MAAKA LIKE THIS...
...I CAN FORGET ABOUT THE PAST. I CAN BE HAPPY.
AND IF I'M HAPPY, I WON'T MAKE HER BLOOD INCREASE. I WON'T HURT HER.

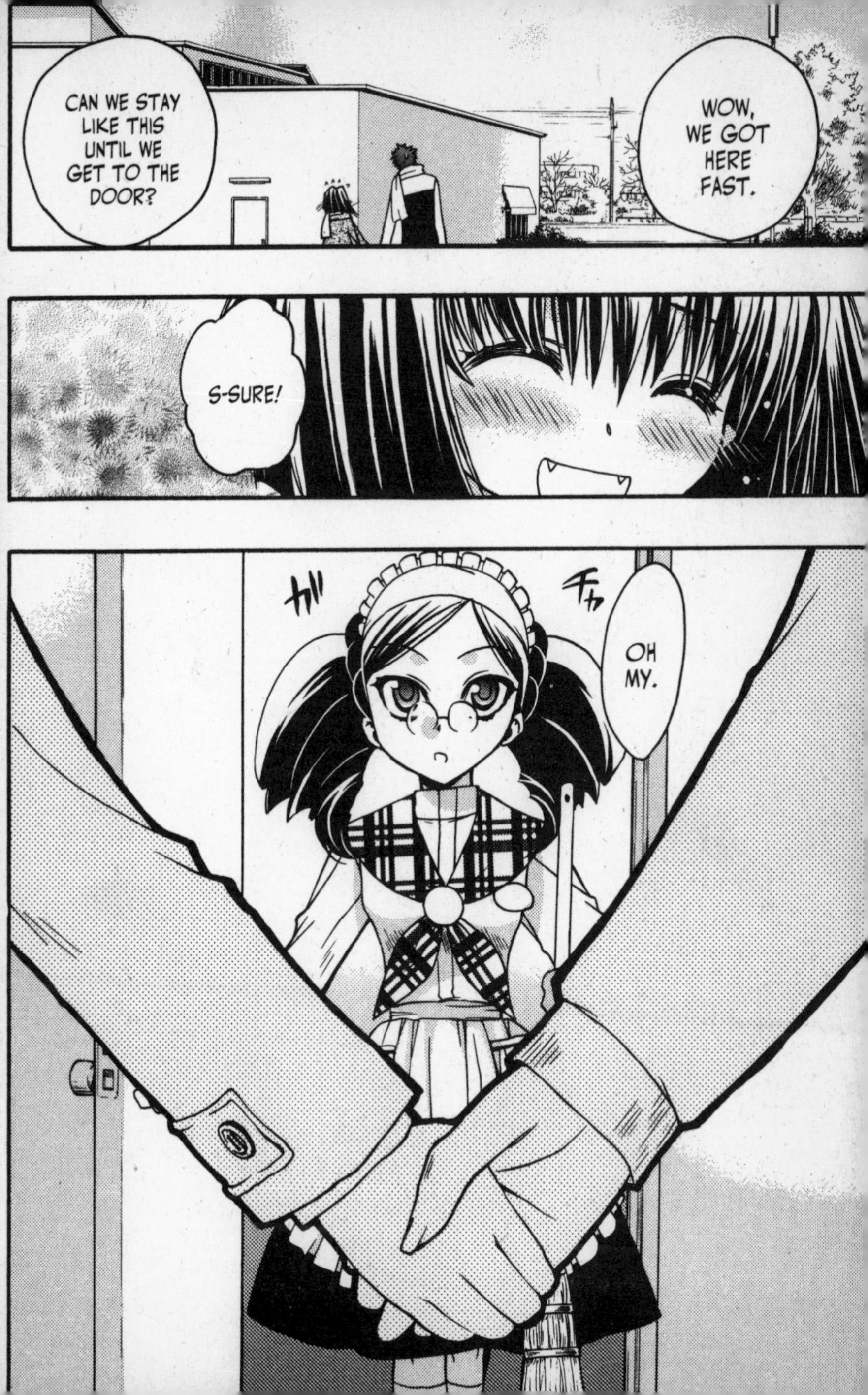
WOW, WE GOT HERE FAST.
CAN WE STAY LIKE THIS UNTIL WE GET TO THE DOOR?
S-SURE!
OH MY.

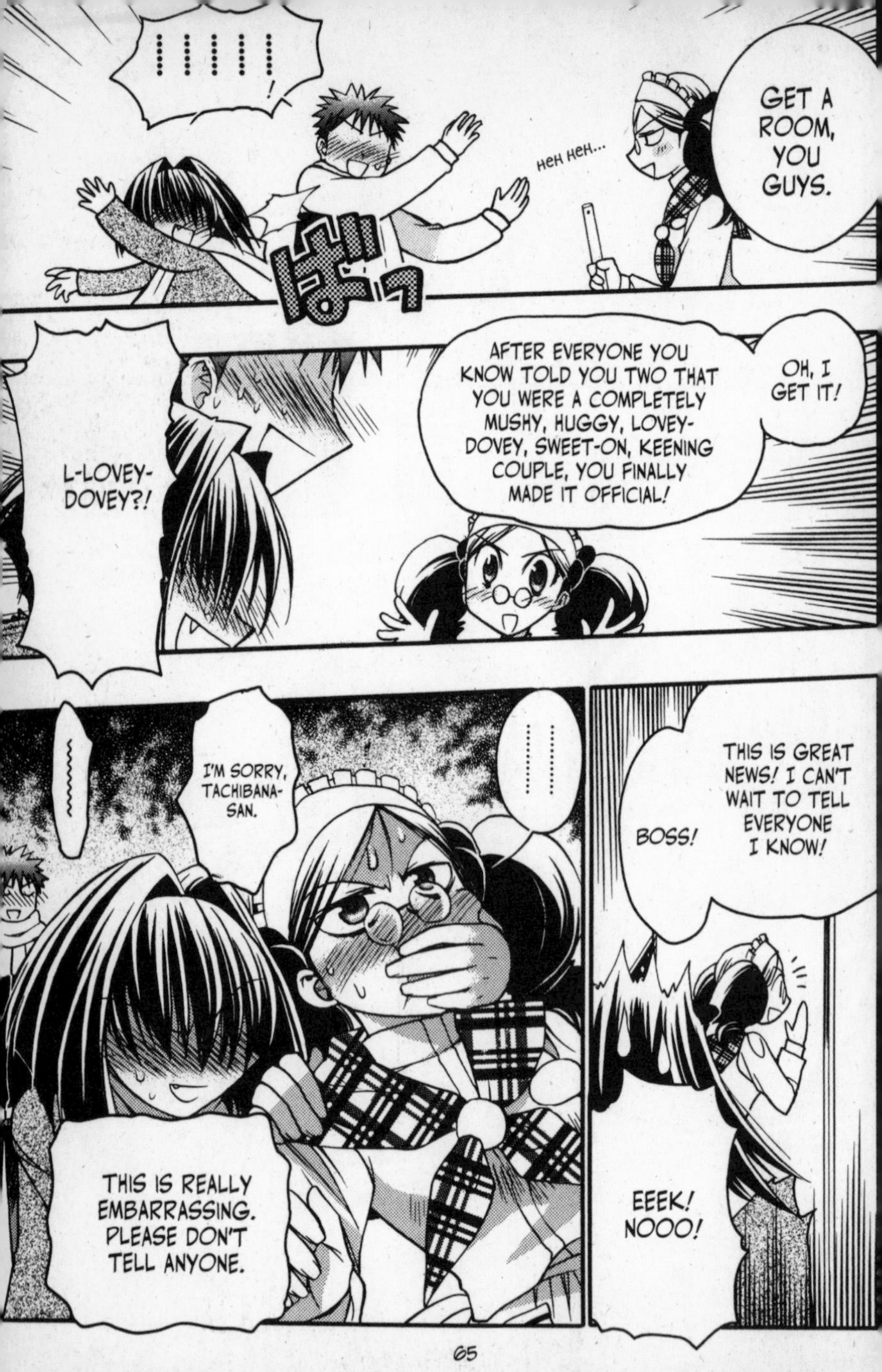
GET A ROOM, YOU GUYS.
HEH HEH...
ぱっ
OH, I GET IT!
AFTER EVERYONE YOU KNOW TOLD YOU TWO THAT YOU WERE A COMPLETELY MUSHY, HUGGY, LOVEY-DOVEY, SWEET-ON, KEENING COUPLE, YOU FINALLY MADE IT OFFICIAL!
L-LOVEY-DOVEY?!
THIS IS GREAT NEWS! I CAN'T WAIT TO TELL EVERYONE I KNOW!
BOSS!
EEEK! NOOO!
I'M SORRY, TACHIBANA-SAN.
THIS IS REALLY EMBARRASSING. PLEASE DON'T TELL ANYONE.

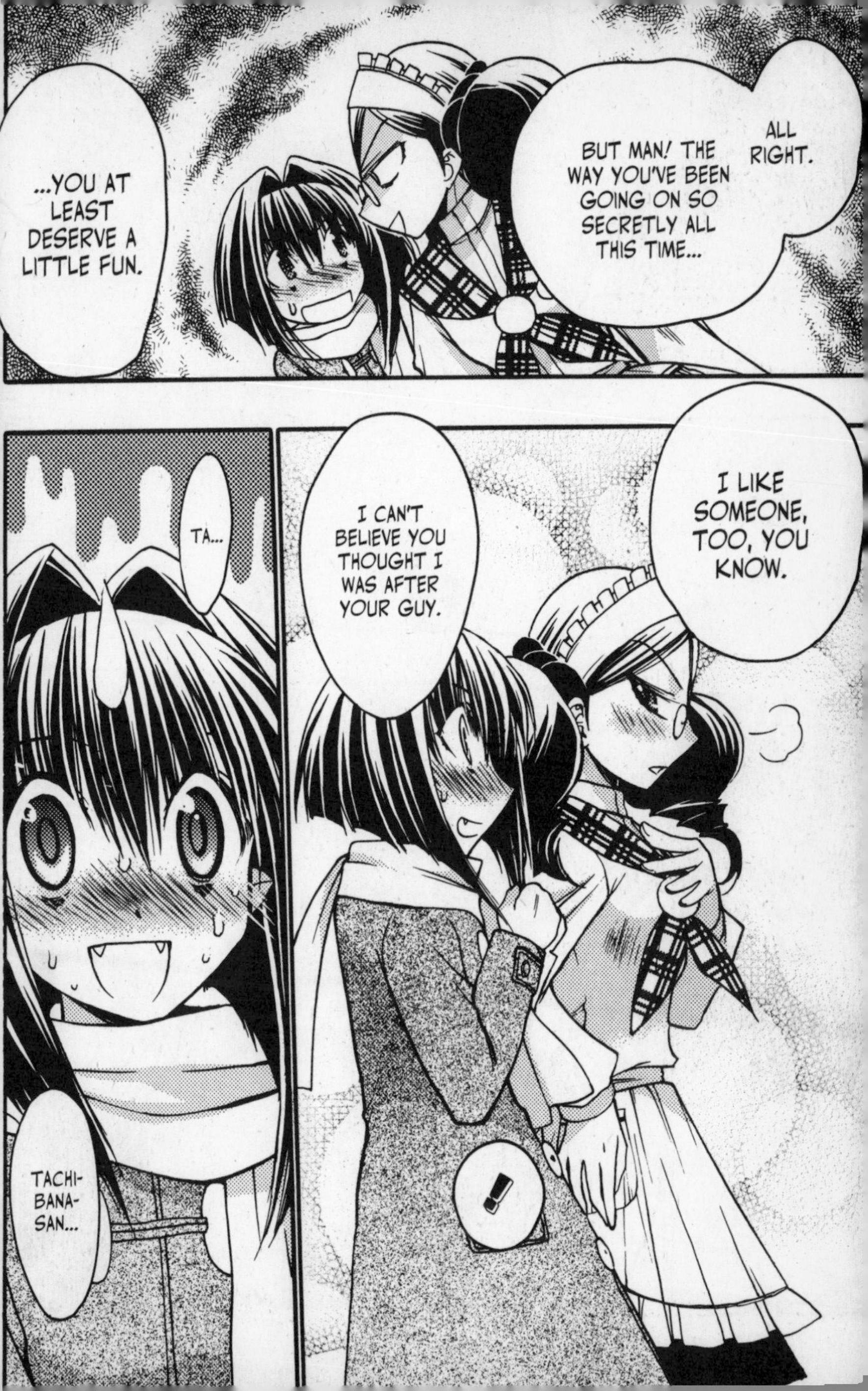
ALL RIGHT.
BUT MAN! THE WAY YOU'VE BEEN GOING ON SO SECRETLY ALL THIS TIME...
...YOU AT LEAST DESERVE A LITTLE FUN.
I LIKE SOMEONE, TOO, YOU KNOW.
I CAN'T BELIEVE YOU THOUGHT I WAS AFTER YOUR GUY.
!
TA...
TACHIBANA-SAN...

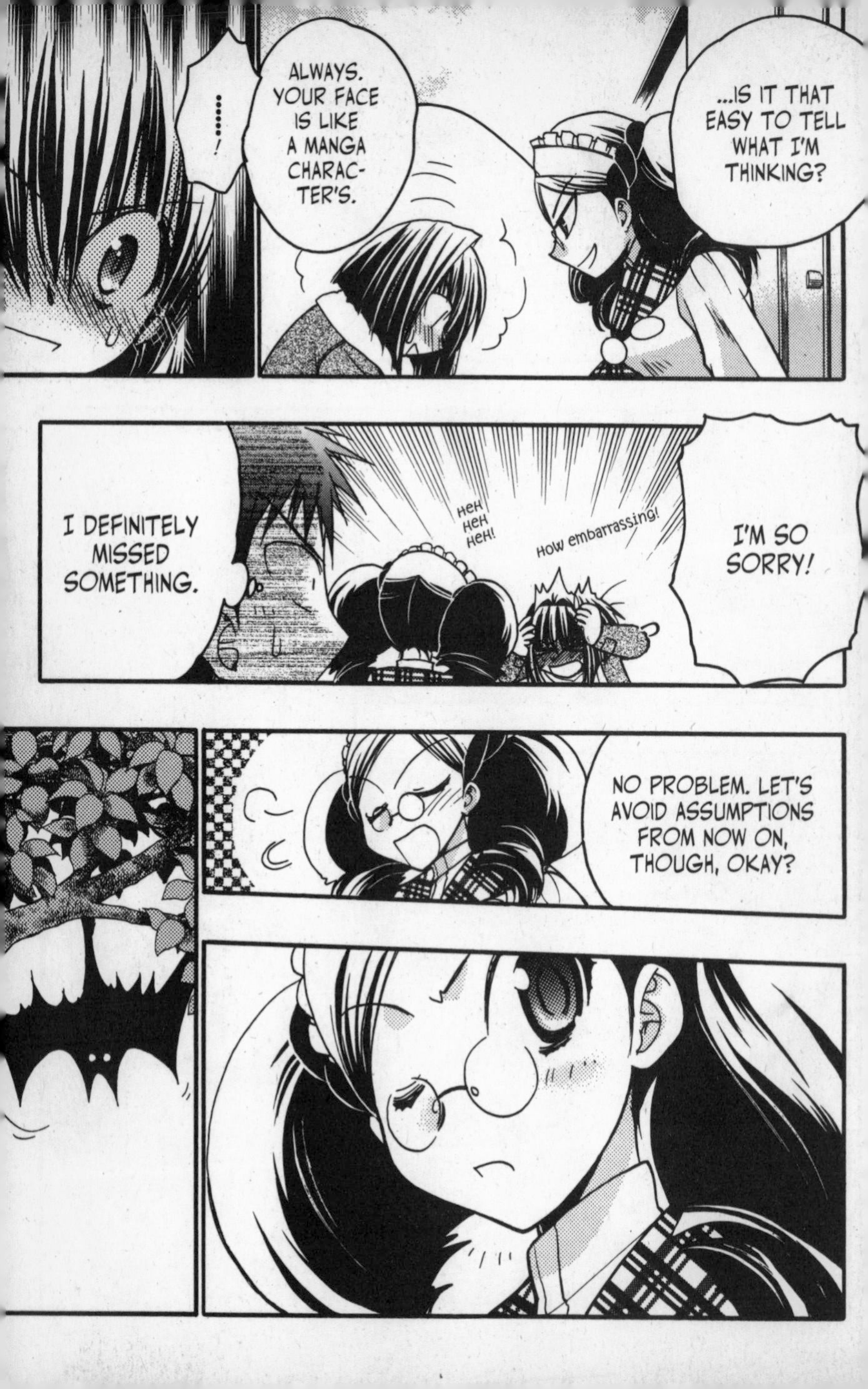
...IS IT THAT EASY TO TELL WHAT I'M THINKING?
ALWAYS. YOUR FACE IS LIKE A MANGA CHARACTER'S.
......!
I'M SO SORRY!
How embarrassing!
HEH HEH HEH!
I DEFINITELY MISSED SOMETHING.
NO PROBLEM. LET'S AVOID ASSUMPTIONS FROM NOW ON, THOUGH, OKAY?

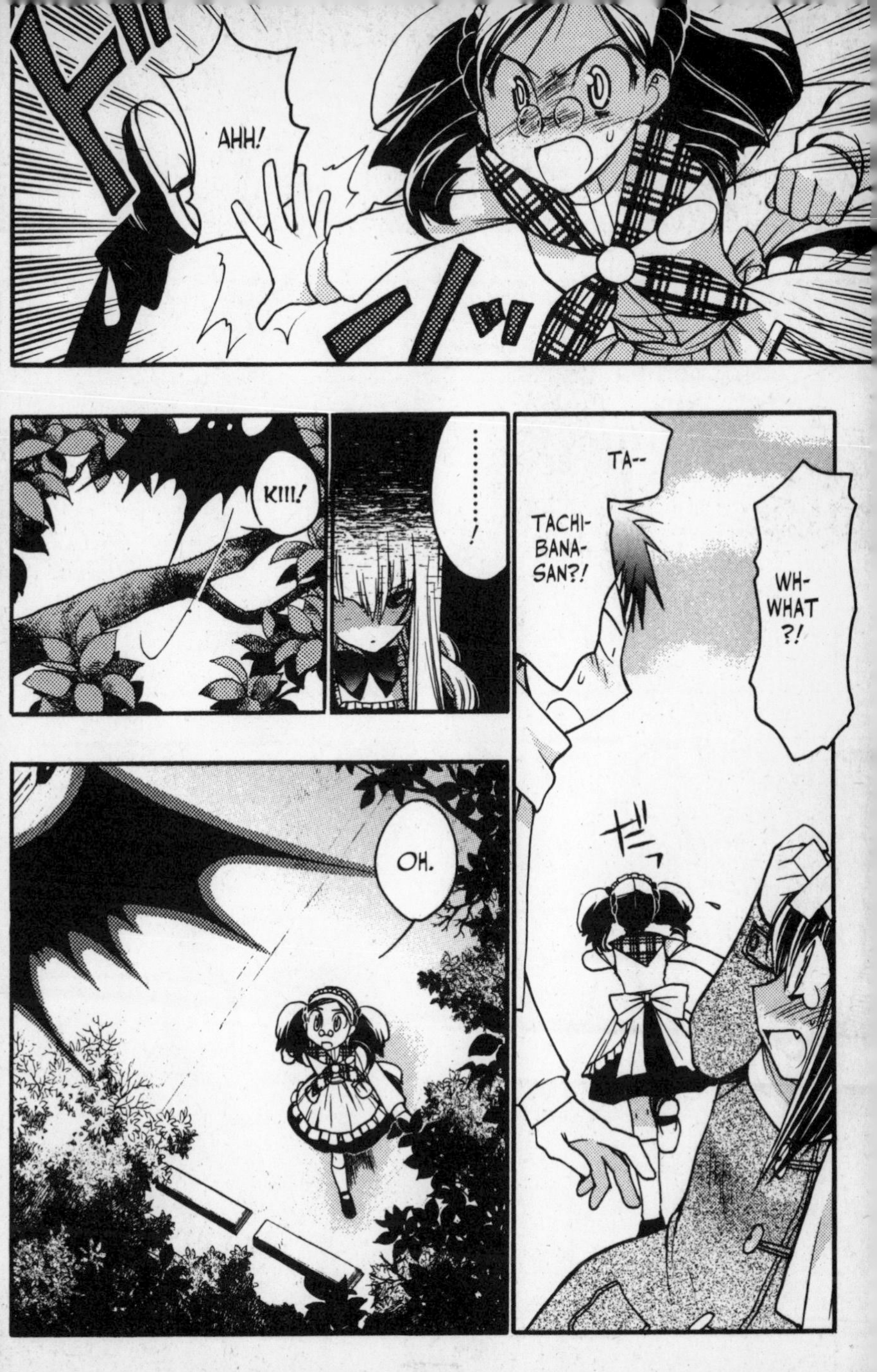
AHH!
WH-WHAT ?!
TA--
TACHIBANA-SAN?!
......!
KIII!
OH.

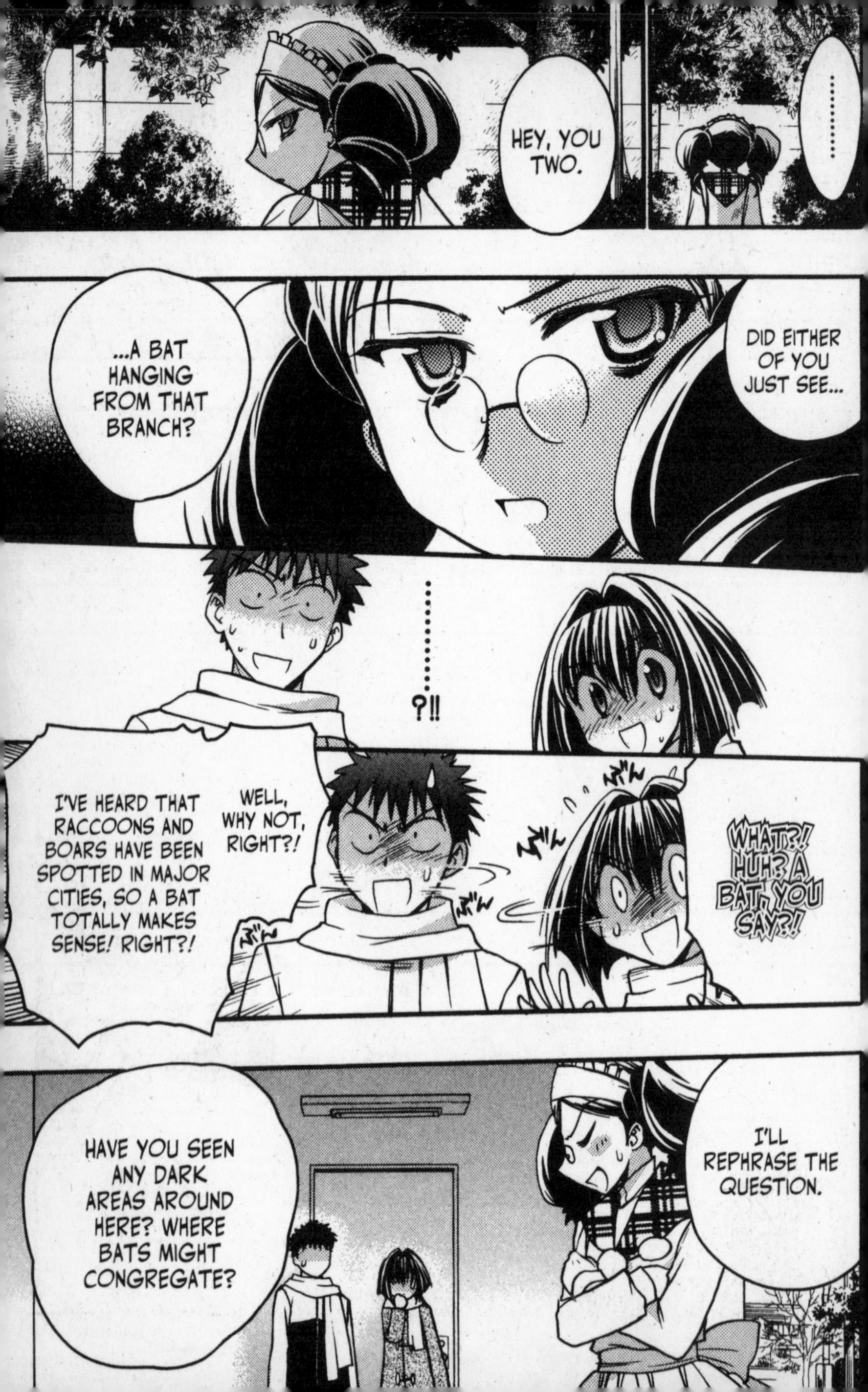
......
HEY, YOU TWO.
DID EITHER OF YOU JUST SEE...
...A BAT HANGING FROM THAT BRANCH?
......?!!
WHAT?! HUH? A BAT, YOU SAY?!
WELL, WHY NOT, RIGHT?!
I'VE HEARD THAT RACCOONS AND BOARS HAVE BEEN SPOTTED IN MAJOR CITIES, SO A BAT TOTALLY MAKES SENSE! RIGHT?!
I'LL REPHRASE THE QUESTION.
HAVE YOU SEEN ANY DARK AREAS AROUND HERE? WHERE BATS MIGHT CONGREGATE?

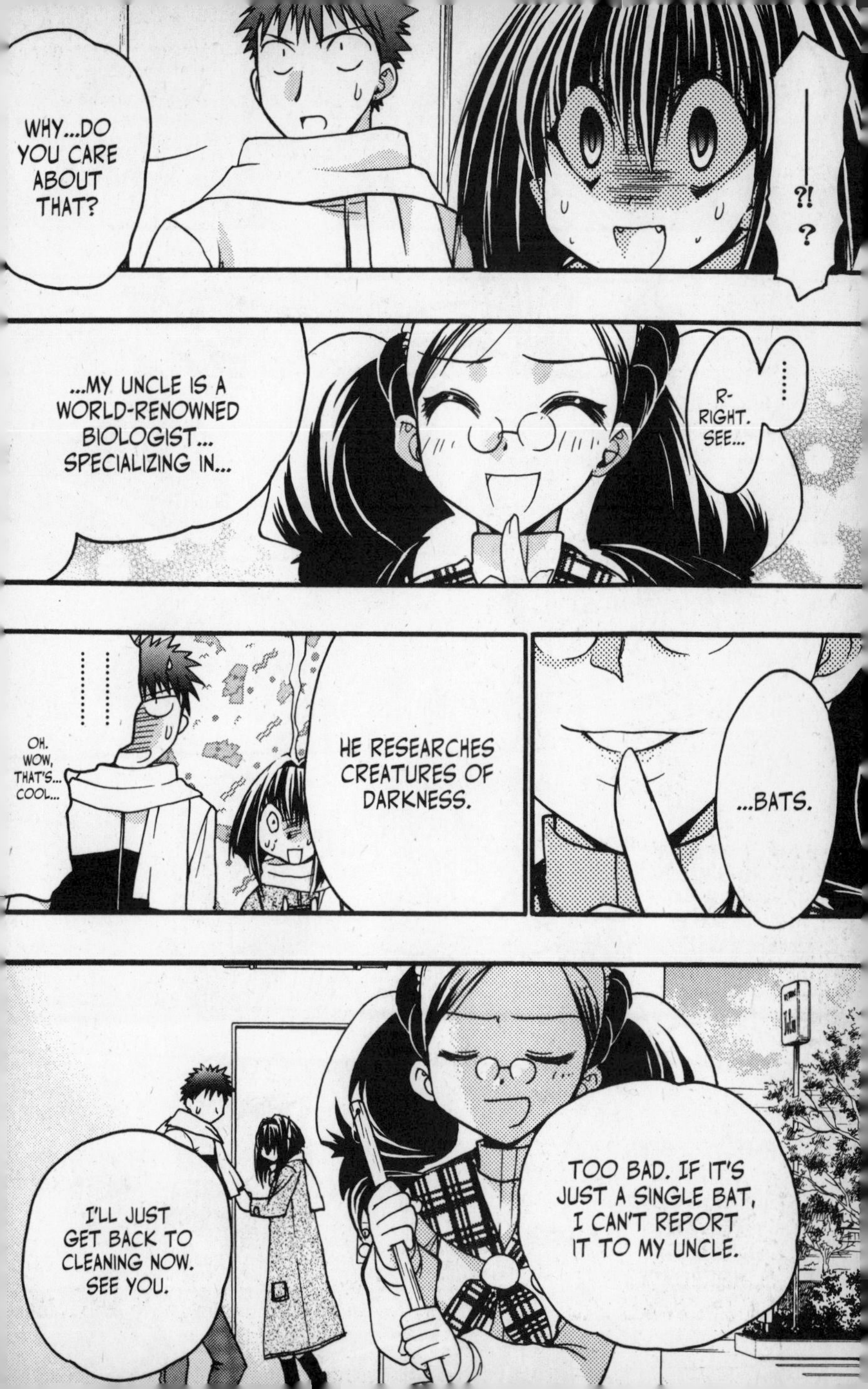
?!
?
WHY...DO YOU CARE ABOUT THAT?
......
R-RIGHT. SEE...
...MY UNCLE IS A WORLD-RENOWNED BIOLOGIST... SPECIALIZING IN...
...BATS.
HE RESEARCHES CREATURES OF DARKNESS.
....
OH. WOW, THAT'S... COOL...
TOO BAD. IF IT'S JUST A SINGLE BAT, I CAN'T REPORT IT TO MY UNCLE.
I'LL JUST GET BACK TO CLEANING NOW. SEE YOU.

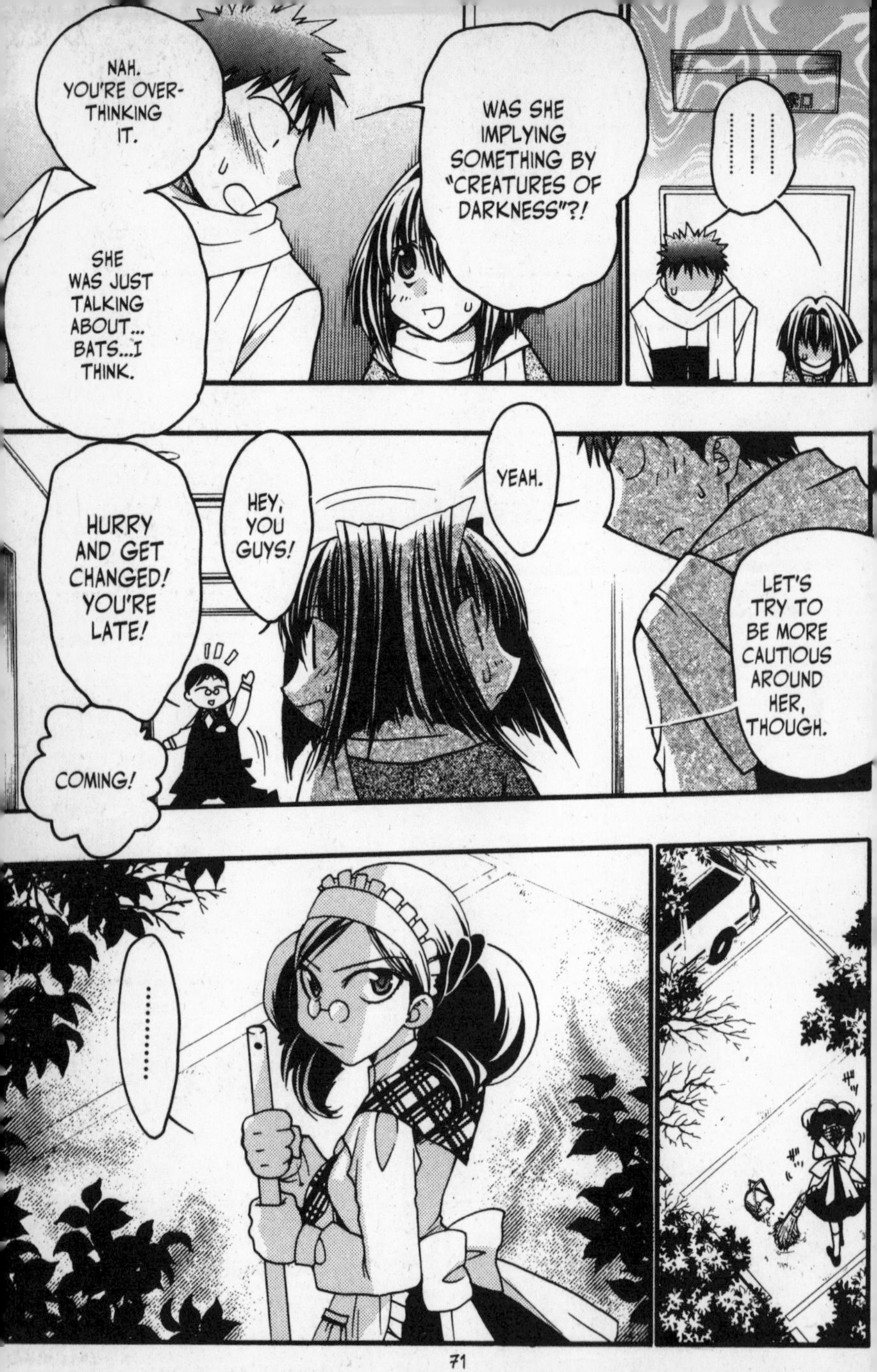

......
WAS SHE IMPLYING SOMETHING BY "CREATURES OF DARKNESS"?!
NAH. YOU'RE OVER-THINKING IT.
SHE WAS JUST TALKING ABOUT... BATS...I THINK.
LET'S TRY TO BE MORE CAUTIOUS AROUND HER, THOUGH.
YEAH.
HEY, YOU GUYS!
HURRY AND GET CHANGED! YOU'RE LATE!
COMING!
....

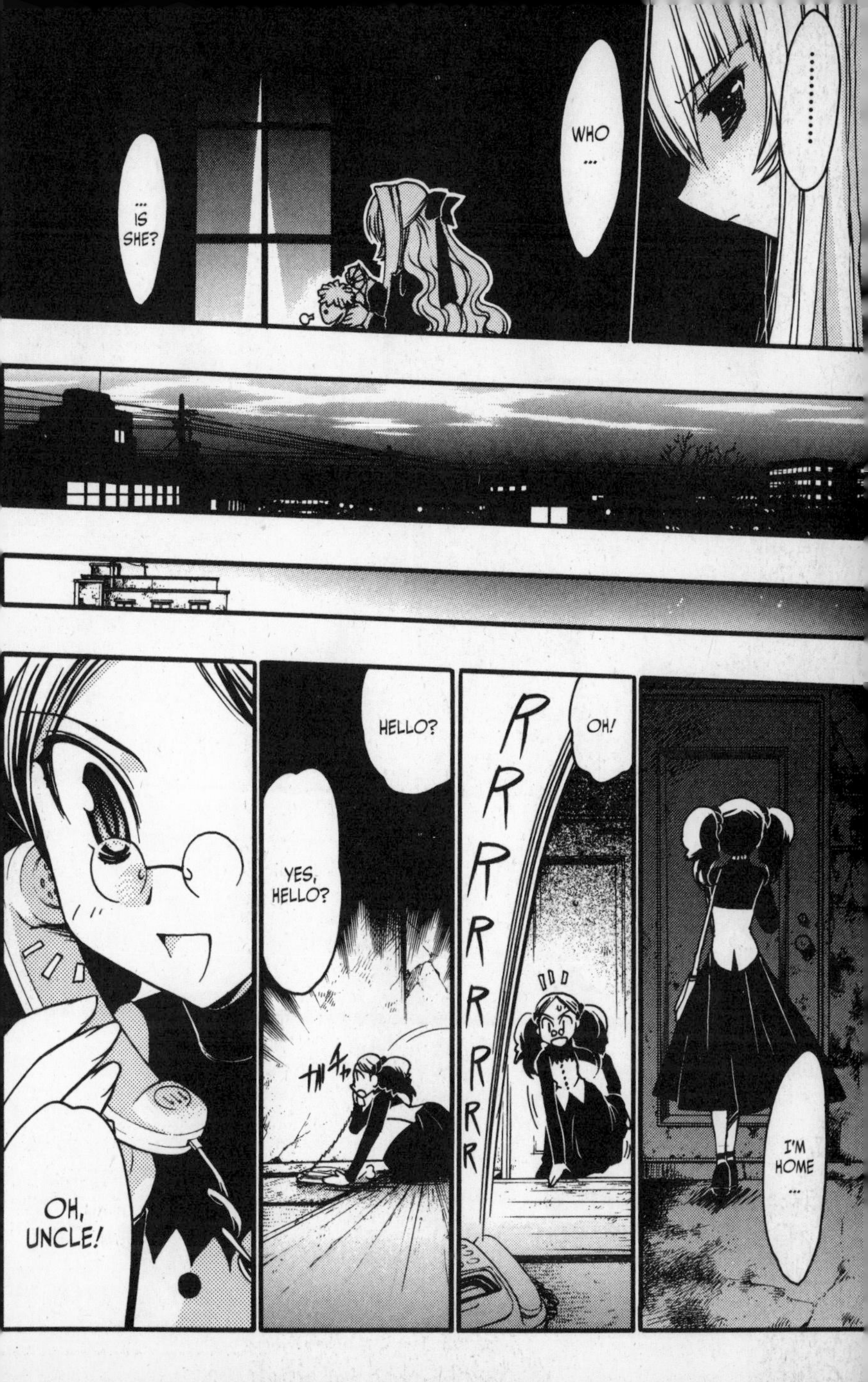
……
WHO ...
... IS SHE?
I'M HOME ...
OH!
RRRRRRRR
HELLO?
YES, HELLO?
OH, UNCLE!

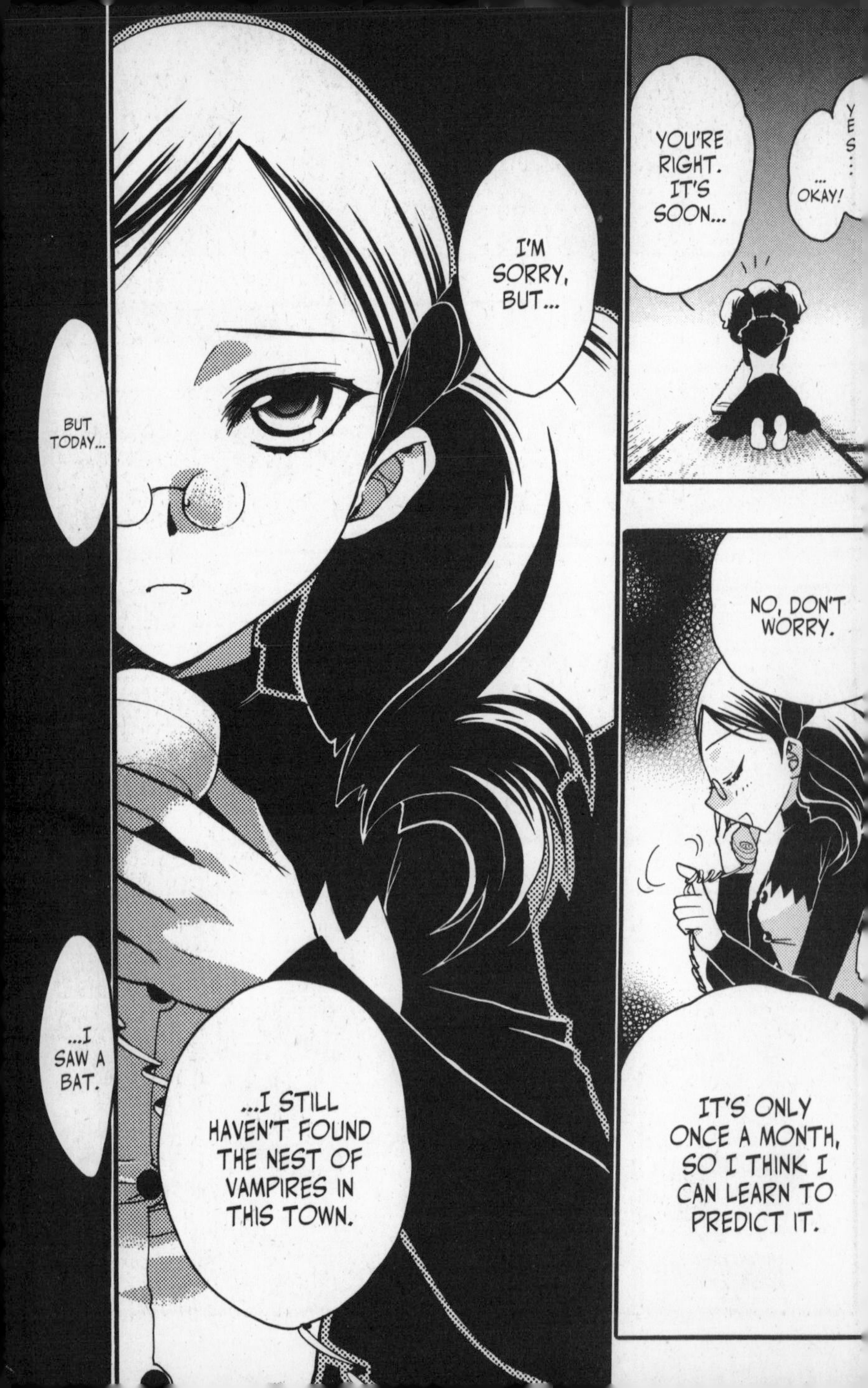
YES... ...OKAY!
YOU'RE RIGHT. IT'S SOON...
NO, DON'T WORRY.
IT'S ONLY ONCE A MONTH, SO I THINK I CAN LEARN TO PREDICT IT.
I'M SORRY, BUT...
...I STILL HAVEN'T FOUND THE NEST OF VAMPIRES IN THIS TOWN.
BUT TODAY...
...I SAW A BAT.

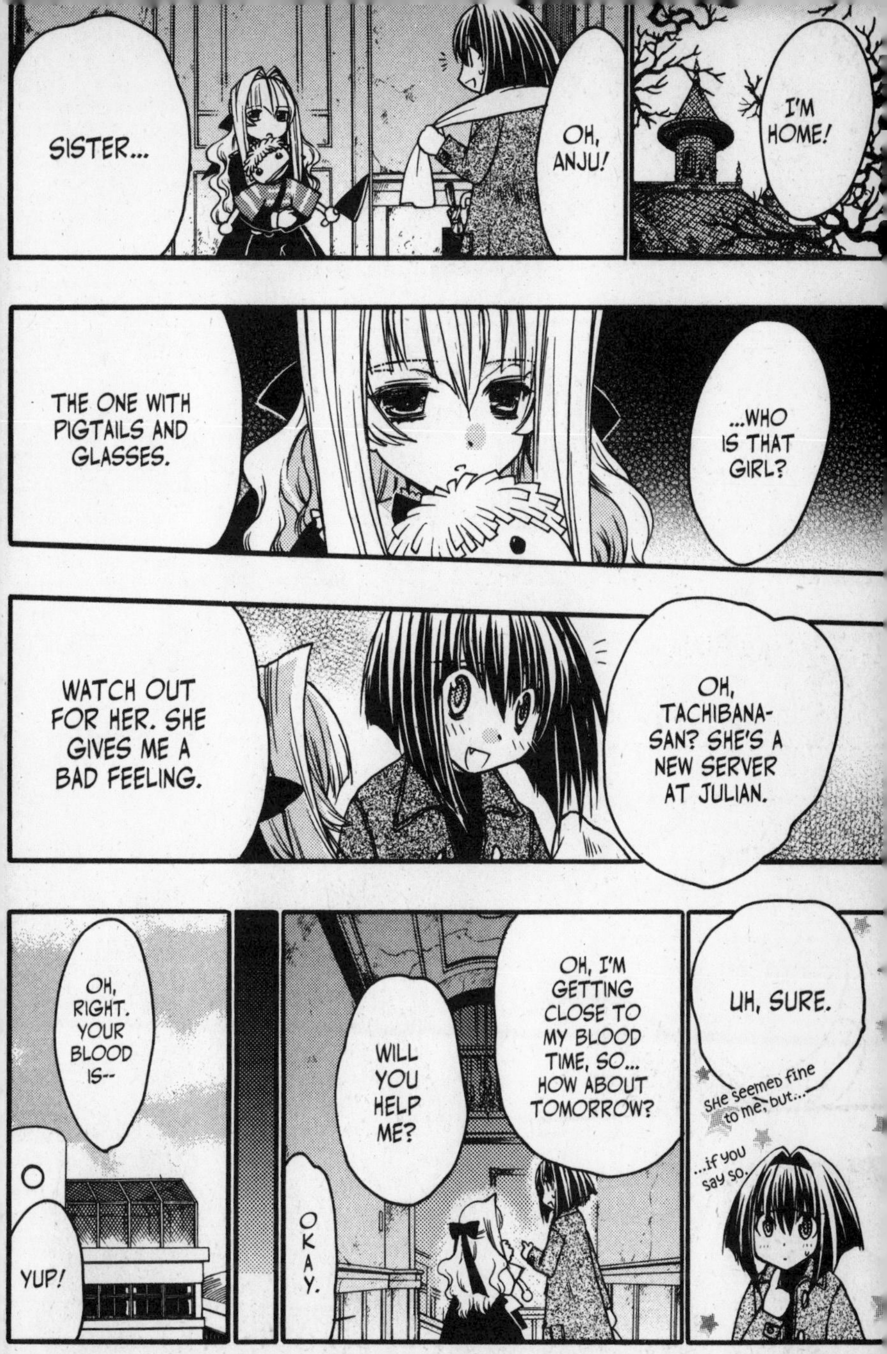
I'M HOME!
OH, ANJU!
SISTER...
...WHO IS THAT GIRL?
THE ONE WITH PIGTAILS AND GLASSES.
OH, TACHIBANA-SAN? SHE'S A NEW SERVER AT JULIAN.
WATCH OUT FOR HER. SHE GIVES ME A BAD FEELING.
UH, SURE.
She seemed fine to me, but...
...if you say so.
OH, I'M GETTING CLOSE TO MY BLOOD TIME, SO... HOW ABOUT TOMORROW?
WILL YOU HELP ME?
OKAY.
OH, RIGHT. YOUR BLOOD IS--
YUP!

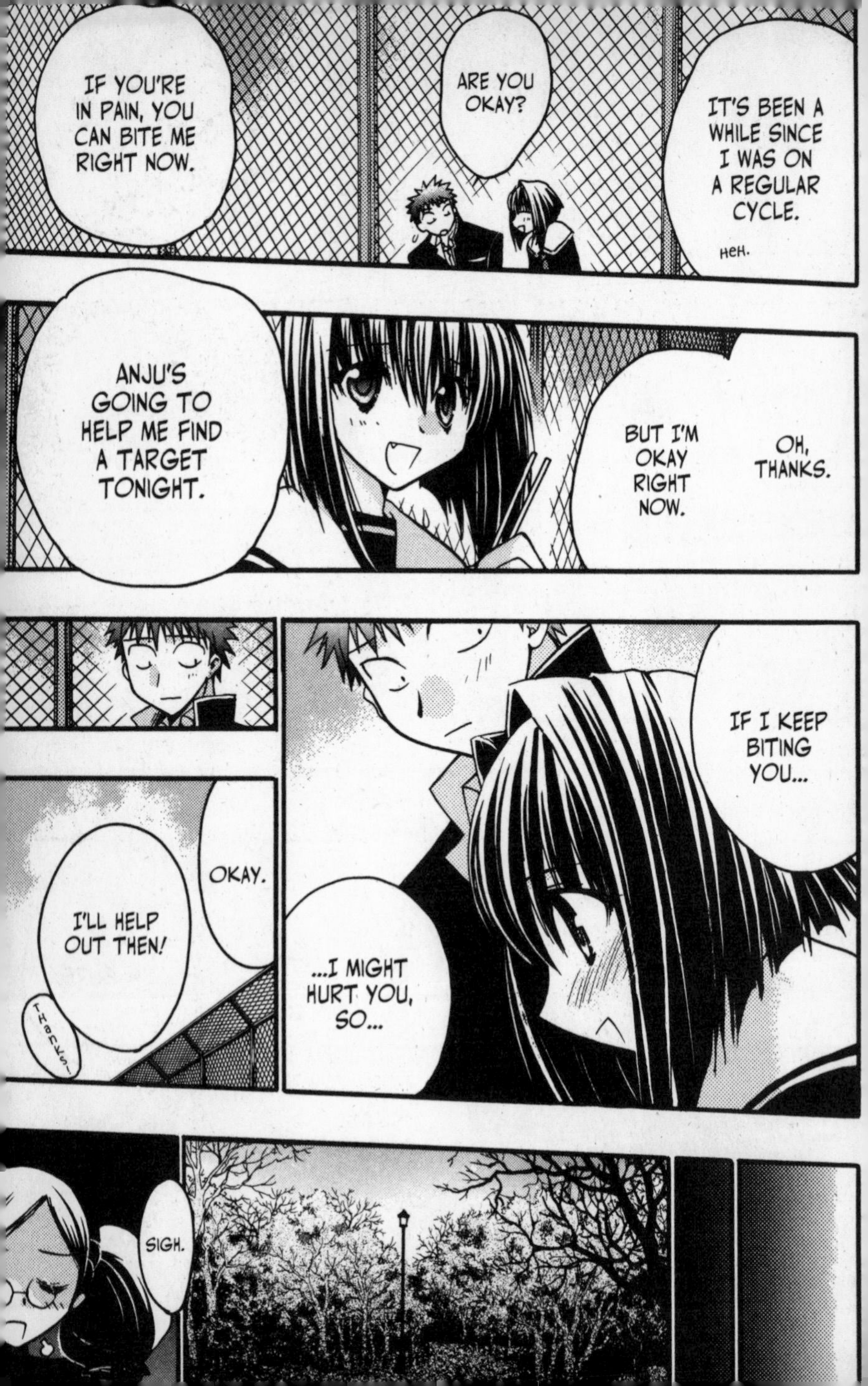
IT'S BEEN A WHILE SINCE I WAS ON A REGULAR CYCLE.
HEH.
ARE YOU OKAY?
IF YOU'RE IN PAIN, YOU CAN BITE ME RIGHT NOW.
OH, THANKS.
BUT I'M OKAY RIGHT NOW.
ANJU'S GOING TO HELP ME FIND A TARGET TONIGHT.
IF I KEEP BITING YOU...
...I MIGHT HURT YOU, SO...
OKAY.
I'LL HELP OUT THEN!
Thanks!
SIGH.

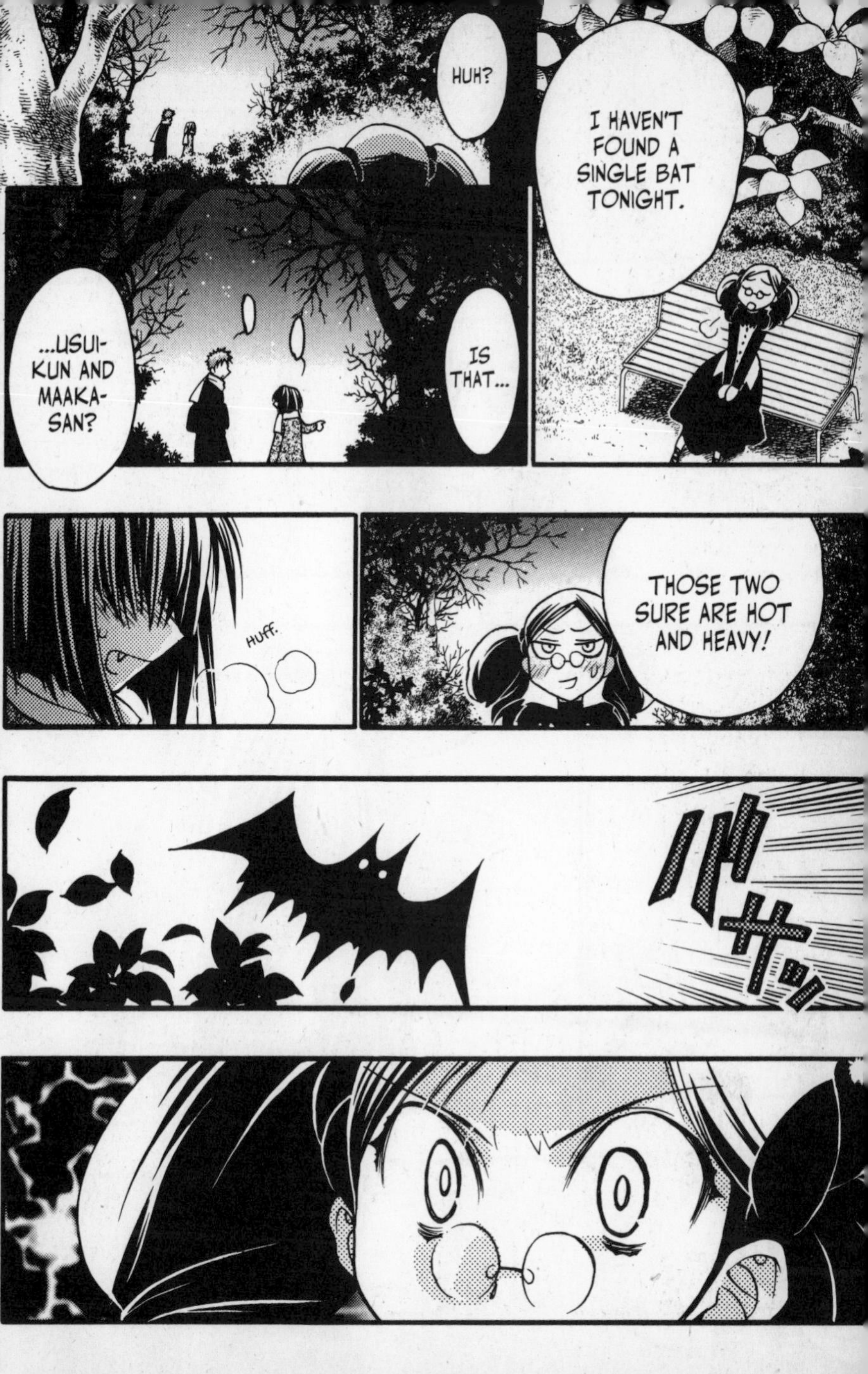
I HAVEN'T FOUND A SINGLE BAT TONIGHT.
HUH?
IS THAT...
...USUI-KUN AND MAAKA-SAN?
THOSE TWO SURE ARE HOT AND HEAVY!
HUFF.
バサッ

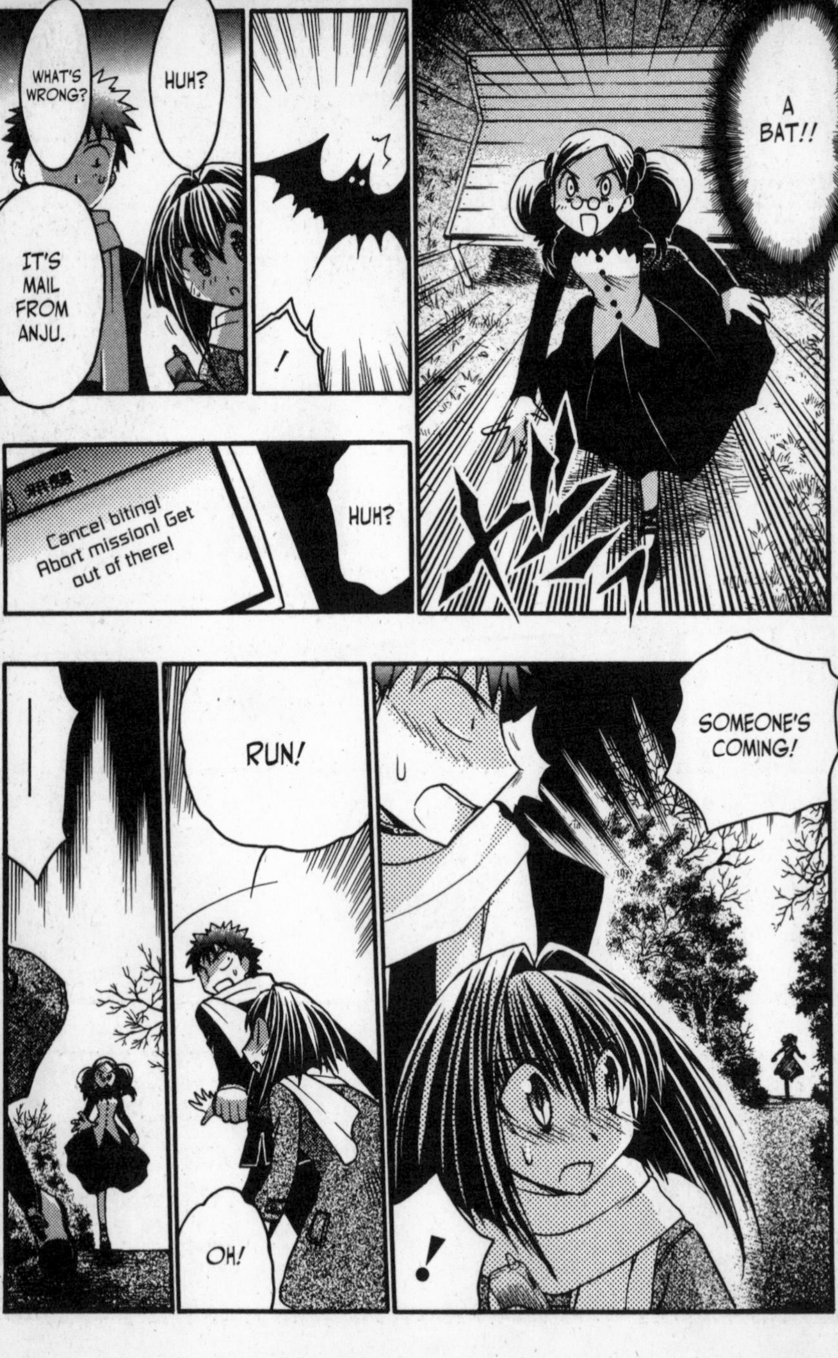
A BAT!!
!
HUH?
WHAT'S WRONG?
IT'S MAIL FROM ANJU.
HUH?
Cancel biting! Abort mission! Get out of there!
SOMEONE'S COMING!
!
RUN!
OH!

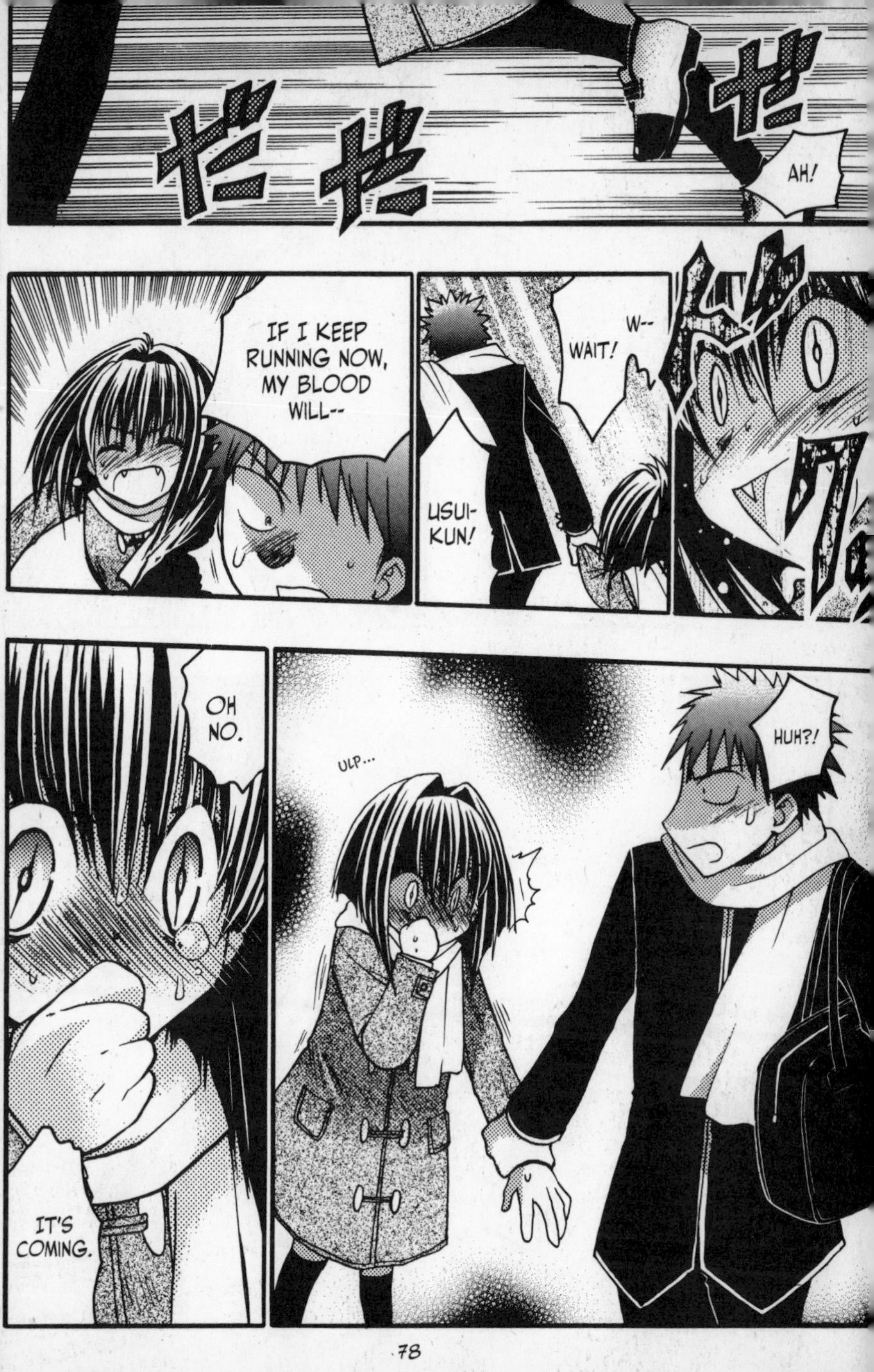
AH!
W-- WAIT!
USUI-KUN!
IF I KEEP RUNNING NOW, MY BLOOD WILL--
HUH?!
ULP...
OH NO.
IT'S COMING.

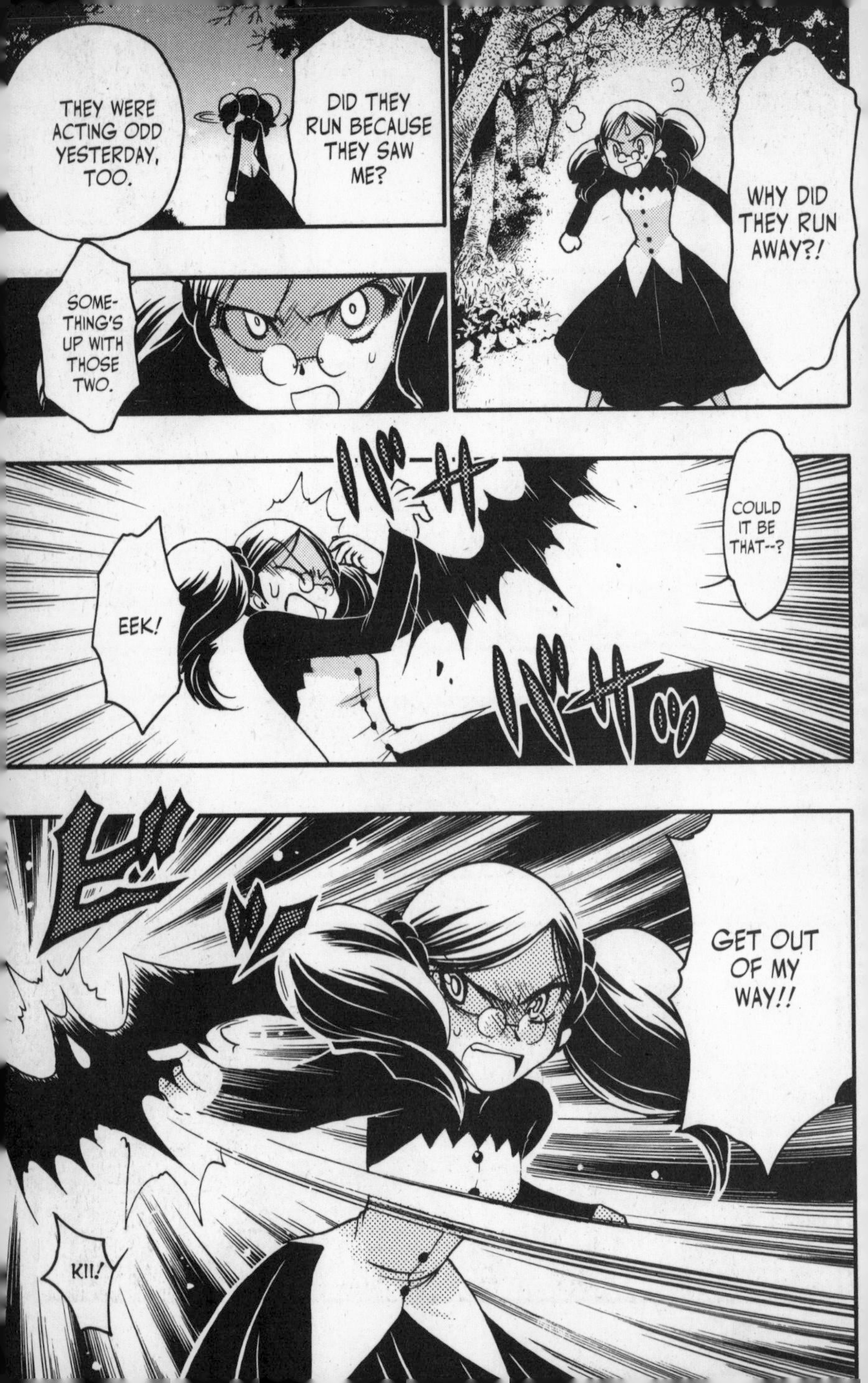
WHY DID THEY RUN AWAY?!
DID THEY RUN BECAUSE THEY SAW ME?
THEY WERE ACTING ODD YESTERDAY, TOO.
SOME-THING'S UP WITH THOSE TWO.
COULD IT BE THAT--?
EEK!
GET OUT OF MY WAY!!
KII!

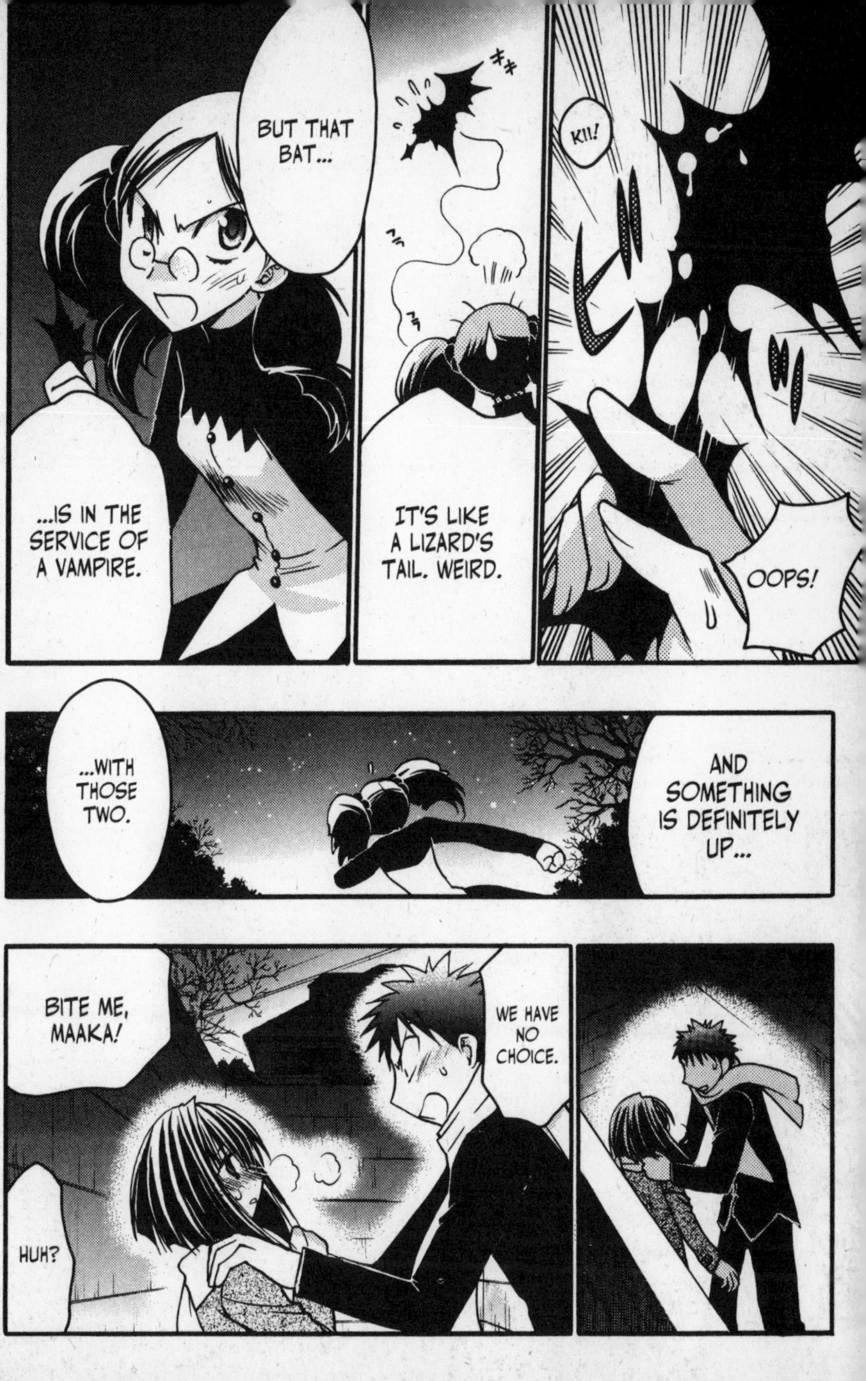
KII!
OOPS!
IT'S LIKE A LIZARD'S TAIL. WEIRD.
BUT THAT BAT...
...IS IN THE SERVICE OF A VAMPIRE.
AND SOMETHING IS DEFINITELY UP...
...WITH THOSE TWO.
WE HAVE NO CHOICE.
BITE ME, MAAKA!
HUH?

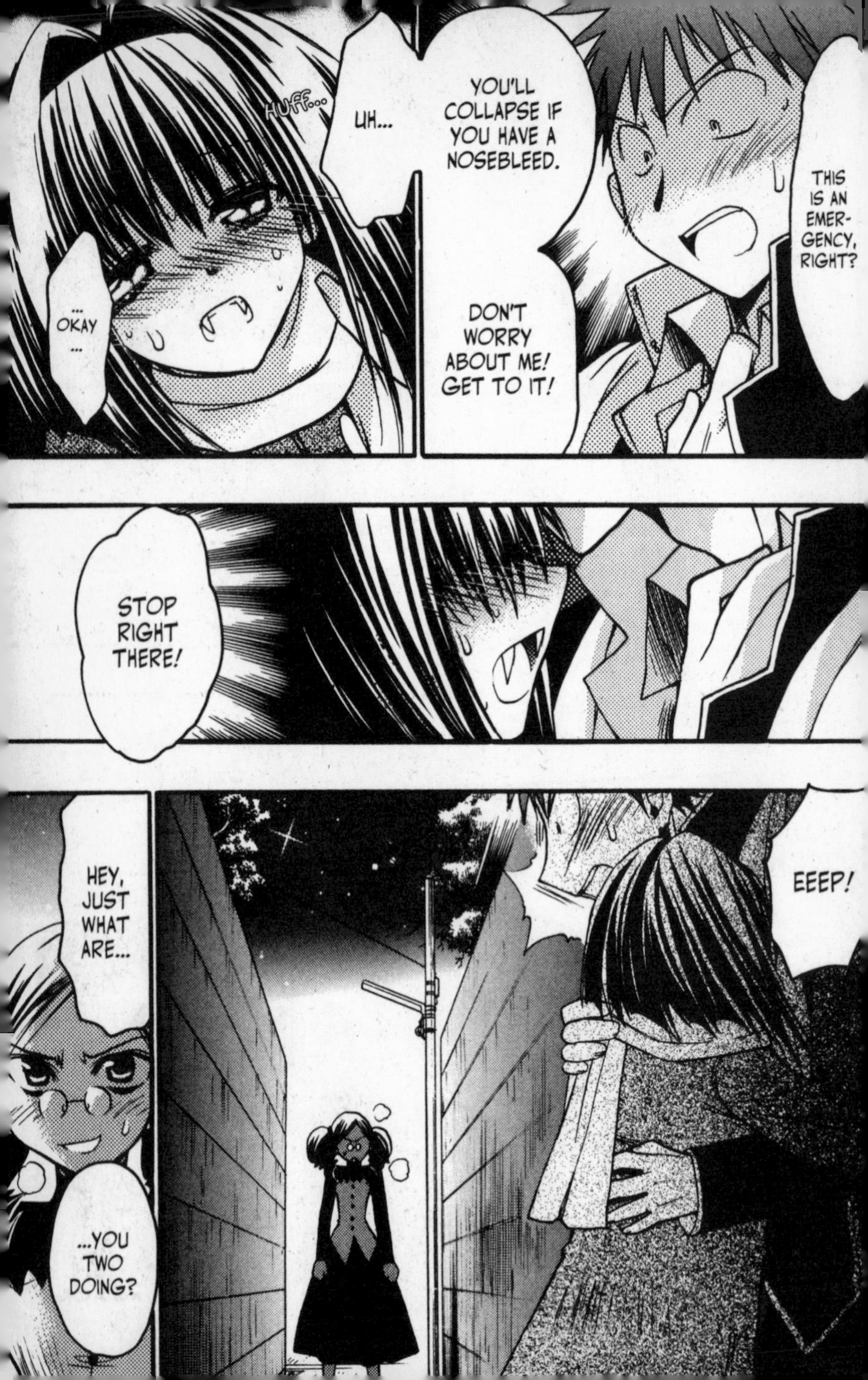
THIS IS AN EMERGENCY, RIGHT?
YOU'LL COLLAPSE IF YOU HAVE A NOSEBLEED.
DON'T WORRY ABOUT ME! GET TO IT!
HUFF...
UH...
...OKAY...
STOP RIGHT THERE!
EEEP!
HEY, JUST WHAT ARE...
...YOU TWO DOING?

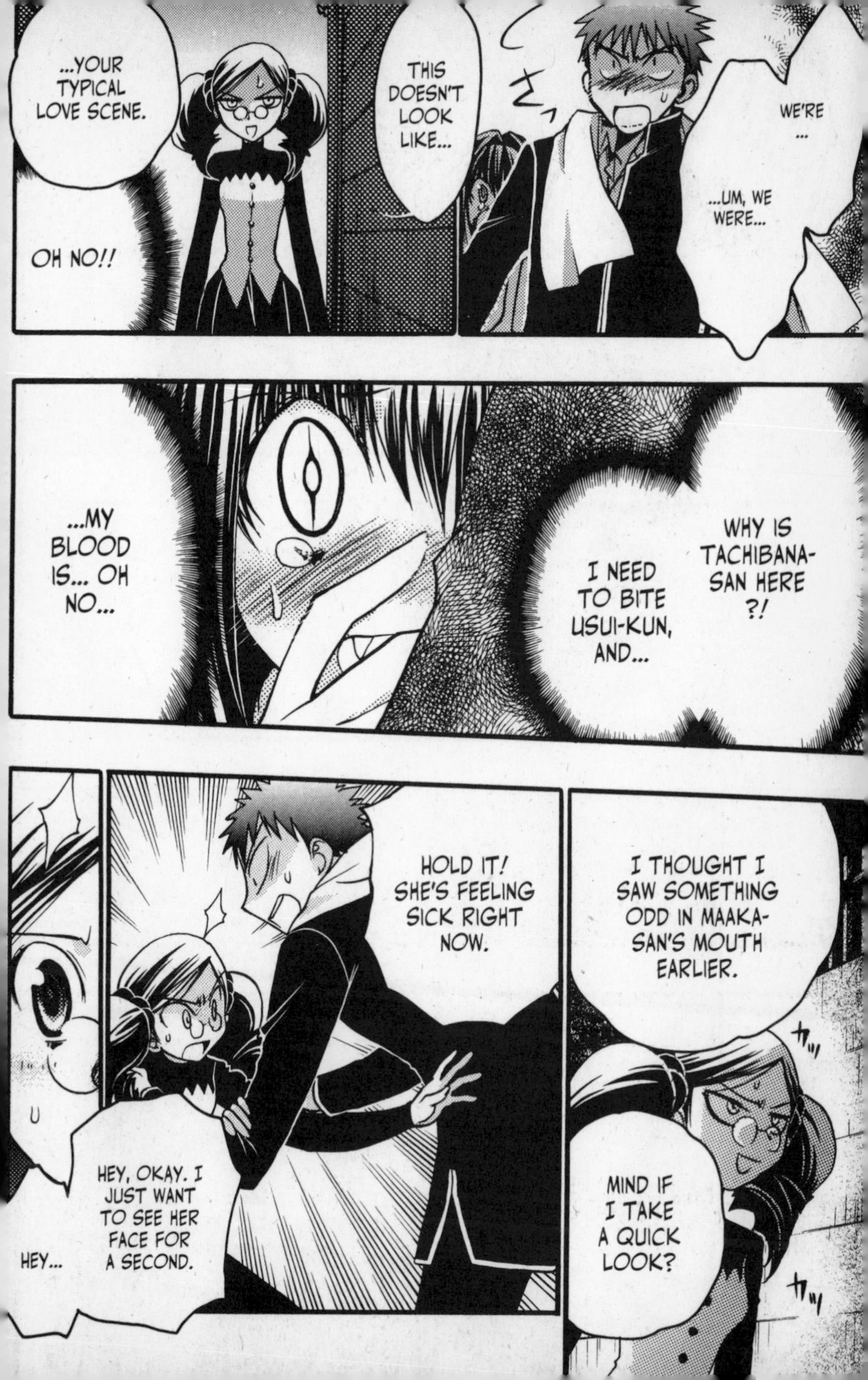
WE'RE ...
...UM, WE WERE...
THIS DOESN'T LOOK LIKE...
...YOUR TYPICAL LOVE SCENE.
OH NO!!
WHY IS TACHIBANA-SAN HERE?!
I NEED TO BITE USUI-KUN, AND...
...MY BLOOD IS... OH NO...
I THOUGHT I SAW SOMETHING ODD IN MAAKA-SAN'S MOUTH EARLIER.
MIND IF I TAKE A QUICK LOOK?
HOLD IT! SHE'S FEELING SICK RIGHT NOW.
HEY, OKAY. I JUST WANT TO SEE HER FACE FOR A SECOND.
HEY...

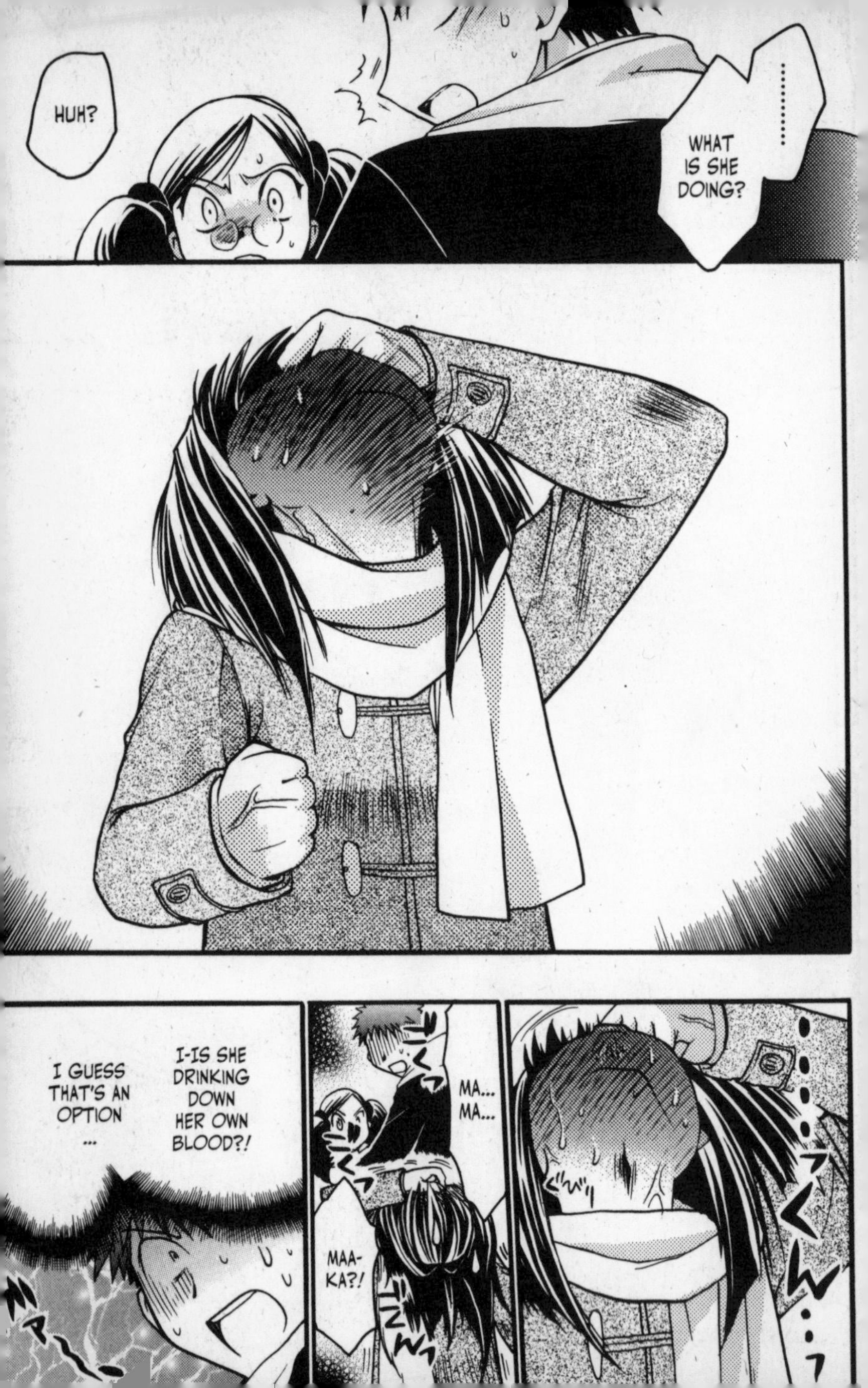
......
WHAT IS SHE DOING?
HUH?
......
MA... MA...
MAA-KA?!
I-IS SHE DRINKING DOWN HER OWN BLOOD?!
I GUESS THAT'S AN OPTION ...

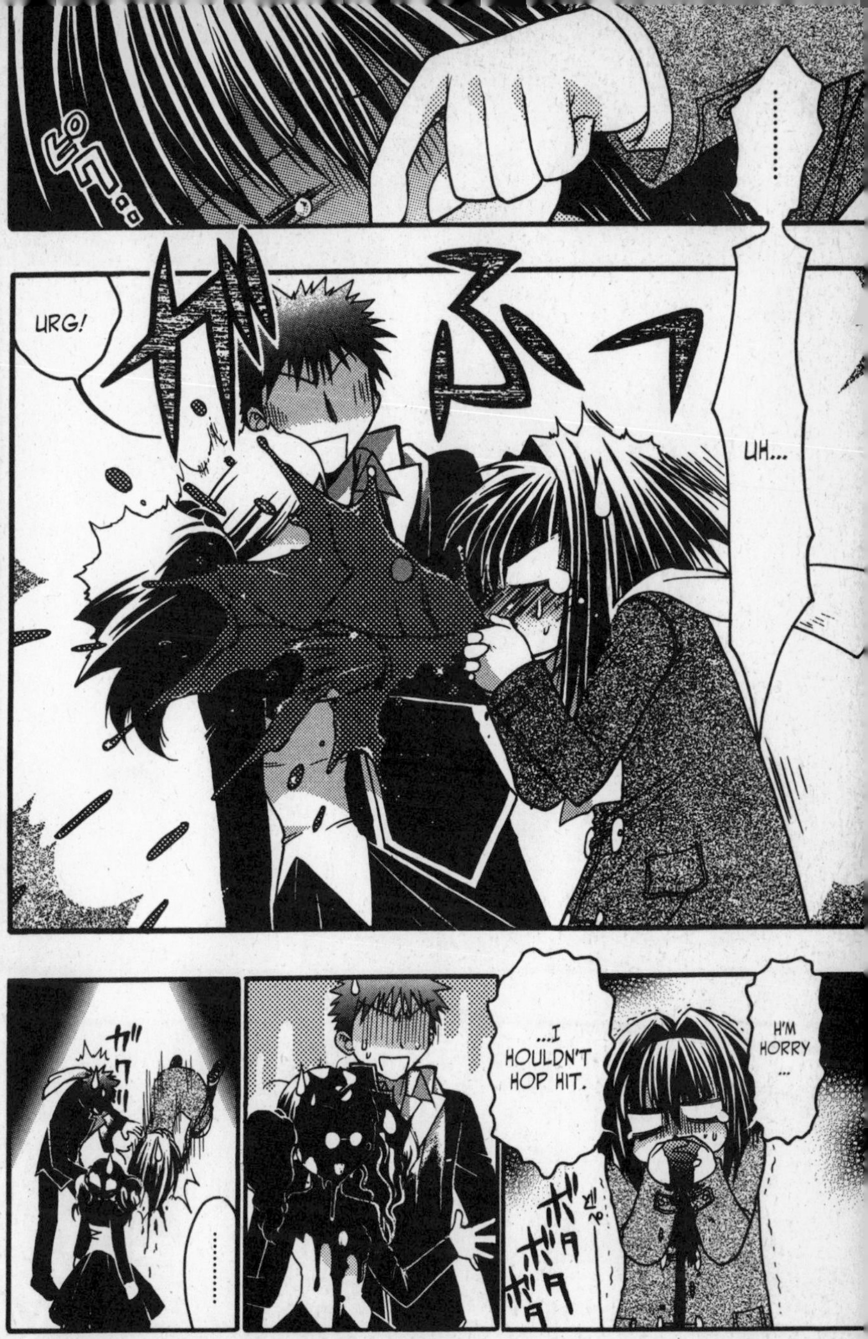
......
UH...
URG!
H'M HORRY ...
...I HOULDN'T HOP HIT.
......

37TH EMBARRASSMENT END

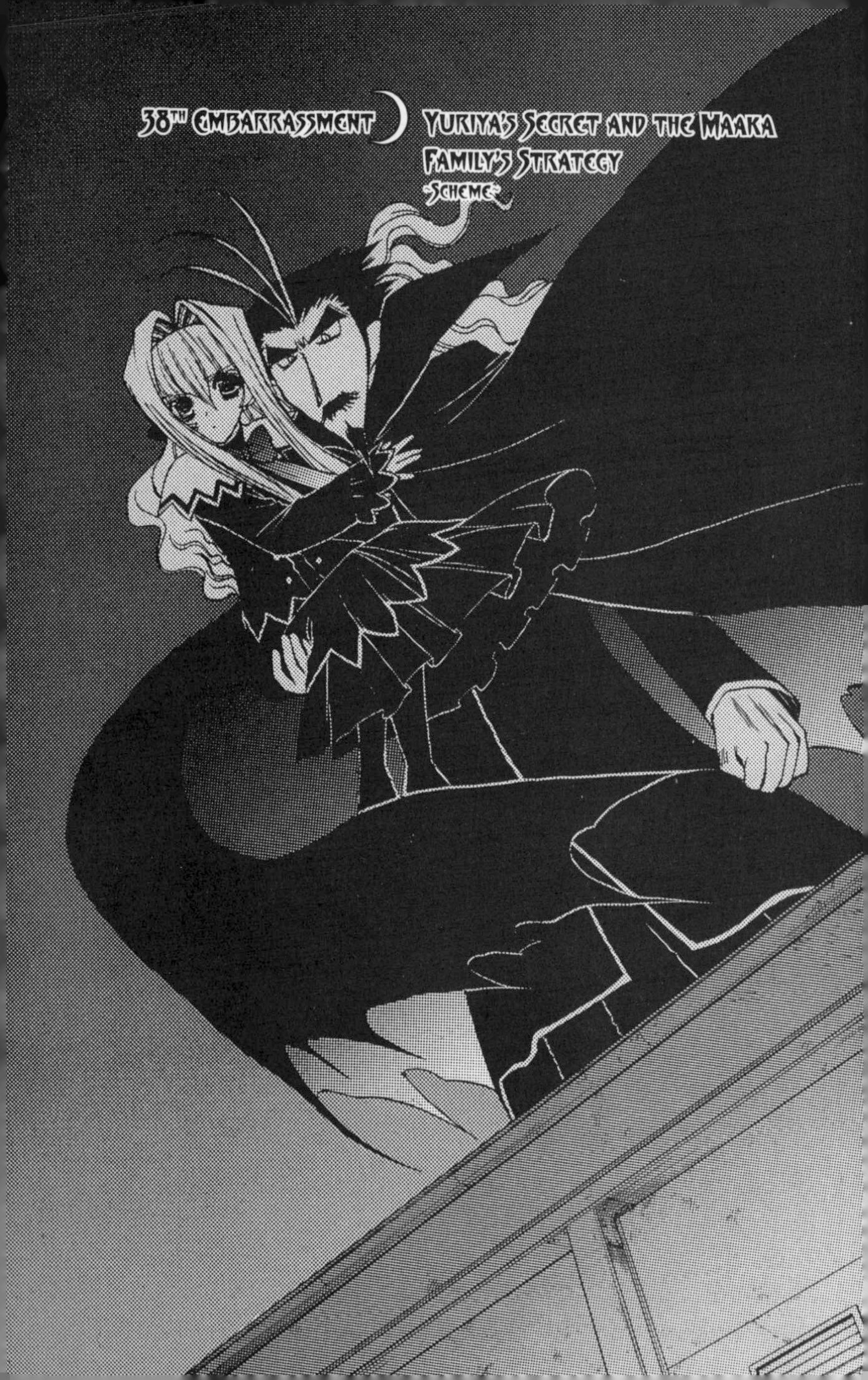
38th Embarrassment
Yuriya's Secret and the Maaka Family's Strategy
~Scheme~

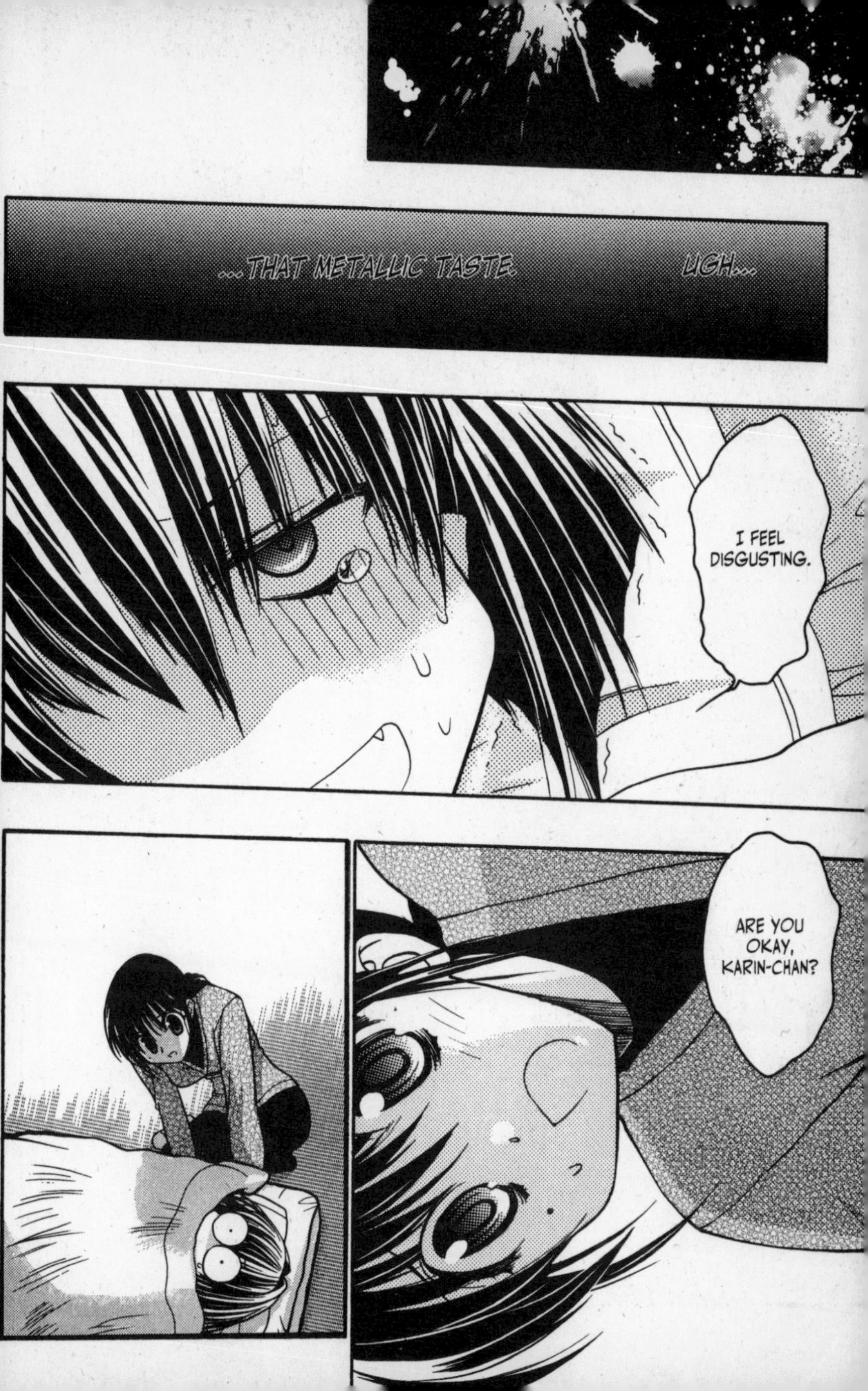
...THAT METALLIC TASTE.
UGH...
I FEEL DISGUSTING.
ARE YOU OKAY, KARIN-CHAN?

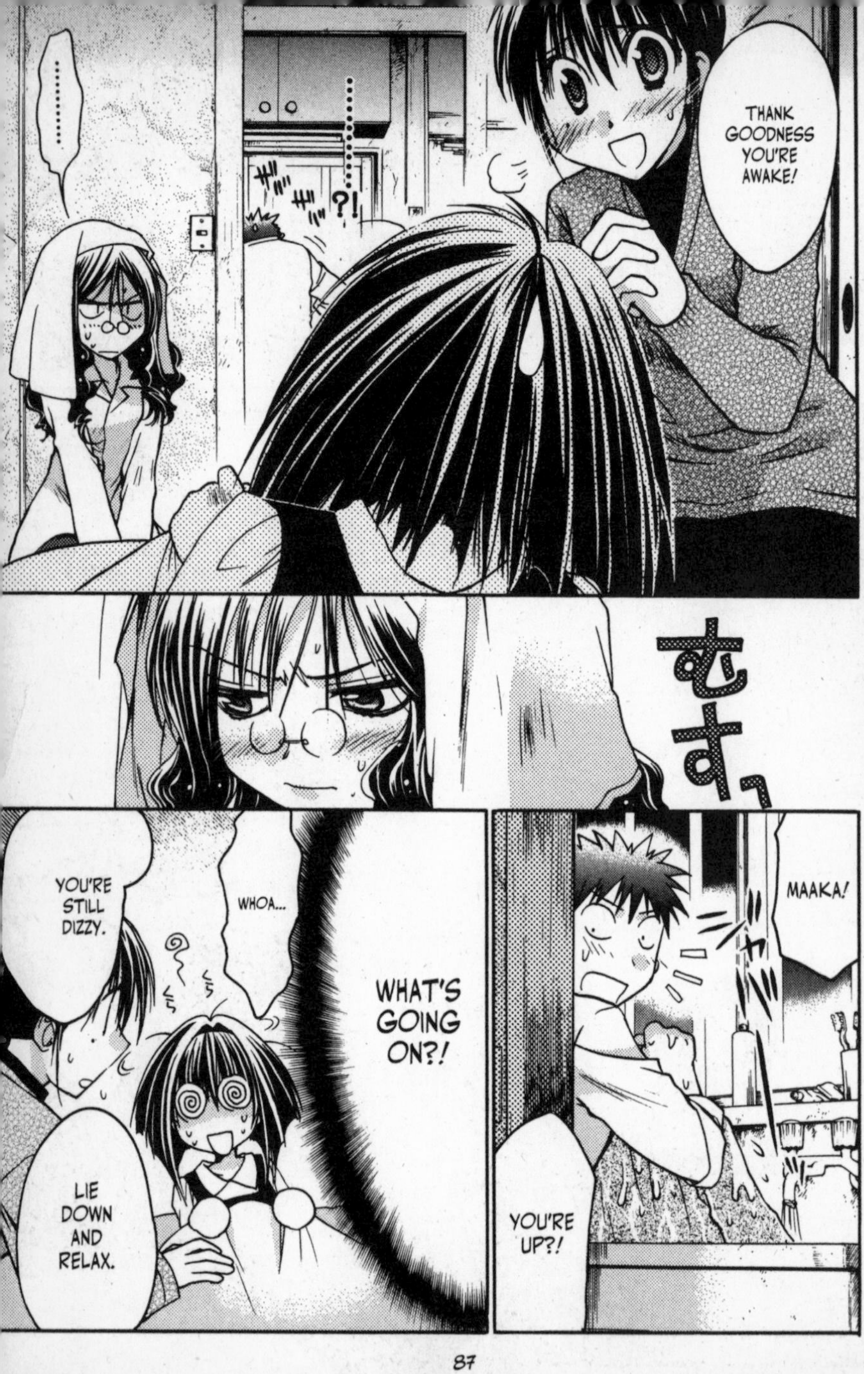

THANK GOODNESS YOU'RE AWAKE!
......?!
......
むすっ
MAAKA!
YOU'RE UP?!
WHAT'S GOING ON?!
WHOA...
YOU'RE STILL DIZZY.
LIE DOWN AND RELAX.

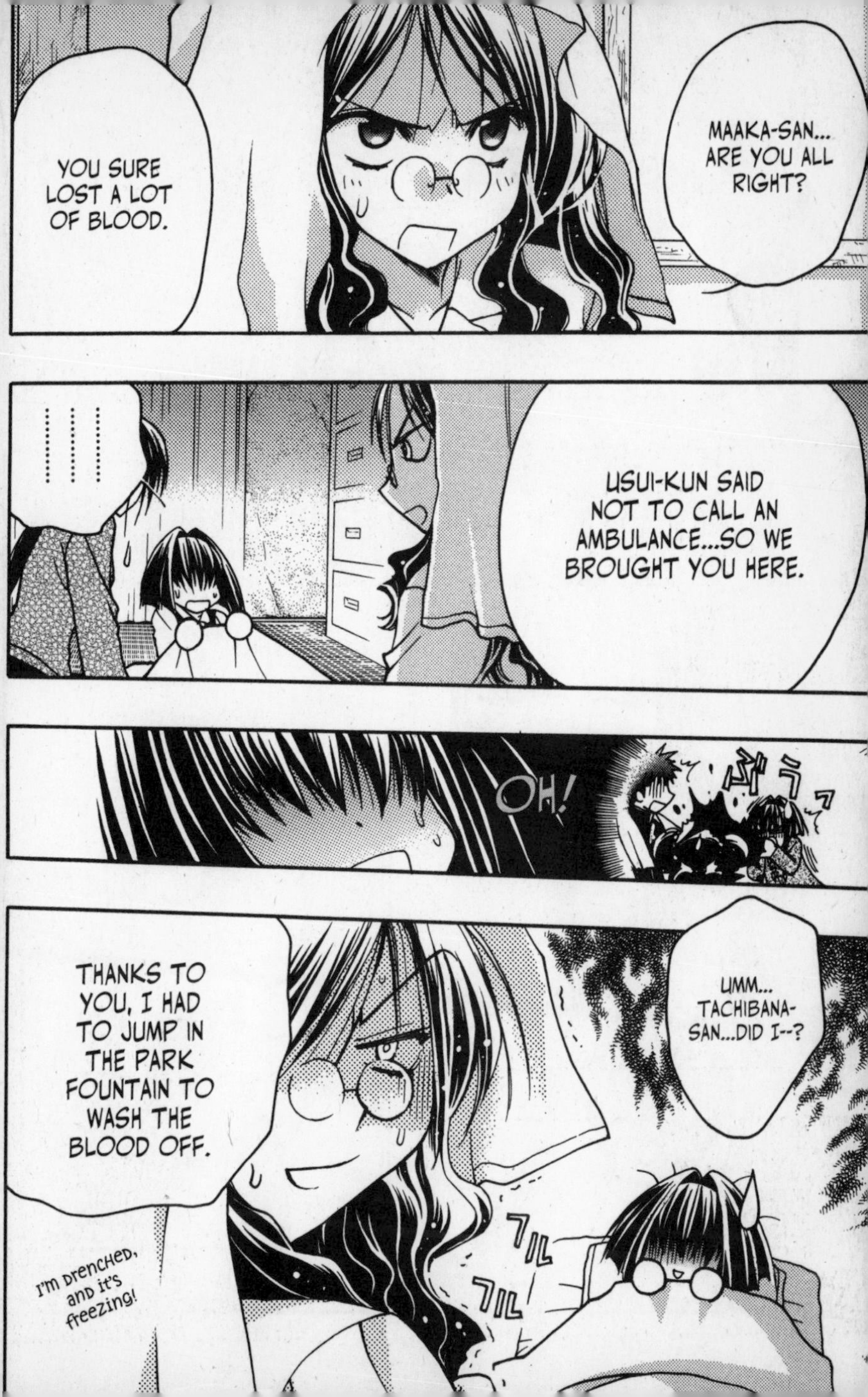
MAAKA-SAN... ARE YOU ALL RIGHT?
YOU SURE LOST A LOT OF BLOOD.
USUI-KUN SAID NOT TO CALL AN AMBULANCE...SO WE BROUGHT YOU HERE.
......
OH!
UMM... TACHIBANA-SAN...DID I--?
THANKS TO YOU, I HAD TO JUMP IN THE PARK FOUNTAIN TO WASH THE BLOOD OFF.
フル
フル
I'm drenched, and it's freezing!

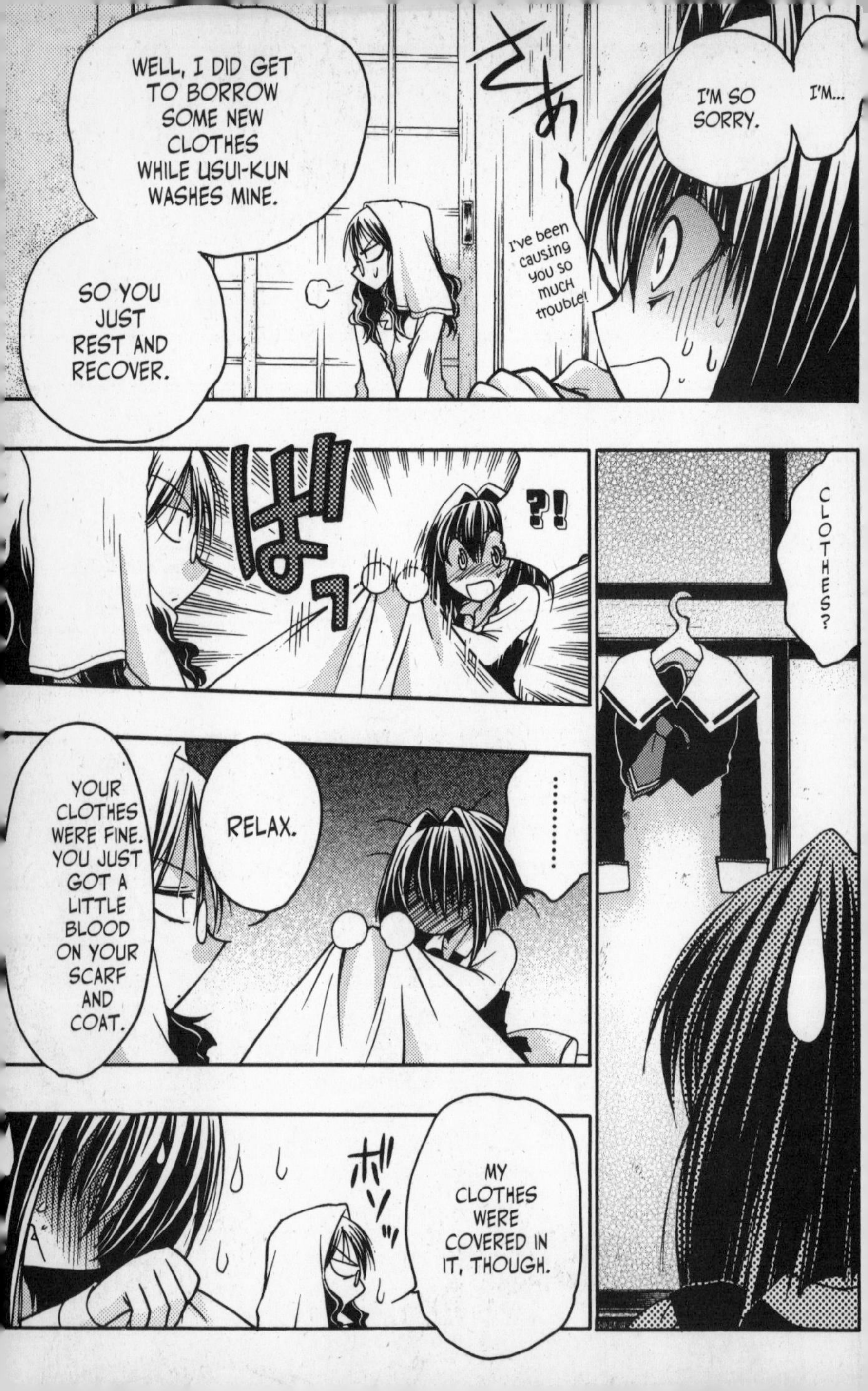
I'M...
I'M SO SORRY.
さあ
I've been causing you so much trouble!
WELL, I DID GET TO BORROW SOME NEW CLOTHES WHILE USUI-KUN WASHES MINE.
SO YOU JUST REST AND RECOVER.
CLOTHES?
?!
ぱっ
......
RELAX.
YOUR CLOTHES WERE FINE. YOU JUST GOT A LITTLE BLOOD ON YOUR SCARF AND COAT.
MY CLOTHES WERE COVERED IN IT, THOUGH.
ボソッ

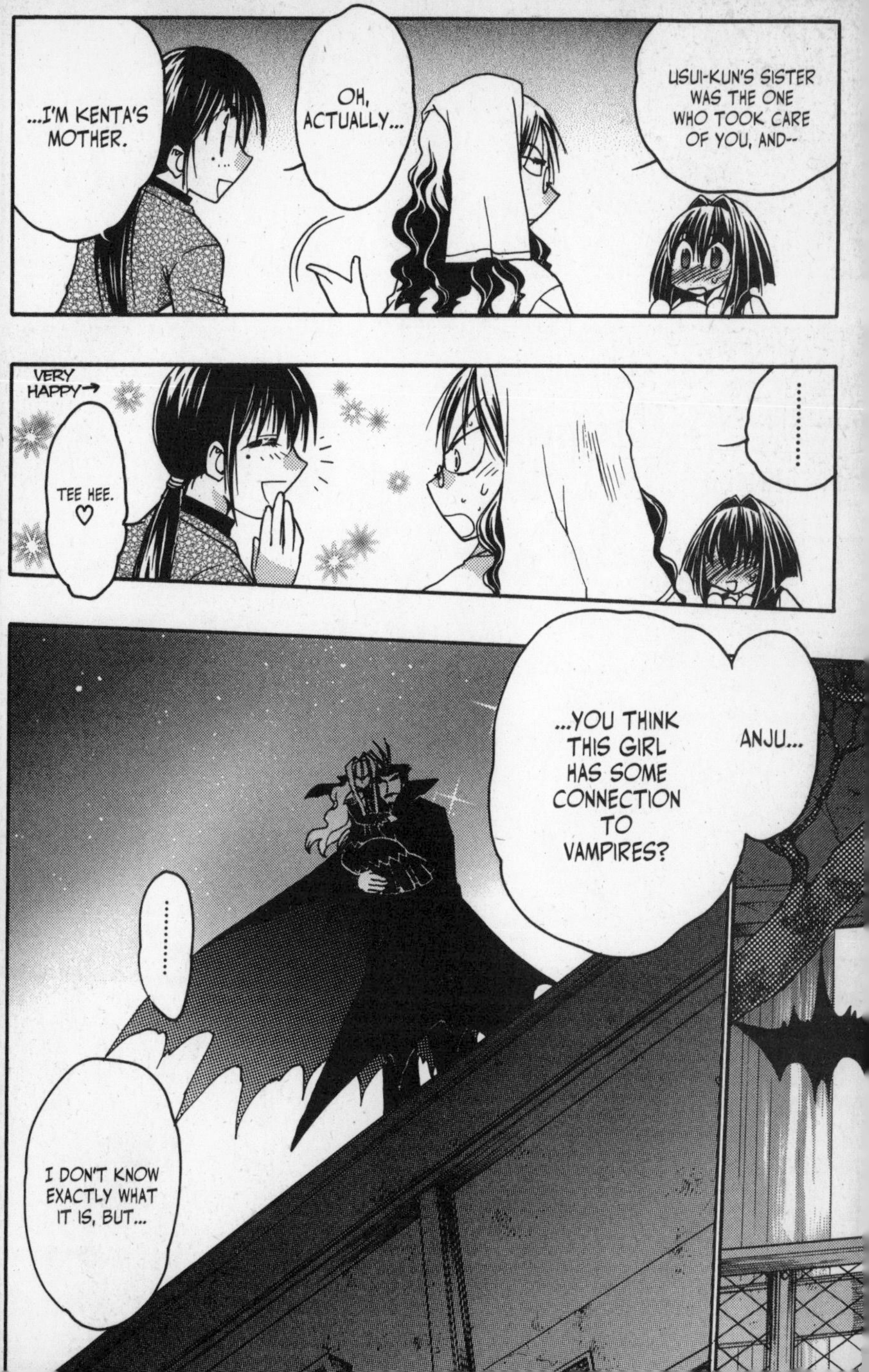
USUI-KUN'S SISTER WAS THE ONE WHO TOOK CARE OF YOU, AND--
OH, ACTUALLY...
...I'M KENTA'S MOTHER.
......
VERY HAPPY→
TEE HEE. ♡
ANJU...
...YOU THINK THIS GIRL HAS SOME CONNECTION TO VAMPIRES?
......
I DON'T KNOW EXACTLY WHAT IT IS, BUT...

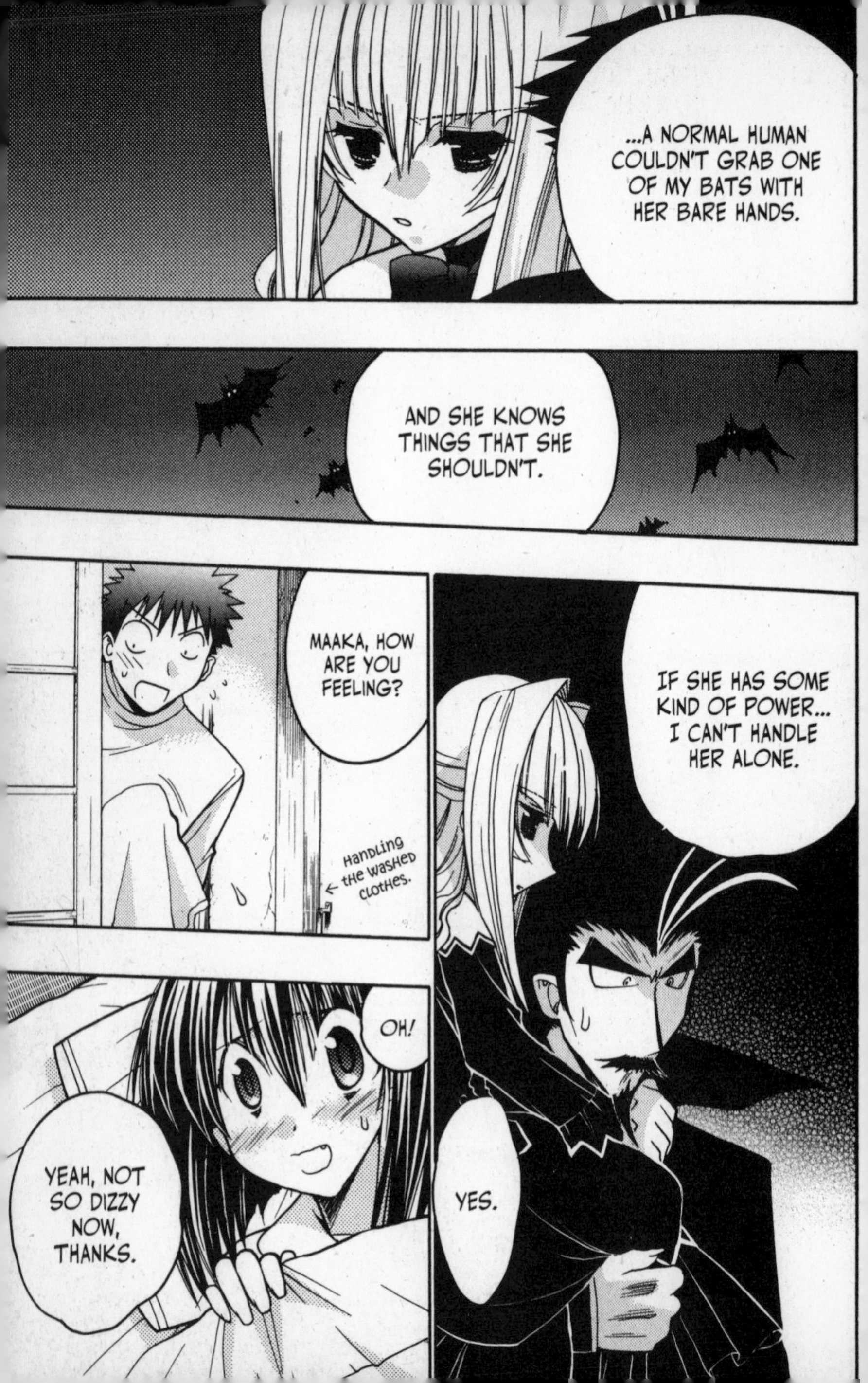
...A NORMAL HUMAN COULDN'T GRAB ONE OF MY BATS WITH HER BARE HANDS.
AND SHE KNOWS THINGS THAT SHE SHOULDN'T.
IF SHE HAS SOME KIND OF POWER... I CAN'T HANDLE HER ALONE.
YES.
MAAKA, HOW ARE YOU FEELING?
Handling the washed clothes.
OH!
YEAH, NOT SO DIZZY NOW, THANKS.

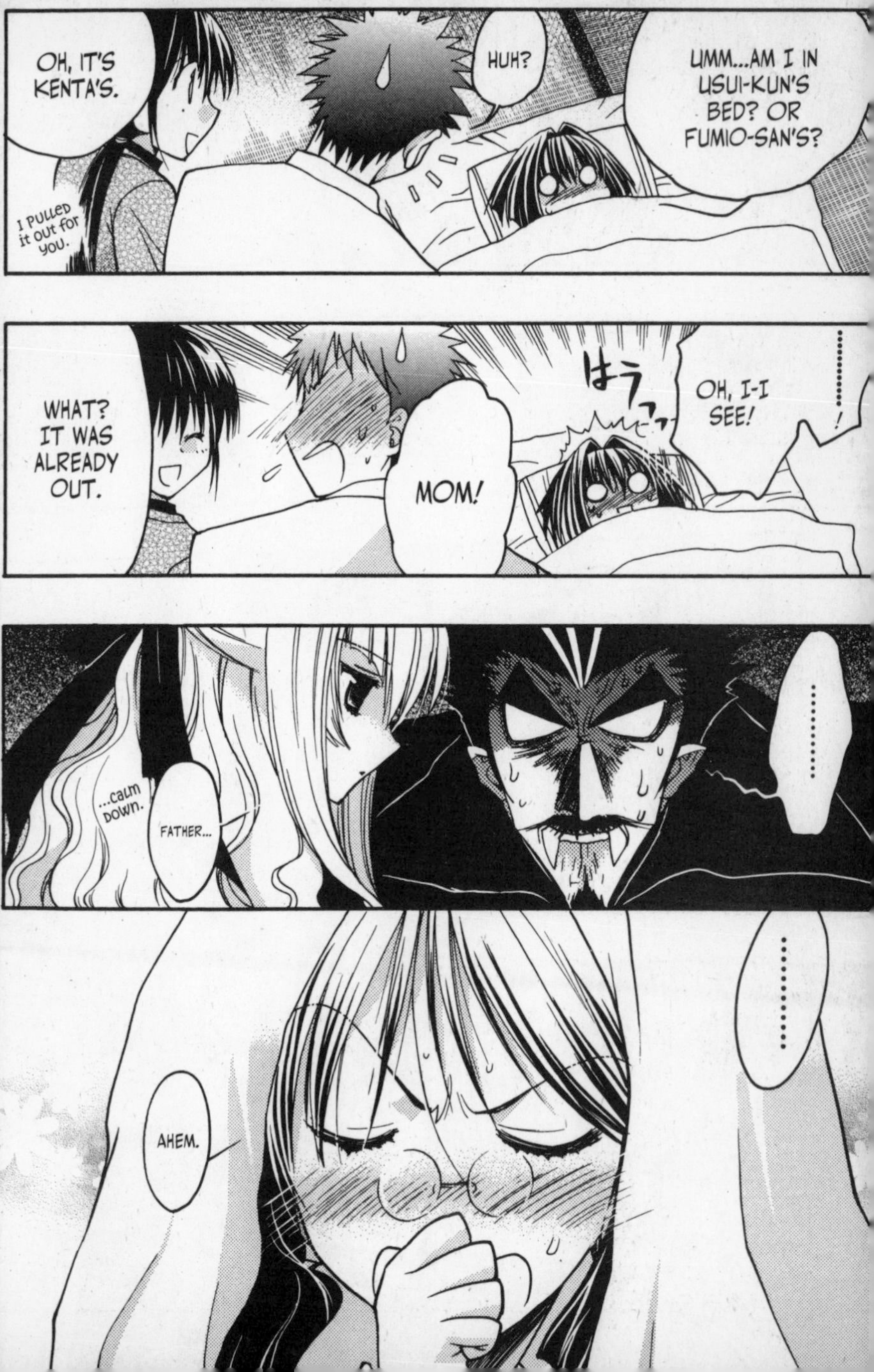
UMM...AM I IN USUI-KUN'S BED? OR FUMIO-SAN'S?
HUH?
OH, IT'S KENTA'S.
I PULLED IT OUT FOR YOU.
.........!
OH, I-I SEE!
はうっ
MOM!
WHAT? IT WAS ALREADY OUT.
....
FATHER...
...calm down.
....
AHEM.

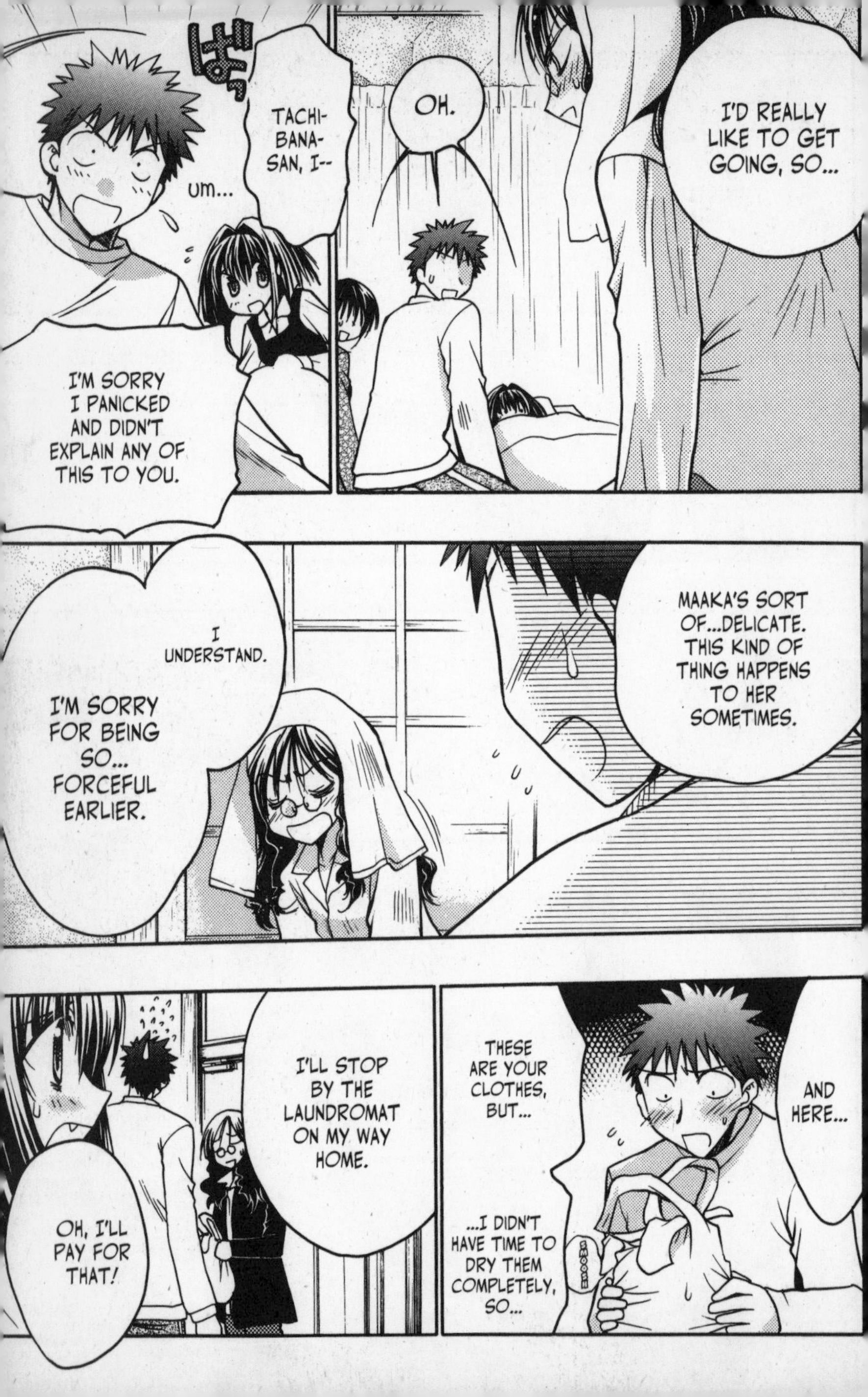
I'D REALLY LIKE TO GET GOING, SO...
OH.
ぱっ
TACHI-BANA-SAN, I--
UM...
I'M SORRY I PANICKED AND DIDN'T EXPLAIN ANY OF THIS TO YOU.
MAAKA'S SORT OF...DELICATE. THIS KIND OF THING HAPPENS TO HER SOMETIMES.
I UNDERSTAND.
I'M SORRY FOR BEING SO... FORCEFUL EARLIER.
AND HERE...
THESE ARE YOUR CLOTHES, BUT...
...I DIDN'T HAVE TIME TO DRY THEM COMPLETELY, SO...
I'LL STOP BY THE LAUNDROMAT ON MY WAY HOME.
OH, I'LL PAY FOR THAT!

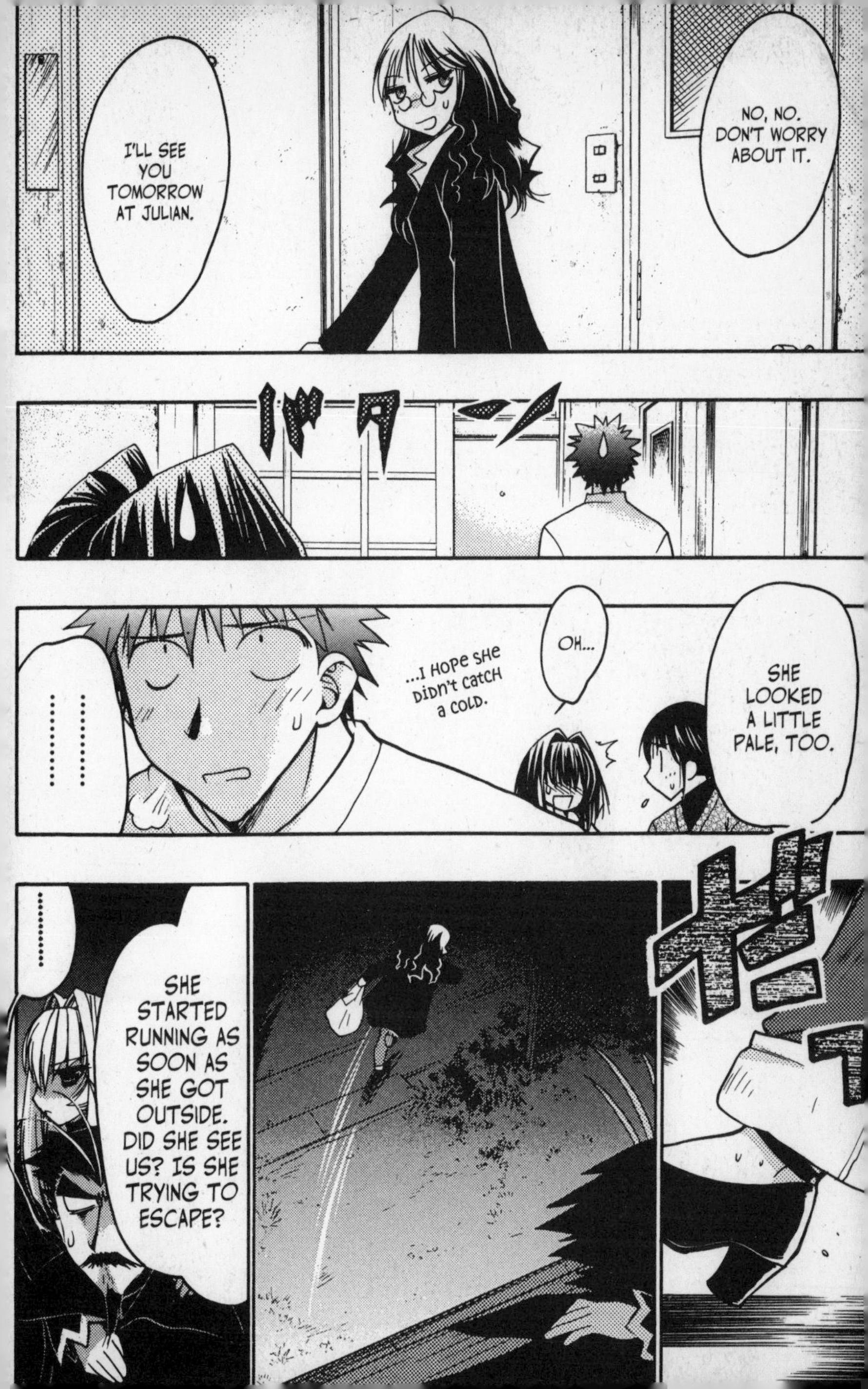
NO, NO. DON'T WORRY ABOUT IT.
I'LL SEE YOU TOMORROW AT JULIAN.
SHE LOOKED A LITTLE PALE, TOO.
OH...
...I HOPE SHE DIDN'T CATCH A COLD.
....
SHE STARTED RUNNING AS SOON AS SHE GOT OUTSIDE. DID SHE SEE US? IS SHE TRYING TO ESCAPE?
....

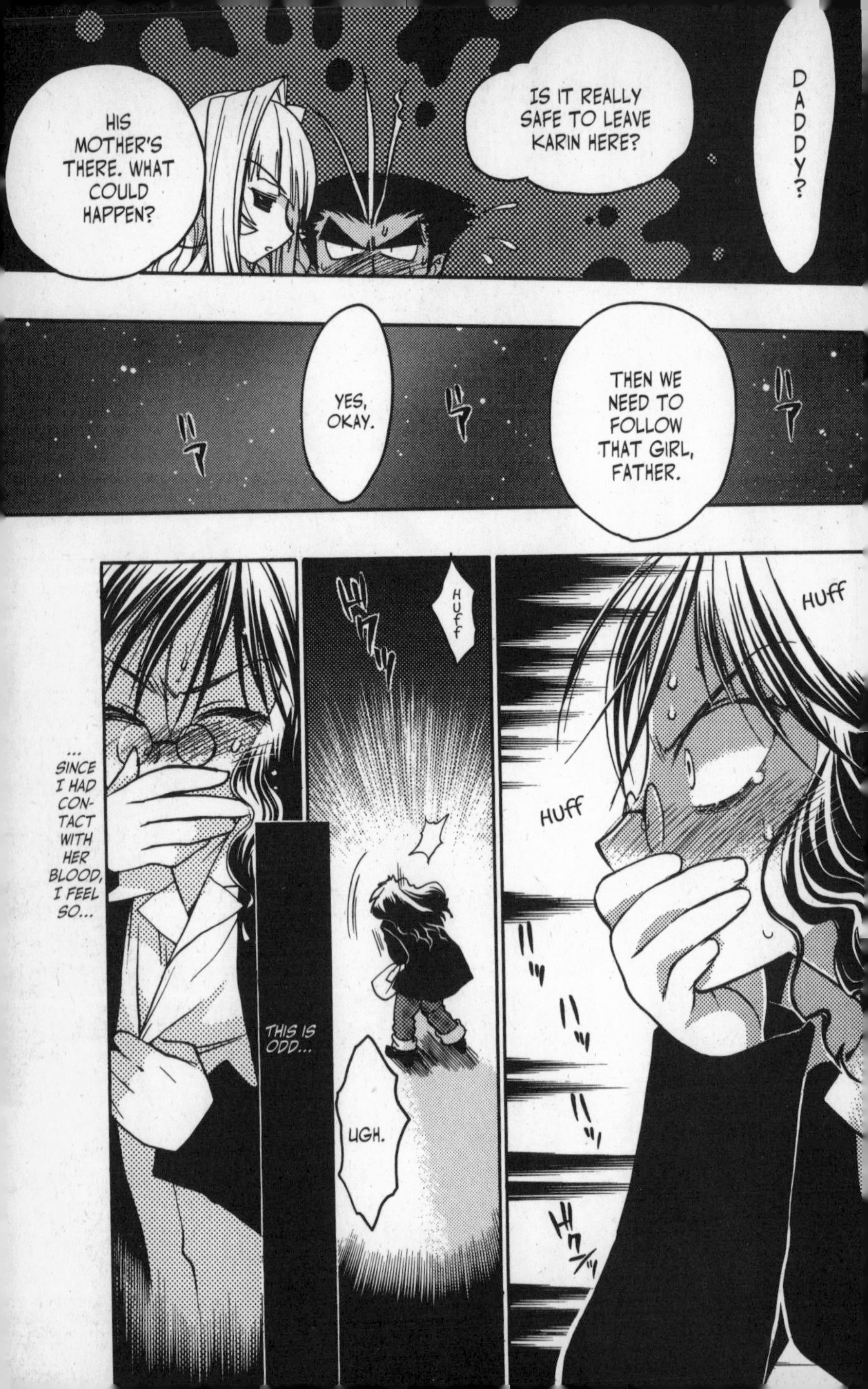
DADDY?
IS IT REALLY SAFE TO LEAVE KARIN HERE?
HIS MOTHER'S THERE. WHAT COULD HAPPEN?
THEN WE NEED TO FOLLOW THAT GIRL, FATHER.
YES, OKAY.
HUFF
HUFF
HUFF
UGH.
THIS IS ODD...
...SINCE I HAD CONTACT WITH HER BLOOD, I FEEL SO...

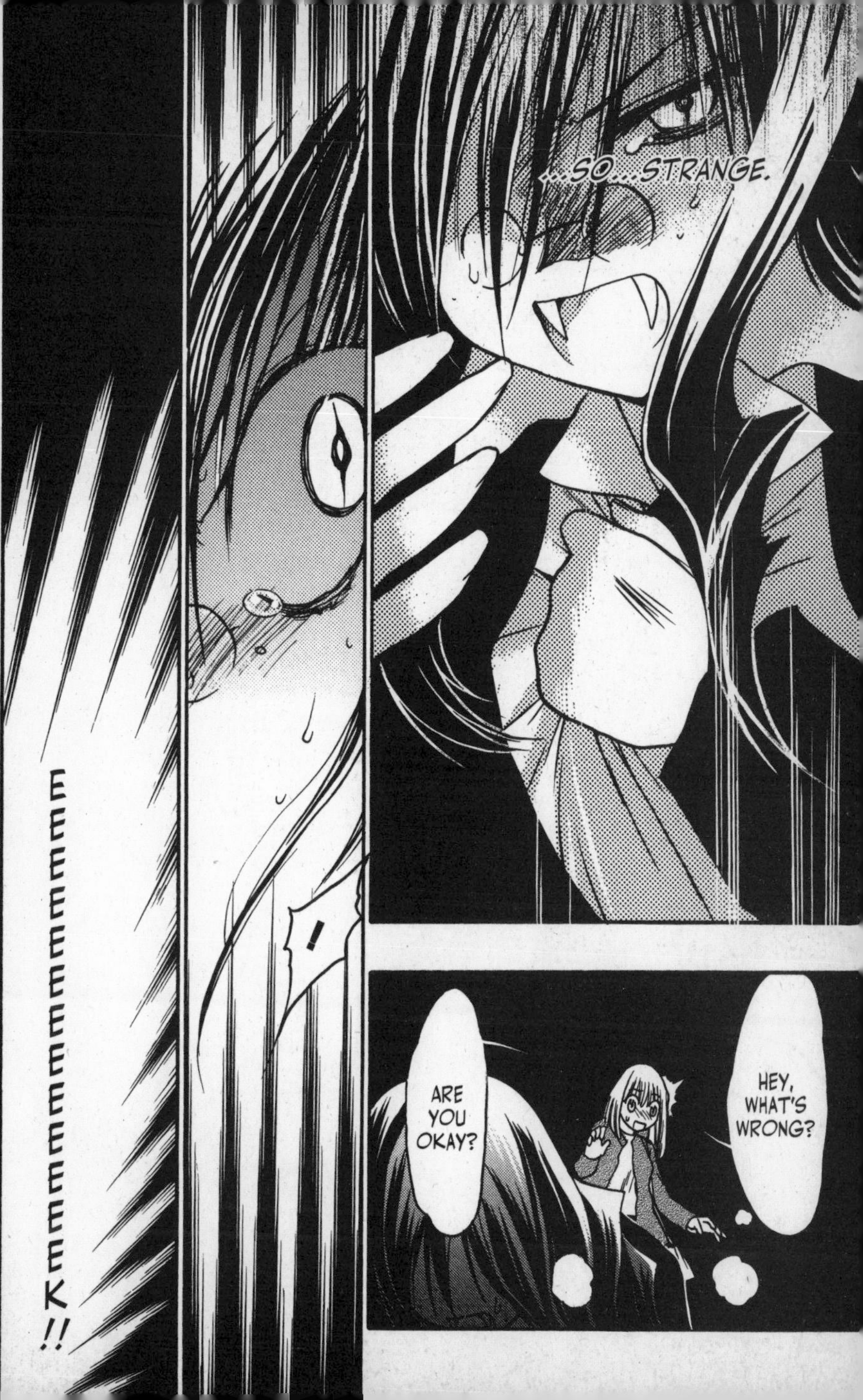
...SO...STRANGE.
HEY, WHAT'S WRONG?
ARE YOU OKAY?
!
EEEEEEEEEEEEEEEEEK!!

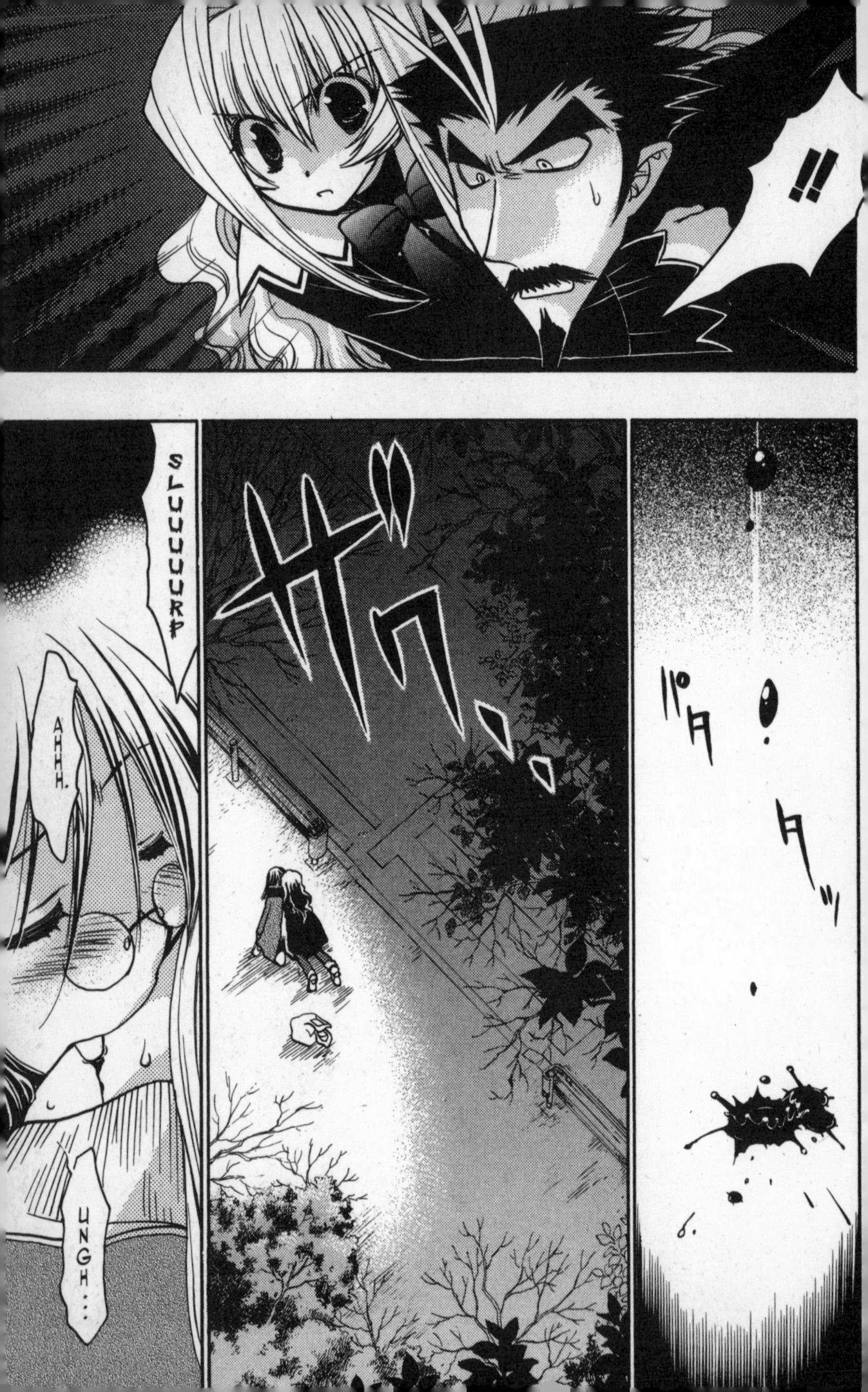
!!
パタ
タッ
ザク..
SLUUUUURP
AHHH.
UNGH...

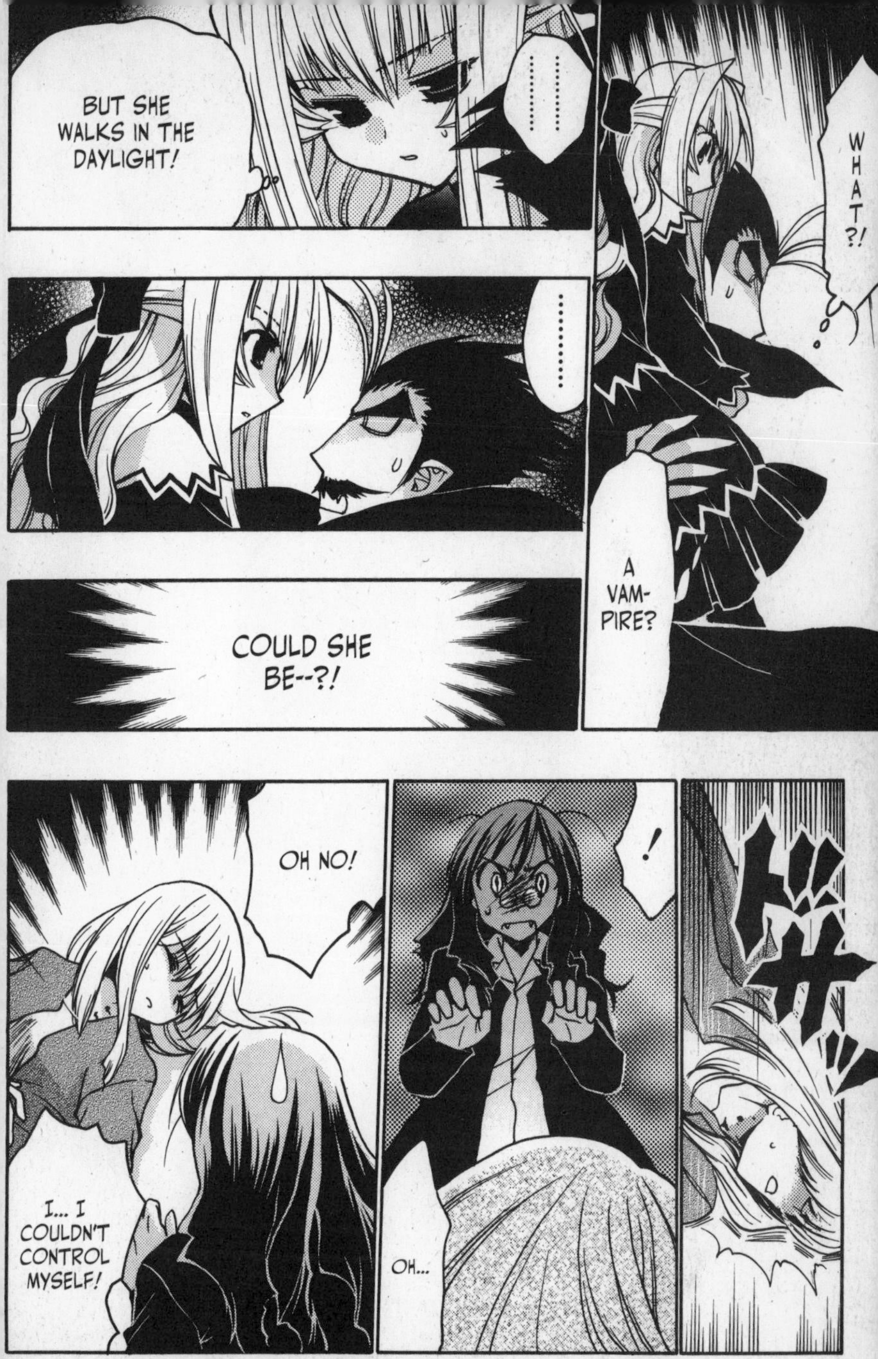
WHAT?!
A VAMPIRE?
......
BUT SHE WALKS IN THE DAYLIGHT!
......
COULD SHE BE--?!
!
OH...
OH NO!
I... I COULDN'T CONTROL MYSELF!

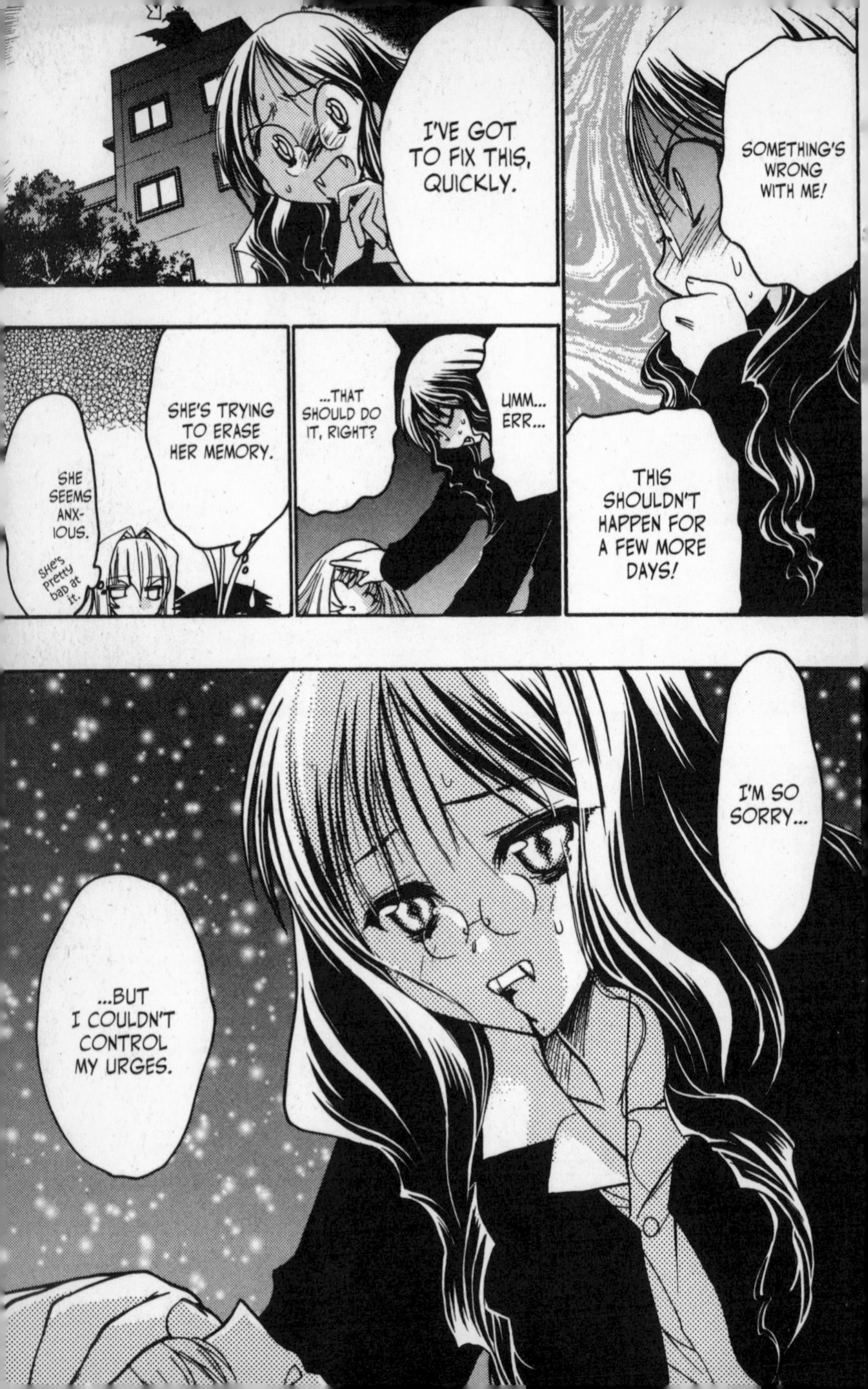
SOMETHING'S WRONG WITH ME!
THIS SHOULDN'T HAPPEN FOR A FEW MORE DAYS!
I'VE GOT TO FIX THIS, QUICKLY.
UMM... ERR...
...THAT SHOULD DO IT, RIGHT?
SHE'S TRYING TO ERASE HER MEMORY.
SHE SEEMS ANX-IOUS.
She's pretty bad at it.
I'M SO SORRY...
...BUT I COULDN'T CONTROL MY URGES.

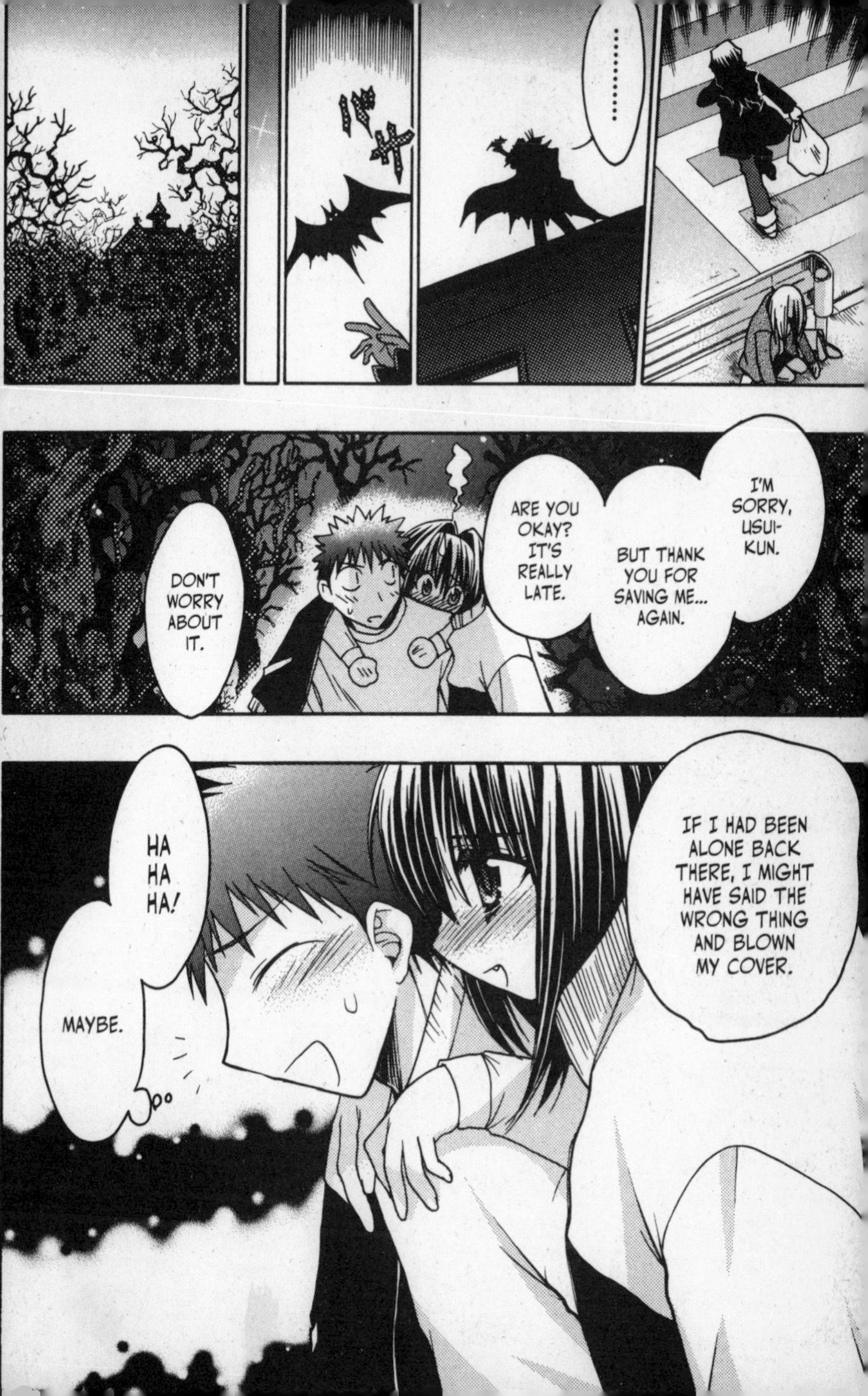
......
I'M SORRY, USUI-KUN.
BUT THANK YOU FOR SAVING ME... AGAIN.
ARE YOU OKAY? IT'S REALLY LATE.
DON'T WORRY ABOUT IT.
IF I HAD BEEN ALONE BACK THERE, I MIGHT HAVE SAID THE WRONG THING AND BLOWN MY COVER.
HA HA HA!
MAYBE.

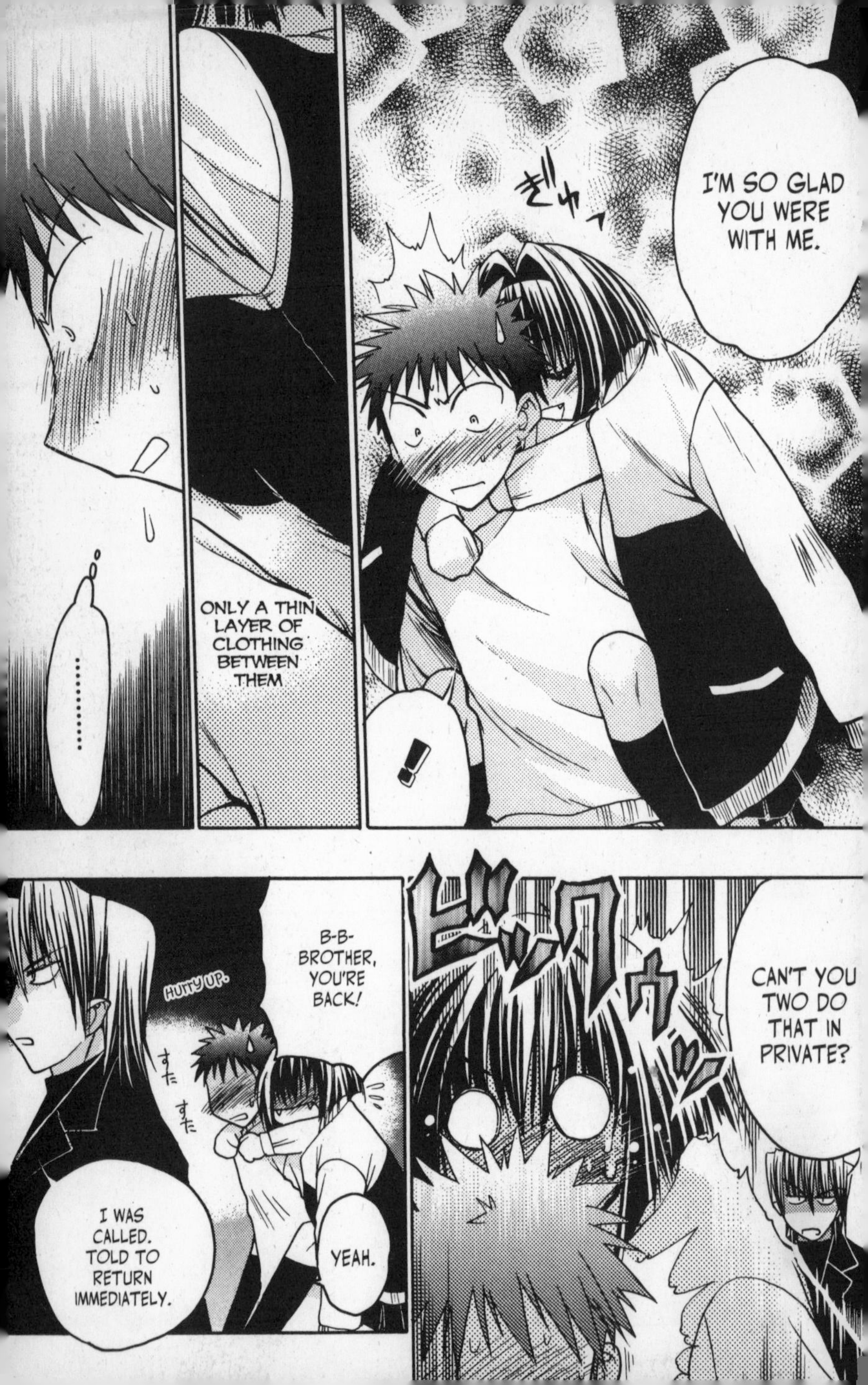
I'M SO GLAD YOU WERE WITH ME.
ぎゅ
!
ONLY A THIN LAYER OF CLOTHING BETWEEN THEM
......
CAN'T YOU TWO DO THAT IN PRIVATE?
ビクゥッ
B-B-BROTHER, YOU'RE BACK!
HUTTY UP.
すた すた
YEAH.
I WAS CALLED. TOLD TO RETURN IMMEDIATELY.

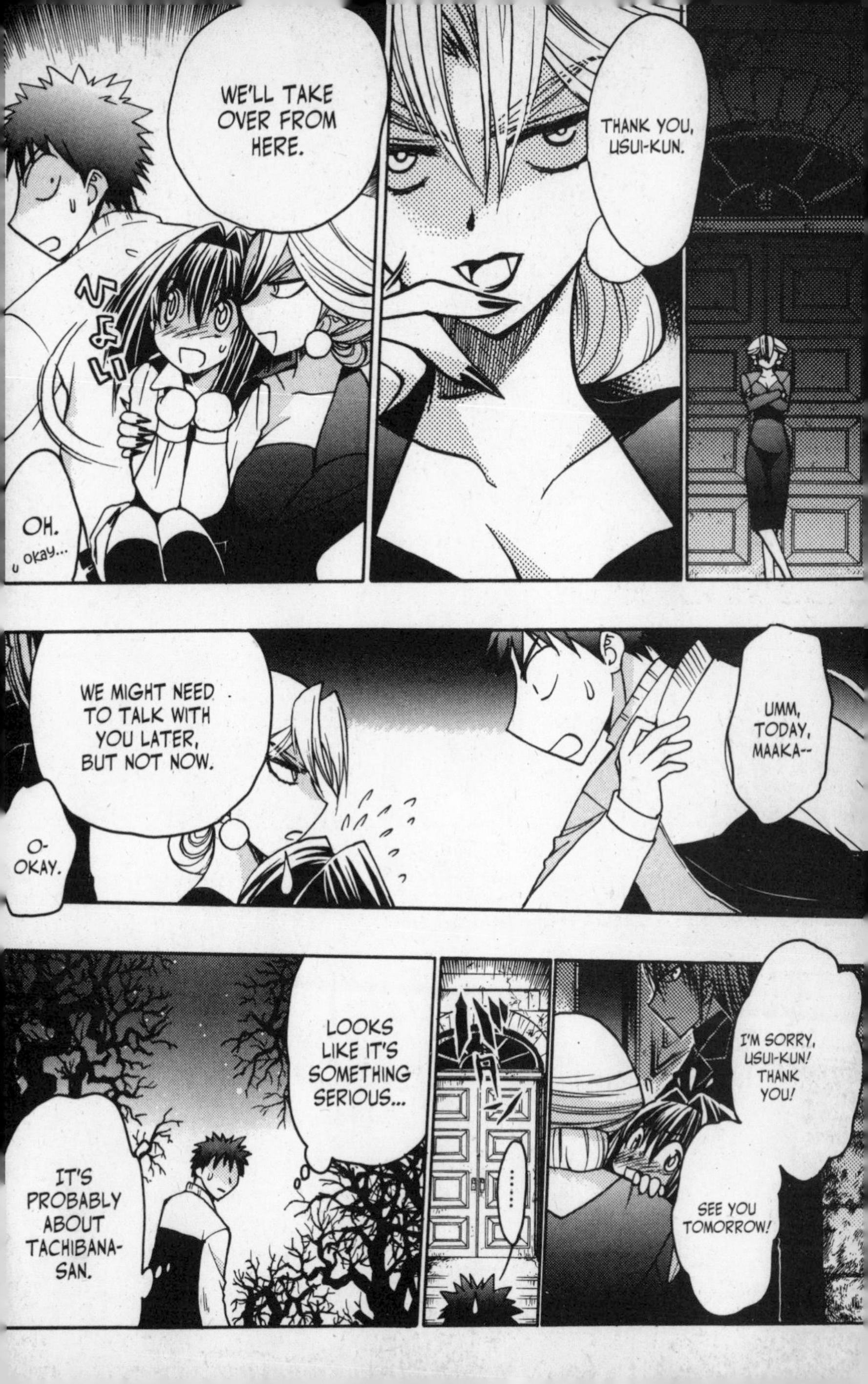
THANK YOU, USUI-KUN.
WE'LL TAKE OVER FROM HERE.
OH.
okay...
UMM, TODAY, MAAKA--
WE MIGHT NEED TO TALK WITH YOU LATER, BUT NOT NOW.
O-OKAY.
I'M SORRY, USUI-KUN! THANK YOU!
SEE YOU TOMORROW!
......
LOOKS LIKE IT'S SOMETHING SERIOUS...
IT'S PROBABLY ABOUT TACHIBANA-SAN.

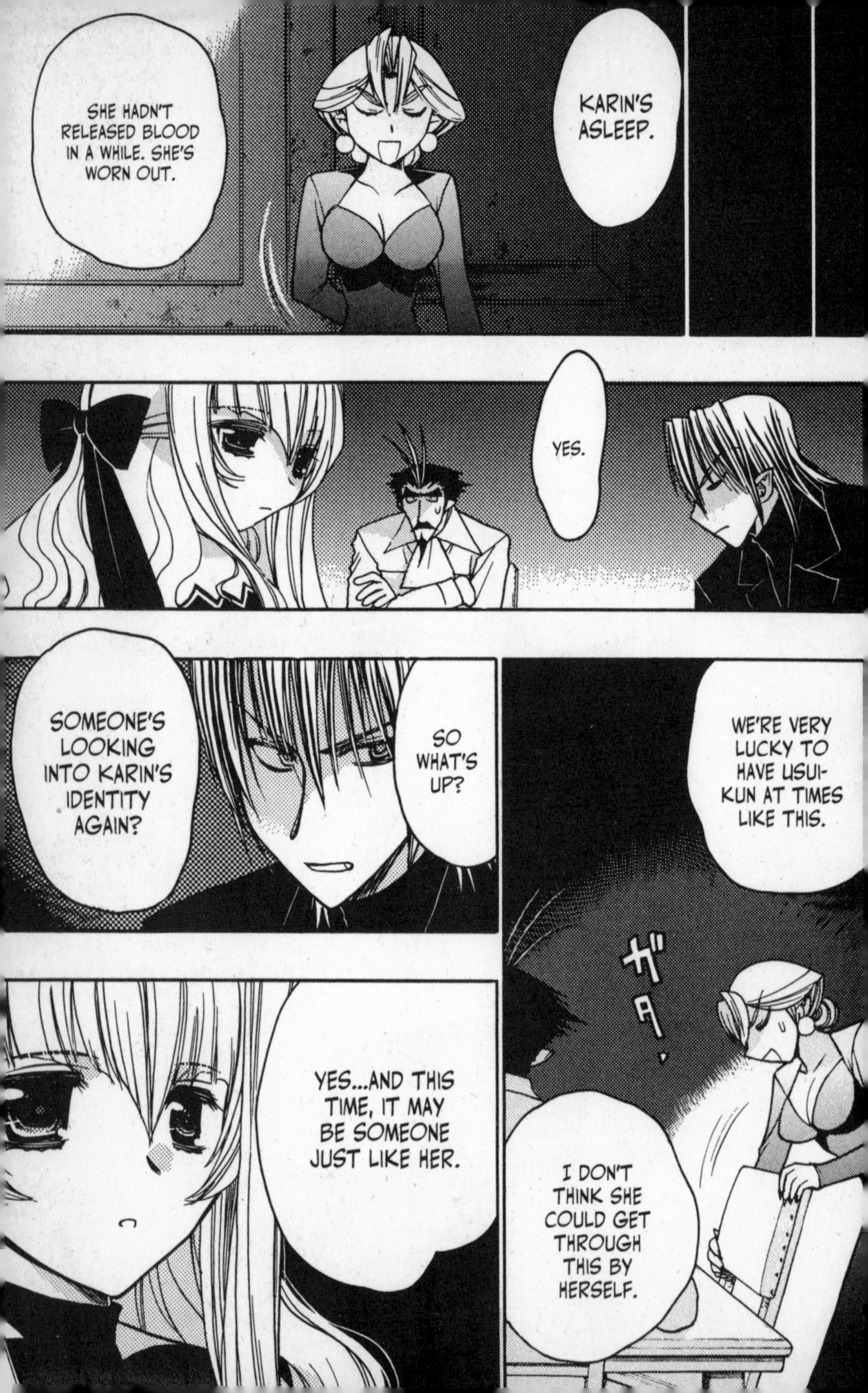
KARIN'S ASLEEP.
SHE HADN'T RELEASED BLOOD IN A WHILE. SHE'S WORN OUT.
YES.
WE'RE VERY LUCKY TO HAVE USUI-KUN AT TIMES LIKE THIS.
ガタ
I DON'T THINK SHE COULD GET THROUGH THIS BY HERSELF.
SO WHAT'S UP?
SOMEONE'S LOOKING INTO KARIN'S IDENTITY AGAIN?
YES...AND THIS TIME, IT MAY BE SOMEONE JUST LIKE HER.

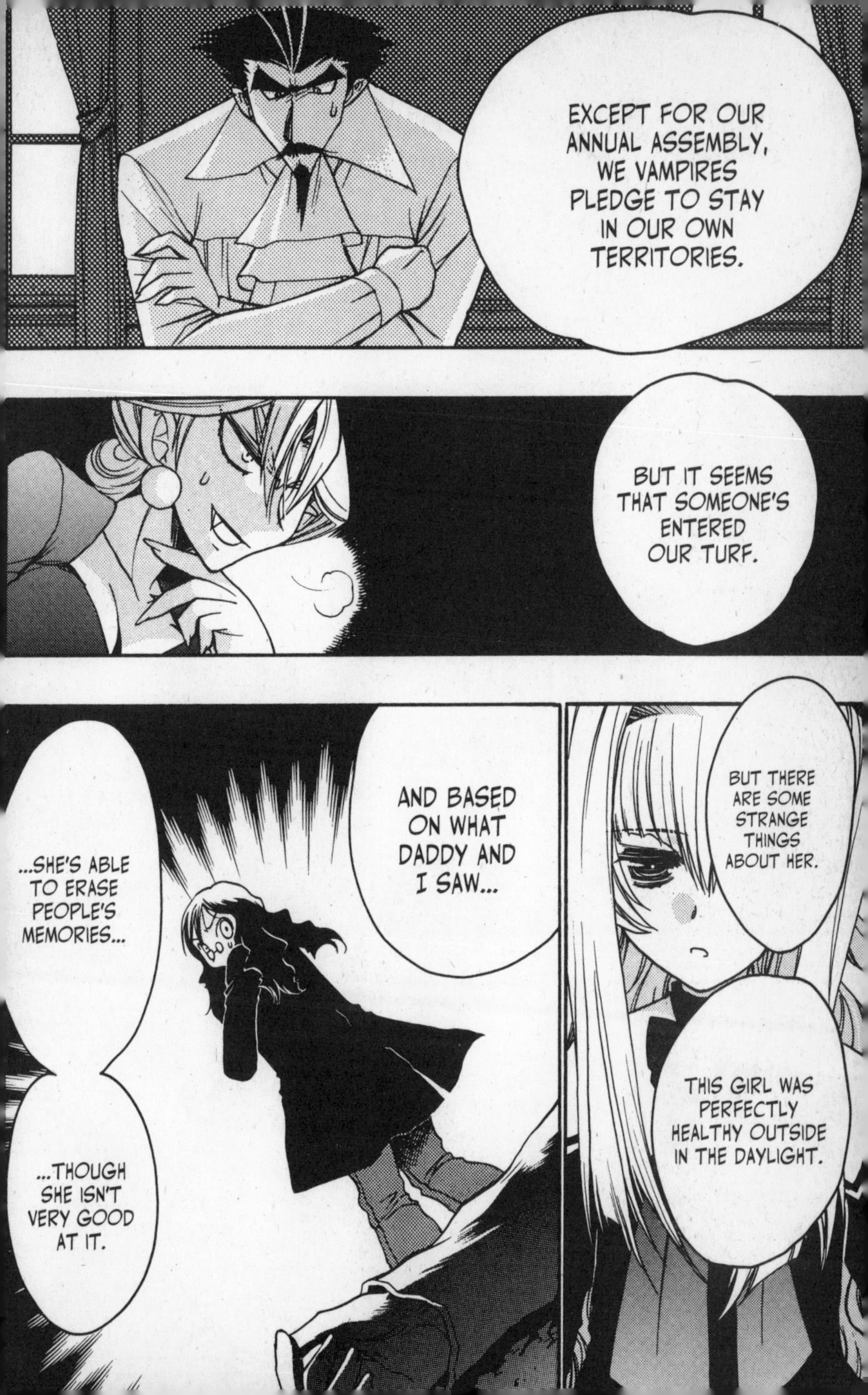
EXCEPT FOR OUR ANNUAL ASSEMBLY, WE VAMPIRES PLEDGE TO STAY IN OUR OWN TERRITORIES.
BUT IT SEEMS THAT SOMEONE'S ENTERED OUR TURF.
BUT THERE ARE SOME STRANGE THINGS ABOUT HER.
THIS GIRL WAS PERFECTLY HEALTHY OUTSIDE IN THE DAYLIGHT.
AND BASED ON WHAT DADDY AND I SAW...
...SHE'S ABLE TO ERASE PEOPLE'S MEMORIES...
...THOUGH SHE ISN'T VERY GOOD AT IT.

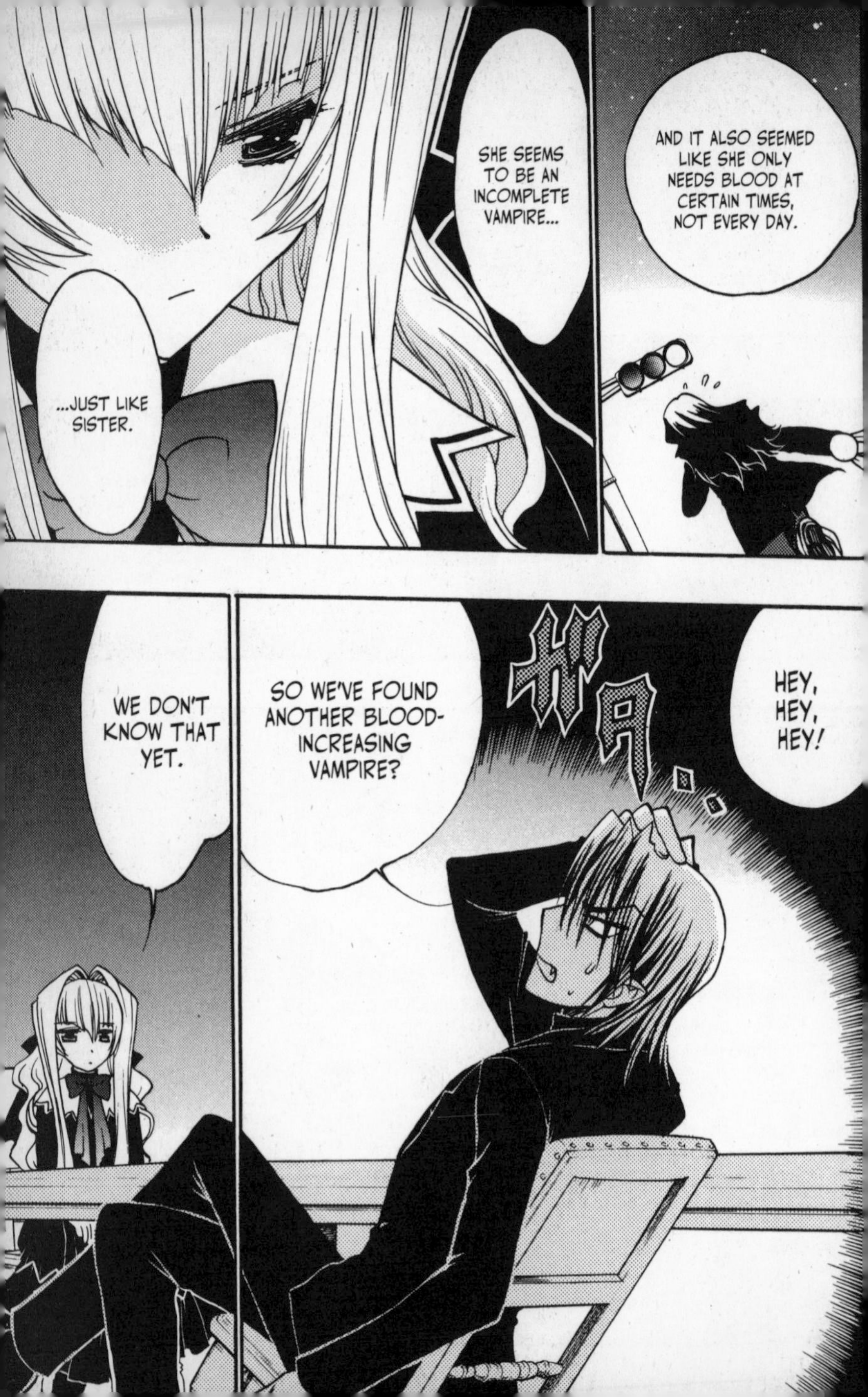
AND IT ALSO SEEMED LIKE SHE ONLY NEEDS BLOOD AT CERTAIN TIMES, NOT EVERY DAY.
SHE SEEMS TO BE AN INCOMPLETE VAMPIRE...
...JUST LIKE SISTER.
HEY, HEY, HEY!
SO WE'VE FOUND ANOTHER BLOOD-INCREASING VAMPIRE?
WE DON'T KNOW THAT YET.

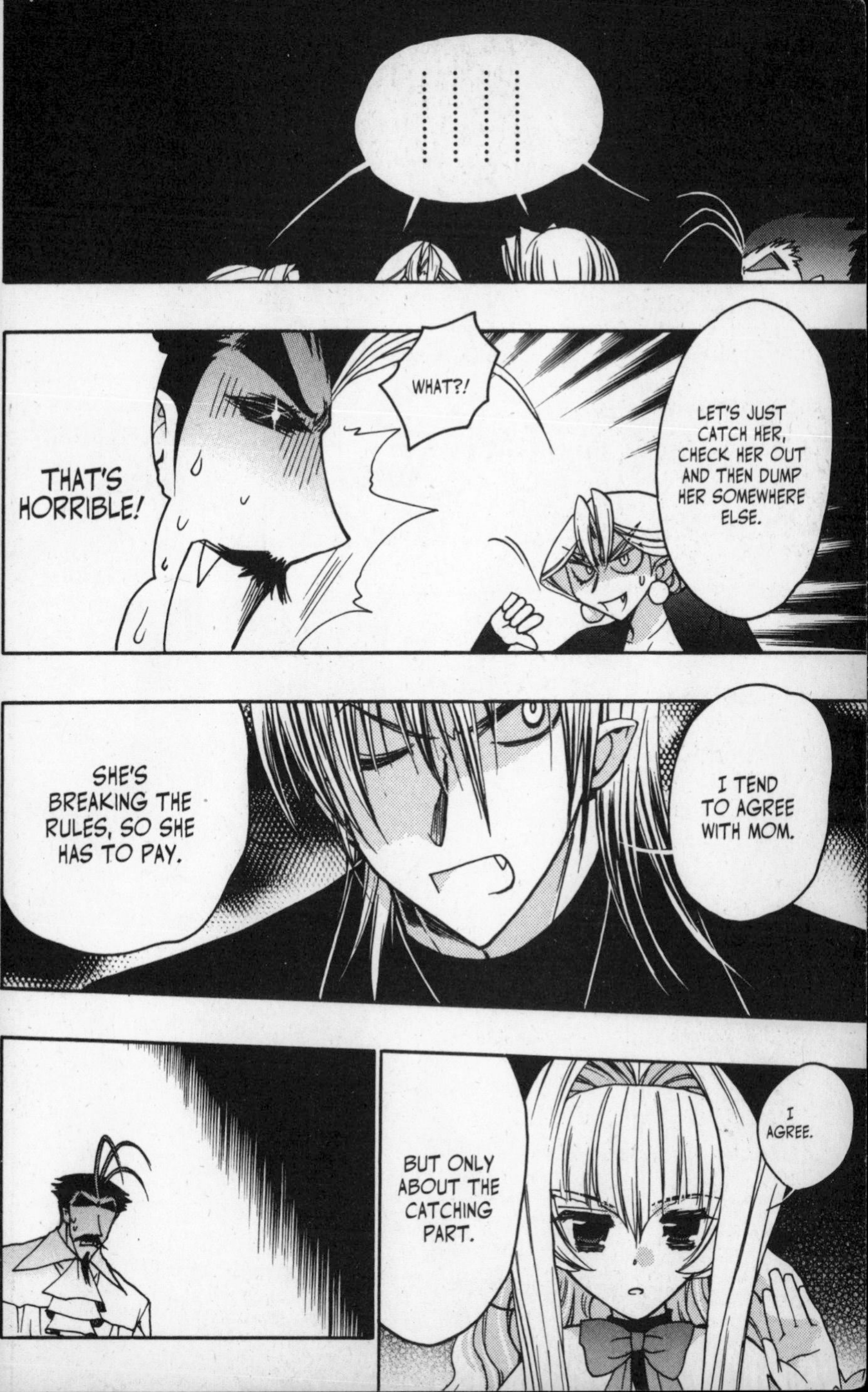
.....
LET'S JUST CATCH HER, CHECK HER OUT AND THEN DUMP HER SOMEWHERE ELSE.
WHAT?!
THAT'S HORRIBLE!
I TEND TO AGREE WITH MOM.
SHE'S BREAKING THE RULES, SO SHE HAS TO PAY.
I AGREE.
BUT ONLY ABOUT THE CATCHING PART.

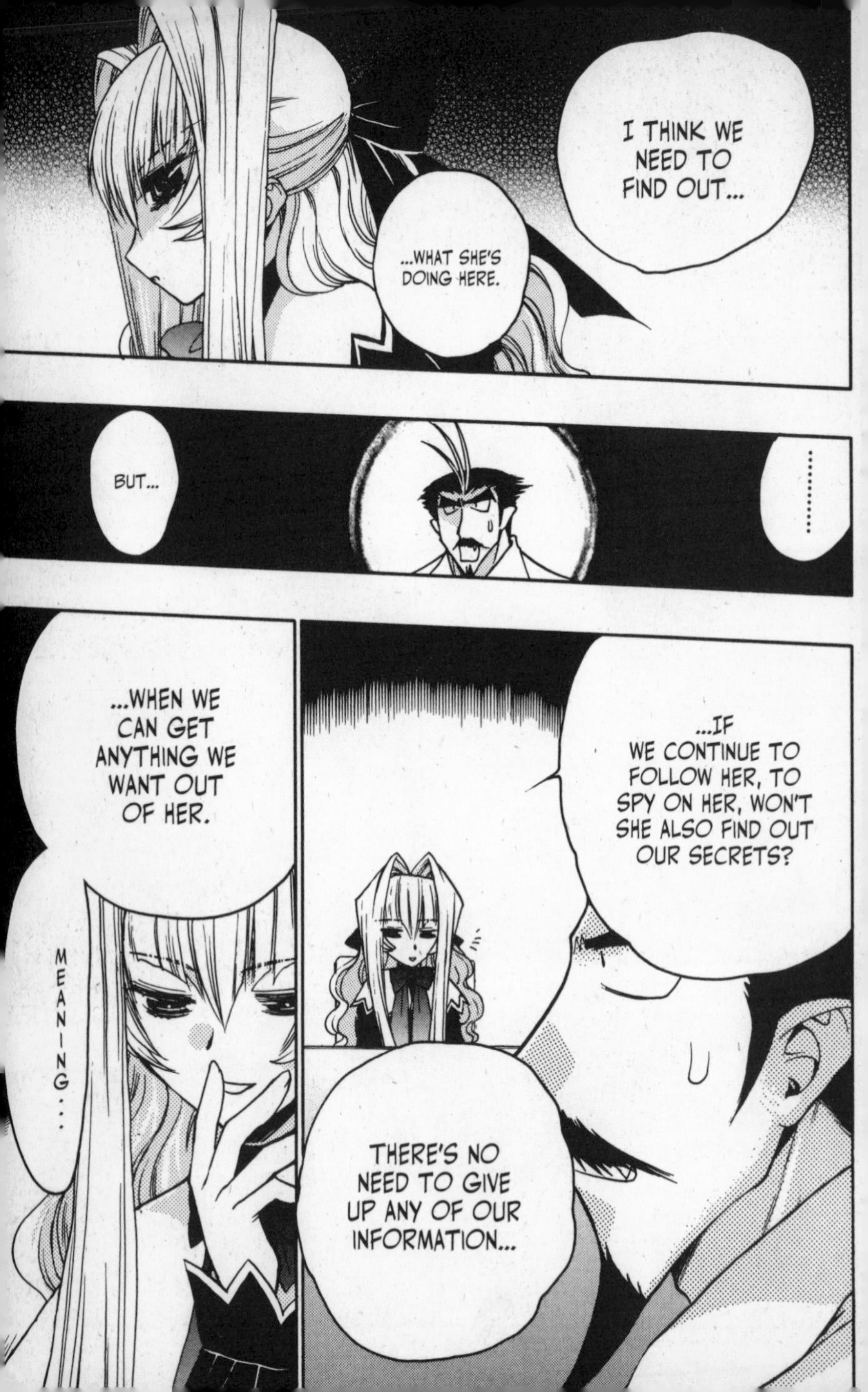
I THINK WE NEED TO FIND OUT...
...WHAT SHE'S DOING HERE.
....
BUT...
...IF WE CONTINUE TO FOLLOW HER, TO SPY ON HER, WON'T SHE ALSO FIND OUT OUR SECRETS?
THERE'S NO NEED TO GIVE UP ANY OF OUR INFORMATION...
...WHEN WE CAN GET ANYTHING WE WANT OUT OF HER.
MEANING...

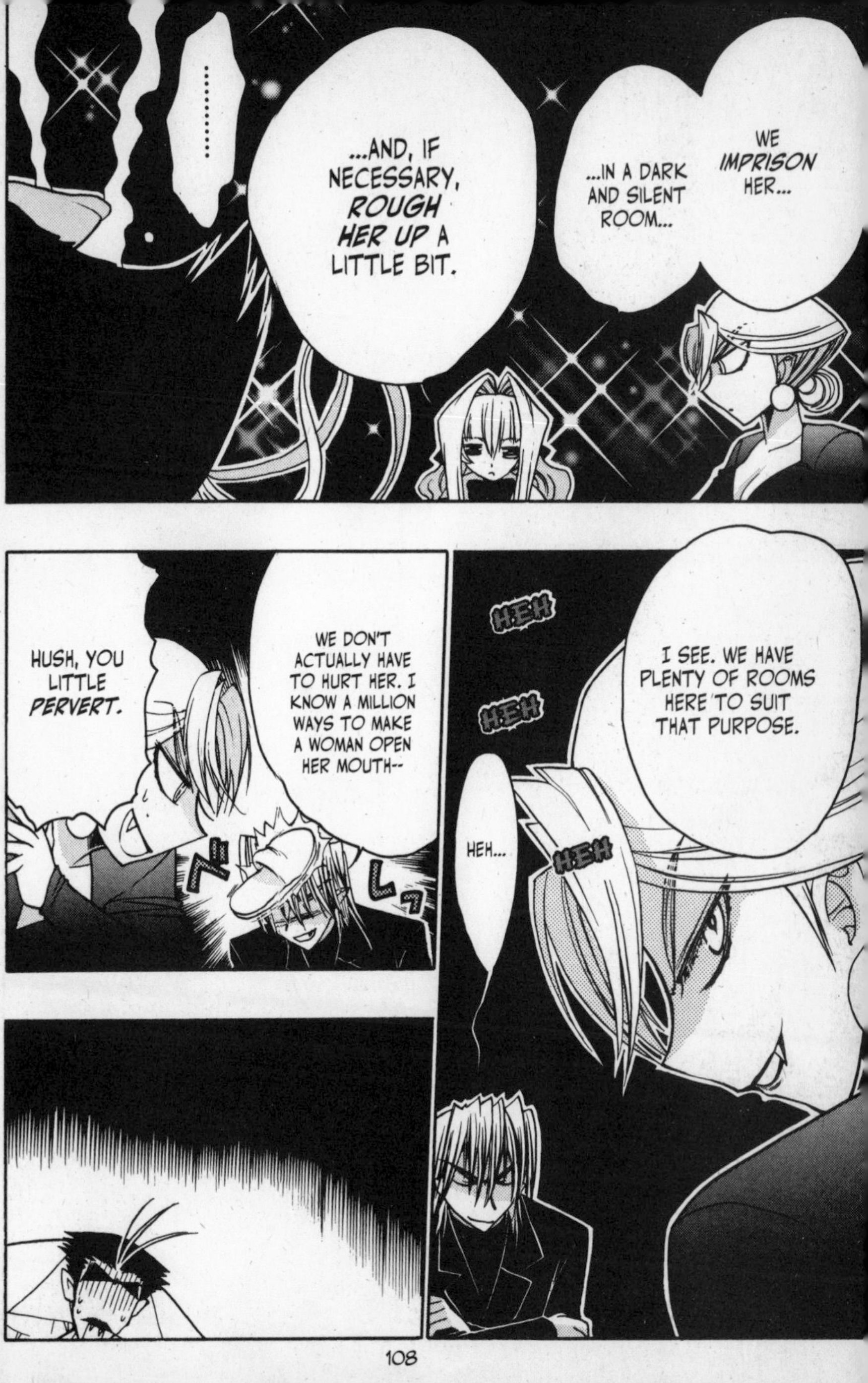
WE *IMPRISON* HER...
...IN A DARK AND SILENT ROOM...
...AND, IF NECESSARY, *ROUGH HER UP* A LITTLE BIT.
......
I SEE. WE HAVE PLENTY OF ROOMS HERE TO SUIT THAT PURPOSE.
HEH
HEH
HEH
HEH...
WE DON'T ACTUALLY HAVE TO HURT HER. I KNOW A MILLION WAYS TO MAKE A WOMAN OPEN HER MOUTH--
HUSH, YOU LITTLE *PERVERT.*

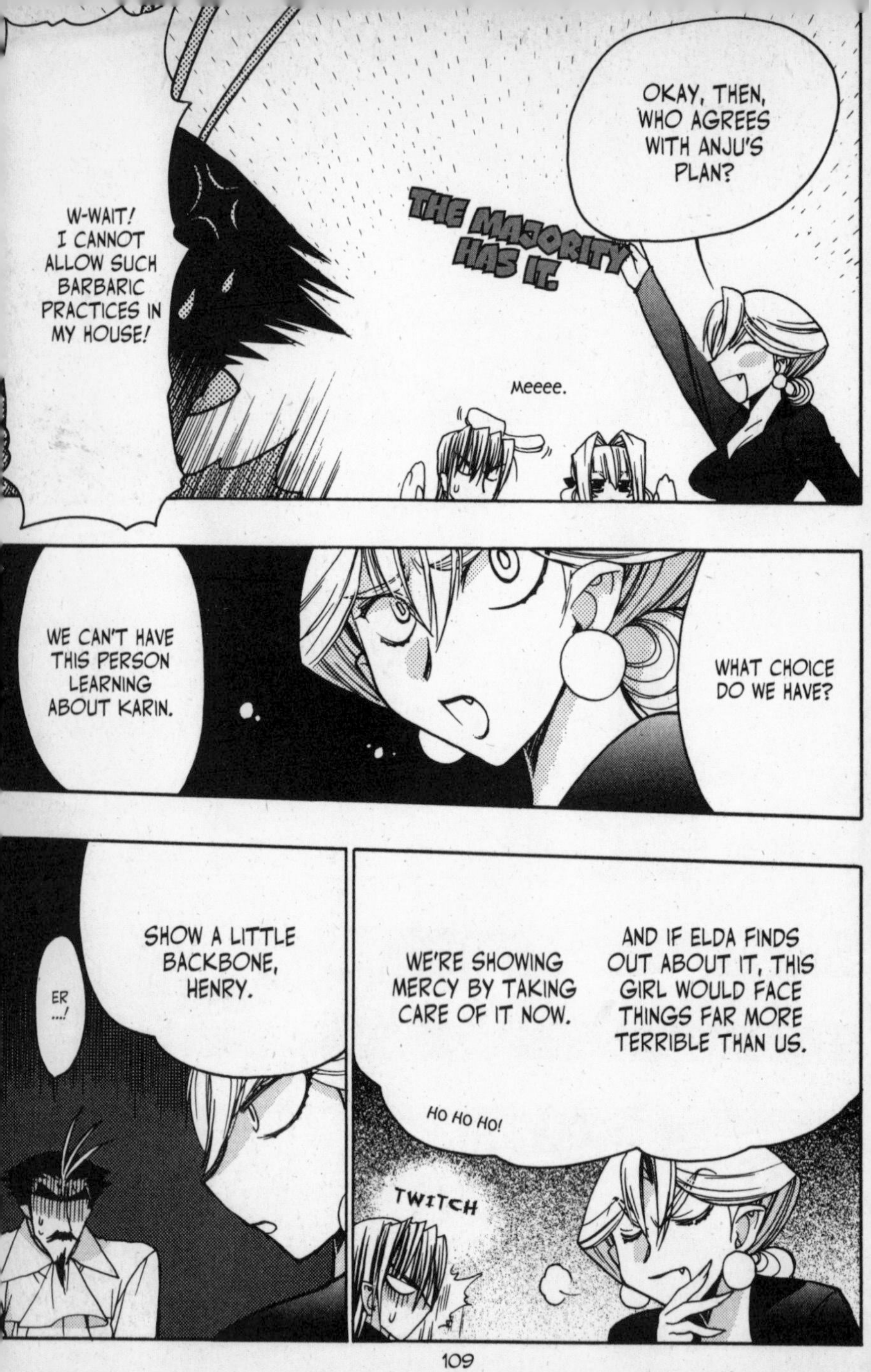
OKAY, THEN, WHO AGREES WITH ANJU'S PLAN?
THE MAJORITY HAS IT.
Meeee.
W-WAIT! I CANNOT ALLOW SUCH BARBARIC PRACTICES IN MY HOUSE!
WHAT CHOICE DO WE HAVE?
WE CAN'T HAVE THIS PERSON LEARNING ABOUT KARIN.
AND IF ELDA FINDS OUT ABOUT IT, THIS GIRL WOULD FACE THINGS FAR MORE TERRIBLE THAN US.
WE'RE SHOWING MERCY BY TAKING CARE OF IT NOW.
HO HO HO!
TWITCH
SHOW A LITTLE BACKBONE, HENRY.
ER ...!

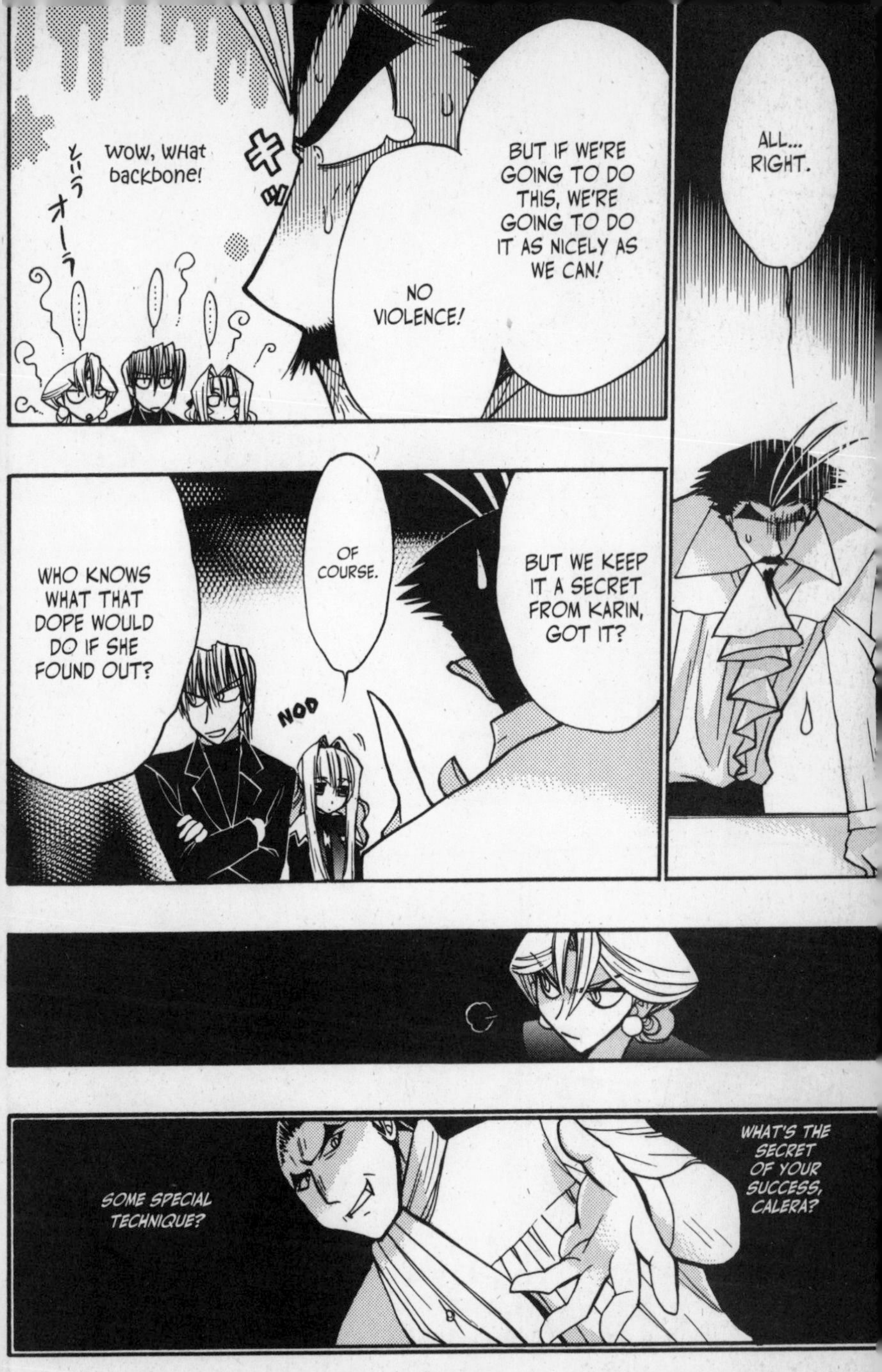
BUT IF WE'RE GOING TO DO THIS, WE'RE GOING TO DO IT AS NICELY AS WE CAN!
NO VIOLENCE!
WOW, WHAT backbone!
というオーラ
ALL... RIGHT.
BUT WE KEEP IT A SECRET FROM KARIN, GOT IT?
OF COURSE.
WHO KNOWS WHAT THAT DOPE WOULD DO IF SHE FOUND OUT?
NOD
WHAT'S THE SECRET OF YOUR SUCCESS, CALERA?
SOME SPECIAL TECHNIQUE?

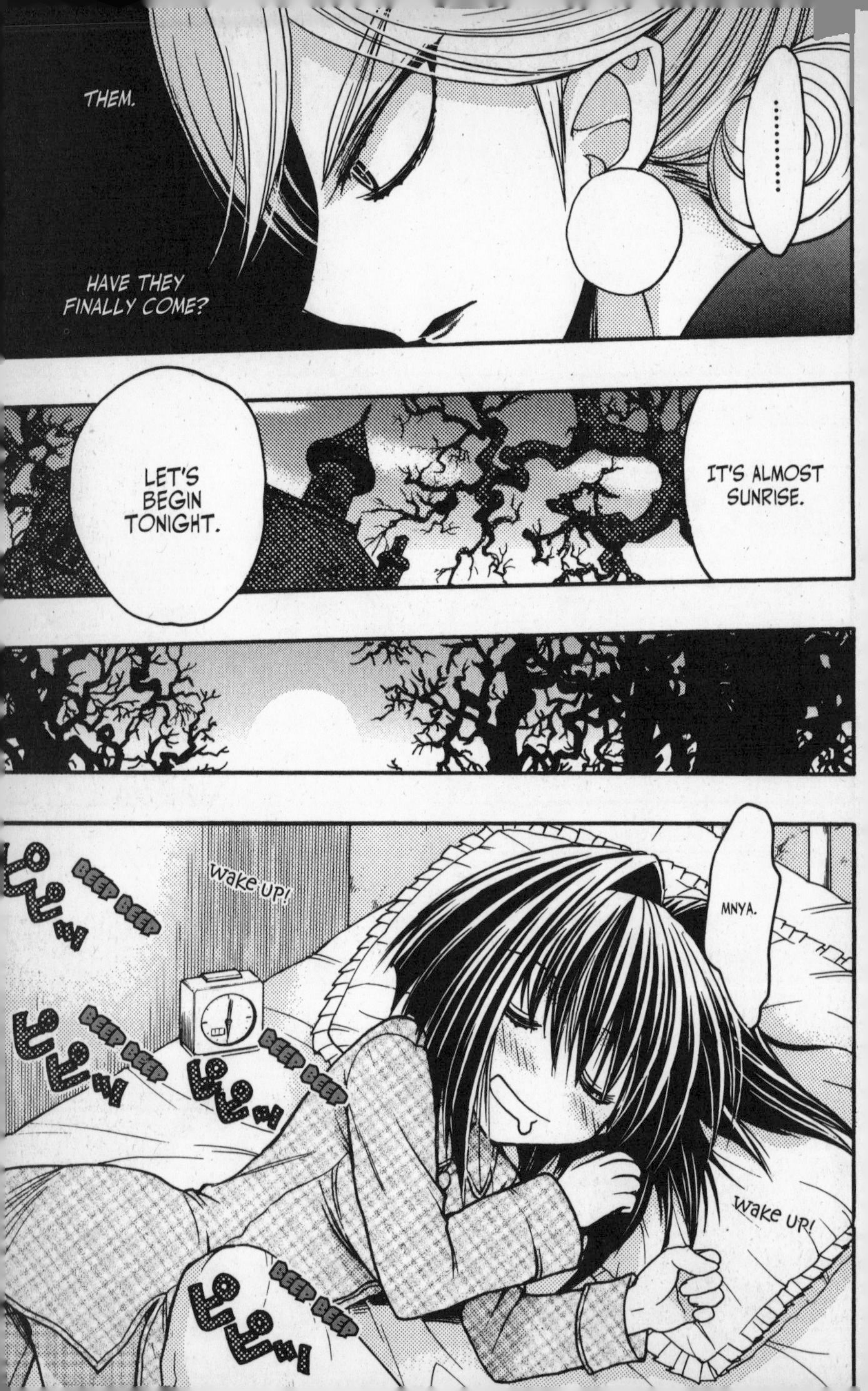
......
THEM.
HAVE THEY FINALLY COME?
IT'S ALMOST SUNRISE.
LET'S BEGIN TONIGHT.
MNYA.
wake up!
BEEP BEEP
BEEP BEEP
BEEP BEEP
wake up!
BEEP BEEP

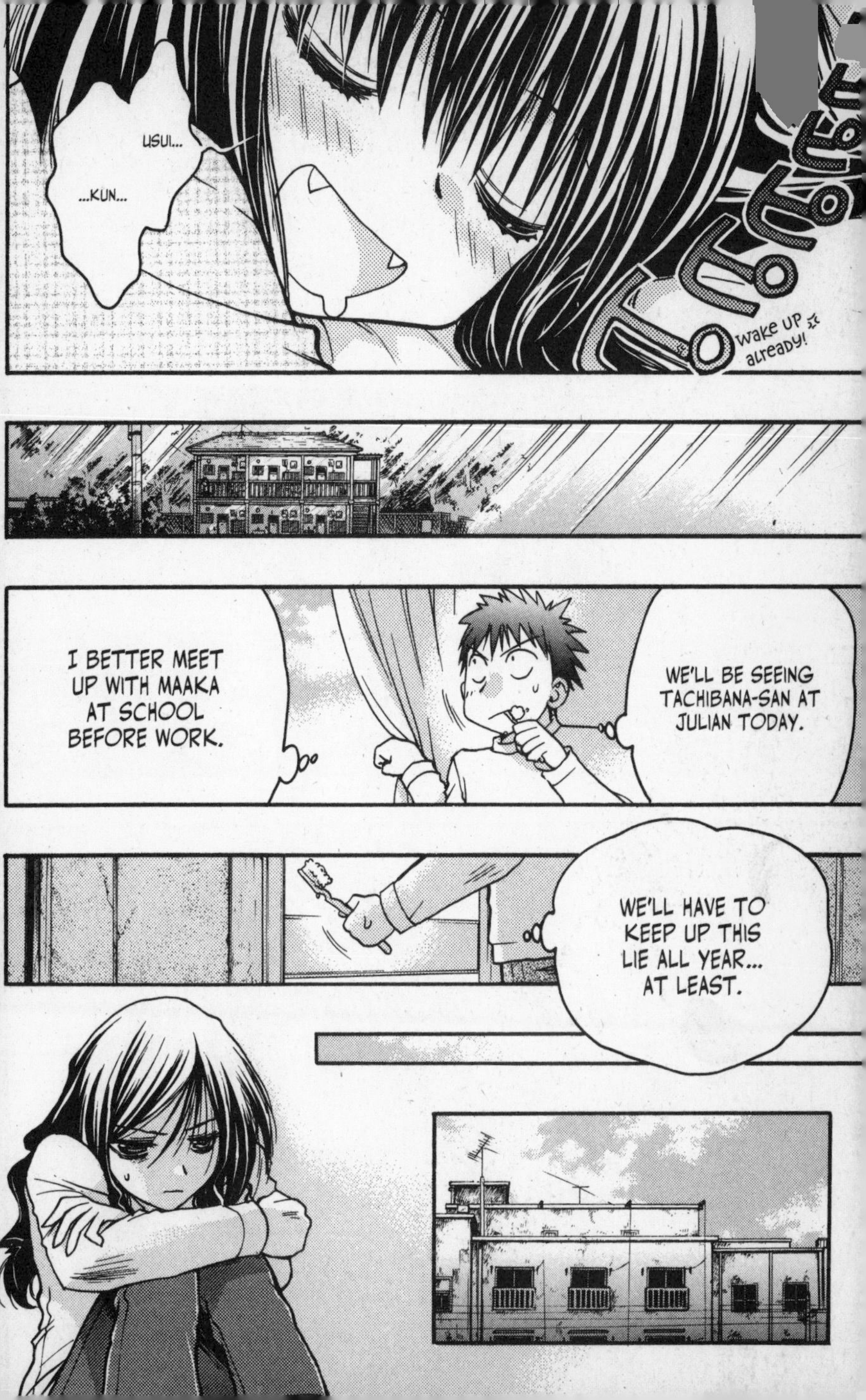
wake up already!
USUI...
...KUN...
WE'LL BE SEEING TACHIBANA-SAN AT JULIAN TODAY.
I BETTER MEET UP WITH MAAKA AT SCHOOL BEFORE WORK.
WE'LL HAVE TO KEEP UP THIS LIE ALL YEAR... AT LEAST.

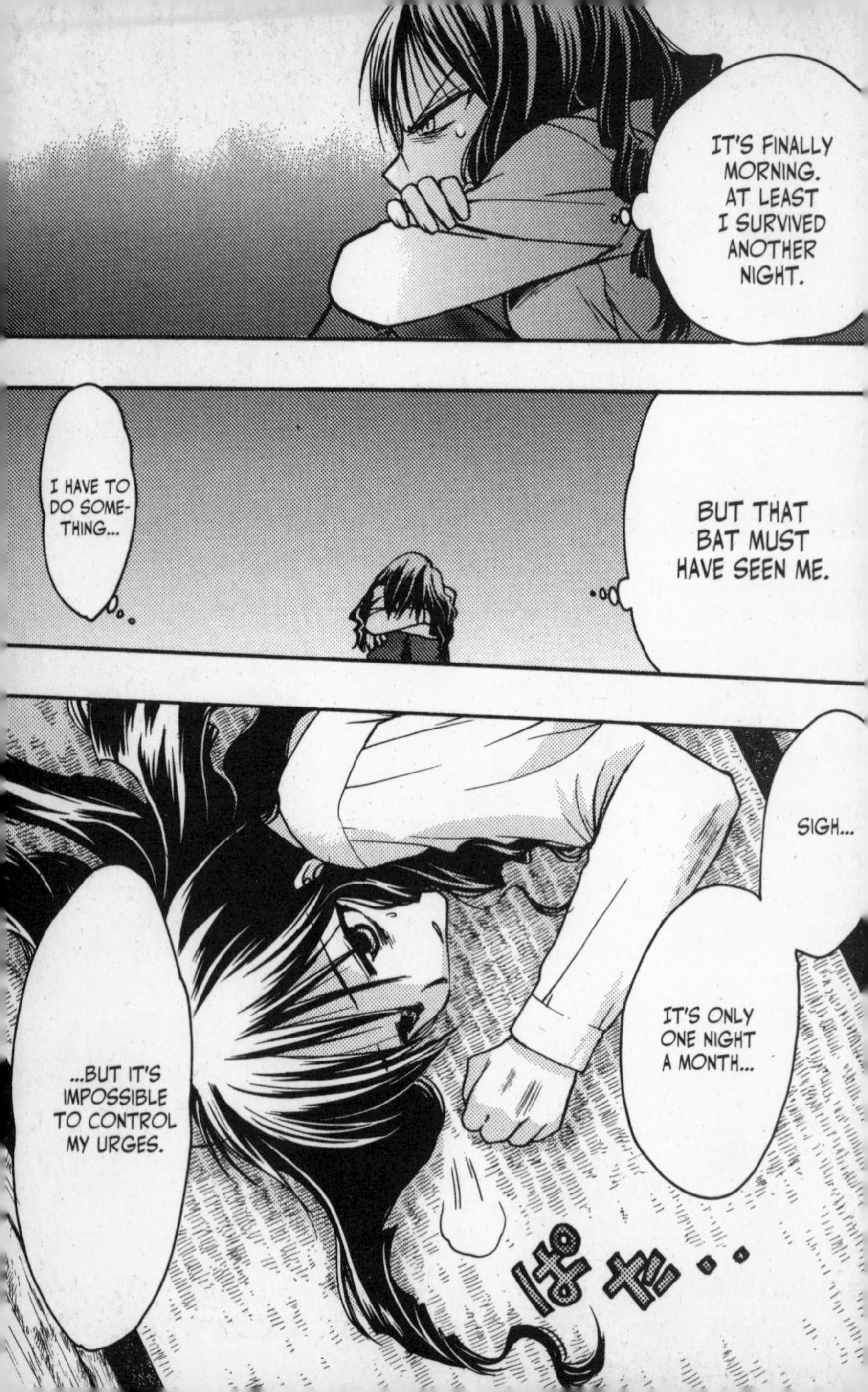
IT'S FINALLY MORNING. AT LEAST I SURVIVED ANOTHER NIGHT.
BUT THAT BAT MUST HAVE SEEN ME.
I HAVE TO DO SOME-THING...
SIGH...
IT'S ONLY ONE NIGHT A MONTH...
...BUT IT'S IMPOSSIBLE TO CONTROL MY URGES.

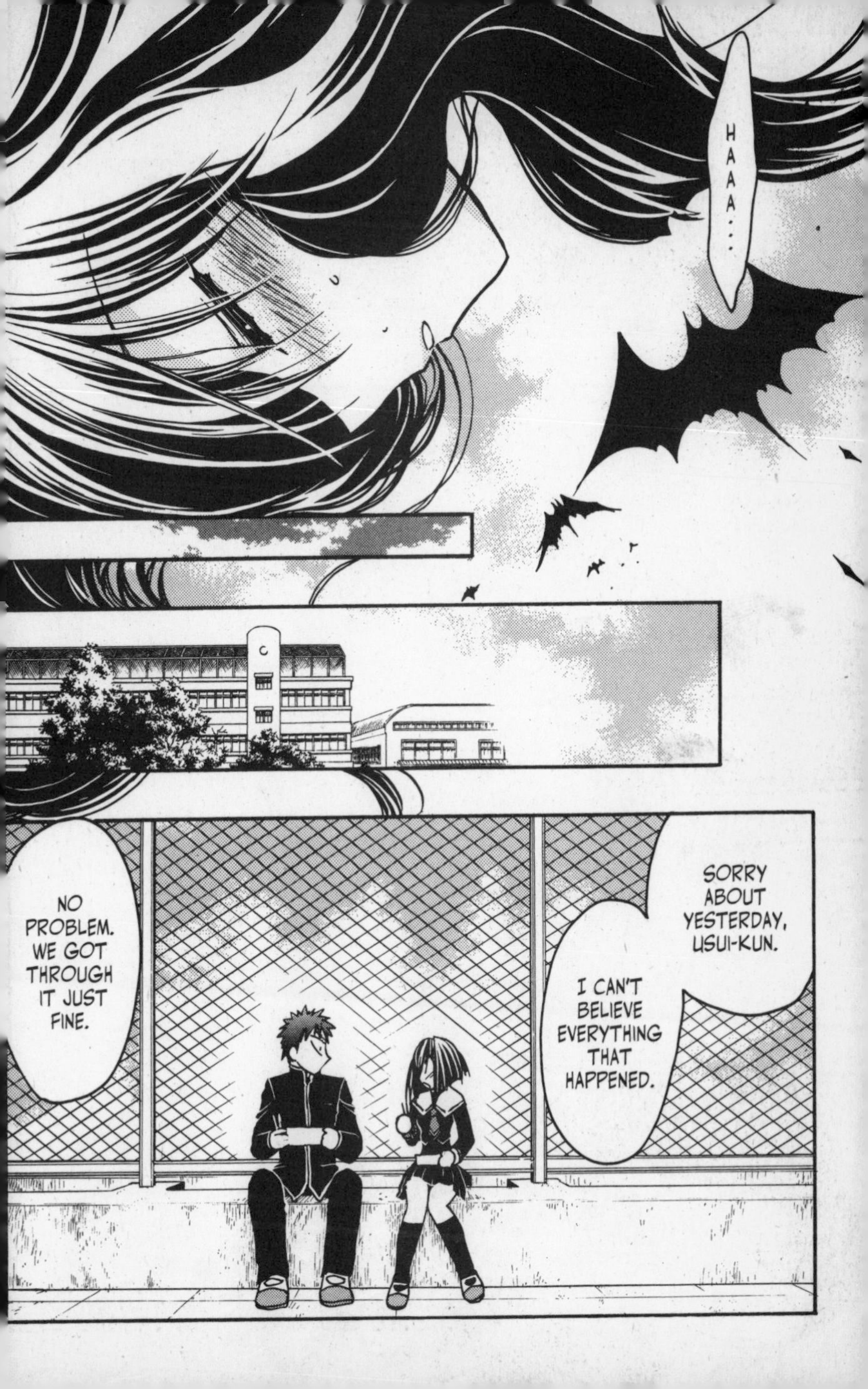
HAAA...
SORRY ABOUT YESTERDAY, USUI-KUN.
I CAN'T BELIEVE EVERYTHING THAT HAPPENED.
NO PROBLEM. WE GOT THROUGH IT JUST FINE.

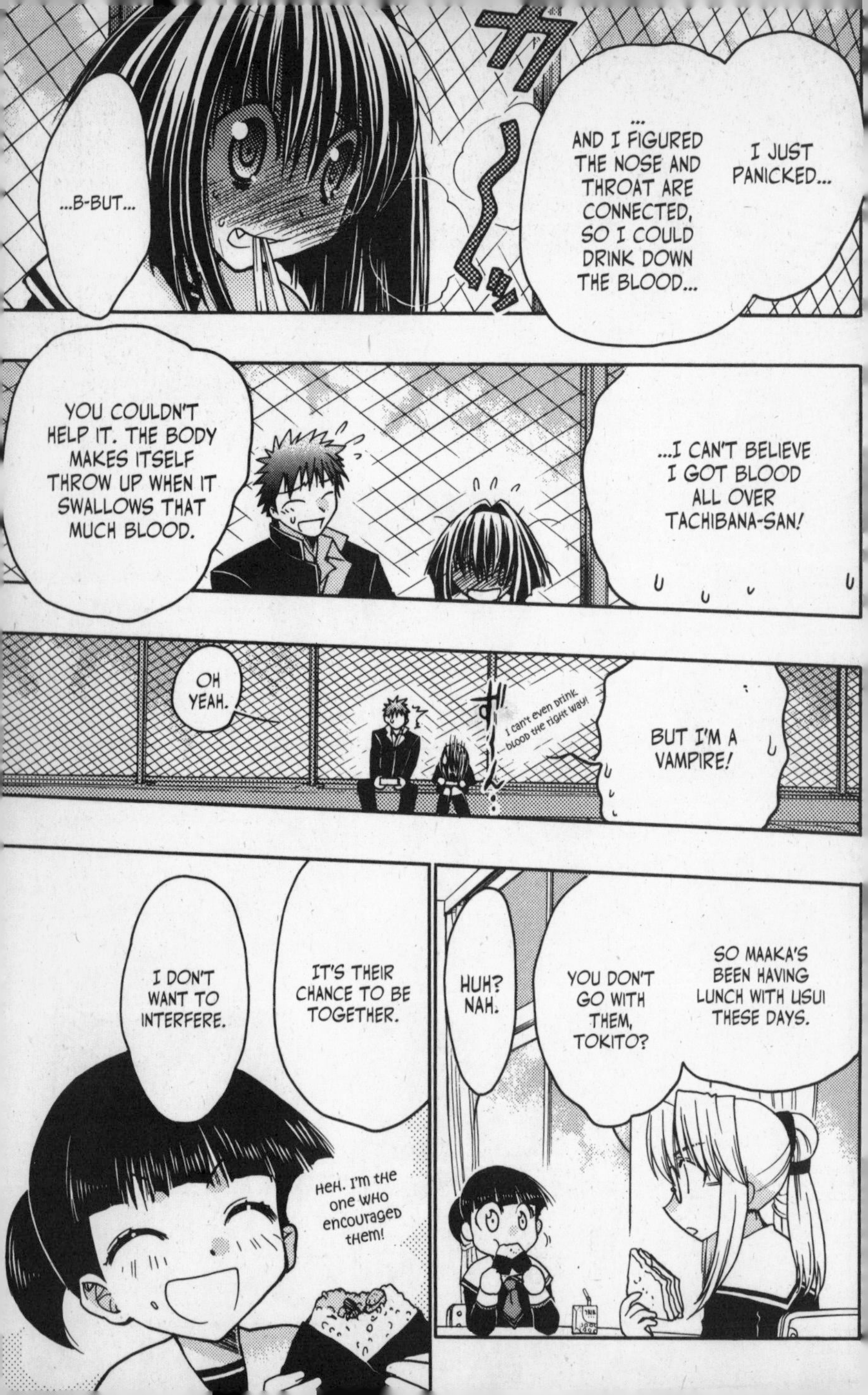
I JUST PANICKED...
... AND I FIGURED THE NOSE AND THROAT ARE CONNECTED, SO I COULD DRINK DOWN THE BLOOD...
...B-BUT...
...I CAN'T BELIEVE I GOT BLOOD ALL OVER TACHIBANA-SAN!
YOU COULDN'T HELP IT. THE BODY MAKES ITSELF THROW UP WHEN IT SWALLOWS THAT MUCH BLOOD.
BUT I'M A VAMPIRE!
I can't even drink blood the right way!
OH YEAH.
SO MAAKA'S BEEN HAVING LUNCH WITH USUI THESE DAYS.
YOU DON'T GO WITH THEM, TOKITO?
HUH? NAH.
IT'S THEIR CHANCE TO BE TOGETHER.
I DON'T WANT TO INTERFERE.
HEH. I'M THE ONE WHO ENCOURAGED THEM!

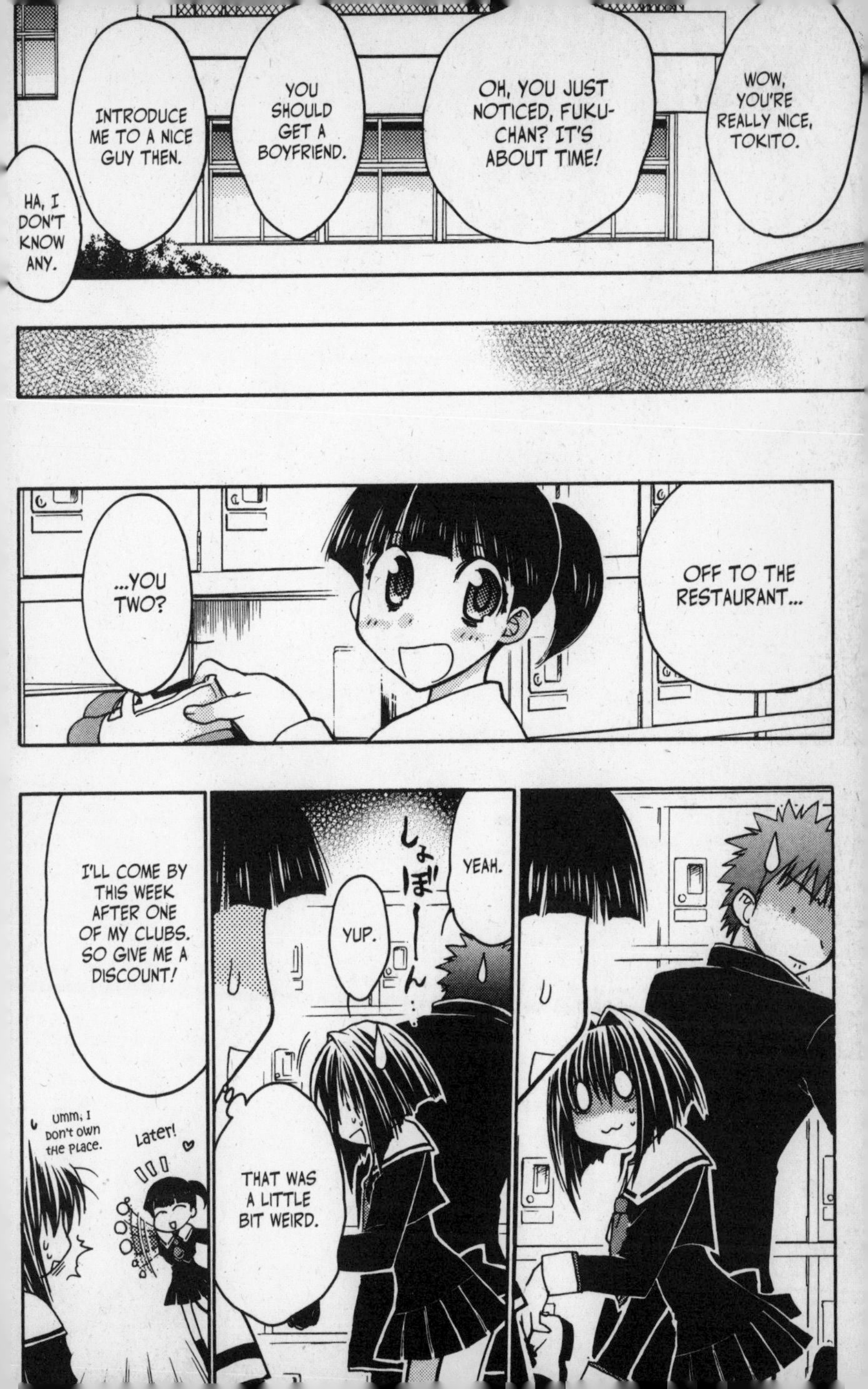
WOW, YOU'RE REALLY NICE, TOKITO.
OH, YOU JUST NOTICED, FUKU-CHAN? IT'S ABOUT TIME!
YOU SHOULD GET A BOYFRIEND.
INTRODUCE ME TO A NICE GUY THEN.
HA, I DON'T KNOW ANY.
OFF TO THE RESTAURANT...
...YOU TWO?
YEAH.
しょぼーん…
YUP.
THAT WAS A LITTLE BIT WEIRD.
I'LL COME BY THIS WEEK AFTER ONE OF MY CLUBS. SO GIVE ME A DISCOUNT!
Later!
Umm, I don't own the place.

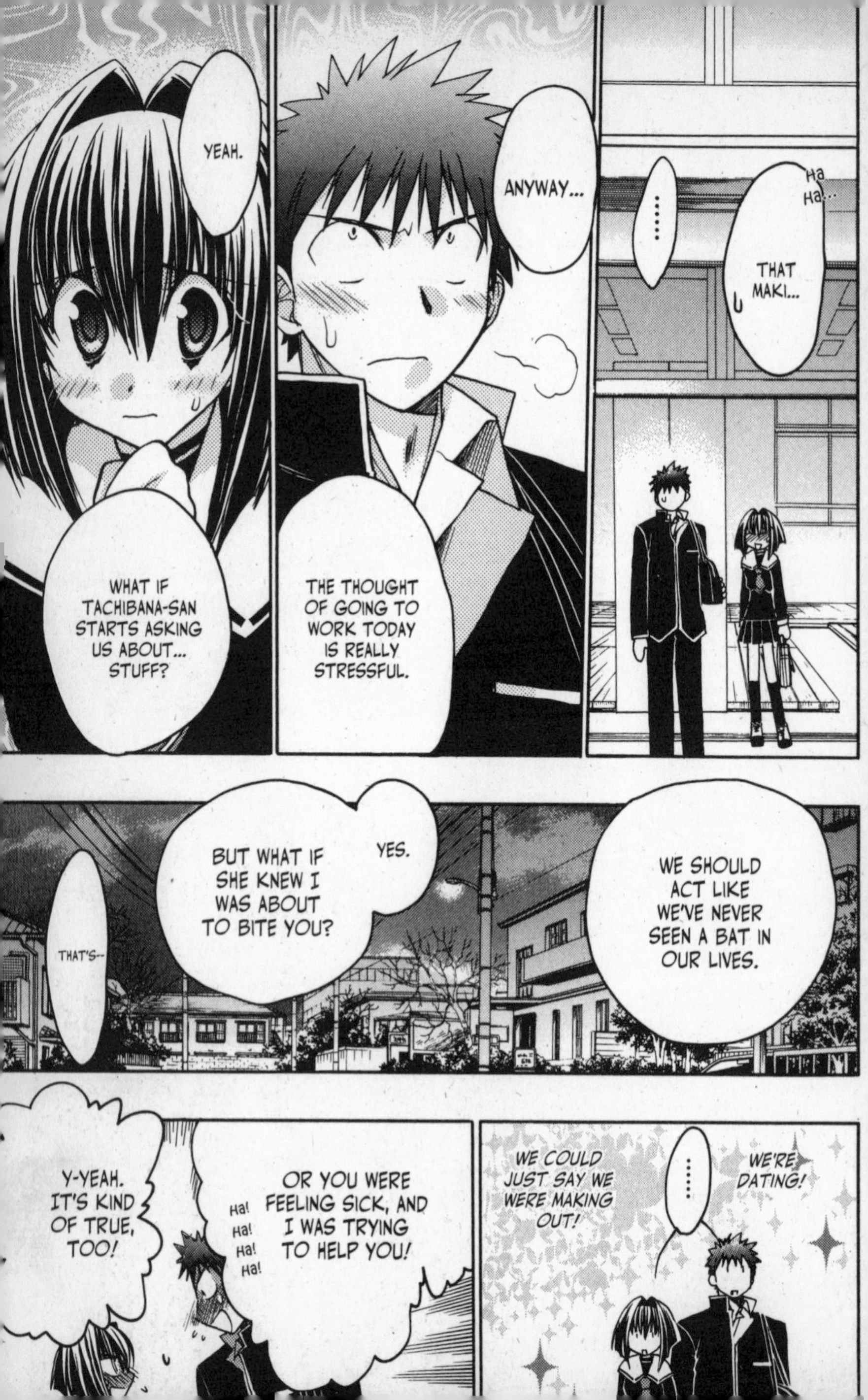

Ha Ha...
THAT MAKI...
U
......
ANYWAY...
THE THOUGHT OF GOING TO WORK TODAY IS REALLY STRESSFUL.
YEAH.
WHAT IF TACHIBANA-SAN STARTS ASKING US ABOUT... STUFF?
WE SHOULD ACT LIKE WE'VE NEVER SEEN A BAT IN OUR LIVES.
YES.
BUT WHAT IF SHE KNEW I WAS ABOUT TO BITE YOU?
THAT'S--
WE'RE DATING!
......
WE COULD JUST SAY WE WERE MAKING OUT!
OR YOU WERE FEELING SICK, AND I WAS TRYING TO HELP YOU!
Ha! Ha! Ha! Ha!
Y-YEAH. IT'S KIND OF TRUE, TOO!

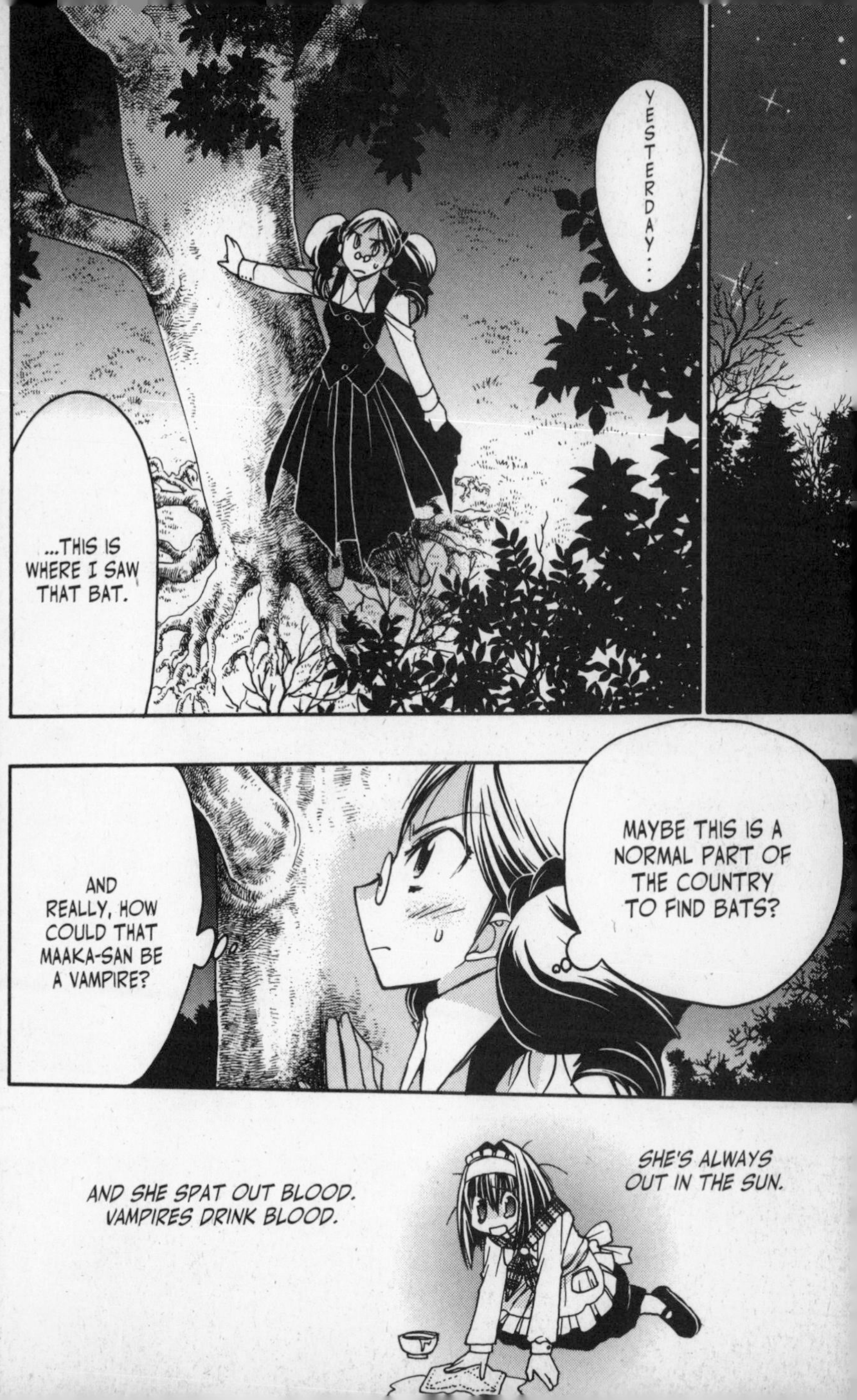
YESTERDAY...
...THIS IS WHERE I SAW THAT BAT.
MAYBE THIS IS A NORMAL PART OF THE COUNTRY TO FIND BATS?
AND REALLY, HOW COULD THAT MAAKA-SAN BE A VAMPIRE?
SHE'S ALWAYS OUT IN THE SUN.
AND SHE SPAT OUT BLOOD. VAMPIRES DRINK BLOOD.

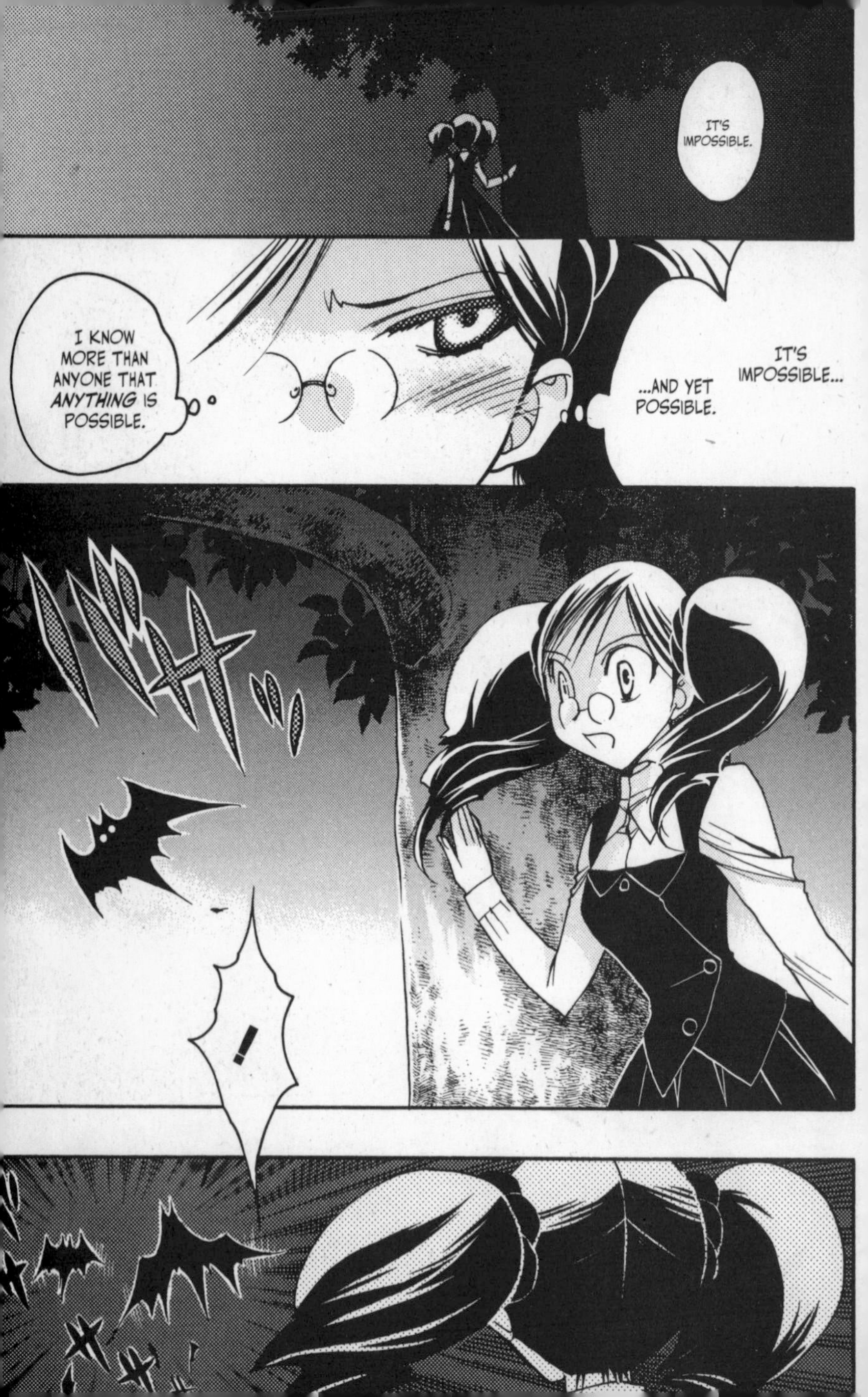
IT'S IMPOSSIBLE.
IT'S IMPOSSIBLE...
...AND YET POSSIBLE.
I KNOW MORE THAN ANYONE THAT *ANYTHING* IS POSSIBLE.
!

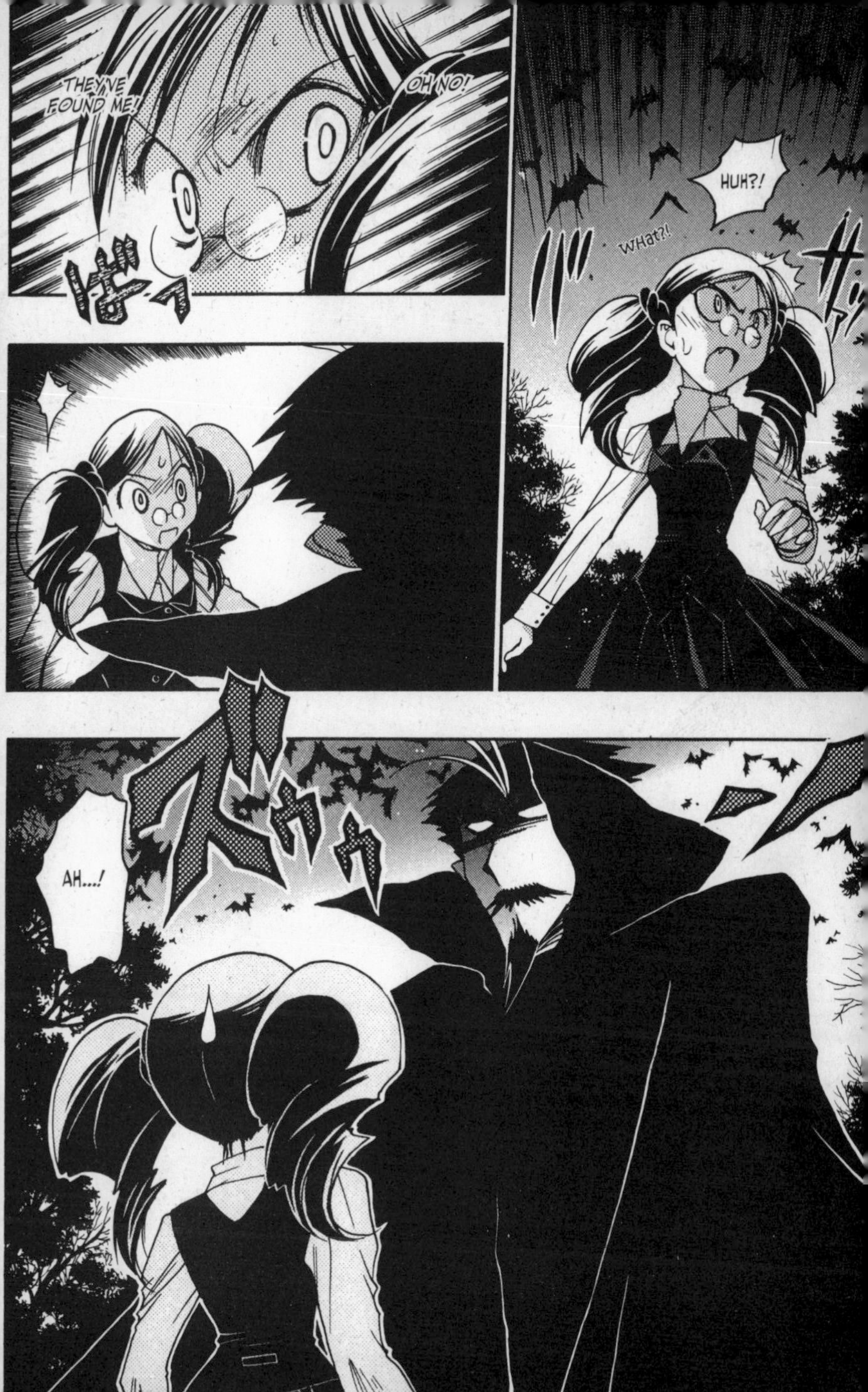
HUH?!
WHAT?!
OH NO!
THEY'VE FOUND ME!
AH...!

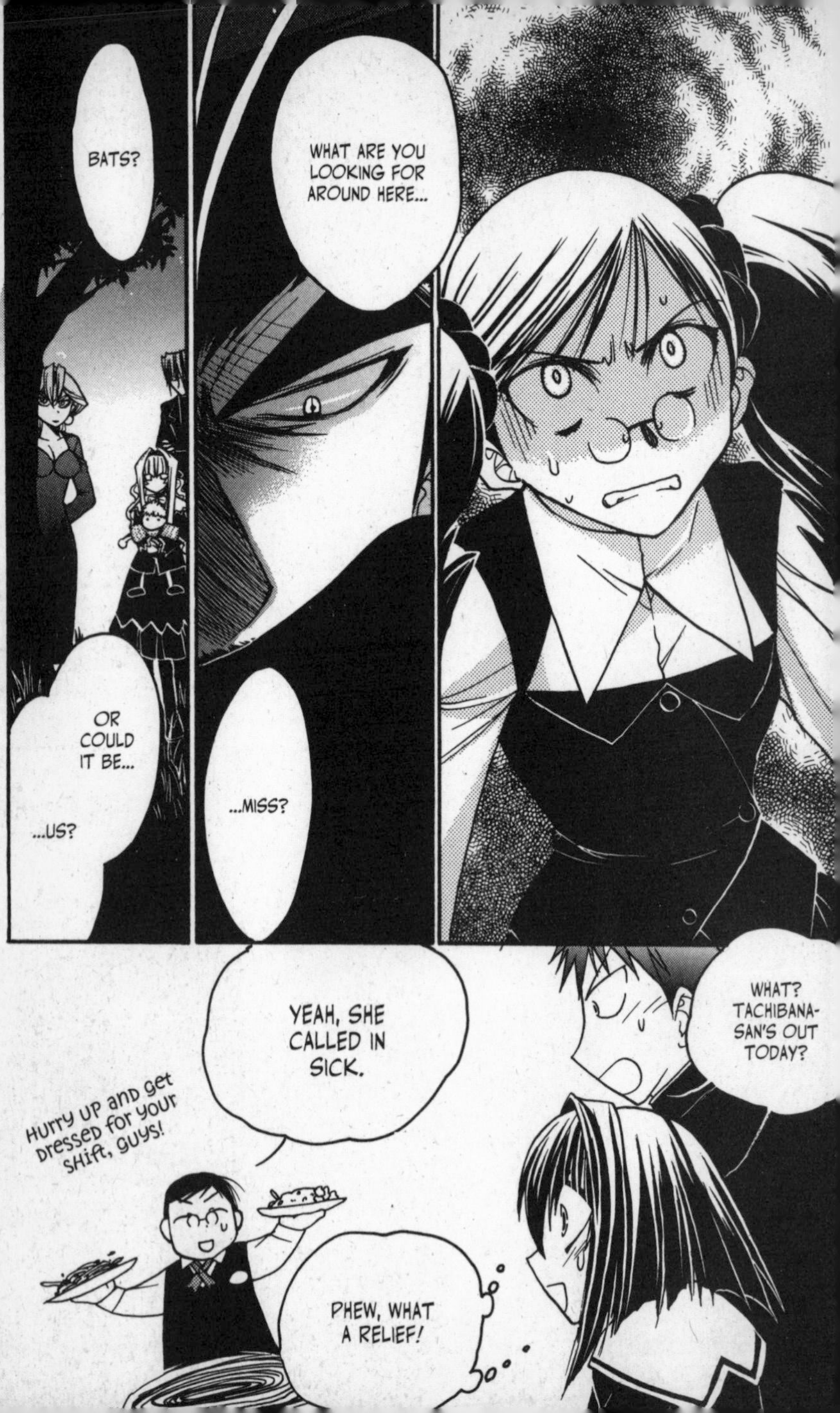
WHAT ARE YOU LOOKING FOR AROUND HERE...
...MISS?
BATS?
OR COULD IT BE...
...US?
WHAT? TACHIBANA-SAN'S OUT TODAY?
YEAH, SHE CALLED IN SICK.
Hurry up and get dressed for your shift, guys!
PHEW, WHAT A RELIEF!

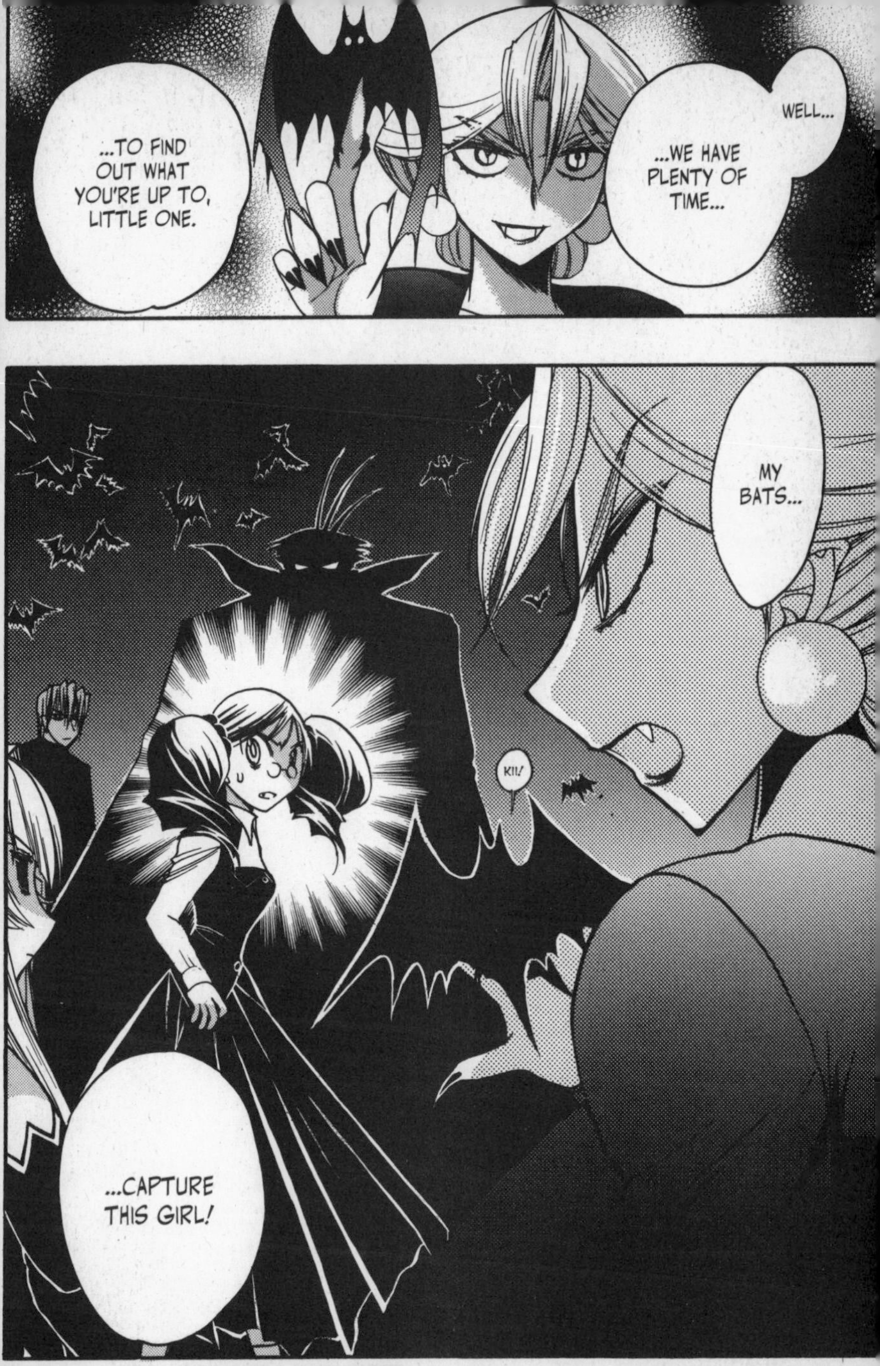
WELL...
...WE HAVE PLENTY OF TIME...
...TO FIND OUT WHAT YOU'RE UP TO, LITTLE ONE.
MY BATS...
KII!
...CAPTURE THIS GIRL!

38TH EMBARRASSMENT END

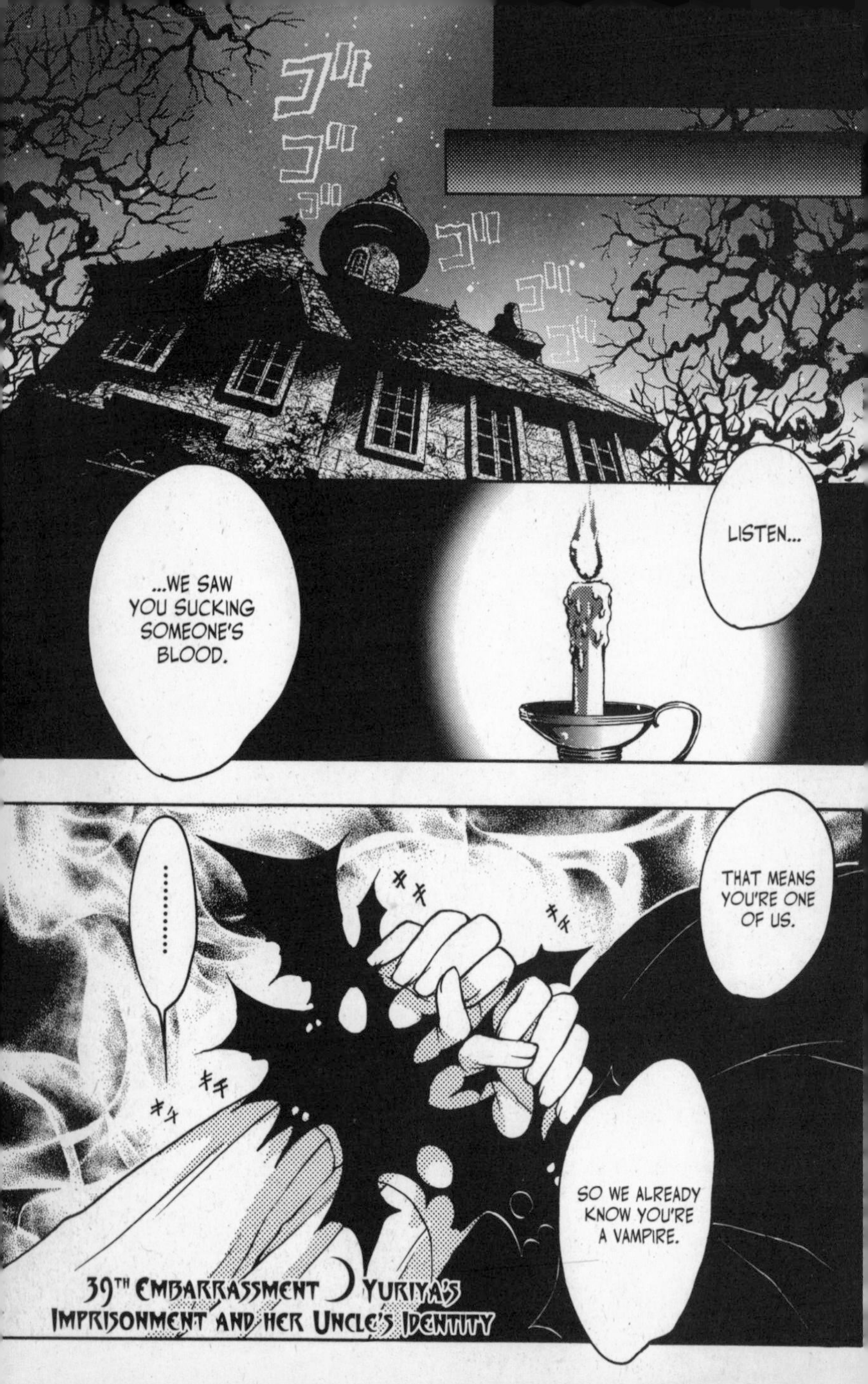
LISTEN...
...WE SAW YOU SUCKING SOMEONE'S BLOOD.
THAT MEANS YOU'RE ONE OF US.
SO WE ALREADY KNOW YOU'RE A VAMPIRE.
......
39TH EMBARRASSMENT YURIYA'S IMPRISONMENT AND HER UNCLE'S IDENTITY

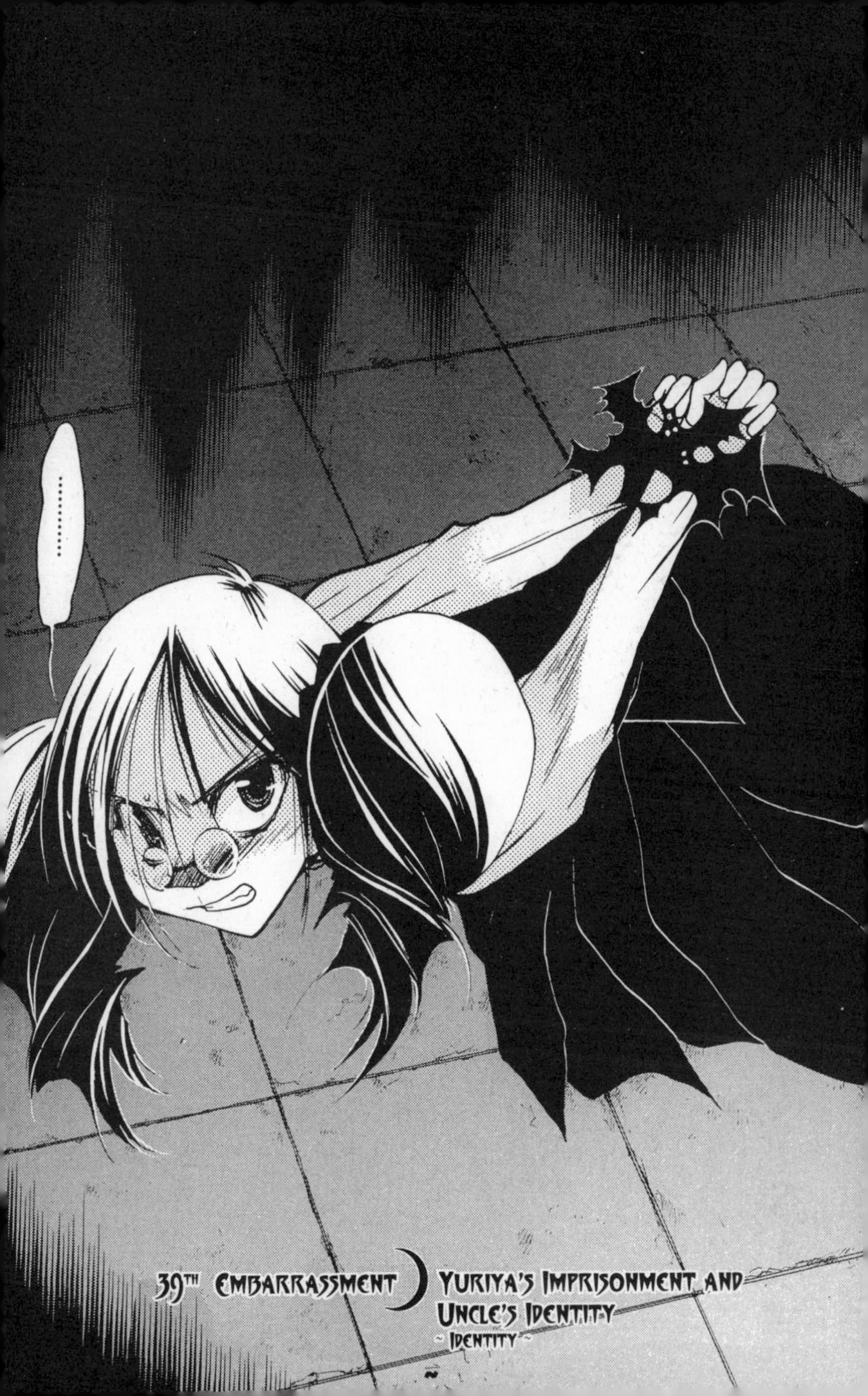
......
39th Embarrassment Yuriya's Imprisonment and Uncle's Identity
~ Identity ~

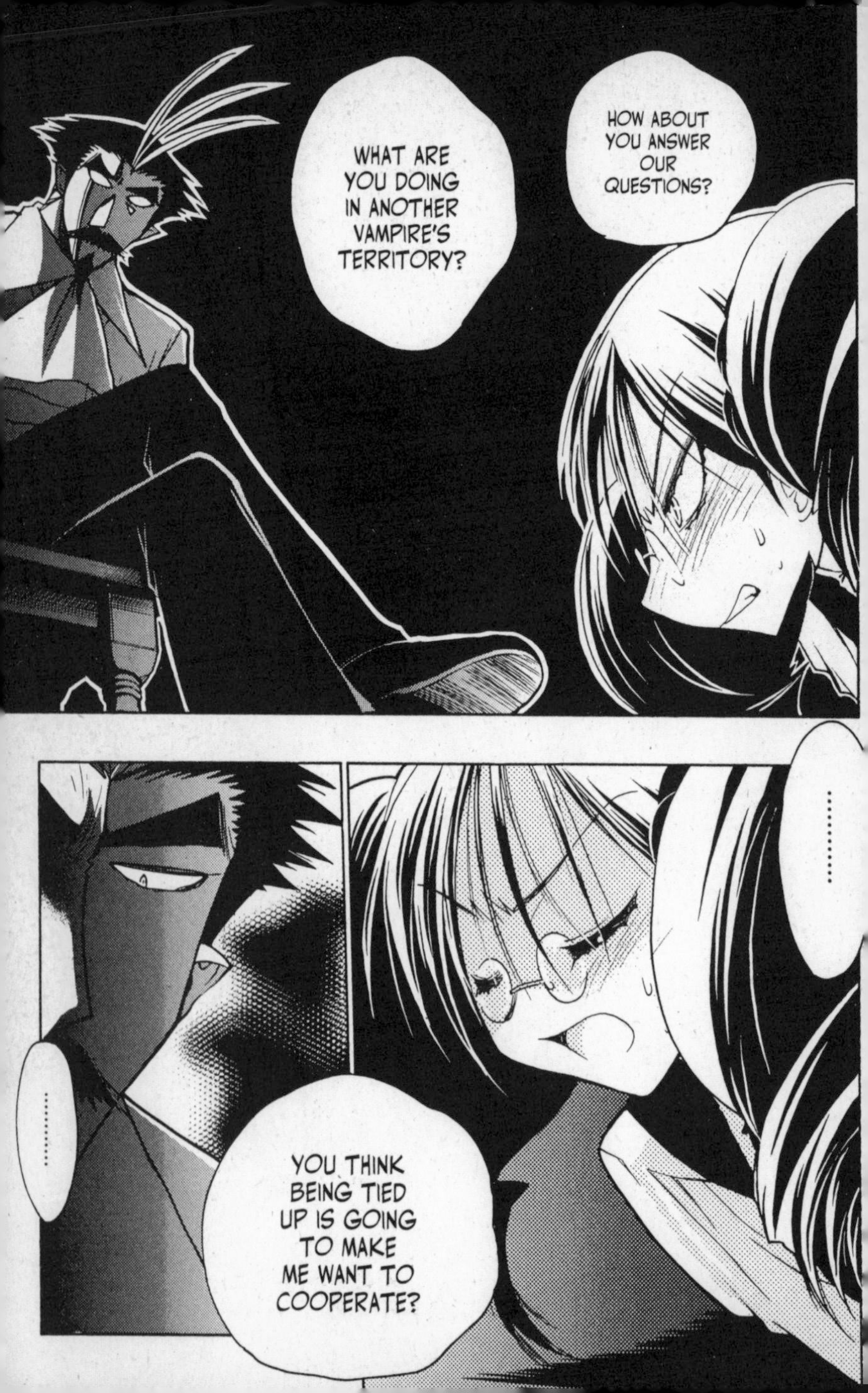
HOW ABOUT YOU ANSWER OUR QUESTIONS?
WHAT ARE YOU DOING IN ANOTHER VAMPIRE'S TERRITORY?
......
YOU THINK BEING TIED UP IS GOING TO MAKE ME WANT TO COOPERATE?
......

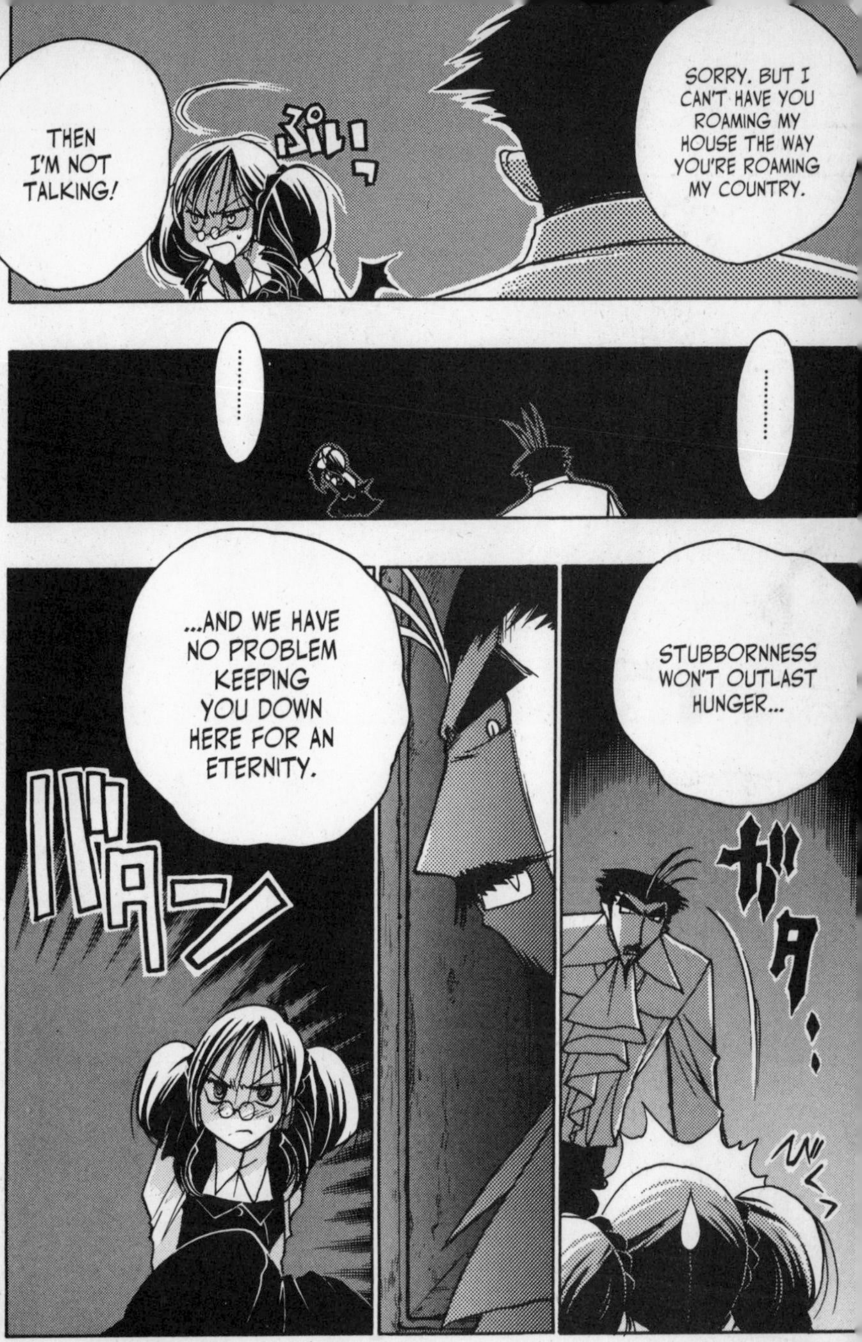
SORRY. BUT I CAN'T HAVE YOU ROAMING MY HOUSE THE WAY YOU'RE ROAMING MY COUNTRY.
ぷいっ
THEN I'M NOT TALKING!
......
......
STUBBORNNESS WON'T OUTLAST HUNGER...
ガタ..
...AND WE HAVE NO PROBLEM KEEPING YOU DOWN HERE FOR AN ETERNITY.
バターン

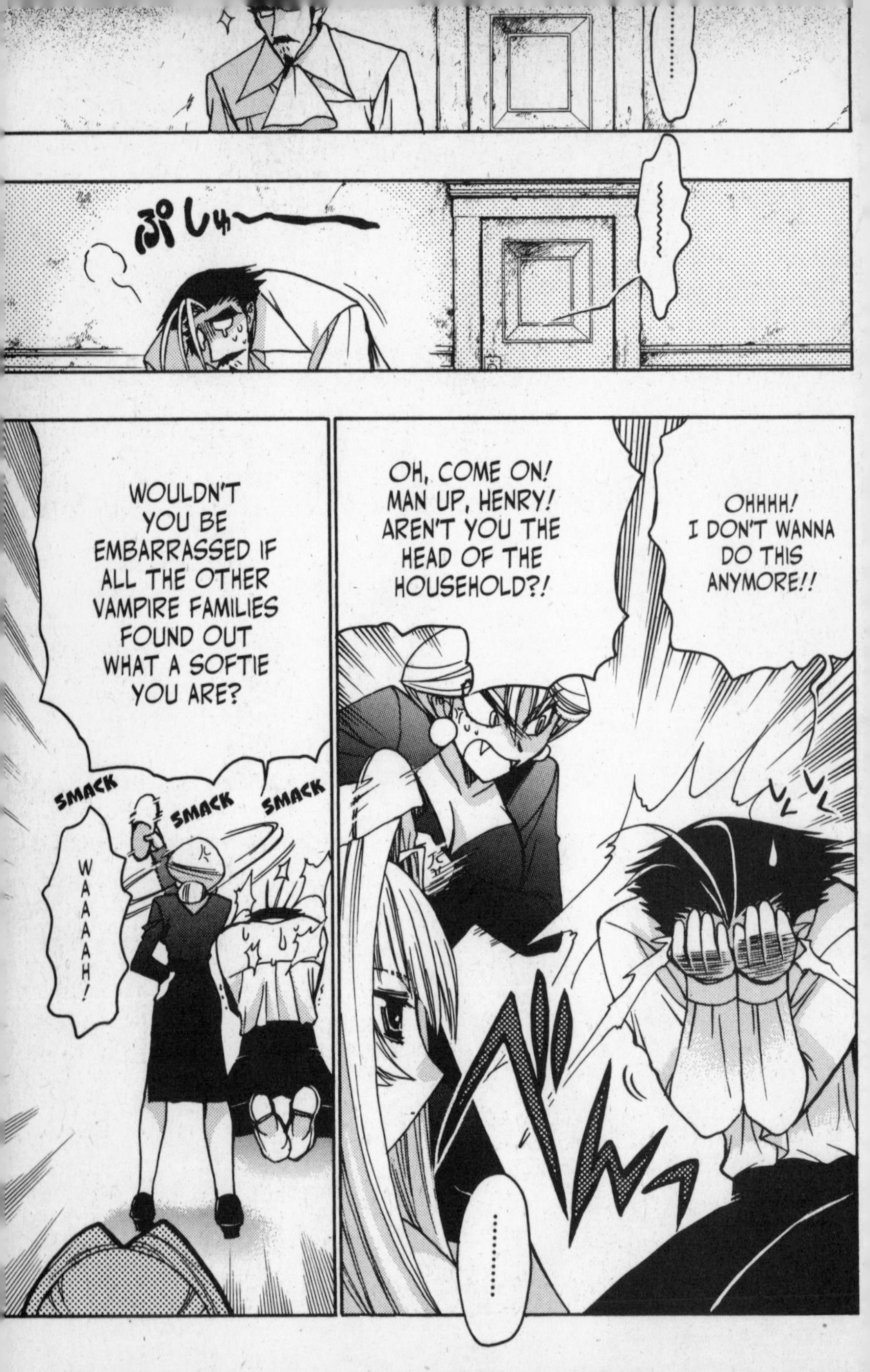
......
ぷしゅ〜〜
OHHHH! I DON'T WANNA DO THIS ANYMORE!!
OH, COME ON! MAN UP, HENRY! AREN'T YOU THE HEAD OF THE HOUSEHOLD?!
......
WOULDN'T YOU BE EMBARRASSED IF ALL THE OTHER VAMPIRE FAMILIES FOUND OUT WHAT A SOFTIE YOU ARE?
SMACK
SMACK
SMACK
WAAAAAH!

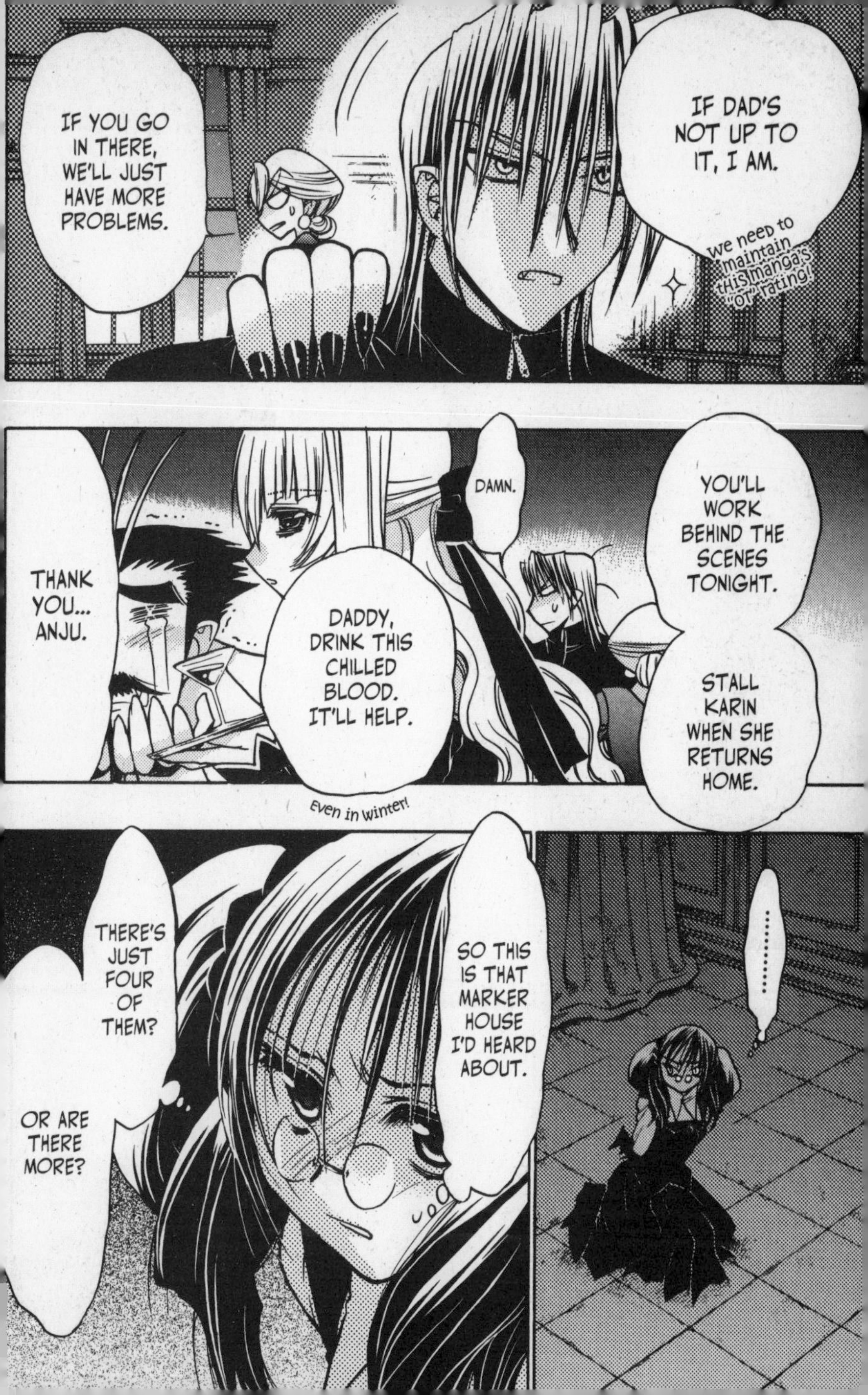
IF DAD'S NOT UP TO IT, I AM.
We need to maintain this manga's "OT" rating!
IF YOU GO IN THERE, WE'LL JUST HAVE MORE PROBLEMS.
YOU'LL WORK BEHIND THE SCENES TONIGHT.
STALL KARIN WHEN SHE RETURNS HOME.
DAMN.
DADDY, DRINK THIS CHILLED BLOOD. IT'LL HELP.
Even in winter!
THANK YOU... ANJU.
......
SO THIS IS THAT MARKER HOUSE I'D HEARD ABOUT.
THERE'S JUST FOUR OF THEM?
OR ARE THERE MORE?

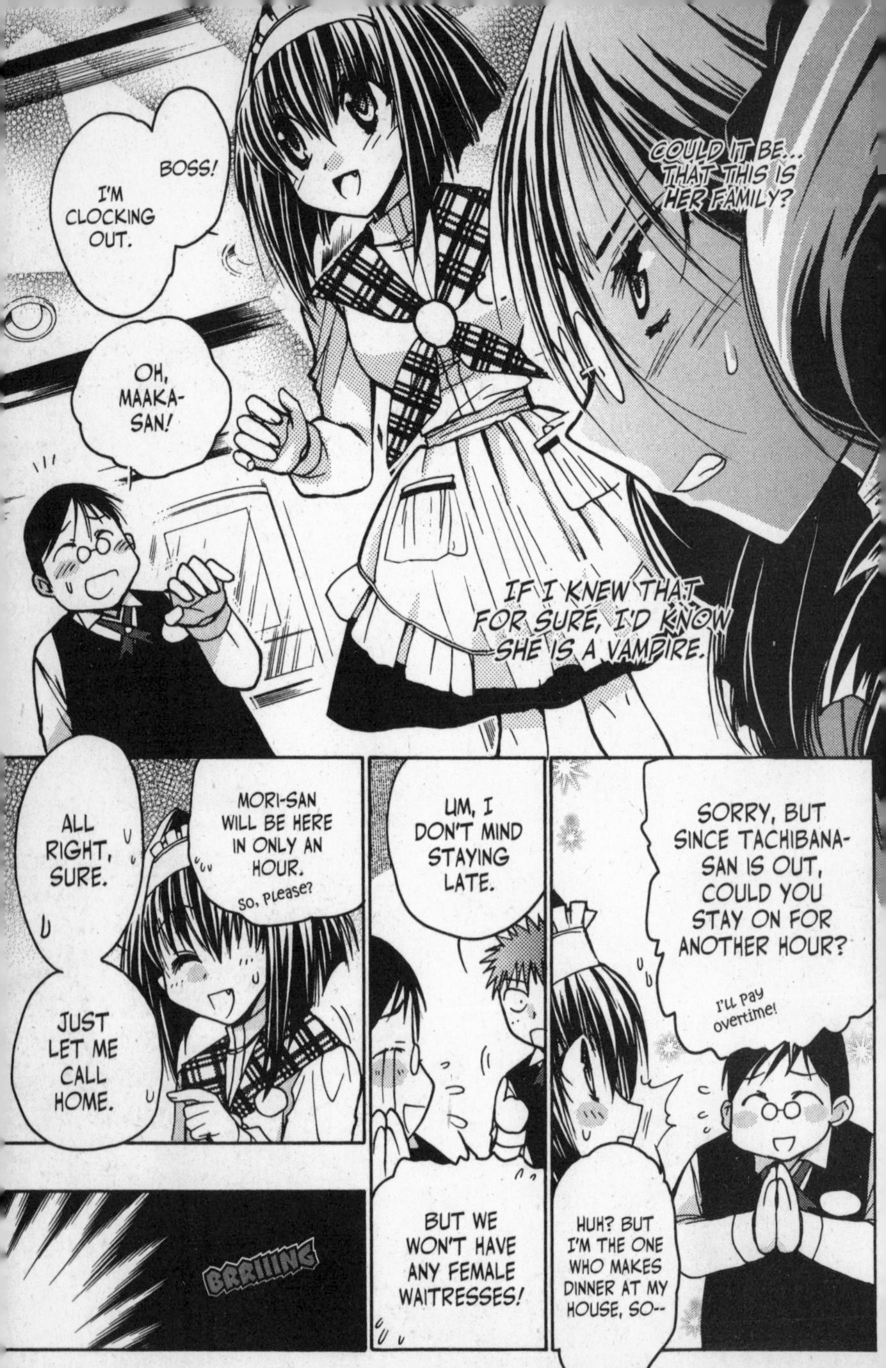
COULD IT BE... THAT THIS IS HER FAMILY?
BOSS! I'M CLOCKING OUT.
OH, MAAKA-SAN!
IF I KNEW THAT FOR SURE, I'D KNOW SHE IS A VAMPIRE.
SORRY, BUT SINCE TACHIBANA-SAN IS OUT, COULD YOU STAY ON FOR ANOTHER HOUR?
I'll pay overtime!
HUH? BUT I'M THE ONE WHO MAKES DINNER AT MY HOUSE, SO--
UM, I DON'T MIND STAYING LATE.
BUT WE WON'T HAVE ANY FEMALE WAITRESSES!
MORI-SAN WILL BE HERE IN ONLY AN HOUR.
So, please?
ALL RIGHT, SURE.
JUST LET ME CALL HOME.
BRRIIING

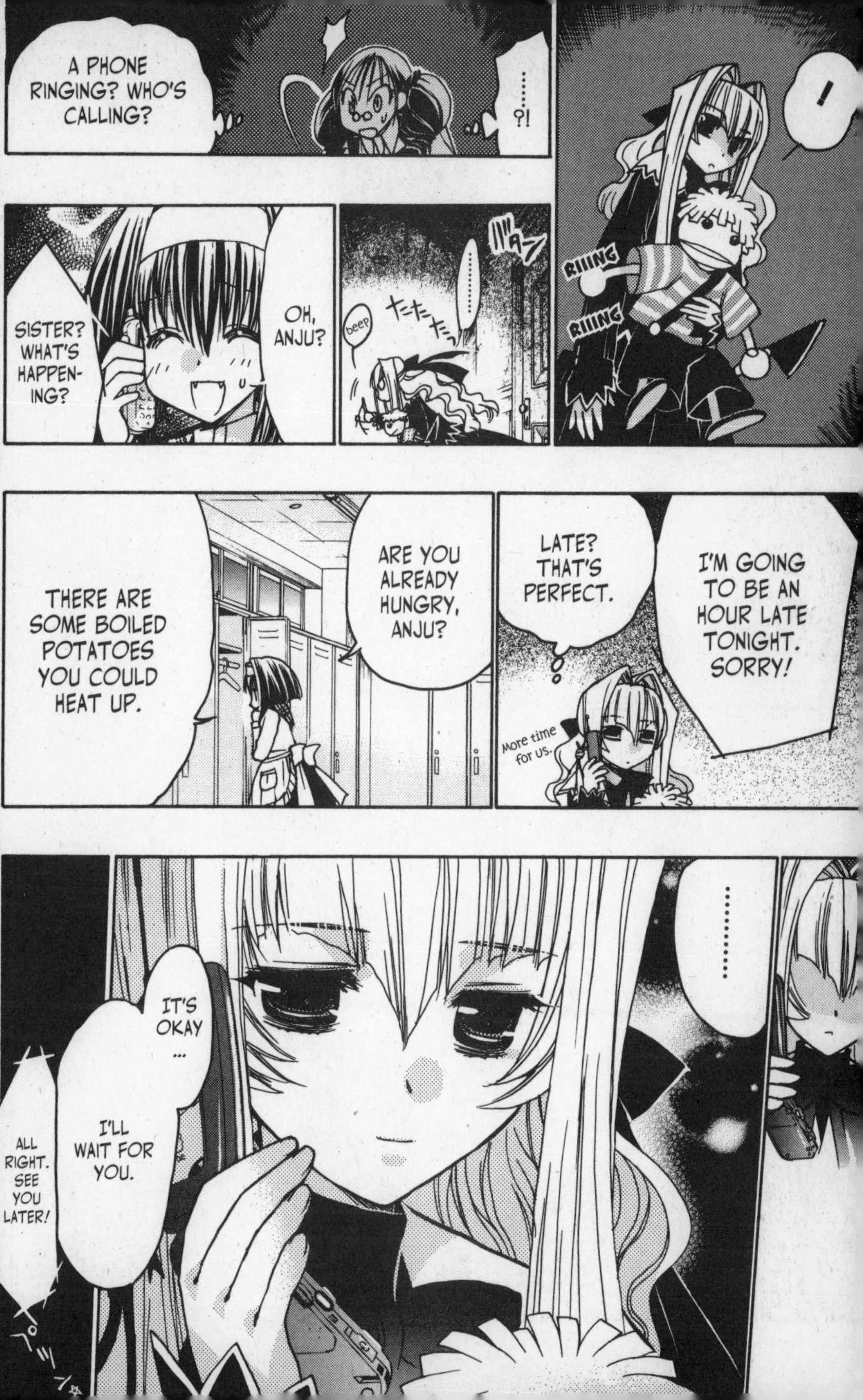
!
RIIING
RIIING
......?!
A PHONE RINGING? WHO'S CALLING?
......
beep
OH, ANJU?
SISTER? WHAT'S HAPPENING?
I'M GOING TO BE AN HOUR LATE TONIGHT. SORRY!
LATE? THAT'S PERFECT.
More time for us.
ARE YOU ALREADY HUNGRY, ANJU?
THERE ARE SOME BOILED POTATOES YOU COULD HEAT UP.
......
IT'S OKAY ...
I'LL WAIT FOR YOU.
ALL RIGHT. SEE YOU LATER!

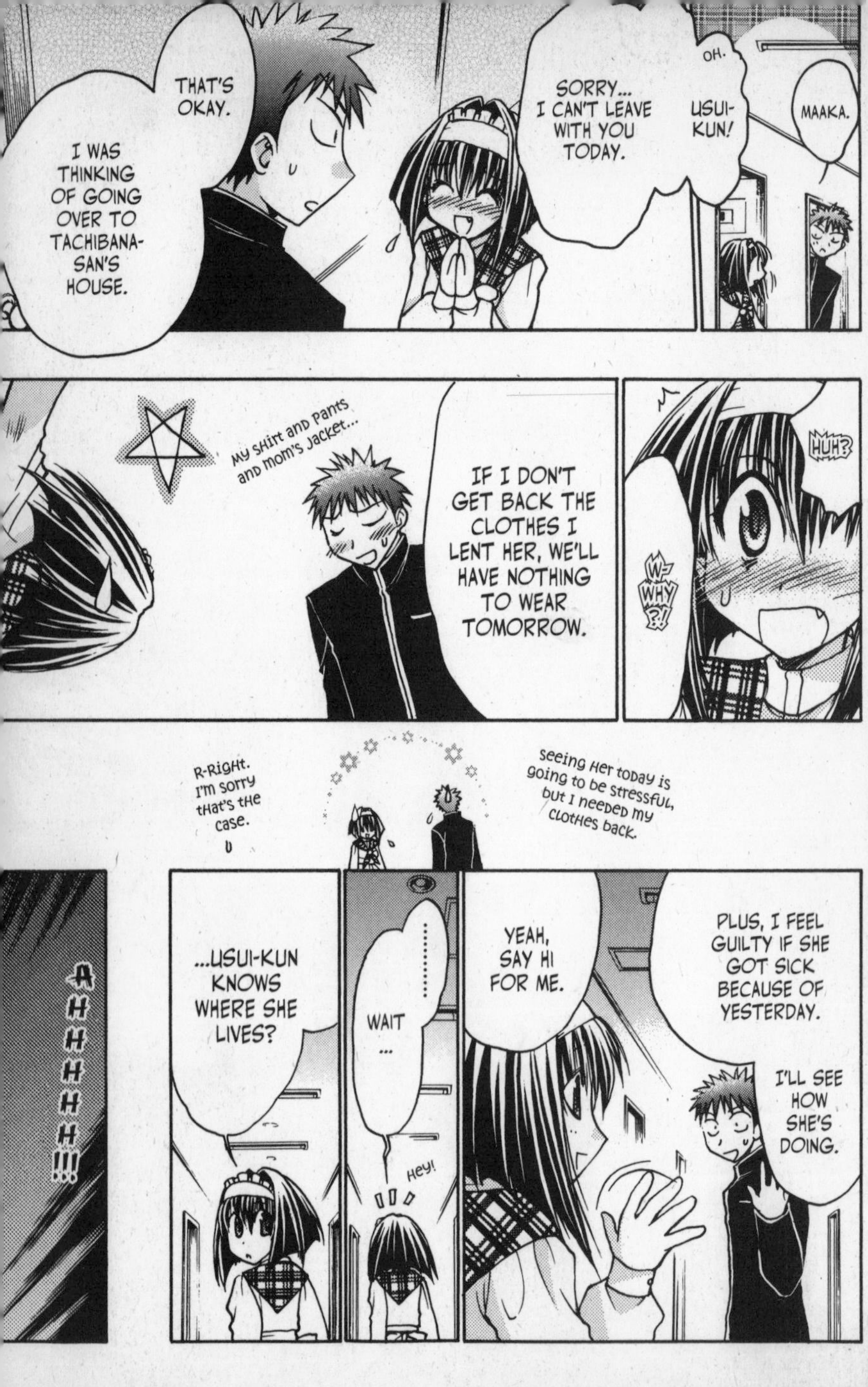
MAAKA.
OH. USUI-KUN!
SORRY... I CAN'T LEAVE WITH YOU TODAY.
THAT'S OKAY.
I WAS THINKING OF GOING OVER TO TACHIBANA-SAN'S HOUSE.
HUH?
W-WHY?!
IF I DON'T GET BACK THE CLOTHES I LENT HER, WE'LL HAVE NOTHING TO WEAR TOMORROW.
My shirt and pants and mom's jacket...
Seeing her today is going to be stressful, but I needed my clothes back.
R-Right. I'm sorry that's the case.
PLUS, I FEEL GUILTY IF SHE GOT SICK BECAUSE OF YESTERDAY.
I'LL SEE HOW SHE'S DOING.
YEAH, SAY HI FOR ME.
....
WAIT...
Hey!
...USUI-KUN KNOWS WHERE SHE LIVES?
AHHHHHHH!!!

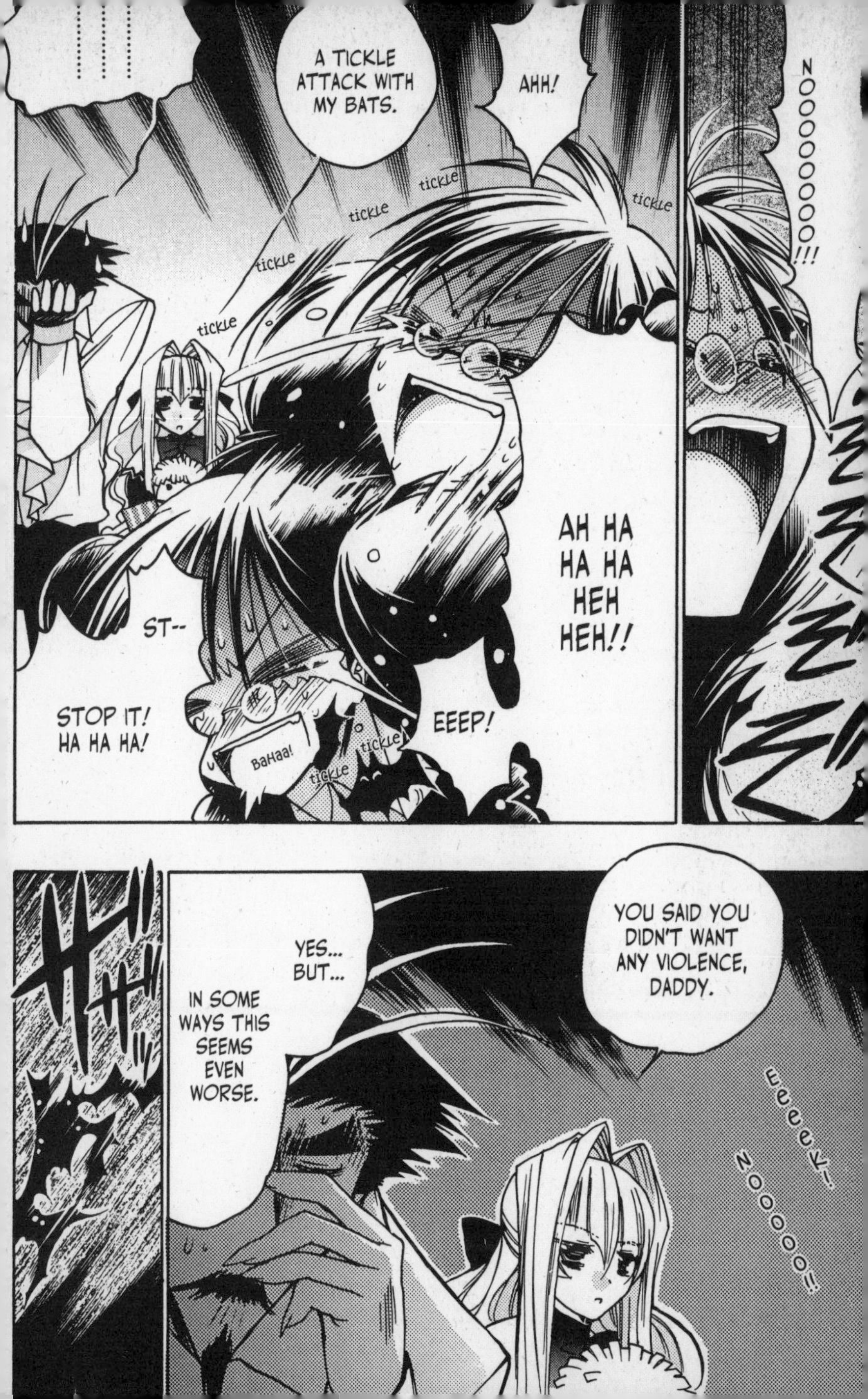
NOOOOOOOOO!!!
AHH!
A TICKLE ATTACK WITH MY BATS.
tickle
tickle
tickle
tickle
tickle
AH HA HA HA HEH HEH!!
EEEP!
ST--
STOP IT! HA HA HA!
tickle
tickle
BaHaa!
YOU SAID YOU DIDN'T WANT ANY VIOLENCE, DADDY.
Eeeek! NOOOOOO!!
YES... BUT...
IN SOME WAYS THIS SEEMS EVEN WORSE.

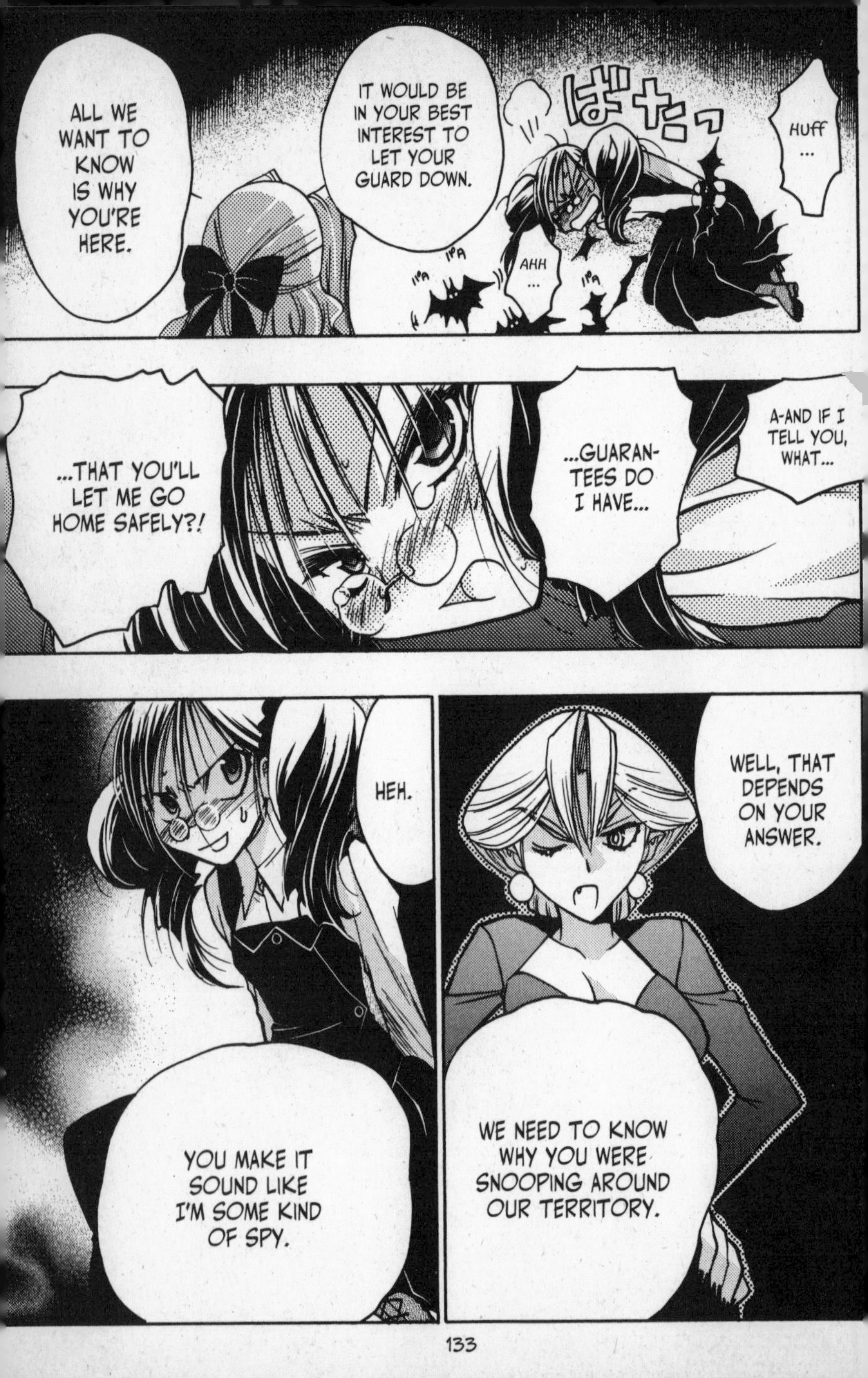
HUFF ...
ばたっ
IT WOULD BE IN YOUR BEST INTEREST TO LET YOUR GUARD DOWN.
AHH ...
IPA
IPA
IPA
IPA
ALL WE WANT TO KNOW IS WHY YOU'RE HERE.
A-AND IF I TELL YOU, WHAT...
...GUARANTEES DO I HAVE...
...THAT YOU'LL LET ME GO HOME SAFELY?!
WELL, THAT DEPENDS ON YOUR ANSWER.
WE NEED TO KNOW WHY YOU WERE SNOOPING AROUND OUR TERRITORY.
HEH.
YOU MAKE IT SOUND LIKE I'M SOME KIND OF SPY.

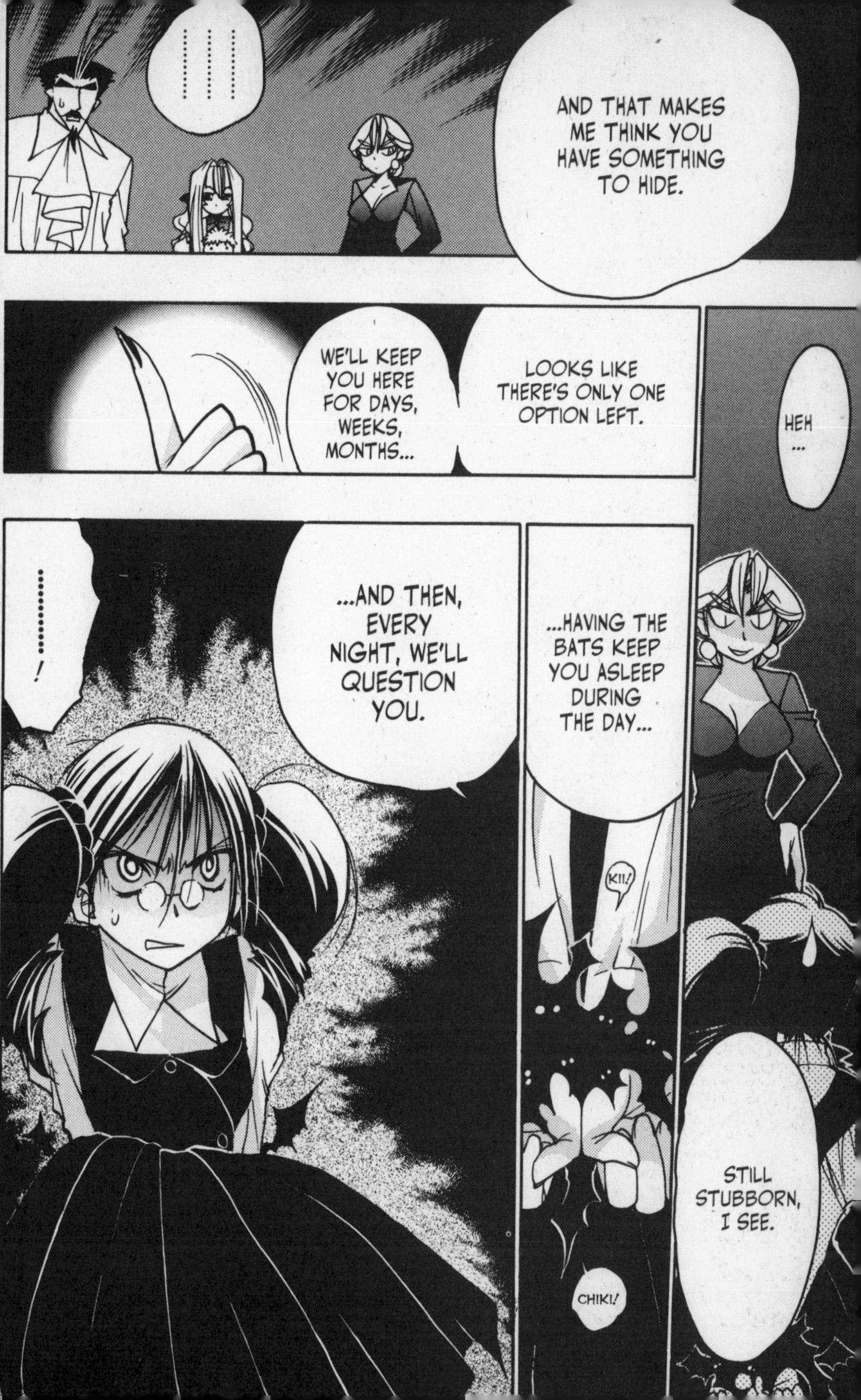
AND THAT MAKES ME THINK YOU HAVE SOMETHING TO HIDE.
......
HEH...
STILL STUBBORN, I SEE.
LOOKS LIKE THERE'S ONLY ONE OPTION LEFT.
WE'LL KEEP YOU HERE FOR DAYS, WEEKS, MONTHS...
...HAVING THE BATS KEEP YOU ASLEEP DURING THE DAY...
KII!
CHIKI!
...AND THEN, EVERY NIGHT, WE'LL QUESTION YOU.
.........!

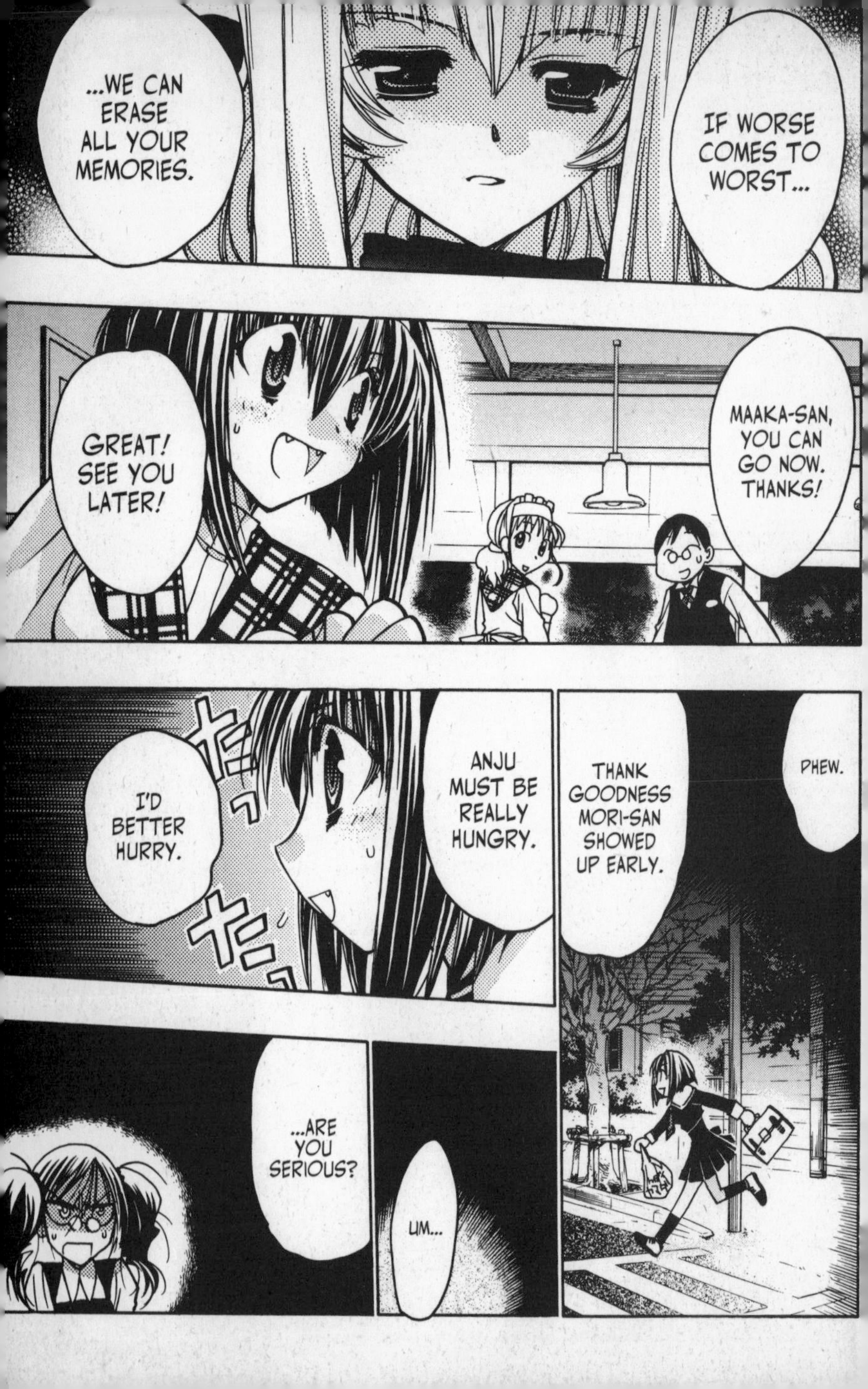
IF WORSE COMES TO WORST...
...WE CAN ERASE ALL YOUR MEMORIES.
MAAKA-SAN, YOU CAN GO NOW. THANKS!
GREAT! SEE YOU LATER!
PHEW.
THANK GOODNESS MORI-SAN SHOWED UP EARLY.
ANJU MUST BE REALLY HUNGRY.
I'D BETTER HURRY.
UM...
...ARE YOU SERIOUS?

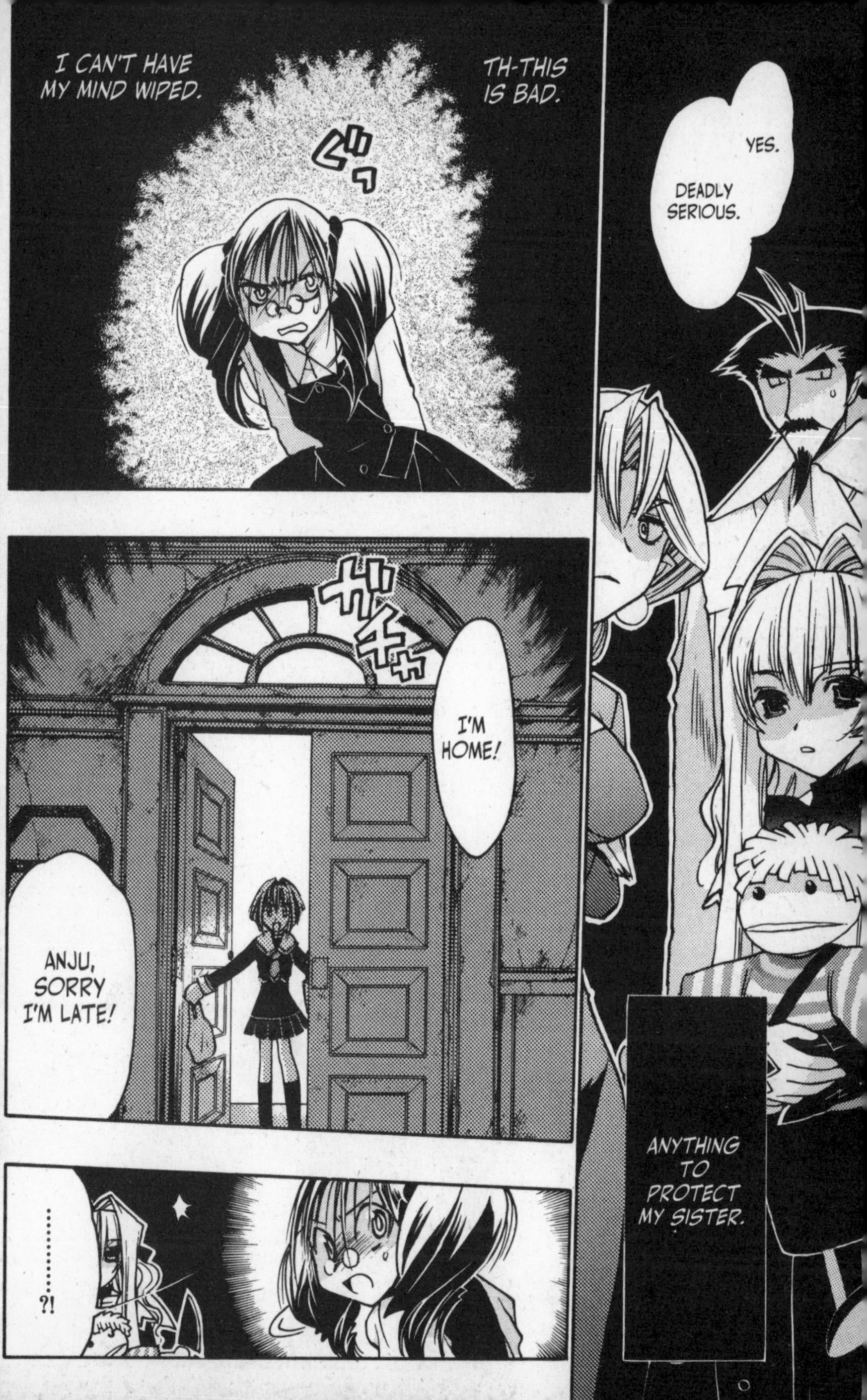
YES.
DEADLY SERIOUS.
ANYTHING TO PROTECT MY SISTER.
TH-THIS IS BAD.
I CAN'T HAVE MY MIND WIPED.
ぐっ
ガチャ
I'M HOME!
ANJU, SORRY I'M LATE!
....
?!

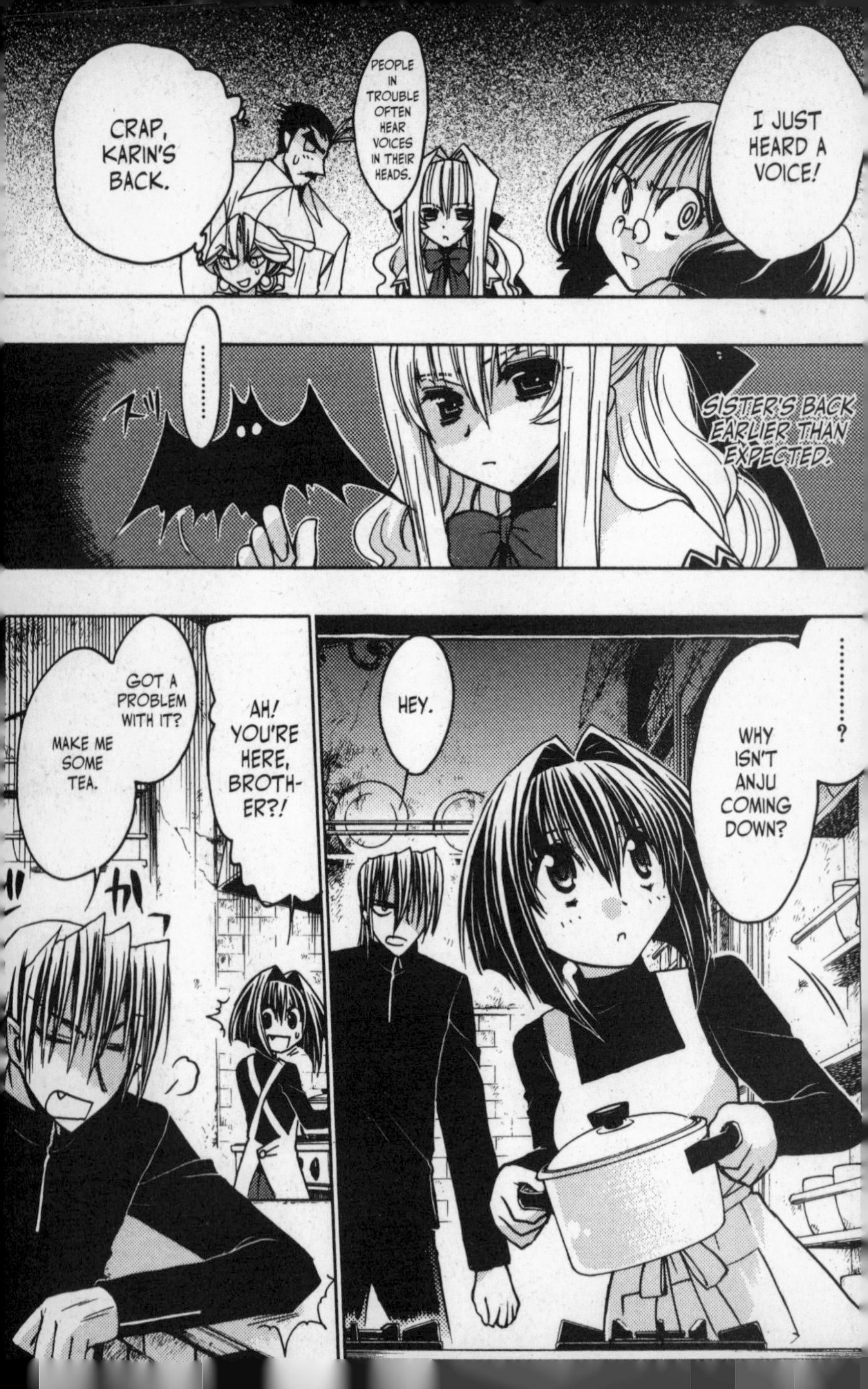
I JUST HEARD A VOICE!
PEOPLE IN TROUBLE OFTEN HEAR VOICES IN THEIR HEADS.
CRAP, KARIN'S BACK.
SISTER'S BACK EARLIER THAN EXPECTED.
......
......?
WHY ISN'T ANJU COMING DOWN?
HEY.
AH! YOU'RE HERE, BROTHER?!
GOT A PROBLEM WITH IT?
MAKE ME SOME TEA.

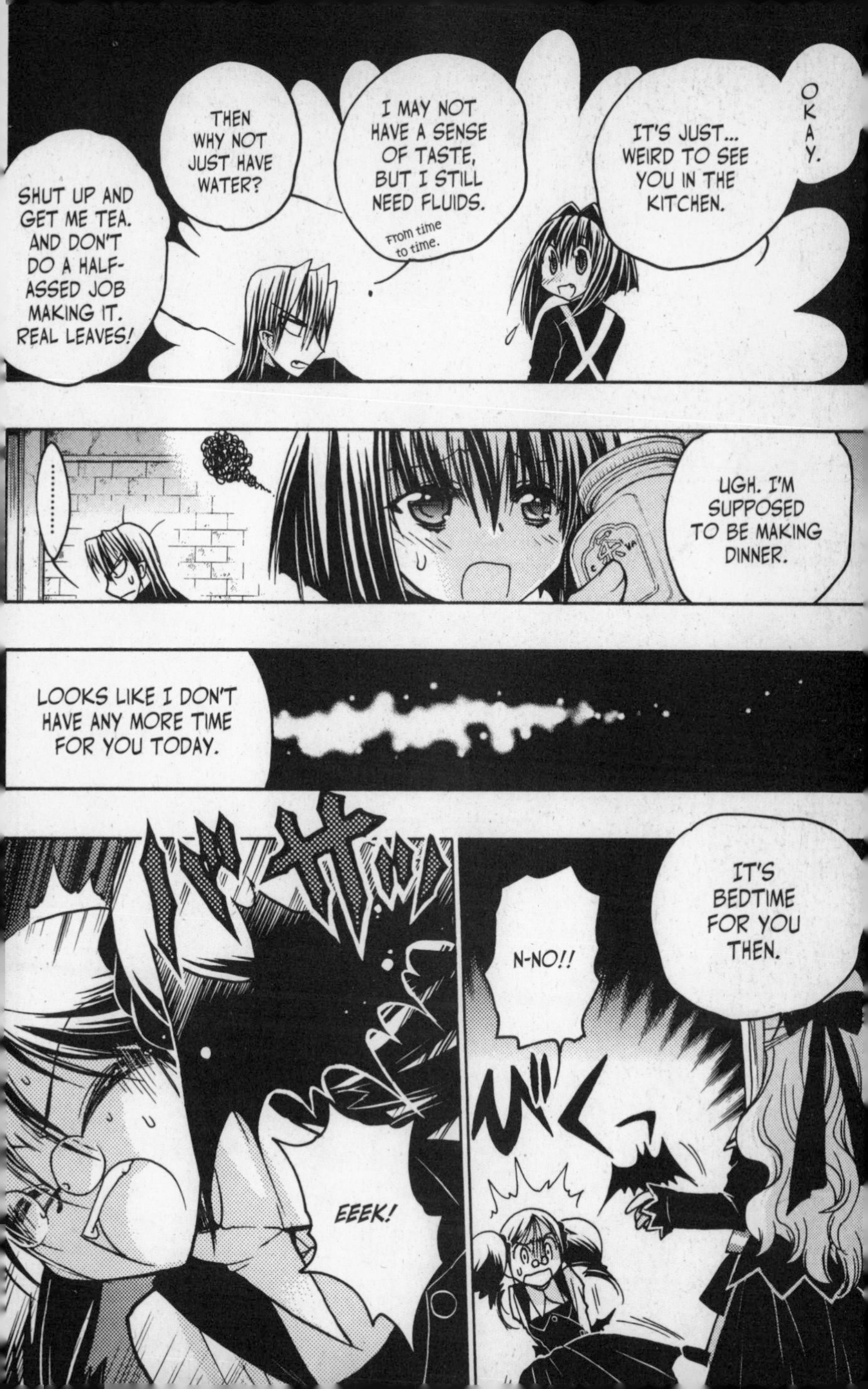
OKAY.
IT'S JUST... WEIRD TO SEE YOU IN THE KITCHEN.
I MAY NOT HAVE A SENSE OF TASTE, BUT I STILL NEED FLUIDS.
From time to time.
THEN WHY NOT JUST HAVE WATER?
SHUT UP AND GET ME TEA. AND DON'T DO A HALF-ASSED JOB MAKING IT. REAL LEAVES!
UGH. I'M SUPPOSED TO BE MAKING DINNER.
....
LOOKS LIKE I DON'T HAVE ANY MORE TIME FOR YOU TODAY.
IT'S BEDTIME FOR YOU THEN.
N-NO!!
EEEK!

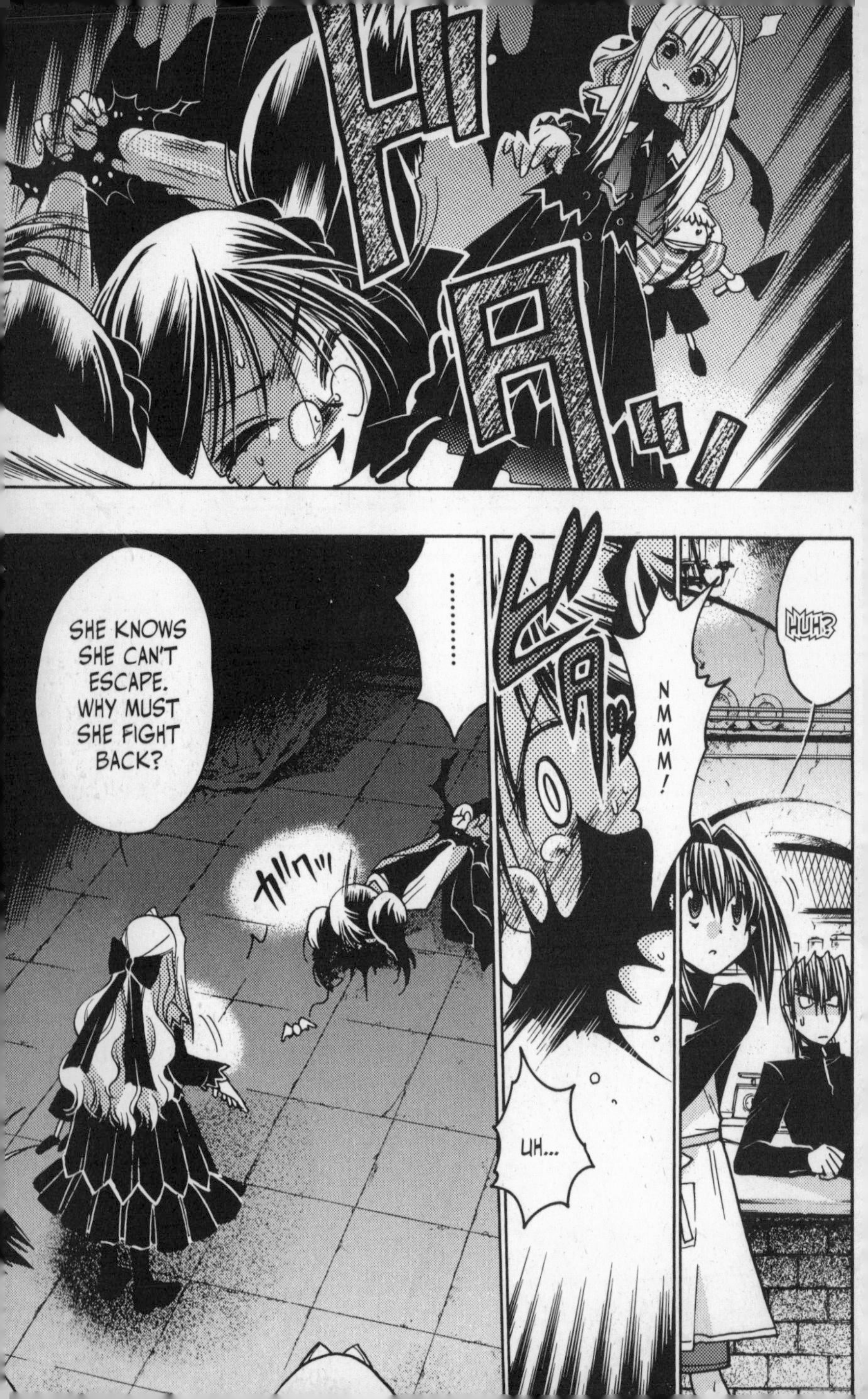
HUH?
NMMMM!
UH...
......
SHE KNOWS SHE CAN'T ESCAPE. WHY MUST SHE FIGHT BACK?
カリッ

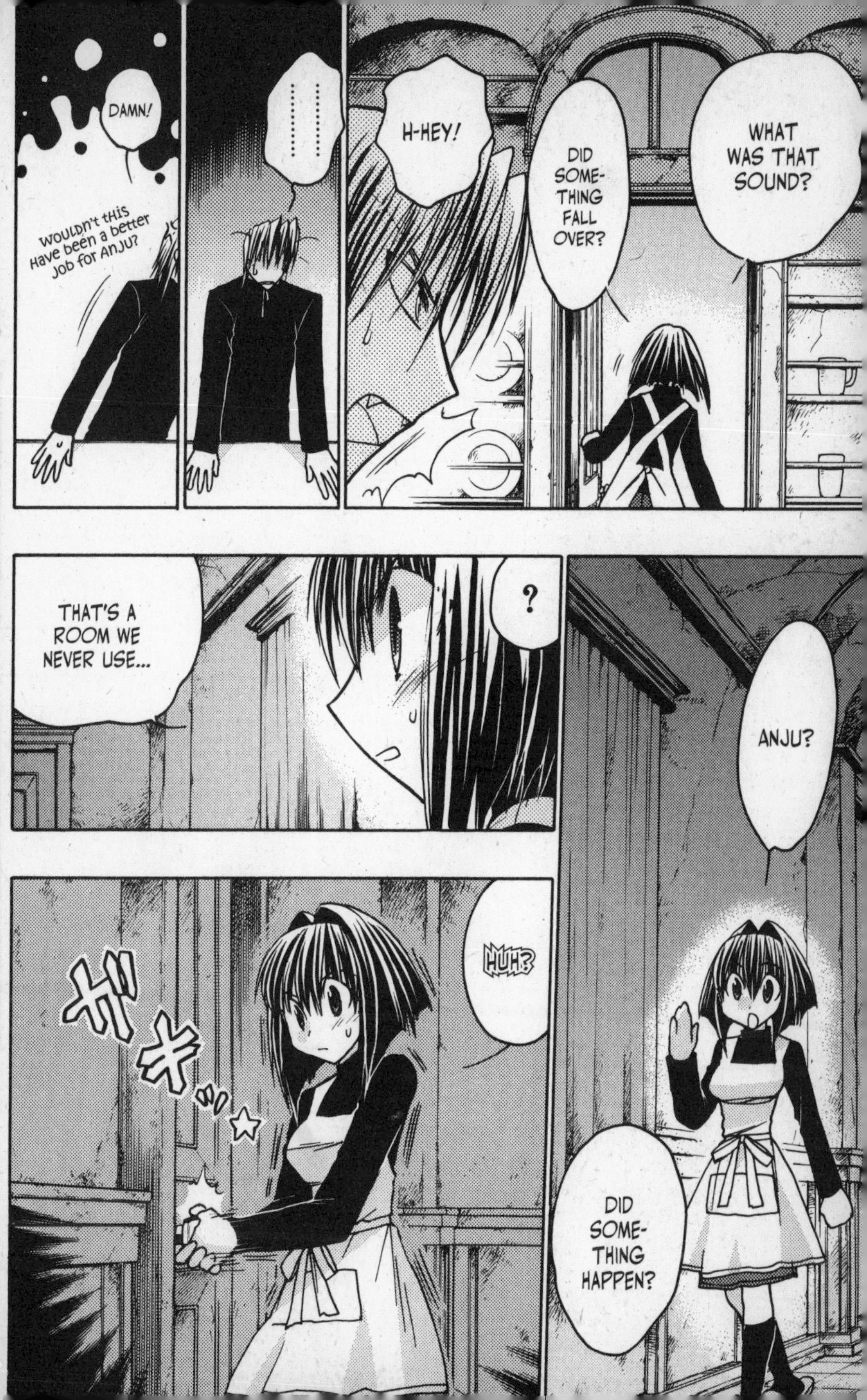

WHAT WAS THAT SOUND?
DID SOMETHING FALL OVER?
H-HEY!
……
DAMN!
Wouldn't this have been a better job for Anju?
ANJU?
DID SOME-THING HAPPEN?
?
THAT'S A ROOM WE NEVER USE...
HUH?
ガキ…☆

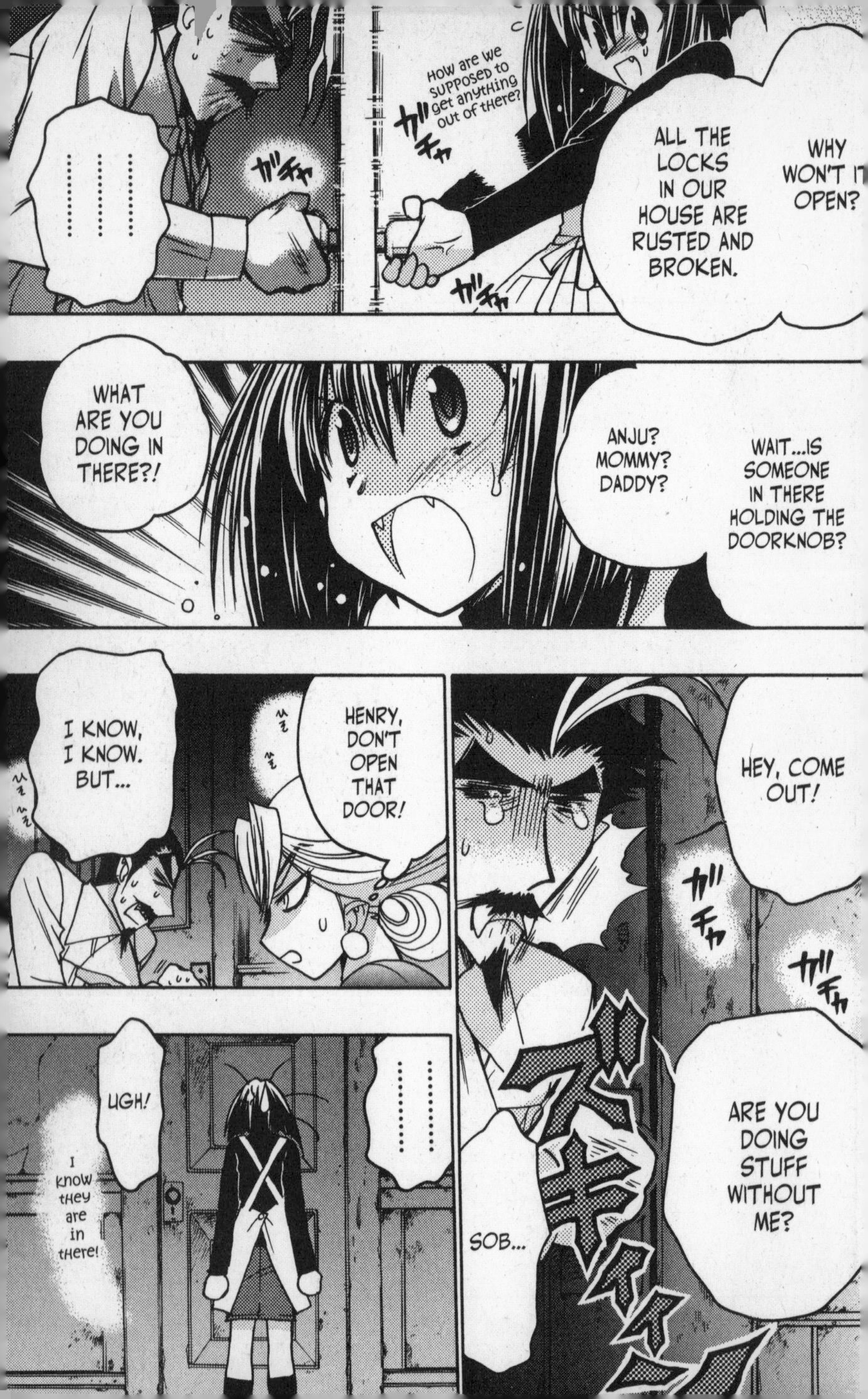
WHY WON'T IT OPEN?
ALL THE LOCKS IN OUR HOUSE ARE RUSTED AND BROKEN.
How are we supposed to get anything out of there?
ガチャ
ガチャ
......
ガチャ
WAIT...IS SOMEONE IN THERE HOLDING THE DOORKNOB?
ANJU? MOMMY? DADDY?
WHAT ARE YOU DOING IN THERE?!
HEY, COME OUT!
ガチャ
ガチャ
ARE YOU DOING STUFF WITHOUT ME?
SOB...
HENRY, DON'T OPEN THAT DOOR!
I KNOW, I KNOW. BUT...
......
UGH!
I know they are in there!

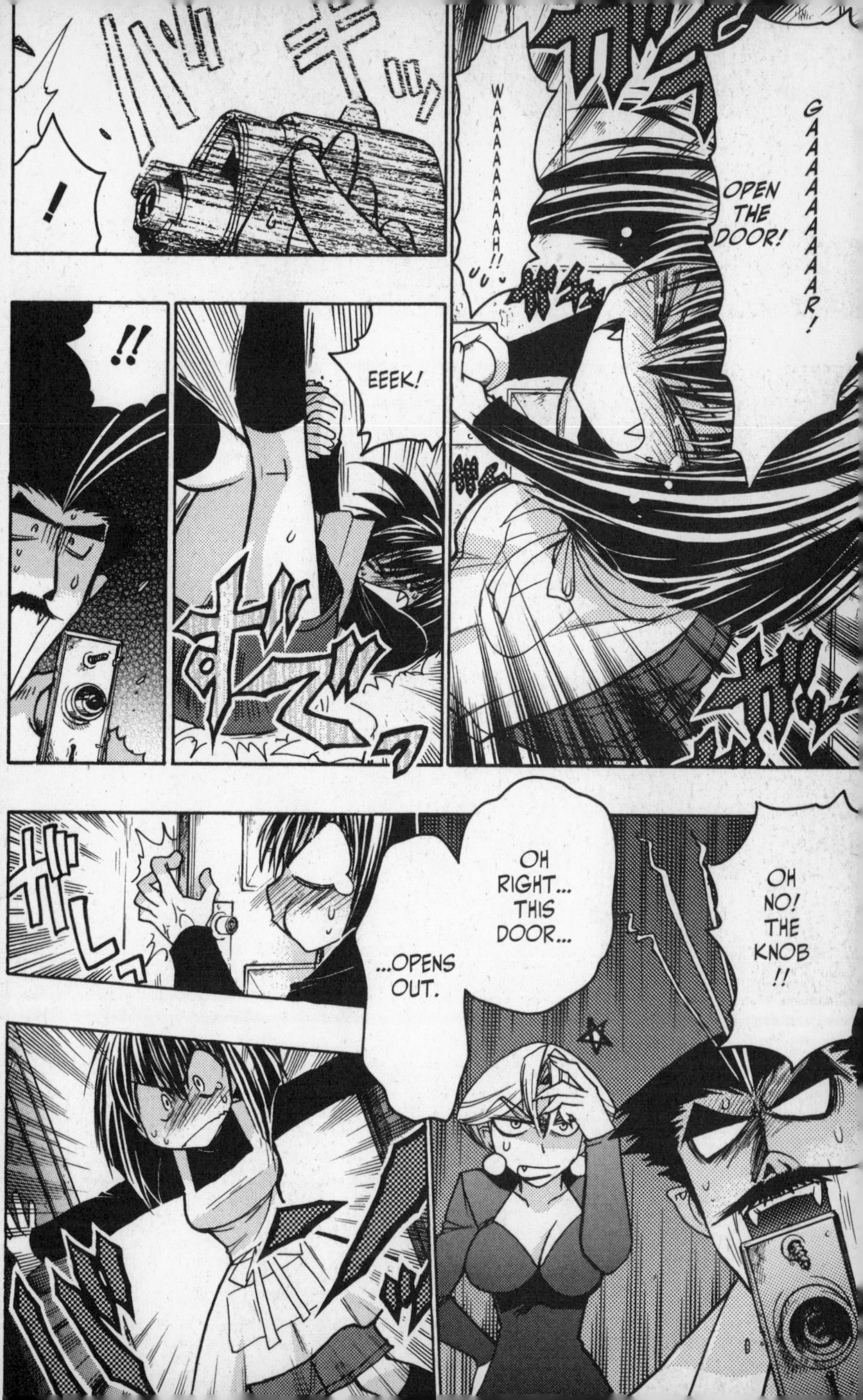
GAAAAAAAAAAR!
OPEN THE DOOR!
WAAAAAAAAAAH!!
!
EEEK!
!!
OH NO! THE KNOB!!
OH RIGHT... THIS DOOR...
...OPENS OUT.

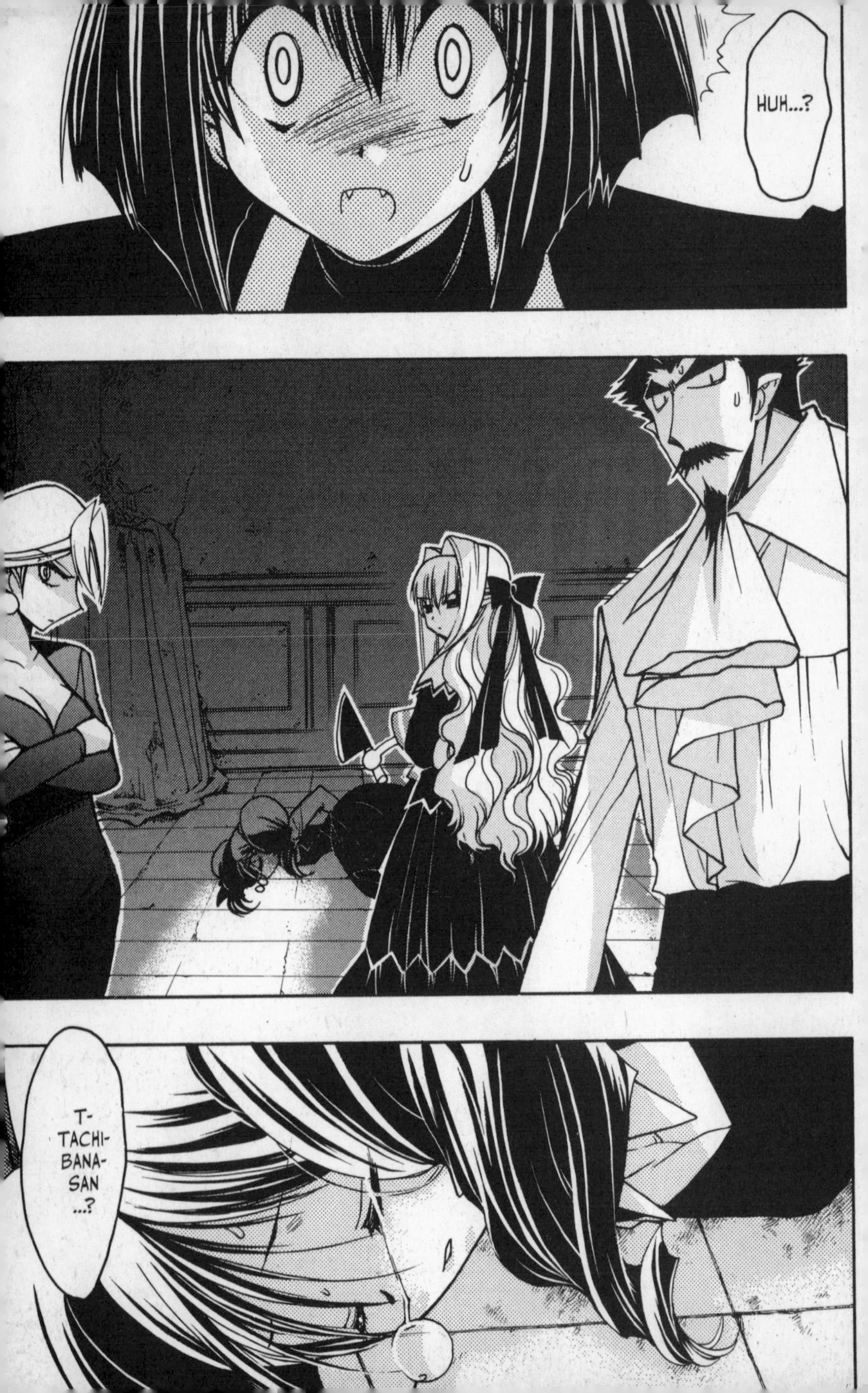
HUH...?
T-TACHI-BANA-SAN...?

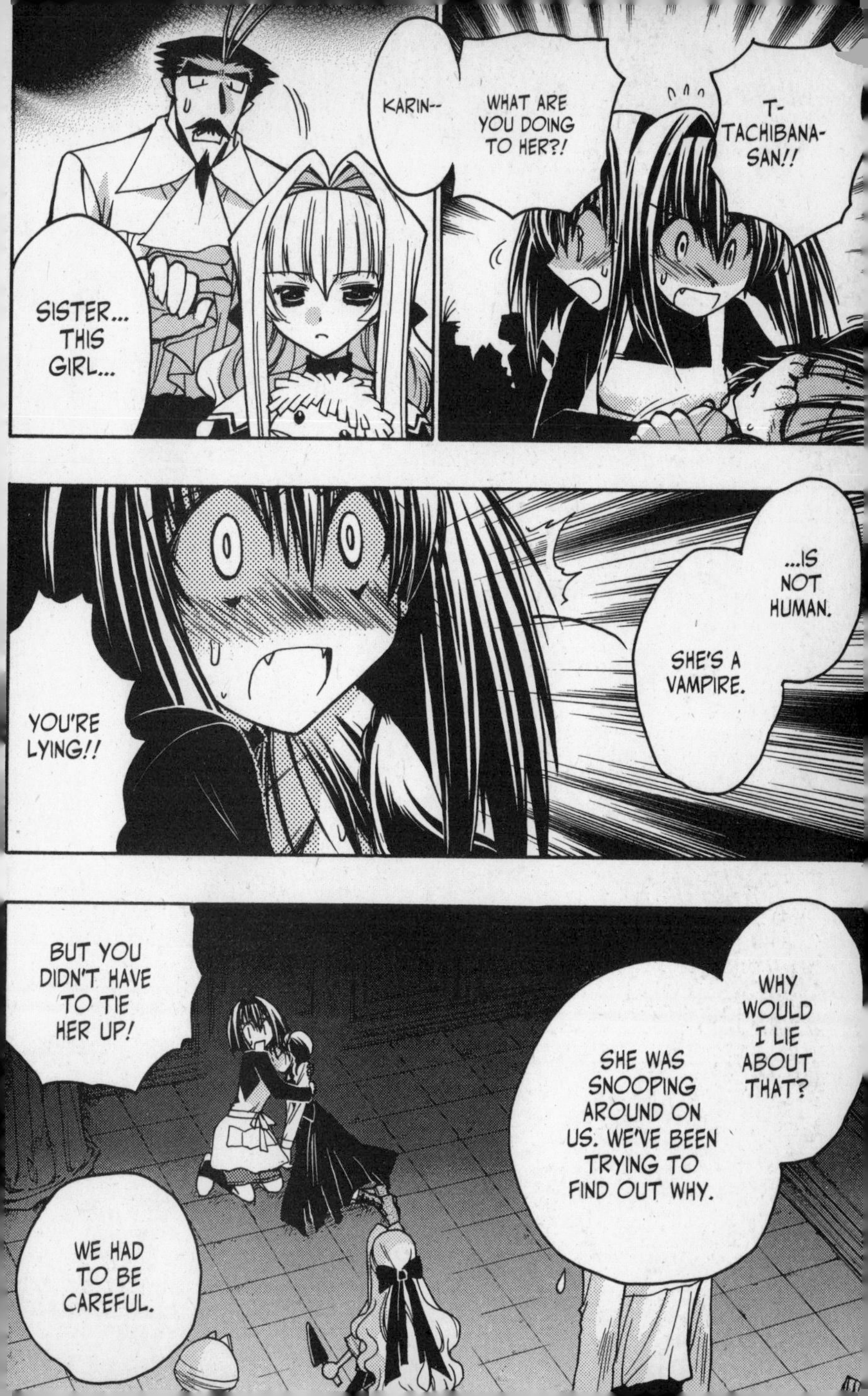
T-TACHIBANA-SAN!!
WHAT ARE YOU DOING TO HER?!
KARIN--
SISTER... THIS GIRL...
...IS NOT HUMAN.
SHE'S A VAMPIRE.
YOU'RE LYING!!
WHY WOULD I LIE ABOUT THAT?
SHE WAS SNOOPING AROUND ON US. WE'VE BEEN TRYING TO FIND OUT WHY.
BUT YOU DIDN'T HAVE TO TIE HER UP!
WE HAD TO BE CAREFUL.

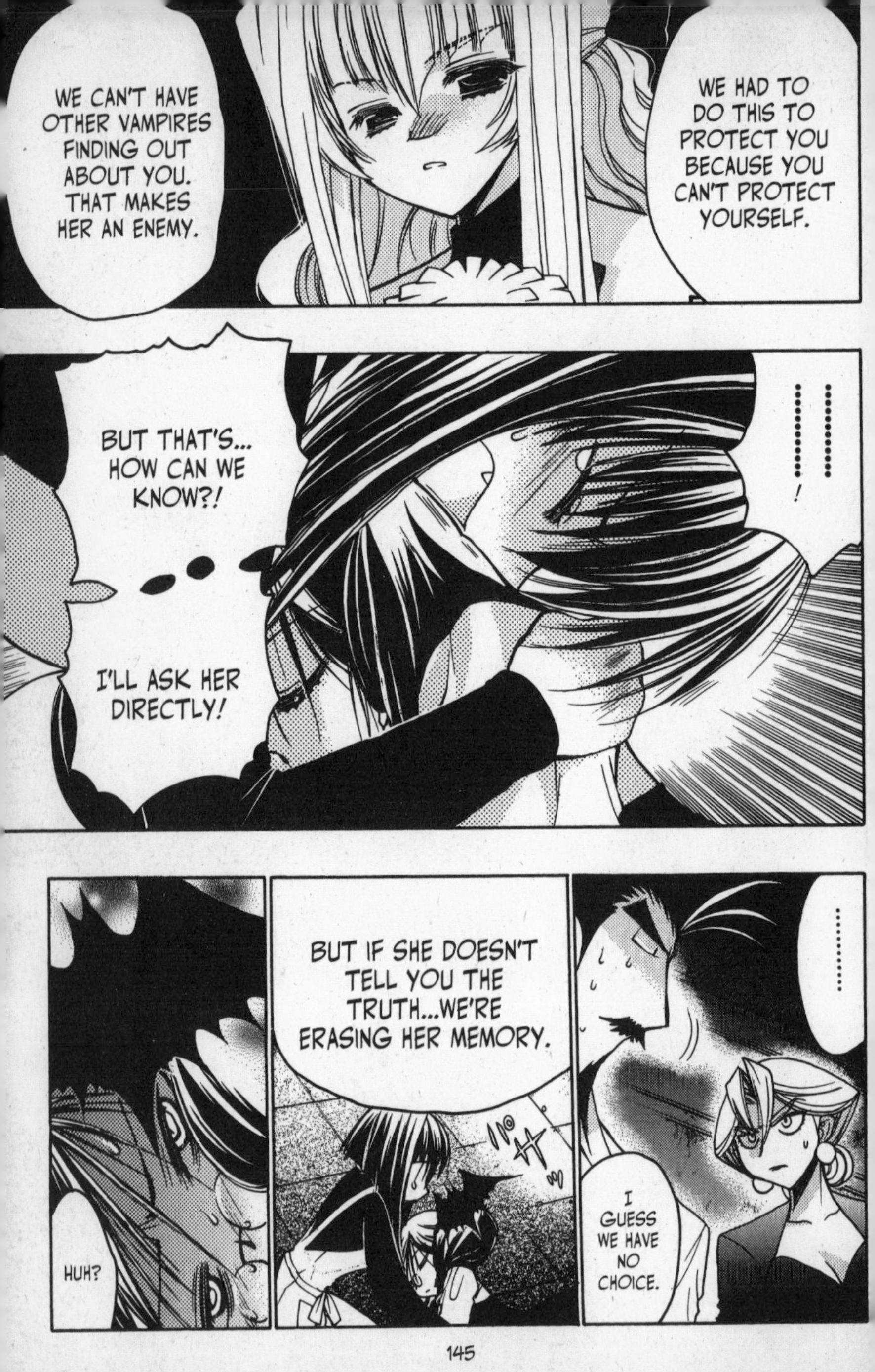
WE HAD TO DO THIS TO PROTECT YOU BECAUSE YOU CAN'T PROTECT YOURSELF.
WE CAN'T HAVE OTHER VAMPIRES FINDING OUT ABOUT YOU. THAT MAKES HER AN ENEMY.
..........!
BUT THAT'S... HOW CAN WE KNOW?!
I'LL ASK HER DIRECTLY!
....
I GUESS WE HAVE NO CHOICE.
BUT IF SHE DOESN'T TELL YOU THE TRUTH...WE'RE ERASING HER MEMORY.
HUH?

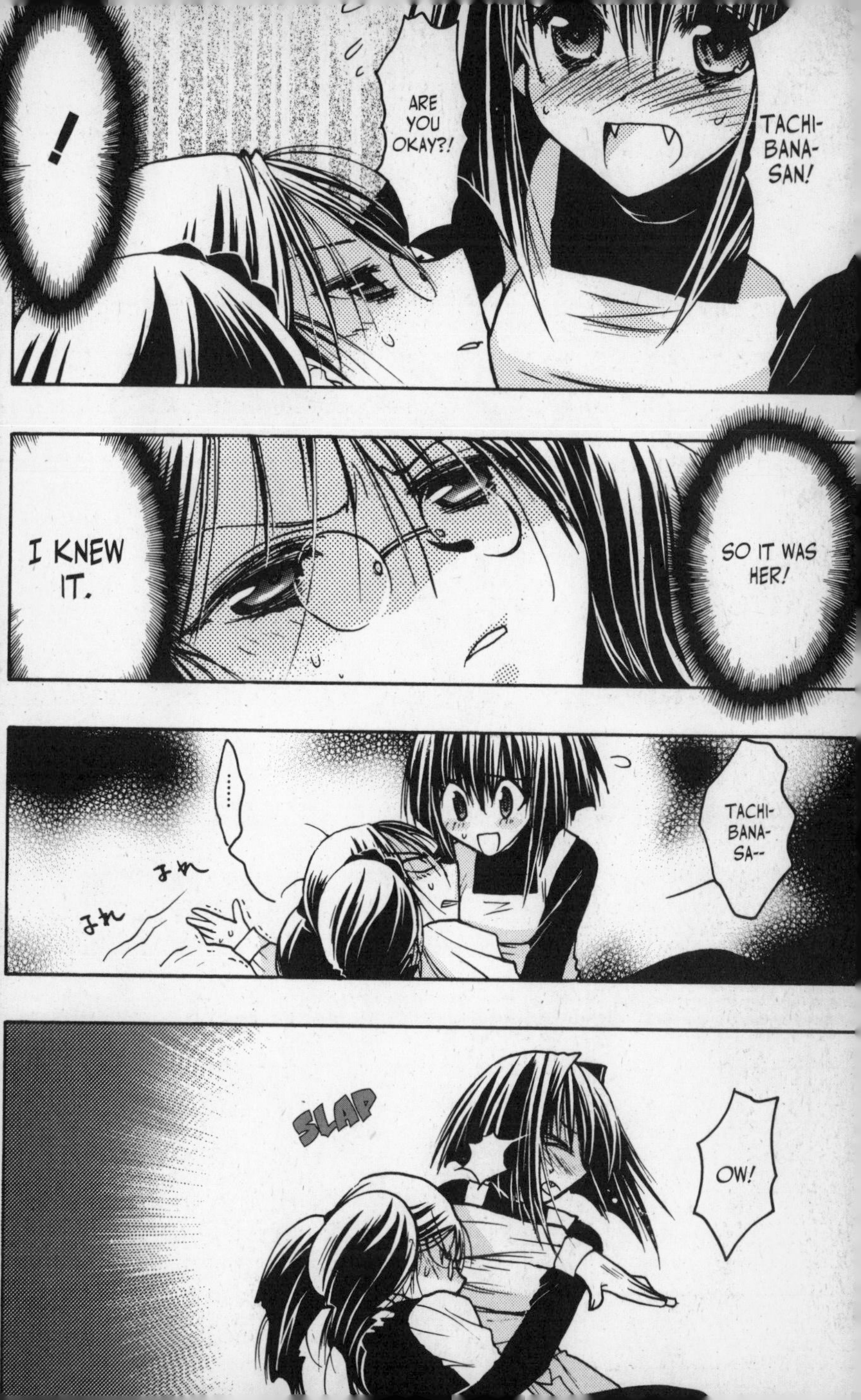
TACHI-BANA-SAN!
ARE YOU OKAY?!
!
SO IT WAS HER!
I KNEW IT.
TACHI-BANA-SA--
......
OW!
SLAP